Beachhead

Also by Jack Williamson

Firechild

Beachhead

Jack Williamson

A TOM DOHERTY ASSOCIATES BOOK
NEW YORK

For Patrice

This is a work of fiction. All the characters and events
portrayed in this book are fictitious and any resemblance
to real people or events is purely coincidental.

BEACHHEAD

Copyright © 1992 by Jack Williamson

Map copyright © 1992 by Ron Miller

This book was printed on acid-free paper.

A Tor Book
Published by Tom Doherty Associates, Inc.
175 Fifth Avenue
New York, N.Y. 10010

TOR® is a registered trademark of Tom Doherty Associates, Inc.

Library of Congress Cataloging-in-Publication Data

Williamson, Jack.
    Beachhead / Jack Williamson.
        p.   cm.
    "A Tom Doherty Associates book."
    ISBN 0-312-85154-5
    I. Title.
    PS3545.I557B4 1992
    813'.52—dc20   92-3275
                                                        CIP

Printed in the United States of America

0 9 8 7 6 5 4 3 2

Contents

Foreword 7

Introduction 9

1. The Authority 17
2. The Corps 26
3. Moon Dust 34
4. Farside 41
5. Moon Day 49
6. Profile 57
7. Windows 63
8. The Crew 75
9. The *Ares* 86
10. The Company 97
11. Reaction 105
12. The Cost 114
13. Mars 120
14. Magellan 132
15. Quarters 146
16. Planum Australe 153
17. Coprates 165
18. Periapsis 181

6 · Contents

19. Paralife   189
20. Biosphere   196
21. Mars Time   204
22. Habitat   214
23. Gardens   226
24. Alien Air   231
25. Motion   242
26. Anomaly   249
27. Propulsion   259
28. Creation   271
29. Sammy   281
30. Winter   290
31. Regression   301
32. Year Two   309
33. Citizen   317
34. Olympus   329
35. Bubble   337
36. Conjunction   353

Foreword

The inspiration for this novel came from a tour of Biosphere II, the experimental habitat then under construction at Oracle, north of Tucson, Arizona. A sealed environment, with 2.5 acres under glass, it is designed to be an independent ecosystem. Eight volunteers have been sealed inside to stay two years, along with a few goats and dwarf pigs and the green plants intended to supply them all with oxygen and food.

My nephew, Larry Littlefield, was installing its elaborate Hewlett-Packard computer system. He spent a day showing me over the multimillion-dollar installation and introduced me to the director, Margret Augustine, the architect, Phil Hawes, members of the staff, and the waiting volunteers. I found that many of them conceived it as a pilot project for future habitats to be built on the Moon or Mars.

This novel is the story of the first expedition to Mars and the attempt to plant the first human colony as I imagine future space history may happen, with no space aliens or petrified cities or surviving Martians, though I have allowed myself one surprise. I've tried hard to respect what is known, depending on such sources as the NASA *Atlas of Mars,* by Batson, Bridges, and Inge; *The Surface of Mars,* by Michael H. Carr; and NASA's *Viking: The Exploration of Mars.* My thanks are due to all these people and many others. I am especially indebted to Geoffrey A. Landis for a copy of the NASA workshop report, *Lunar Helium-3 and Fusion Power.*

I trust that the actual first explorers will be more fortunate than some of my own people. If what they find on the actual planet is not exactly what I've described, I'm sure it will be equally exciting and certainly worth the cost of the expedition.

—Jack Williamson

Introduction
by Arthur C. Clarke

Some little while ago, when I was a gangling farm boy of 14, I came across a copy of *Amazing Stories* containing a tale I still remember, despite the millions of words that have since passed before my eyes. It was written by one Jack Williamson and was called "The Green Girl". Thereafter I kept meeting Jack's stories all over the place: the one which made the greatest impact on me was "The Moon Era", in which the hero goes back in time to the period when the Moon was a living world. Perhaps the years have given this tale a magic which would not survive re-reading, but it seems to me that in "The Mother" Jack created one of the first memorable *alien* beings in science fiction—comparable to Weinbaum's famous "Tweel". There is a sadness and tenderness about this story which still lingers with me.

Very different was Jack's collaboration with Dr. Miles J. Breuer in "The Birth of New Republic"—a re-enactment of the American Revolution on the Moon. The struggle for independence of mankind's colonies from another world is a common theme in science fiction, but this may well have been its earliest treatment. Looking back over Jack's long career (now entering its *seventh* decade!) I am astonished to see how many themes he has explored, and even originated. "The Humanoids" remains a classic study of man-machine relationships, and *Seetee Shock* developed the technology of contra-terrene matter—a subject of considerable interest in connection with advanced space propulsion systems. We can now actually manufacture small quantities of "C.T. matter", albeit at enormous expense; long ago, Jack explored the tricky—indeed hair-raising—technology of handling it. And "The Legion of Time" may have been one of the earliest explorations of alternative universes—again a subject now very much in the forefront of modern physics.

On looking back over his long and influential career, I have no hestitation in placing Jack on a level with the two other American giants, Isaac Asimov and Robert Heinlein. And now, in his eighty-third year, he has shown that he has lost none of his old skills.

The first flight to the Moon was a major theme in science fiction right up to the 1960s. Now the first expedition to Mars is *the* topic for the closing decade of this century—and the opening one of the next. Although there are quite a few points over which I'd love to have a friendly argument with Jack, *Beachhead* is an exciting and enjoyable dramatization of the first Mars expedition.

I use that word "dramatization" deliberately. Anyone writing about Mars today is labouring under a severe disadvantage, from which his/her precursors like Wells, Burroughs and Bradbury were happily free. We now know that, alas, there aren't any Martian princesses, ruined cities or vast canal systems—or indeed any atmosphere worth talking about. It's quite a challenge, therefore, to write an exciting story about the exploration of Mars, without inventing implausibilities which may be refuted in a few years' time. Jack has managed very well to maintain suspense and momentum, while at the same time giving a vivid picture of Mars as it *really* is—a rugged, colourful world, which will continue to unfold its mysteries for decades to come.

To plug a book of one's own in an introduction to a fellow author's may be regarded as scaling new heights of *chutzpah*. However, I think the unique manner in which I'm writing this introduction fully justifies such effrontery. . . .

I'm reading Jack's manuscript in truly extraordinary circumstances, which would have been pure science fiction only 20 years ago. Virtual Reality Laboratories of San Luis Obispo, California, recently sent me their amazing VISTAPRO computer program, which allows one to take the topographical maps of Mars obtained from the Mariner and Viking missions, and to generate incredibly realistic images of them from any viewpoint: some of these are so good that they could easily be mistaken for actual colour photographs. More than that, one can modify the images in an almost infinite number of ways—introducing vegetation, water, trees, clouds etc. In fact, I've been busy terraforming Mars to produce the illustrations for a book I've entitled *The Snows of Olympus: A Garden on Mars.*

Even with the fastest AMIGA3000 east of Suez, it may take up 30 minutes for a complete picture to appear on the monitor, so I have been reading Jack's manuscript while waiting for the program to run. And since we both, for obvious reasons, have chosen the most spectacular areas of Mars, I've had the uncanny experience of reading about such places as the Coprates Canyon and Olympus Mons *while they were slowly materializing on the monitor beside me.*

Thank you, Jack, for a memorable experience, and also for inventing the very word 'terraforming' half a century ago! The best of luck for your latest opus—not, I'm sure, your last. . . .

Arthur C. Clarke
Colombo, Sri Lanka
17 December 1991

Beachhead

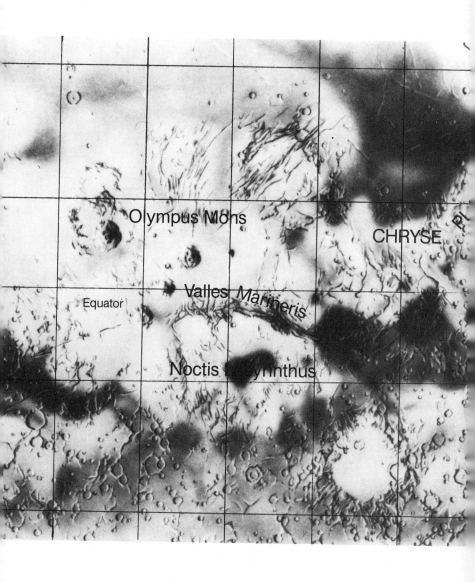

Olympus Mons

CHRYSE PL

Equator

Valles Marineris

Noctis Labyrinthus

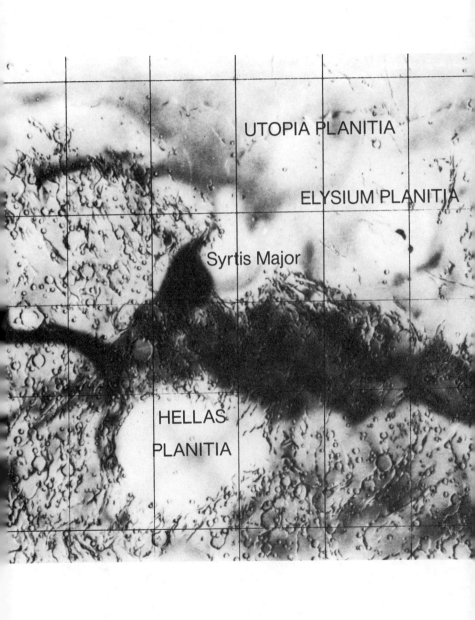

1

The Authority

The Mars Authority was a consortium formed to support the exploration and ultimate colonization of Mars. It had four members: United Europe, Russia, Japan, and America. Unfortunately, it was already bankrupt and near collapse before the first explorers took off.

Sam Houston Kelligan. Sam to his father, Houston to his mother, Hew to most of his friends. A quiet slim young chap with sandy hair and an open smile. Born heir apparent to the billion-dollar Kelligan empire, he disappointed everybody, growing up with his imagination fixed on Mars.

His parents and LeeAnn: he loved all three. In their different ways, all three loved him. But they wanted him here on Earth, not risking his fool neck on one more crazy escapade.

On that early summer morning in the old Fort Worth mansion, he came down for breakfast in his blue dress uniform. His father, already in the kitchen, looked up from the morning papers spread over half the table, grinning at his rows of Mars Corps award ribbons.

"Como 'sta, Moonboy?"

"Okay, sir." He tried to ignore the sarcasm. "I'm flying back to White Sands this morning. We're checking in for the Moon flight today."

Roberto had the Texas breakfast ready: ham and eggs

and redeye gravy hot on the stove, biscuits still warm in the oven, coffee made, chilled orange juice in a tub of ice. He filled his plate and brought it to the table.

"Damfool stunt!" his father snorted, jabbing a finger at a bold headline. "Look at this."

MARS EXPLORERS
RACING ON MOON

"A test, sir." His father had taught him to say sir when he was three years old. "To see how ready we are for Mars. We build the rovers and drive them across the far side of the Moon."

"A lunatic scheme!" His father scowled across the table through black-rimmed glasses. "We saw it on TV last night, and your mother's sick about it. I promised to have a word with you."

"We've had words enough." Houston shrugged. "Sorry, sir."

"Listen to the facts." His father's blunt forefinger jabbed at him. "Scientists call it idiotic. Congress is cutting support for your grand Authority. You've got just one ship, the other still in pieces on the Moon. Listen, boy—"

Flushed pink, he caught a raspy breath. Used to giving orders, he didn't like to beg. Houston felt sorry for him.

"Can't you see?" Grimly, he went on. "See the pure asinine stupidity? Risking your life on the Moon, just to get your chance to die on Mars?"

"We've talked enough about it, sir." He kept his voice down. "Let's not fight again. Not this morning."

"Please, Sam, take a minute." His father's voice wavered between pleading and command. "Remember who we are."

"I remember."

"We Kelligans helped found the Republic of Texas."

Silently, Houston buttered a biscuit. He had heard the words all his life. Stephen Austin Kelligan, named for the first founder of the state, was the founder himself of a corporate empire. Sitting erect across the cluttered table now, he was sternly handsome in profile, his silvery hair worn long. A man of achievement all his life, though always here on Earth and first of all in Texas. An honored cadet commander long ago at College Station, he had read Latin, studied Caesar's campaigns, and called himself a modern Roman. Nearly sixty now, once a state senator, he still relished the title.

"Some of our kin did go to seed." Awkwardly, he groped for understanding. "Your mother and I did have to scrimp and save when we first began, but I worked years south of the border. Earned new respect for the old family name. Created Kelligan Resources. Even rebuilt the old family mansion. All for you, Sam."

The pride gave way to vexation.

"You're a Kelligan and Texan. Come to your senses! Carry on, Sam-boy, and you can be the richest man in the state."

"Which isn't—isn't what I want." He gulped to curb his impatience. "We've talked enough about it, and you know I'm trained for Mars. I hope to go out on the *Ares*. If I fail to make the grade—" Shoulders hunching, he laid his fork down. "That's when I'll have to opt for something else."

But not for Kelligan Resources. With that silent resolution, he bent again to his ham and eggs. His father had always fought to shape his life, and he had always fought for freedom.

"About this race?" His father pushed the bifocals down to frown at the paper. "Here's this engineer saying the Mars Corps is taking foolhardy risks to get the expedition into space while it can."

"There has to be a risk."

"Risk?" His father mocked his tone. "Your risks have always killed your mother. Ski jumping. Flying those idiot kite contraptions you used to build. That tomfool hang gliding. Now this wild-haired game on the Moon. Can't you grow up?"

"Sir—" He drew a long breath. "Planting the first Mars colony is certainly more than a game. The test is a trial run, planned to pick survivor types for Mars. People that should have the best chance there."

"Must you run it on the Moon?"

"They're a lot alike, sir, Mars and the Moon. Both dead worlds. Smaller than Earth. Gravity weaker. No air a man can breathe. No liquid water. No natural screen against radiation."

"If that's what you want—" His father paused to polish the black-rimmed glasses on his wide maroon necktie and peer across the empty dishes as if finally trying to understand. "How do you pick these survivor types?"

"We run a five-hundred kilometer course laid out across the other side of the Moon. I don't know where they plan to start us, but our finish point will be the Farside Observatory."

"How many miles?" His father had refused to learn the metric system.

"Around three hundred, sir."

"Three hundred?" His father's voice lifted with startled concern. "Across the Moon? An area you've never seen?"

"We have maps, sir. Photos taken from space. The hazards have to be there to make it a test, but we've all lived and worked on the Moon. I've been flying there, testing the laser spectrometer. We were granted a million apiece, to build our vehicles and buy equipment."

"A million to squander?" A scornful sniff. "That's what's killing your Authority!"

"A million wasn't too much, sir. Not considering the

conditions we had to meet. Complete life support. Adequate range and power. Total weight under a hundred and eighty kilos. That's for the vehicle, suit, supplies. Everything."

"If you've got to do it—" Absently, Kelligan polished has glasses again. "What are the odds?"

"Thirty-two people will be competing, sir. Eight from each power. Only two Americans will be chosen to go. With luck enough, I'll be one of them."

Roberto had appeared at the door.

"Luck, boy, if your mother can't stop you." His father rose abruptly, thrusting out a heavy, black-haired hand. Religiously, he was in his downtown office well before eight, five mornings a week. "With better luck, you'll soon be back, training yourself to compete with Marty to be our next CEO."

♂

Marty Gorley.

The son of Lucina Gorley. Once Kelligan's private secretary, Lucina was now, as he called her, his right-hand man. Houston had never much liked her, and he had hated Marty as much as he could hate anybody, ever since a day when he was four years old.

His fourth birthday. His mother had given him a set of brightly-colored building blocks and a picture book of the planets. He built towers and forts and cities with the blocks, but the book was more exciting. He made his mother explain the pictures and read the words aloud. He begged people to help him find Mars in the sky. His mother couldn't find it, and his father never had time to look, but one dark night he slipped out into the back yard after dinner and saw a bright red star that had to be Mars.

He tried to show the star to Marty, who came along to

play with him when Lucina was working on papers with his father. Marty didn't care about Mars or any planet. What he wanted was to play with the neat bright blocks. Houston let him help build a city on the floor. On Mars, Houston told him. That was silly, Marty said. Mars was a star somewhere off in the sky where nobody could go.

"Maybe not yet," Houston said. "But I'm going to build a Mars ship and fly there when I'm grown up."

"Like hell you will." Marty liked bad words. "Mother says you're *no bueno por nada.* She says you'll die in jail, because they spoil you rotten."

"Tell her to wait and see," Houston answered. "I heard my mother tell her bridge ladies you're a rotten apple."

"If you're so smart—" Marty came running. "Look at your city!"

Marty kicked the city. The blocks went flying, and Houston balled his fists.

"You can't hit me." Marty backed hastily away. "Your mother won't let you. I'm littler."

Houston let him run away to the room where Lucina was shut up with his father. He gathered the little blocks and built another city, placing the buildings in a neat little circle, like he thought they should be on Mars.

Growing up, he never liked Lucina, not even when she brought him little gifts from Mexico and said how smart he was. He never really made friends with Marty, even when they had to share rooms for one semester at College Station.

He had never forgotten the way Marty laughed and kicked his city.

♂

His mother came down as she always did to kiss his father dutifully and walk with him out to the waiting car.

She was still in her pajamas and her favorite old blue silk robe, her face not yet made, though her fine white hair was already neat. Not quite fifty, she looked years older.

"Your father talked to you?" When the car was gone, she came back with a cup of hot water and a tea bag to the kitchen table. She stood a moment scanning him with pale, troubled eyes. "What did he say?"

She had been a Bascomb, one of her forebears a captain in the Mexican War, her great-grandfather a Texas Ranger, her father a rancher and a federal judge. Her inheritance had been the seed of the Kelligan fortune. Meeting her haunted eyes, Houston wondered how she had ever loved his father.

"Nothing to change anything." He shrugged, unhappy with the moment. "I'm catching my flight this morning. Checking in this afternoon. Medicals tomorrow. Our equipment's already inspected. We'll be on our way to the Moon by the end of the week."

"We hoped you might resign."

"Mother—" He reached for her hand. Its thin flesh felt lax and cold. "You know I can't."

"Houston—" She sat down slowly, with a hopeful glance at his face. "Don't you care for LeeAnn?"

"She's okay."

"She's beautiful!" A tone of hurt protest. "She adores you. She always did."

"We're good friends." He smiled and nodded, trying to soften her disappointment. "I like her a lot and I know what she means to you. Old Texas. Neighbors when your father owned the ranch. I guess it's no secret she always wanted us to marry."

"Houston, why don't you—"

"Because I'd have to give up—everything." He shrugged, a gesture of denial. "Space. Mars. All I ever hoped for. She'd want a home in the suburbs. Golf and dances at the country club. Fort Worth society. I'd have to go into business. Probably with my father."

"We'd be so happy!" The anxious smile dimmed into her set look of passive endurance. "I couldn't help hoping, but I'll try to understand." She turned with a tired little sigh to sip at her tea. "I used to hope you'd wake up, at least for your father's sake, but I guess you never will."

"I don't expect to."

"I remember—" She paused to peer at him, her pale eyes wistful. "The first time you said you were going to Mars. It was here in this same room. Your father had scolded you. He said you'd been impertinent."

"I'd called him a fat nincompoop." He grinned. "I'd heard the word from Marty."

"There was some book you were reading—"

"Heinlein," he said. "A story about the red planet. I wanted to go there."

"You were so young." Her wan smile reflected his. "Only six."

"Even then, Mars was real to me." He spoke softly, but then his voice lifted. "I always read about it, dreamed about it. NASA broke my heart, killing their manned programs, but now there's this one last chance."

"I know." Her thin fingers caught his arm, pulling him back from the dream of space, back to the kitchen table and her look of saddened resignation. "Your father calls it craziness. You've never made him happy, but I try to understand."

"I hope you can." He leaned to kiss her dry blue lips. "I'll feel better if you do."

"Can I ask you, Houston?" Her troubled eyes came back to his face. "About this Authority? Your father gets upset when I want to know about it."

"He hates paying taxes. Exploring space costs money. That's the why of the Mars Authority. It spreads the load four ways. Our ship's the *Ares*. We've made most of the components on the Moon and assembled it in orbit. The last six months I've been out there, working at the helium plant and learning to fly shuttle craft."

"On the Moon?" She was distressed. "Already? Your father never told me."

"Mom, you worry too much."

"LeeAnn has been telling me things you and your father wouldn't. She's afraid you're going to be in terrible danger. Houston—" She had to pause, blue lips quivering. "What's going to happen to you? Out on Mars?"

"Quién sabe, as Father likes to say." She didn't answer his smile, and he told her more seriously, "Whatever happens, I don't mean to be sorry."

"It could be—bad?"

"We just don't know, but this Moon test is to pick the best crew possible. We'll have fine equipment, and we're all trained for it. I hope you'll be proud if I get to go, because it's a great thing, Mom. Great for humankind!"

She lifted her empty teacup and set it down again, rattling in the saucer.

"When—" A sob broke her voice. "When?"

"If—" He shrugged and grinned, but still she wouldn't smile. "We'll all be back at White Sands for the final physicals and briefings. The *Ares* is taking on water right now, mass for the helium drive. The crew can go aboard as soon as they are chosen."

"My child!" She reached again for her cup, but it slipped out of her fingers and shattered on the floor. She seemed not to notice. "My only child."

With no more he could say, he put his arm around her. He caught her scent, the jasmine his father always bought her. She trembled against him, thin frail bones in thin frail flesh. Holding her, he grasped to understand all he couldn't share: the pain she had endured, the hopes she must have lost, the fears that still haunted her.

In a moment she moved again, wiping at her tears with

the sleeve of the worn blue robe. With a silent shrug, he let her go. His world was space, hers this old house. The gulf between had grown too wide for them to cross.

"I'm sorry!" Bravely, she was trying at last to smile. "I can't—can't help what I feel." She caught her breath. "When is your flight?"

"Ten forty-five. LeeAnn is coming to drive me."

2

The Corps

The Mars Corps was a tiny force of picked men and women trained to undertake the exploration and colonization of the planet. The few who finally got there were cynically betrayed.

White Sands Spacebase, once the White Sands Missile Range, was now Mars Command. Many of the buildings were old and shabby, but there was a huge new hangar for the spaceplanes. A wide new runway arrowed through ten kilometers of sparse desert brush toward old desert mountains and the new worlds beyond. The new Goddard Tower, all bright aluminum and glass, held Authority headquarters and Mission Control.

After chow that evening, Houston sat with three Corps friends in the Starways Lounge on the top floor of the tower, looking down across the tarmac at the tiny silver blade of the spaceplane standing in front of the hangar, ready to take them toward the Moon.

A Russian, an East Asian, another American, all three on edge.

"To the winners!" Lavrin had offered to share his bottle of vodka, but Ram Chandra wanted white soda.

Houston and Martin Luther White ordered Mexican
beer. "Us!"

The others drank, but White sat glaring at his beer, his
scarred features moodily grim. A muscular giant born in
Baltimore, he had shrugged off a big league baseball
contract to earn his chance at Mars. The past year he had
been away, on duty on the Moon.

"I'm out of the race," he told them glumly. "Got the
word before I left Farside."

"Out?" Shocked, they stared at him. "How?"

Jaws bleakly set, he merely shrugged.

"Hard luck," Houston told him. "I'm sorry."

"You needn't grieve." Wryly, he grinned. "Fact is,
Hew, you ought to be happy. With me sitting out, you've
got your own chance to make the American twosome."

"Maybe." Houston laughed. "If you think you're a
better man than I am. Anyhow, the race is yet to run, and
I wish you were still with us."

Close companions, the four had trained together since
enlistment, in barracks and classrooms, spacecraft and
labs, deserts and mountains and even undersea, with
special duty tours on the Moon.

The Russian was Arkady Lavrin. A red-haired giant,
he was the son of a Swedish mother and a Ukrainian
diplomat who carried Viking genes from the blond in-
vaders who brought their dragon ships down the Dnieper
a thousand years ago. Never happy at home in Kiev or
anywhere on Earth, he had spent his boyhood exiled to
military schools and more years advising guerrilla groups
in Africa before he got sick of tribal feuds, and fixed his
mind on Mars. He liked his vodka, played wicked chess,
and had a gift for command.

Ram Chandra was born in Calcutta but educated on
Asia Island. That was the floating nation built to be the
new Hong Kong, now the commercial hub of the whole
Pacific and capital of the East Asian Union. A hollow

square, it was five kilometers on a side and twelve decks high, supported on submerged pontoons, with airstrips along three sides and a seaport in the center.

At the Starways table now, White sat staring wistfully though the windows at the spaceplane on the tarmac and that runway to the planets. Lavrin ordered more beers for him and Houston and poured another vodka for himself—the Corps didn't mind a drink or two after duty, though many more washed you out. Nervously, he drained his soda. They sat watching in awkward silence till he turned slowly back.

"Cheer up, starbirds." He grinned. "A hard lump for me, but nobody's funeral. I may be the lucky one when the whole story's told."

"How come?" English was the language of the Corps. Lavrin had learned it on training tours at Texas Tech, and his Russian accent was nearly gone except in moments of emotion. "Or can't you talk?"

"Shouldn't," he muttered. "But don't cry for me. I've already made my name, whenever the Authority decides to let you know."

Down on the tarmac, mechanics were opening an access door to load the heavy little green-painted cylinders of helium-3. White watched them sadly, lips pressed tight.

"Here's what I can tell." He looked up last. "I've been on special duty out at the Farside labs. Assigned to study the rocks and dust the probes brought back from Mars. Held there in quarantine, to keep hostile Mars bugs off the Earth. A wise idea, I guess, seeing what happened to me."

"Something we should know?"

"You will." He nodded. "In due time, whoever makes the team will get a secret briefing. Probably just before the takeoff."

"Why secret?" They all stared across the table. "Those bugs—they're real?"

White shrugged and turned again to gaze at the spaceplane and the endless runway and the brassy desert sky above the far brown mountain.

"If they are," Lavrin said, "we've got a right to know."

"I guess you do." He turned soberly back to drain his beer. They were alone at the end of the long room, but he lowered his voice. "You won't talk about anything I spill?"

"Of course not," Lavrin said. "Agreed."

Chandra and Houston nodded, listening.

"No actual bugs," he said. "But there is something in the dust. Not as totally dead as was first reported."

"Life?"

"Not exactly." White shook his head, still hesitant. "Nothing like ours, anyhow. You have to understand that the research is still incomplete. Preliminary conclusions are still classified. I don't want to say more than I have to. Any public hint would be terrible PR. Could even kill the expedition."

"I see." Lavrin looked behind him to be sure they were still alone. "But since you've said this much—"

"A molecule." White nodded. "One we isolated from the dust. Something that can replicate, placed in the right medium. It has to have water, nitrogen, carbon, and at least a trace of iron. Strange and very primitive. Simpler than any life on Earth, but perhaps the first step toward the evolution of a different sort of life. We were debating what to call it. Protolife, or maybe paralife."

"I don't see—" Lavrin's red eyebrows lifted. "How could that discovery wash you out?"

"The protolife did." His face twitched. "We'd decided the dust was harmless. I exposed myself. I'm infected, or maybe allergic to it. Something new and confusing to the docs. They never agreed what it was. No treatment, of course. I was hospitalized for a couple of weeks. Cough, fever, skin eruptions."

Troubled, they studied him.

"You look okay." Houston grinned and gripped his massive arm. "You feel okay. Fit enough to take us all."

"Fit for Mars." A rueful shrug. "I begged for my chance, but I'm still the guinea pig. They're holding me here for more observation. Taking half a liter of my blood every other week, for a vaccine they're trying to produce."

"If it's that bad—" Chandra pushed his empty glass away. "It's a crime to keep it secret."

"What I thought." White nodded. "The general called me in when he heard about it. My own advice was to go public. Delay the launch till we could finish the study and try to make a vaccine. He wasn't convinced. It's now or never, so he says. Do or die."

"He has no right—" Chandra muttered. "Not to choose for us."

"You'll get your choice if you make the team," White promised him. "And you can see the general's problem. The flight window's open now. We have to launch in the next few weeks or wait two years."

"I'd wait. In two years we could have the *Nergal* complete. Two ships instead of one. Double our chance. And maybe that vaccine."

"The general says we can't wait two years. Too many cost overruns. Too many delays already, even to get the *Ares* off the Moon. Two more years, he thinks, and we're dead."

"Better to die of the dust?"

"Up to you." White shrugged. "After you're briefed. After all, I'm not dead. Not even any major complications—none the docs can find. If we do get a vaccine, we can ship it out on the *Nergal* when the next window opens. If the Authority is still alive by then, and *Nergal* actually ready.

"That's the story, anyhow." With a defiant scowl at the bar machine, he clicked his credit code to order one more beer. "Just in case you want to resign."

He saw their faces and shook his head.

"Not that I thought you would."

"Thanks for the facts," Houston said. "Now what's ahead for you?"

"I'm still with you, at least as far as the Moon," White said. "They need to keep me in reach as long as they want my blood. I'm to be a deputy mission commander on the Moon mission."

"Our boss?" Houston waved him an ironic Corps salute. "Orders for us, sir?"

"I do have instructions for you." White frowned, serious again. "The Authority is staging another publicity blitz. Tomorrow's media day. They're inviting critics to tour the facility; interview the teams."

"Nothing I like." Chandra scowled. "Can't we hide?"

"Better be charming," White urged him. "If you want to keep us alive. If the public and the congress cut off the money—which could happen in a minute if they hear about the protolife—Mars will be dying on the vine."

♂

Next day Houston found himself escorting a heavy, sweaty, blue-jowled newsman named Nicholas Blink, who wanted to know what on Mars could be worth forty billion American dollars.

He took Blink aboard the spaceplane and recited facts about it. Construction time, empty weight, fuel load, rocket thrust, Mach speed at shift from ramjets to scramjets, titanium skin temperature at hypersonic velocities, flight time to LEO. Blink, he saw, didn't understand or care.

"Fuel?" He pointed at a yellow-painted pump truck. "What does it burn?"

"That's water," Houston told him. "Reaction mass for the rocket engine. In the rocket jet, it's turned to superheated plasma—"

"Water?" Blink took it as a joke. "You're flying to the Moon with water in the tank?"

He tried to explain the helium fusion engine, but Blink's newspaper was *The Keyhole Spy,* aimed at supermarket shoppers who wanted spice instead of space.

"This damn hellhole!" he grumbled. "Get me out of the heat and find me a beer."

Houston took him to the air-conditioned Starways Lounge for the beer and gave him a press kit.

"All about the Moon run," he said. "A fact sheet, photos, even a video disk. The object, of course, is to pick the best people for the Mars team."

Blink unbuckled his belt to ease his considerable belly and squinted at a spidery Moon rover.

"That's what the taxpayers get for all their billions? A car race across the back the Moon?"

"It's a planet they're buying." Houston tried to swallow his impatience. "Read the facts and run the disk. Space does cost a lot, but what we've already spent is wasted unless we do get there."

Blink gurgled his beer.

"We will get there," Houston promised him. "We'll build habitats, explore the planet, establish a permanent colony. A second human world—"

"This Moon race?" He wasn't listening. "A great sports event, if I could get there."

"Sorry, sir," Houston said. "But the Moon's no picnic for anybody. Facilities are limited. No accommodations for the media."

"You don't have to coddle me." Blink raised his nasal whine. "I've never ducked a risk. I've been down in subs and ridden a balloon over Everest. If you really want publicity, get me to the Moon."

"Sorry, sir. But you'll find background on the Mars Corps in the press kit. The test is to choose eight volunteers for this first expedition. We have a few hundred more in training, hoping to follow when they can—"

"These eight?" Blink squinted at him shrewdly. "Are they married?"

"They aren't even selected yet."

"Four couples, I understand?"

"Four men and four women."

"That could be a story for us." Blink nodded to accept another beer. "Eight people cooped up together, away from the world for two long years. What will they do about sex?"

"Their own business," Houston said. "Not that I think it's a problem. They'll have enough to do without—"

"There's our story!" Blink broke in. "A psychologist I interviewed last week said all eight should agree to a sort of group marriage. To prevent the violence that might result from natural sexual jealousies. In other words, a free love society."

"A nut," Houston said. "We can do without his advice. The team members will be free—"

"Free!" Blink echoed him. "That's my point. They'll be off the Earth, outside of public notice and beyond any law. Like the old *Bounty* mutineers. What is to restrain them?"

"Their own decency. The discipline they've learned. Their mission is Mars, and they aren't going there for any sex orgy—"

"Sex orgy!" Blink grinned, murmuring the words. "Sex orgy on Mars! That's what I came for."

3

Moon Dust

The wealth of the Moon is the helium-3 in its surface regolith, the dust ground fine by four billion years of meteoric impacts. That helium isotope, rare on Earth but brought to the Moon by the solar wind, yields fusion power that may someday replace depleted fossil fuels.

The spaceplane was a taxi from Earth to low orbit. Burning liquid hydrogen and atmospheric oxygen on takeoff and shifting to helium-3 fusion boosters in the stratosphere, it could lift off an eight-kilometer runway, carry ten tons of passengers and freight out to Goddard Station, and come back whole.

Houston's heart skipped a beat when he walked aboard next morning and saw Jayne Ryan. Another beat when she smiled with the green-gray eyes he recalled, and nodded at the vacant seat beside her.

"Sam Houston?"

"Jayne! So you do remember?"

"From four years ago, when we were still green cadets." The recollection seemed to please her. "I'd just finished survival school and you were back from arctic training."

The event returned, still fresh in his imagination. He had glimpsed her first in the arms of Arkady Lavrin, dancing here in the Starways Lounge. Generously, Lavrin had let him have the next dance. He had never forgot-

ten the warm timbre of her voice, the good-scented soft-
ness of her hair, the feel of her body, light and quick
against him.

In lonely moments on the Moon, he could always
recall the laughing quirk of her full lips, the inquisitive
tilt of her nose, the small brown mole beside it on her
Moon-tanned cheek.

"I love your voice." Happy with her, he had felt free
to say anything. "So different from Texas."

"The accent?" She laughed. "Two grandmothers took
turns keeping me. One Irish, the other Italian. I used to
imitate them both. I guess they're still with me."

She liked the music, a fiddler and guitarist recalling
Western tunes of many years ago, and they talked of the
adventures and small disasters of their training. Intox-
icated with her, he felt that she was opening a new chapter in his life, but she had been gone next day, to altitude
training in Tibet.

♂

In the seat beside him now, she was as splendid as the
image he had cherished, her blue skin-tight moonsuit
arrayed with achievement ribbons and shaped to perfection by the woman inside.

"Good of Arkady to introduce us." With a wistful
grin, he shook his head at her. "But after a couple of
dances he took you away. Where have you been?"

"Out on the Moon," she said. "Bottling helium-3 for
the *Ares*. And then at Farside, watching a dust storm on
Mars."

"I heard about the dust. Trouble waiting for us."

"Quite a monster. Spread across both hemispheres. So
thick you could see nothing for months except the tops of
Olympus and the Tharsis volcanos. But it has finally
cleared."

She looked up the aisle as if expecting someone else. Anxious not to lose her, he asked, "You're on the Moon run?"

"And running just now from an pretty obnoxious reporter." She turned back to him, her fair skin flushed. "What a jerk! Wanted a shot of me in the door of the plane. A sexy pose, to make the most of the moonsuit!" Her head tossed with indignation. "Got hot when I told him no thanks."

"Media day!" He shrugged. "We'd need a media year to educate the world."

"No educating that duck!" Anger still edged her voice. "Though I did try to explain the rocket engine. How we use helium fusion to turn water into plasma for the jet. He cut me off. Said his public wouldn't understand and didn't give a damn. He sure didn't. Wanted to know what kind of water we drank."

"I think I met the same man. Nicholas Blink?"

"That's the moron." She made a face. "Writes for something called *The Keyhole*—"

Leaning to look at his own service ribbons, she had seen his name. Her face changed.

"Kelligan?" Something chilled her voice. "I thought your name was Houston."

"Sam Houston Kelligan."

"The Texan Blink spoke about?" She had drawn away, frowning at him critically. "Son of Austin Kelligan, the Fort Worth billionaire."

"Guilty." He shrugged. "If that's a crime."

"Blink was asking if I knew you." She refused to smile. "He was calling you a billionaire playboy. Wanted to know why you were in the Corps."

"The same reason I imagine you are," he told her soberly. "I want to see Mars."

"I think—" She scrutinized his face. "I think I've seen

pictures of you. At sports events. Winning a glider race. Or maybe a ski event."

"I used to fly gliders," he said. "Built one myself. And I do like to ski."

"Blink said his paper keeps a file on you rich kids that play life like a game, with never a day's work to earn your way."

"Our training?" He felt defensive. "Do you call that play? I used to work summers for my father, running errands and driving trucks and packing boxes in a warehouse—till I decided I'd had enough of Kelligan Resources."

"So you found better games to play?" He heard scorn in her voice. "Scuba diving? Hang gliding? Climbing mountains?"

"Things I used to love." He searched for words to make her understand. "Back before the Corps, when Mars was just a dream. I got a little legacy from my grandmother. Spent it doing what I wanted—which didn't make my father very happy. No business of Blink's."

"His editor wants a story on you." With a hint of malice in her eyes, she watched his reaction. "He's calling you a planetary playboy. You're in the Corps, he says, just for the hell of it, with Mars just one more of your daredevil games."

"I suppose I do like to test myself." He had to nod. "To prove what I am. I imagine most of us in the Corps feel pretty much the same. How about you?"

"Perhaps." Her indifferent shrug dismissed his argument. "Getting back to Blink, he's hung up on what he imagines about the life we expect to lead on the ship and out on Mars. Beyond society, he kept saying. Beyond the law."

She flushed again.

"The dirty-minded bastard! Hinting we'd be staging sex orgies on Mars. Said you'd spoken of them—"

"I didn't!" he told her hotly. "Or rather, I was denying—"

No longer listening, she was looking up the aisle again, waving to Chandra and Kim Lo, who were coming aboard together. He called his own greeting and watched them find a seat. Both were on the East Asian team. Chandra had taken him to meet Kim's father, who had designed the system of anchor blocks and cables that held Asia Island in place above the Magellan Seamount.

Hopefully, he turned again to Jayne.

"Mars itself is a sort of game for all of us," he said. "I think most of us are in it for its own sake. Because it's the greatest thing a human being can undertake. Certainly nothing we're doing to interest Nicholas Blink."

"That—" She swallowed the half-spoken expletive.

"Let's forget him. Tell me about yourself. You never said where you're from, or what got you into the Corps."

"If you care. Nothing exciting."

"I'd like to know."

"Okay." She shrugged, with another expectant glance toward the door. "Born in Lakefield, Ohio. On the skids since Lakefield Sheet and Beam went out of business. A union town till then. My great-grandfather was killed by a company cop. Which may explain what turned me against big companies.

"We were an Irish blue-collar family, though Grandpa married a Polish girl. I grew up with four brothers and no money. We had to fight for what we wanted. Won sometimes, more often didn't. I took care of Mom till cancer killed her. I was working my way through college when I qualified for the Corps."

A quizzical grimace at him wrinkled her nose.

"So why should I love rich Texans?"

"Please!" he begged her earnestly. "I've left the Kelligan company behind."

"Maybe. If you win. If you lose, you're still a rich Texan. If I do, there's nothing."

"You'll never lose!" He waved his hand against her mocking shrug and added on impulse, "I hope we both win—and get to Mars together."

"Good luck, Mr. Kelligan." She gave him a level look and slowly shook her head. "But even on Mars, you'd still be a wealthy Texan."

"Texans are human." He tried to speak lightly, but a tremor crept into his voice. "Even my father. It might surprise you, but I got him to let his aerospace division bid on the Authority contracts. The company has been fabricating titanium skins for the landers."

"But not for love, Mr. Kelligan." She spoke the name with forbidding emphasis, and paused to consider him again before she added, "We have to get along because we're in the Corps together, but Mars will never be a group marriage—"

"Please forget that!"

"It sticks in my head." She shrugged his protest away. "For a very good reason, if you want to know."

"I do."

"Nothing I like remembering." She frowned and bit her lip and finally asked, "You know a Martin Gorley?"

"Marty?" He stared. "I know him, rather too well."

"Here's what happened." Her voice turned harder. "And what I think of Kelligans." She frowned. "I suppose you know your company has a big resort on a Pacific island they call Shangri-La?"

"I've seen the brochures." She said nothing, and he went on, "A pet project of Marty's. Close enough to Asia Island, which has no runways long enough for spaceplanes. He built a spaceplane terminal and a luxury hotel and casino complex, hoping to steal tourist traffic."

"If you like that sort of luxury!" She spoke with bitter force. "The PR people sent a dozen of us out to their grand opening. Two nights in Shangri-la. All free; booze and casino chips and big-time entertainment. A lot of people drunk. Among them your Mr. Gorley."

"Back at home, his mother keeps him sober."

"He tried to rape me." He flinched from the anger in her eyes, and saw her lip curl with a bleak satisfaction. "Next day he had a black eye."

"I saw that when he got back." He grinned. "He's been a bully all his life. But please—" He caught an uneasy breath. "I'm not Marty."

"Listen, Mr. Kelligan." She spoke his name with a cool finality. "That's how I feel. I'm happy in the Corps and I want to make the crew for Mars. That's all I really care about. Something I hope you understand. And now—"

She was suddenly smiling, looking toward the door again.

"Would you mind, Mr. Kelligan?" Arkady Lavrin was in the aisle, waving at her. "Could you find another seat?"

"If you wish." Unwillingly, he rose.

"Thanks, Hew." Lavrin gave him a one-sided grin. "Thoughtful of you."

Farther down the aisle, he saw a vacant seat beside Irina Barova. A striking blonde on the Russian team, she had been pictured in Blink's newspaper as "killer queen of the Corps."

"Sorry, Houston." She gave him a dazzling smile, but waved him away from the seat. "Otto's coming."

She enjoyed captivating men, and Otto Hellman was now her slave. A thickset, black-haired German, he came striding down the aisle with only a curt nod for Houston before he settled into the seat with a muscular arm around her.

Farther back, Houston took the last vacant seat, across from Chandra and Kim Lo. A gong pealed. A robotic voice warned them to secure themselves. The closing doors muffled the screaming engines. The cabin was windowless, but he felt the plane lurch and sway, felt the thrust of the jets hurling them down the long runway, toward the naked desert mountains and low Earth orbit and the Moon.

4

Farside

The Moon, with its helium-3 and the easy lift out of its shallow gravity well, became the doorway to space. The window was Farside Observatory, around on the face where Earth never rises and instruments are shielded from its disturbing radiations.

Jayne and Lavrin left the spaceplane ahead of him at Goddard Station. In spite of her coolness he couldn't help longing for another moment with her, but they had vanished before he found his gear.

He had to wait a dozen hours for the Moon shuttle, a larger, low-thrust craft. Roaming the station, getting used to free fall again, he drank a squeeze-bottle beer in the bar with Martin Luther White and clung a long time to a holdfast in the passenger lounge, absorbed in the white-and-blue splendor of the Earth rolling under him: huge and beautiful, nearly close enough to touch, yet not Mars.

He saw Jayne just once, leaving the cafeteria with Lavrin. Lavrin hailed him heartily, but she gave him only an unsmiling nod.

Grow up! he told himself. *She doesn't care for Kelligans. Accept the fact, and keep your mind on Mars.*

He found old friends, joked with them about their training days, all of them trying to seem more carefree and confident than they could have been. Yet his untamed heart still paused when he thought he saw her anywhere.

The shuttle came, and he went aboard to share a narrow cabin with White. Here water mass for the fusion engines was as precious as helium, because no water had been found on the Moon. Tanker craft had to lift it out from Earth.

Hoarding water, the shuttle took three days to reach lunar orbit. He watched the slow rotation of the dwindling Earth and the slower creep of sunlight across the impact scars of the swelling Moon. He worked out in the gym. He stood watches with the pilot, a Brazilian volunteer who still dreamed of his own chance at Mars.

Landers took them down from orbit, half a dozen at a time. Jayne and Lavrin disembarked ahead of him again, and he called himself a fool again because her distance hurt. When his own turn came, he went off with White.

The lander dropped to snag a braking cable that guided them over a safety net stretched across a crater and finally down to the terminal dock. A tunnel car took them on to Farside. Most of it was buried deep beneath the lunar regolith, safe from radiation, but the quartz dome above the main habitat let him see the dead-gray moonscape and the scattered installations.

He knew it from training here, yet the stark contrasts still entranced him. The high-tech hardware, mirror-domed labs and instrument shelters, the great radio dish suspended inside its own crater pit, the optical telescopes and dipole antennas arrayed like robot armies on a wide crater floor, the X-ray and gamma-ray telescopes. He felt a moment of pride and a shock of reality. For all the

high-tech power, it was still only a small and lonely outpost against the dead black sky, the desolate waste of
broken rock and dead gray dust, the ink-black shadows
cast by the savage sun just rising.

Reporting for his turn in the underground Corps complex, he unpacked his gear, checked what he could see of
his crated rover, inspected the power cells and filters for
his air unit, tried the fit of his yellow pressure suit. On the
day before the run, White called him away from breakfast in the mess hall to receive a personal laserphone call.

"Houston?" Marty Gorley's whining nasal twang had
come a quarter-million miles out from Earth and on
around the Moon, but it seemed almost at his ear. "Are
you there? Your mother and Miss Halloran want to talk.
Priorities don't come easy, but I've wangled three minutes."

"I'm here."

Three long seconds to wait, while the lasers bounced
his voice to far Fort Worth, and his mother's thin-voiced
question came back.

"Hew?" He heard her anxiety. "You're really out there
on the Moon?"

"Back side of the Moon. Just at breakfast."

"Hew, here's LeeAnn."

"Houston?" Her voice was tight and breathless, like
his mother's. "Are you okay?"

"Better than ever," he told her. "Gear checked and
ready. Final physicals passed. Only one last briefing, and
I'm ready for the run."

"Sorry if we spoiled your breakfast, but your
mother—we both had to talk to you. This race—it's so
dreadful! We hadn't realized, but the news is full of the
dangers. Killer particles from storms on the sun. Such
awful country! No air to breathe if anything goes wrong.
Nobody to help. Hew, are you sure—"

Her voice trembled and failed.

"I'll make it," he said. "Bear up, Lee. And please do what you can for Mom. Too bad she takes it so hard, but I can't give up my life. Help her understand."

The long seconds stretched until he thought they had been cut off.

"Houston—" Her voice came faintly at last. "If you lose your race—" Sobs broke it again. "If you get back safe—and don't make the Mars crew—I love you, Hew! I always will."

"Lee, please—"

He was glad when the operator cut them off.

Returning to the mess hall at the cautious lunar shuffle that kept his head from bumping the tunnel roof, he found the two images side by side in his imagination, as if he had a choice. LeeAnn, the friend since childhood, tall and blonde, hard to beat at tennis, quietly intense at everything she did, always smiling happily to see him. Jayne Ryan, who didn't seem to care how she looked and hated corporations and wanted nothing from any wealthy Texan.

Why sweat? he asked himself. *Let the race decide.*

♂

The slow sun had climbed two days higher before White called them in groups of eight into an underground briefing room. He handed them maps and signal codes, and brought them to attention for Colonel Orbeliani, a stout black-moustached Asiatic Georgian whose harsh staccato accents were hard to follow.

"Ready, gentlemen?" Scanning them, he found two female trainees. "Ladies?"

"Sir?" Kim Lo had raised a diffident hand. "May I ask—"

"Let's get on." He ignored her. "You will find Farside located near the center of your map."

Harshly abrupt as he was, Houston felt sorry for him. A pioneer in the Corps, and a brilliant engineer, he had been disqualified for Mars for colorblindness. Still loyal to the Corps, he had never recovered from that bitter disappointment.

"Examine your maps," he went on. "You will find your starting points marked in red. They are five hundred kilometers out, spaced a hundred kilometers apart along a circular perimeter line."

"Our question, Colonel." The man beside Kim Lo called louder. "Please?"

Orbeliani nodded. "Speak."

"Five hundred kilometers, sir? Our suits are good for only forty hours, max. Are we expected to finish in forty hours? Five hundred—"

"Not so!" he barked. "You each will have a spare carbon filter and a spare power cell. The rating is thirty hours per unit, average safety margins ten hours. You have eighty hours, plus or minus."

"Other questions?" He didn't wait. "You have been briefed on the rules. Each of you will find his own way from the starting line to Farside. Any contacts or attempts at mutual aid may be penalized. Your finish line is the perimeter circle round Farside installations. Observers will be stationed along it to report arrival times."

At last he let Kim Lo speak.

"Sir?" Here without Chandra, who was in another group, she looked lost. "Is it fair, sir? If we don't all run the same course?"

"Mars itself will not be fair." The colonel shrugged. "You have been trained to take what comes. Starting stations for the run have been assigned at random, by computer."

"If we have trouble?"

"Some of you will." He shrugged. "Expecting that, we are issuing each of you a shelter bag and a rocket flare.

The flare can rise thirty kilometers, lighting the area for several minutes. The balloon bag is equipped with an emergency oxygen bottle, a signal strobe, and a radio. A good ten hours of life, while you wait for rescue. That will be attempted. However—"

Scowling at her, he shook his black-maned head.

"Remember, we are choosing crew for Mars. No rescue tenders waiting there. We need no people who expect them. Ask for aid, you're out of the Corps."

♂

First in the ready room, he called greetings as others arrived to wait for the tender: Ken Caulfield, a jovial rival who wanted to bet a beer on the race; Rosa Waldencraft, the sturdy Australian girl who had worked with White at the Farside exobiology lab and somehow escaped infection; Hiro Yanaga and Mayo Watanabe, who sat murmuring together.

All wore tight blue skinsuits. The eight pressure suits hung in a row behind their chairs. Hollow things, stiff yellow plastic and grotesquely sagging, they looked to him like the empty hides of slaughtered animals. He shoved aside the painful notion.

Andy Petersen sauntered in, grinning cheerily, greeting everybody with some small ironic joke. He was a tall blond Norwegian; he and Houston had skied in Colorado before they were sworn into the Corps. Adolfo Morelos followed, the silent Spaniard with the agile grace of a *torero,* said to have the best math brain in the Corps. Good companions in training, they were now tense and self-absorbed, merely nodding when they saw him.

One chair was still empty. Waiting for Jayne? He tried to quench the wish to see her, the hope they both might pass the test and go on to Mars together. Up against these keen contenders, he needed no distraction.

"Hallo, sweethearts!"

The lilt of Irina Barova. "Killer queen" to Blink's *Keyhole Spy*. Daughter of a retired cosmonaut turned academician and a failed Moscow actress, she had grown up torn between their desires for her. High science or higher art? Ambitious enough to try for both, she had mastered science enough for the Corps and studied her mother's thespic skills.

"Kelligan?" Lithe blonde perfection in the tight skin-suit, she glided into the empty chair beside him and leaned to dazzle him with a blue-eyed smile. "The billionaire, as the reporter told me? Really the son of the great American industrialist?"

"No billionaire." He shook his head, uncomfortable with her. "Austin Kelligan is my father, but I left his company and his money back on Earth."

"That may be." Her shrug was a sinuous sway, graceful as if practiced for the camera. "Yet you will go home again." She leaned closer and he caught her strong perfume. "Great plans for then?"

"I have none."

"Make them." Others were listening, and she lifted her voice. "Back from the conquest of Mars, you will be a world hero. Add the Kelligan fortune, and you can do or be anything you choose."

"I'm not there yet," he said. "If I do get to Mars, I hope to stay."

Waiting for the tender, he studied the maps and inspected his gear again. The pressure suit had taken a big bite out of his allotted million. Molded to his measure, it was clumsily humped with life-support gear: water bottle and power cell and cooling unit and the catalytic filter that broke down exhaled carbon dioxide and released pure oxygen. *Spacemaster* was the red-and-blue logo across the chest, but it stank of new plastics, less a marvel of high technology than a trial to be endured.

The maps were large-scale photos taken from space, overprinted with contour lines and data. Locating the red dot that marked his starting point, he tried to trace possible routes. None looked easy.

White alerted them at last to board the tender. Shaped a little like some gigantic insect, it was a huge pressure cylinder carried on six long lever legs with great balloon-tired wheels for feet.

"I'm your driver." He herded them inside. "And your squad commander."

His usual disarming grin was gone, and Waldencraft stopped to ask how he felt.

"Okay, okay!" With that impatient mutter, he turned and raised his voice for all to hear. "We've got a lot of kilometers to go. That will take time. Race clocks start when I drop you off. Till then, relax if you can. Your seats recline. You'll find snacks and water in the galley."

He drove fast on the slag-paved road that ran toward the mines. Around the perimeter, however, there was no road. The big machine had to labor, whining and lurching, pitching across the rocks and pits and ridges of the dead moonscape.

In the cab, White was moodily silent. Houston joined him for a time, but he didn't want to talk. Simply absorbed in the task of driving? Or depressed over losing his chance at Mars? Thinking of the Mars dust and its "half-bugs," Houston asked for more about it.

"Classified," White said shortly. "Wait for your briefing."

Watching for tracks in the dust, which would last almost forever, Houston saw none at all. Even here, tracing out that imaginary circle on the map, they were already going where no human had ever been. He felt a thrill of adventure, chilled in an instant by the sense of lifeless worlds and lonely stars and the dead black void between, overwhelmed by a universe too vast and alien for human comprehension.

Back in the cabin, he found his companions as self-absorbed as White, silent or quietly murmuring, poring over maps and codes, trying to doze. Called one by one, they got into their gear, sealed their helmets, climbed into the lock. The last to go, he was left alone with White. His own turn came.

"Hard luck, Luth." He waved his farewell. "Wish you were with us."

"Look—" A coughing spasm bent White across the wheel. "Look at this."

He ripped his shirt open to show inflamed and swollen patches on his dark chest.

"Damn that dust! Fever's evidently recurrent." Harshly, he laughed. "Could be I'm the lucky one, staying here at home."

5

Moon Day

The Moon's day is long. Orbiting with the same face always toward Earth, it still turns with respect to the sun, rotating once in twenty-nine and a half days. The lunar day is two weeks of savage sunlight, the night two weeks of killing cold.

Houston waved farewell to White and dragged his crated gear out of the lock and down the ramp to the gray moondust on the floor of a shallow crater. Standing beside it, he watched the tender lumber up the crater ridge, blaze for a moment in the sun, and vanish beyond the near black horizon.

Suddenly alone, chilled with a sense of total isolation, he stood still a moment before he looked around to get his bearings. The sun hung four days high, midway to the black zenith, blinding on this waste of harshly-lit boulders and dead gray dust no living thing had ever tracked. He was five hundred cruel kilometers from the next human face, the next human voice—

So what? He shrugged. *This isn't even Mars.*

Still clumsy in the stiff yellow suit, he bent to unpack and assemble his crated rover. It was something he had practiced twenty times, but here his gloves were too awkward, the sun too dazzling on everything it touched, the shadows too dark. He fumbled a bolt and had to scrabble in the dust for it.

The Mars rovers would be fusion-powered, but helium fusion engines had been beyond his budget for the Moon. His power came from a tall sail, stiff with solar cells. The rover was a flimsy thing, stripped of every needless ounce. Four big-tired wheels on a sprawling, spidery frame that carried the control column, his narrow seat, and a tiny tool locker.

The sail was awkward to hang on the telescoping mast and boom, but he got it up at last, swung it to catch the sun, and climbed into the seat. The wheels turned. He steered out of the crater, toward Farside.

Frail as it was, the rover ran smoothly, but the map was nearly useless. Drawn from space photos, it showed the wide moonscape well enough: craters and ejecta falls he wanted to avoid, paths around them he had hoped to follow. Down here, however, nothing looked like the map. All he saw was chaos. Hot light and black shadow. An endless maze of broken rock and powdery dust, of huge pits and small pits, all sliced off by the close mid-night horizon.

With never a landmark he knew and only his gyrocompass and shadow patterns to guide him, he drove north-east, skirting pits and circling peaks, searching out surfaces fit for the rover. The burning sun hung motion-less, as if time had stopped. Every shadow-bottomed pit and dust-gray ridge came to look like every other.

Grown groggy, he sucked hot coffee out of the nipple and drove on. He sucked fruit juices, nuzzled space bis-cuits and energy wafers out of the dispenser, and still drove on until the rover stalled on an ejecta slope too steep for it. He moved the sail to shade his body, slept till he dreamed that Marty Gorley had won the race and stolen his chance at Mars.

Shocked awake, he drove on.

Sometimes the jolting made him giddy. The moon-scape grew haunting, old and dead and alien as Mars would be. The impacts that shattered this gray rock and powdered this gray dust had struck before life on Earth began. The live world had never even risen in this cold black sky.

Fighting that spell of alien strangeness, he shook him-self and sucked again at his coffee. Finally he stopped to check the gyrocompass and his map again—feeling too dopey to be sure he understood them. He oiled the wheel bearings, though they were meant to need no oil. He inspected the motors and steering gear. They looked okay, but the gritty dust would wear them out.

Again he drove on, always drove on.

Hoarding power, he turned the cooler down until he sweated in the suit and had to turn it up again. Sitting hunched on the pitching seat, he let his mind drift back to the living Earth, to his mother and LeeAnn and their hopeless fretting for him; to his father, nursing disappointment with him; to Marty Gorley, who would doubtless be happy to see him gone to Mars.

Why care? He gripped the wheel and steered around a boulder. *They're all gone behind.*

Or would they ever be? Even if he got to Mars?

♂

Once he dozed and let the rover pitch him off. Awake before he hit the rocks, he scrambled to his feet and pursued it desperately. Too fast for him, it was almost out of sight before it veered and tipped the sail out of the sun to let him overtake it.

He slept again in the shadow of the sail, and steered on northeast through broken half-dreams. The bald and grownup Marty was yelling at him like the four-year-old bully who had run to kick his Martian city; LeeAnn waited for him on a rock ahead with a cold beer in her hand, changing to Jayne Ryan before she turned away and disappeared.

Though the sun seemed frozen in time, the tiny amber numerals danced fast in the clock display below his faceplate. Thirty hours gone. Thirty-five. The bright red needle and the green one crept toward zero, reading the life left in the power cell and the catalytic filter.

He tried to forget them. What he had to watch was the gyrocompass, the angle of his shadow, the slopes and rocks ahead. Yet he found himself staring, till the crimson flicker across the dial struck him like an unkind blow.

WARNING! the red letters flashed. REPLACE CARBON FILTER! REPLACE POWER CELL!

He stopped the rover and tilted the sail for shade while he made the change. Holding the spare cell in his gloves, he rehearsed what he had to do: unlatch the life-pack on his back and hinge it into reach; disconnect the dead cell; unlock the retainers; pull it free; position the fresh cell;

fasten the retainers; hook it up; secure and power the life-pack.

To let him keep on breathing.

The displays went out when he pulled the release lever. The helmet fan stopped its insect whine. The air seemed instantly bad. The spare cell slipped out of his glove—but fell very slowly. He recovered it, got it into the retainers, snapped connectors back to the terminal, repositioned the pack, clicked the switches.

The fan droned, and he could fill his lungs.

But still the air was bad, the carbon filter clogged. Changing it was easier. He held his breath while he bypassed the air unit to snap the new one into place. Sweet air filled the helmet, and again he drove on.

On and on, till it seemed forever. The rover lurched and swayed and tried to toss him off. He dozed and shook himself and dozed again. His muscles cramped. He itched and sweated in the suit. Tight spots rubbed him raw. He watched the red needle and the green one creep across the dial, measuring off the lives of the cell and the filter. Perhaps his own?

Too dull and tired to think or feel or care, he drove on till he saw wheel ruts in a patch of dust. He followed them fifty meters farther and stopped the rover when their meaning hit him.

Wheel tracks!

He blinked his gummy eyes and stared again, sucked more coffee and peered again, finally climbed off the rover to walk ahead and stoop to study them. They were real, made by tires with molded cleats like his own.

Or actually his own? Was he lost, out of his head with fatigue and strain, misreading the map and compass? Had he circled back to his own trail? He turned uncertainly, shading his faceplate to study the gray stone jungle around him, and climbed a boulder to look ahead.

The tracks seemed to run straight, as straight as rocks

and cliffs allowed. He saw no other vehicle. Not yet at the zenith, the sun still burned out of the east. His shortened shadow still lay to the west, accurate as the compass. He felt suddenly certain he had never seen the long ridge beside him, curved like a long railway embankment, made by the ejecta sprayed from the sharp-walled crater behind it. The ruts did run on toward where Farside must lie. Some fellow contestant had been here ahead of him.

Why here?

Starting a hundred kilometers apart, their routes had to converge, but they were not intended to cross. Reeling with fatigue, no longer sure of anything, he climbed back on the rover and followed the trail again till he lost it on a stony slope beyond that dust-floored hollow.

The way grew rougher, the scattered boulders larger. On either hand, naked gray ridges ran closer and closer together, the ring walls of two great craters with only a narrow ravine between them.

They thrust higher, closing in to form a narrow, black-shadowed canyon that rose steeply to the black horizon. He stopped on a boulder pile to look for a way ahead. All he saw was the frozen stone that recorded the cosmic epic of fiery planetesimals falling back together after the cataclysmic impact that split the early Earth to make the Moon. No passage that looked safe. But here, in another scrap of dust, he found the same dark-shadowed ruts.

And the machine that had made them.

Another Moon rover, different in design but flimsy as his own. It lay tipped on its side in a pile of rocks half a kilometer beyond. The driver, a forlorn little figure in a yellow pressure suit, stood beside it, faceplate shaded, staring back at him.

♂

Perhaps as groggy as he was, the driver had tried to follow a narrowing shelf between a room-sized boulder and a crater pit. The front wheel of the rover had failed to clear the boulder. The flimsy little vehicle now lay on the rim of the pit, the sail fallen flat. The driver was squatted now over the twisted wheel.

Houston stopped.

"Can I help?"

"Back off!" He knew the crashing radio voice. "Don't stop."

"Jayne Ryan?" She rose to beckon him away, and he glimpsed her face in the helmet, sweat-beaded and grimly set. "Don't you need—"

"Mr. Kelligan?" A hint of mockery in his name, but then her tone turned imperative. "Drive on! No contacts allowed, if you recall."

"If you're in trouble—"

"Not your business."

She turned to bend over the wreck. The front axle, he saw, was broken. He sat half a minute on his own machine, watching silently. She was right, of course. Accepting aid, she would forfeit her chance at Mars. Offering aid, he might compromise his own.

"I'll report your problem," he called. "If or when I get to Farside."

Busy with the wheel, she ignored him.

He shrugged and backed away to find another route. None proved much better. He came to a scarp too steep to climb and drove many kilometers along it before he found a pass. One of his thin-walled tires exploded, but he had a spare. The rover pitched him off again and overturned. The sun-driven motors were dead when he tried to go on, until he found and patched a broken wire.

Farther on—he was never sure how far—he began hearing voices. They were only in his head, he thought, until at last he recognized them as radio calls from a

lander descending toward Farside. With a directional fix
from that, he turned a little to the left, topped a final
mountain ridge, and found the observatory.

Or only a mirage? He wondered, but it stayed real as
he came down the slope. The big Verne dish, the landing
net, the arrayed optical and radio telescopes spread
across the broad crater floor. Knife-sharp shadows under
the sun, all too real to be a hallucination.

The tender rolled to meet him on the perimeter road,
ten-meter wheels looming huge above him. The lock
opened. The ramp ran down. Haunted with his concern
for Jayne, he loaded the rover into the transport rack and
climbed through the lock. The driver was a new cadet,
hopefully sweating out her own future chance at Mars.

"I want to report a runner in trouble," he told her.
"Jayne Ryan. American team. Her vehicle's wrecked.
She needs help."

"No rovers free." She scanned her monitor. "Reports
enough of runners in trouble, but nothing heard from
Ryan. We'll try to haul her in if she signals, but rescue
squads are taking distress calls in turn."

She made him leave the worn and rock-battered rover
for engineering inspection. Before he could shower or eat
or sleep, he had to let the medics run a routine profile
check and report to Colonel Orbeliani for debriefing.

"Lieutenant Kelligan, sir."

Discipline was seldom formal in the Corps, but Colonel Orbeliani waited for his salute and returned it stiffly.

"Duty completed, Lieutenant." He bent to check
something on a yellow pad. "Dismissed."

"Sir, when will the winners be announced?"

"No winners." He stood waiting till Orbeliani added,
"However, you have qualified."

"Sir?" Here without his pressure gear the world
seemed strange, voices too loud, lights too bright, his

movements uncontrolled. He wasn't sure he understood. "For Mars?"

"Nyet. Not yet."

He kept waiting, swaying on his feet.

"Nineteen so far." Orbeliani scowled at the yellow pad. "Mars Command will pick *Ares* personnel back at White Sands. Final selections wait for total profiles."

6

Profile

The Corps volunteers, "Earth's Selected Best," were chosen to fit physiological and psychological profiles that included physical fitness, intelligence, competence, social compatibility, special skills required, and estimated ability to survive and work under conditions of isolation, hardship, and stress.

Houston slept twelve hours. Awake again, and famished, he came upon Arkady Lavrin in the underground mess hall and asked for news about Jayne.

"Got here ahead of you, and already gone." Lavrin grinned as if amused by his concern. "Caught the lander up two hours ago. Asked me to tell you she made it on her own."

"Thanks." He tried not to show too much emotion. "I saw her in trouble. A wheel off her rover, but she wanted no help."

"Jayne?" Lavrin grinned wider. "A broken axle didn't faze her. Welded it with sunlight and a concave mirror."

♂

The rail gun on the eastern cliffs tossed his own lander back to orbital rendezvous with the *Oberth.* He spent three days aboard the shuttle, another at Goddard, before the spaceplane dropped him back to Earth.

Walking down the ramp at White Sands, he filled his lungs with clean desert air that carried dry fragrances of sage and mesquite. He flung his arms wide, happily free of his stiff pressure gear. The green lawns and green trees here had always seemed extravagant, but he enjoyed them now.

They were alive, a precious anodyne for the Moon's dead and deadening gray monotony. Listening to a mockingbird, he stopped for a moment wondering. If Earth felt so good after only two weeks away, how would he feel coming home from two years on Mars? People grown strange, friends half forgotten, his own bone and muscle weakened from the lesser gravity?

So what?

He shrugged and hurried to reclaim his bag, suddenly six times heavier than when he checked it at Farside. He called his mother. Her voice thin and querulous, she asked when he would be home. He didn't know.

He was two days at White Sands. In the Corps hospital, he endured one more ordeal by clinical test. In debriefing rooms, he faced Corps officers and Corps psychologists and Corps engineers who wanted to know more than he could remember about all he had done to prepare for the run and how he had felt at every moment of it. Corps technicians in the labs wired him to recorders and kept him staring at monitors for hours, while they demanded instant responses to riddles he never entirely understood.

"Congratulations, Kelligan." The last examiner frowned at a desk monitor and rose to shake his hand. "You and your equipment scored well on the Moon. Your lab results look okay. I can place you on the final roster, after one more question."

He waited, while the examiner studied him again.

"Have you named a preferred companion?"

He shook his head unhappily, thinking of Jayne. "Must I?"

"Optional." The examiner shrugged. "The *Ares* crew, as you know, will number eight. One man and one woman from each power's team. We can't ask them to marry—their private lives are their own. But we do have to think of social dynamics. On request, couples may be processed as units."

"If it's optional, leave it blank. I'm not attached."

"Very well." The examiner bent to his keyboard and looked up again. "Report to Armstrong Hall at thirteen hundred."

♂

He found Jayne and Lavrin there ahead of him.

"Hiya, Hew!" Lavrin spoke most of the time in the Southwestern drawl he had picked up at Texas Tech. "Welcome aboard!"

A dozen others were back from the Moon. Martin Luther White, alone in a chair near the podium. Ram Chandra and Kim Lo, seated together. Otto Hellman and Irina Barova. Had Lavrin and Jayne named each other as preferred companions? Russian and American? Would that be allowed?

He couldn't ask, but he stopped where they stood. She looked at him gravely, eyes a little widened as if in surprise to see him here.

"Glad you made it," he told her. "I hated leaving you out there alone."

"Perhaps." She shrugged, reproving him. "But we do have rules, Mr. Kelligan."

"Sorry," he said. "I thought you were in trouble."

"We'll have trouble on Mars, if we get there." Her

tone was flatly matter-of-fact. "To survive, we'll have to follow rules."

♂

Colonel Orbeliani came striding to the lectern when they were seated.

"The final roster." Scowling at a yellow pad, he called their names. "Twenty-one qualified for consideration. Eight will be picked for the *Ares*. Eight more alternates, possible personnel for the *Nergal* when it is completed."

"Sir?" Hellman asked. "Our takeoff date?"

"Launch window open eighteen more days," Orbeliani growled. "All personnel to be aboard seven days early. Crew therefore to leave White Sands next week."

"When will we know?"

"In due time." Curtly abrupt, Orbeliani beckoned White to the podium. "First, however, a most unfortunate development to report. Lieutenant White will brief you."

White rose a little unsteadily, Houston thought. His face looked thinned and flushed, and he wore neat adhesive patches on his forehead and his lower lip. Silent for a moment, collecting himself, he gripped the lectern as if he needed support.

"Sorry as hell." He shook his head, grinning painfully. "Something I hate to be telling you, but Command says you've got to have it now. When you hear it, some of you may want to opt out."

Startled whispers died into silence.

"You know we sent seven—" His voice squeaked, and he stopped for a gulp of water. "Sent seven unmanned probes to Mars. Five got back. They brought instrument records and nearly three hundred kilograms of Martian geology. Compressed atmospheric samples. Rocks, dust, drill cores. Clay, permafrost, water ice and carbon dioxide snow from the polar caps.

"All kept in quarantine for study at the Farside labs. Three of us volunteered for the job. The stuff seemed harmless at first, but we did take precautions. Worked in plastic suits in a sealed room with negative air pressure, behind three sealed doors. Stripped and scrubbed and took antiseptic showers before we got out.

"Interesting chemistry, something expected since the results from the Viking experiments. A lot of surface peroxides and superoxides. But something else was a real surprise. A molecule that replicates when you warm dust samples in water. That excited the team biologist. Life, he thought. It is carbon-based, combined with oxygen, nitrogen and hydrogen, but not structured like anything on Earth. He called it protolife.

"And warned us that it could be deadly. Testing it, we fed it to rats and injected them with it. They all got sick. A lot of them died, but some seemed to recover. Healthy rats were not infected by sick rats caged with them.

"The stuff was poison, we concluded, but no major danger to Earth or even to the expedition. I suppose I got careless." His patched lip twisted. "One day I was using a chisel to crack a sample of surface rock. It shattered into dust. My mask had slipped, and I got a whiff of it."

Wincing, he rubbed the patches on his face.

"I got as sick as our rats. The doc on the team told me it might be only flu, but he kept me on a cot in the quarantine room. Fever, cough, skin lesions."

He shrugged, with a bitter little grin.

"Cost my chance at Mars."

He glanced aside at Orbeliani, who stood watching bleakly.

"Not that it's killing me. After a couple of weeks in isolation, I felt okay. Tests found antibodies to the protolife in my blood but no live organisms. The infected rats, of course, had seemed not to carry any contagion. Finally, when I seemed to be no risk to anybody, they let me out. I came back to Earth—and got hit again. Perhaps not quite so hard, but the infection seems to be recurrent." He paused inquiringly. "Questions?"

Chandra gulped and asked, "What about treatment?"

"They're studying the antibodies in my blood, hoping to develop a vaccine. That will take time. We've found a couple of drugs that kill the bugs in test tubes, but the side effects seem to be worse than the infection. They're tough. Have to be, or they wouldn't be alive—if you call them alive—after a billion years exposed on the surface of Mars."

"Can we survive there?"

"I'm surviving." His patched lip twitched to another stiff grin. "Maybe you can escape it. You'll be living in sealed spaces with positive air pressure. You should be able to avoid much contact with the environment." He shrugged. "Nothing promised."

"Colonel?" Lavrin called to Orbeliani. "Should we delay the flight?"

White sat down as if he needed to.

"Impossible." The colonel stalked back to the podium. "Though this is certainly disturbing. We did consider postponement. For compelling reasons, however, we have agreed that the *Ares* must take off as planned."

"Sir," Lavrin protested, "I see strong reasons for delay. The next window will open in only two years. By then, we should have the vaccine. *Nergal* can be completed. We can go with two ships instead of one. Sixteen people instead of eight, providing a wider safety margin—"

"If we had two years." The colonel's hard voice stopped him. "In the judgment of the Corps, we don't. Too many delays. Too many billion already spent. World support failing. On Mars, you may survive exposure to the protolife. After our review of the evidence, we believe you can. Here on Earth, however, the Authority may not survive."

"Sir, do you expect—"

Orbeliani checked him again, with an impatient gesture.

"Discussion enough. The *Ares* will take off on schedule. You have heard Lieutenant White. We are granting you forty-eight hours for decision. Those who wish may leave the Corps. The Mars team will be selected from those who stay.

"If you wish to be considered, report back within forty-eight hours for final tests and briefings. *Ares* will be ready for flight. A spaceplane will be waiting to carry selected crew directly to it."

"Colonel, please—"

Morelos had another question, but he dismissed them and stalked impatiently away.

"Well, Kelligan?" Jayne Ryan spoke to him as they filed out of the room, a speculative challenge in her green-gray eyes. "What do you think?"

"I don't have to think," he told her. "I'm going to Mars."

7

Windows

Earth, moving faster in orbit, overtakes Mars every 26 months. Launch dates must be calculated to fit these passages, and delays between open windows are thus about two years.

Forty-eight hours: one night at home.

LeeAnn Halloran met him at the airport. Laughing in

happy relief, she opened her arms for his kiss and clung as if afraid to let him go. Her bright blonde hair was fragrant with the expensive scent she called Wildfire. Enveloped in it, wishing she had been Jayne Ryan, he felt a brief stab of guilt.

"Hew!" Her voice was a husky contralto. "Thank God you're safe! We were all worried so. Your mother made me promise to drive you straight home. She's asking both our families to your homecoming dinner."

It was a fine summer day. She led him across the parking lot to her new car, a birthday gift from her father. A sleek red convertible, it still smelled of new leather and she loved it. The top was down, the air warm. He breathed it deep, rejoicing in its winelike scent of new life growing.

"Special weather, just for you!"

She smiled into his face. She had always loved him, and she was splendid now, her fine head high, bright hair free in the wind, the sun caressing her creamy cheek. Yet he felt the tension she was trying to hide, felt her fear of the time when he might leave her for Mars. On impulse, he slid his arm around her and almost said how much he loved her.

Almost—

But not yet. Not unless he found his name missing from that final flight roster.

His mother met them at the door. She looked wan and anxious, dark shadows around her eyes, but she had been busy in the kitchen. The whole house was fragrant with the chocolate-pecan brownies he used to love when he was a child. He found them, hot on a platter in the living room. Maria brought coffee for him and LeeAnn, and hot water to make tea for her.

He ate a brownie he didn't really want, because she was offering them so eagerly, and tried to answer her questions about the run. Suddenly she burst into tears.

"I—I'm sorry, Hew." She wiped at her eyes. "It's just too dreadful."

"Mom, the race wasn't dreadful!" He grinned and raised his hand against her anxiety. "It was what I live for. A wonderful adventure. Of course there was hardship. Maybe danger. But still great fun."

"Are you—" She scanned his face, desperately intent. "Are you home for awhile?"

A hard lump in his throat, he had to shake his head.

"Just overnight. We're due back tomorrow. That's when we find out who's on the Mars crew."

"I was hoping—" Thin lips whispering, she caught her breath and wiped her pale cheeks again. "But I guess you still—"

She couldn't go on.

"If I do get the chance—" Saying nothing of protolife, he shook his head at their tight faces. "I'm going."

"That's the way he always was." His mother turned to LeeAnn, speaking very faintly and half to herself. "Always taking such fearful risks. He never seemed to understand—"

She checked herself and reached for her teacup.

"Or is it just me?" The cup rattled in the saucer. She set it down and looked back at him. "I don't—I just don't—" She rose unsteadily and stood a moment looking sadly down at him. "I'm going up to rest."

He walked with her across the room, his arm around her frail old body, and watched her climb the stair. Standing there till LeeAnn spoke, he wondered what his life might become if the *Ares* went without him, wondered again if he could ever endure the sort of future they kept planning for him.

LeeAnn stayed another hour, but she didn't want to hear any more about the Moon. She kept talking too fast and too brightly instead about the good times she recalled from their childhood and their school vacations.

About the colt named Nero they had broken to the saddle, their rafting trip with their fathers on the Rio Grande, their weekend in Nuevo Laredo. Trying hard, he saw, to make him feel her own fondness for the memories.

He ached for her.

"Listen, LeeAnn—" Finally, he had to interrupt her. "I remember when we promised we'd always be best friends. But you know what Mars means to me. If they let me go, it's probably forever. If they don't—"

He shrugged.

"Thank—thank you, Hew." She stood up, her voice quivering. "You were always honest—and I guess I've always known you'd never fit my dreams. Maybe I'm the fool." She caught a long breath and managed a pale small smile. "See you at dinner."

He walked her out to the red convertible. She clung hard when he kissed her, and he heard her sob when she broke abruptly away.

♂

His father came home from the office with two more guests for dinner, Marty Gorley and Lucina. His mother had not expected them, and he saw Maria rearranging the table. Lucina was a striking, lively woman with keen black eyes and sleek black hair. Marty's mother, she was his father's long-time private secretary. He had learned long ago that she was also his father's mistress.

The shock had come on his twelfth birthday, when the Hallorans still owned their country place, adjoining the Kelligan ranch. LeeAnn had asked him for dinner there and baked her very first cake in his honor. White coconut, with twelve tiny blue candles. They were down in the pasture after dinner, saddling Nero, when she asked him in a solemn half-whisper where his father was.

"In Kansas City," he said. "At some energy convention."

"I don't think so." She shook her head, leaning closer. "My folks saw him Saturday in New Orleans. In a bar on Bourbon Street. Lucina was with him. Mother says she always thought they were having an affair."

He wouldn't believe it. In the den that night, after his mother had gone to bed, he told his father about it, hoping for an angry denial.

"Houston, I guess it's time you knew." His father shrugged as if it shouldn't really matter. "It began before you were born. We'd set up a new sales office in Mexico City. I was there to look it over when I found Lucina." His father's voice softened as he spoke her name. "Hardly twenty, but already assistant sales manager."

He'd stood listening, feeling sick.

"She was stunning then." His father smiled, remembering. "Pure Spanish blood, and proud of it. A fine old family, gone bankrupt. I fell for her. She was willing. I brought her back and made a job for her in the office here."

He shook his head, afraid to believe.

"At your age, I know it's hard for you to understand." His father had seen his pain. "But you'll be learning that men have needs. And Lucina—" His father smiled again. "Really, she's been a great thing for the company. Drive and brains to match her looks. Almost a partner now. She's my right hand in Kelligan Resources."

"All these years—" He couldn't go on.

"Son, it's time you learned." His father's voice grew stern, almost scolding. "Your mother never cared for sex. I have to have it. I'm not ashamed of anything I've done. I'm sorry if you're ashamed of me."

"Does Mother—"

"She knows," his father nodded. "Though I never told her."

♂

That painful secret ached again tonight. Lucina hugged him to welcome him home. She had always seemed too eager for him to like her, smiling too soon with her fine white teeth, flattering him with everything she said. Now she wanted to know all about his test on the Moon, and she had brought a gift to welcome him home, a crudely comic little image of a suited spaceman as imagined by some Taxco silversmith. It was nothing he would want on Mars, or anywhere else, but he thanked her politely.

Marty was almost his own age, a plump energetic blue-jowled man with oily black hair around a huge bald spot and Lucina's flashy smile. A playmate long ago, before he knew about Lucina, Marty had never quite been a friend. Not since he had kicked apart his Martian city.

♂

Dinner tonight was not until eight. The Hallorans had not arrived. His mother was still upstairs, avoiding Lucina. Waiting, they sat in the living room. His father asked how things had been on the Moon, but he and Lucina were soon talking instead about an option on a Canadian oil shale prospect. She had brought a copy of the option, and his father took her up to his own room to discuss what to offer.

He and Marty were left alone together.

"News for you, Houston." Marty's voice dropped confidentially. "Three of your runners died on the Moon."

"Are you sure?" He had heard nothing of the sort.

"My inside line." Kelligan Resources had fabricated titanium skins for the landers the *Ares* and the *Nergal* were to carry, and Marty liked to boast of company

secrets he shared. "Got the facts just today. Three dead."
He counted them on three blunt fingers. "A Japanese,
when his air unit failed. A Frenchman, cooked in the sun
when he lost his suit coolant. A Russian girl, killed under
her vehicle when she ran it off a cliff."

Tanaka? Pierre? Olga? All were old friends from the
hard years of training. He asked anxiously for names, but
Marty hadn't inquired.

"Bad news for your Authority." Not for Marty; his
bulging, dull-colored eyes had narrowed with his habit-
ual knowing squint. "And maybe something worse. How
about these proto-bugs the probes brought back from
Mars?"

"What's that?"

"Really, Hew?" Marty's voice accused him. "Don't
you know?"

He waited till Marty went on.

"Your Colonel Orbel-whatever tried the same ploy.
Stonewalling us. But I've got my own contacts in the
Corps. Got a tip I passed along to a newspaper friend
who picked the facts out of your colonel. Nick Blink.
Said he knew you."

"I've met him."

"If you really didn't know—" Marty paused to squint
again, his voice ironic. "Blink says the bugs cause disease. Says they've already got out of your quarantine lab
on the Moon. Hell to pay, he says, if they ever get to
Earth."

"A *Keyhole* story." Houston shrugged. "Blink will be
claiming we've met green monster-men on Mars."

"Blink prints the truth when he knows the truth."
Marty's fat blue chin jutted smugly. "And I called your
colonel myself. When I put the heat on him, he had to
admit the bugs are a fact. He ain't happy, but he can't
stop Blink. And I think the bugs are bad news for your
Authority."

"We don't need that kind of publicity, but Blink won't stop us." He dropped his voice. "Listen, Marty. Do me a favor, won't you. True or not, this story would upset my mother and LeeAnn. Spoil this last night I expect to have at home. Please don't mention it."

Marty grunted noncommittally.

♂

LeeAnn's parents arrived thirty minutes late in their antique Lincoln. Her mother was a large but willowy blonde. She would be attractive, Houston thought, if she didn't try so hard to seem younger than she was. The image, perhaps, of what LeeAnn might be in another twenty years.

Her father was tall, bald, and slightly stooped. Nicknamed "Judge" in high school for his thick black eyebrows and an air of owlish solemnity, he still enjoyed the title even though he had never held any judicial position. A retired attorney, he had two passions: the early history of the Texas Republic and his daughter's happiness.

Old family friends, they were both a little at odds with him now, the judge because he had never married LeeAnn, the wife because she was afraid he would. His mother was still upstairs, and he made drinks for them, Campari and soda for her, bourbon and branch water for the judge.

LeeAnn had followed them in her own car, looking windblown and flushed with emotion. He wondered if they had quarreled. When Houston offered her a gin and tonic, she gulped it down and wanted another. Her mother frowned to hurry her; dinner was waiting.

Still his mother had not come down. His father finished his own bourbon and water and called them at last into the dining room. Roberto was serving thick steaks, done as he knew each guest preferred them. Marty and

Lucina attacked theirs with gusto, but the meal went dismally.

Though nobody mentioned it, he soon realized that Marty's news had spread. His mother never did come down. His father ate in moody silence, eyes on his plate. Roberto was dismayed when Mrs. Halloran found her steak too rare. The judge left most of his on his plate. LeeAnn had hardly tasted hers before she excused herself and went up to see about his mother.

When the other guests were gone, he found them sitting silently together in her room, a Schubert symphony playing very softly. Their unhappy faces turned together to accuse him when he asked how she was. Her pale lips tightened, and LeeAnn asked, "What's this bug?"

"What bug?"

"This germ from Mars."

Eyes on his mother's tragic face, he could only shake his head.

"Lucina was telling us," LeeAnn said. "Marty told her. A Martian virus that causes what they call Mars-dust fever. Marty says the whole expedition could come down with it. Maybe bring it back to Earth. If they get back to Earth—"

Her troubled eyes searched him. "Is that so, Hew?"

"I've heard about it." He nodded reluctantly. "A new molecule, the beginning of another kind of life that evolved on Mars. It does seem to cause something like an allergic reaction. Unpleasant symptoms, but nothing contagious."

"In spite of it—" She looked away from him and reached for his mother's hand. "You're still going?"

"If I'm chosen. Really, it's nothing we didn't expect. Not since the biology experiments the old *Viking* landers did, back in the nineteen-seventies."

"But you don't know." Her lips quivered. "It could—" Eyes on his mother, she didn't finish.

"Nobody has died from it," he told them. "I hope nobody does." Silent for a moment, he had to add, "There is a risk. We expected risks when we joined the Corps. For me—for all of us—Mars is worth any risk."

"If that's the way you feel—"

Her voice died. With a bleak glance at him, she turned to his mother. They sat silent till his mother spoke suddenly, with a stronger voice than he expected.

"Thank you, Houston. If that's the way it has to be, I'll pray for you. I'm sorry I get so upset, but Lee has found a tranquilizer for me and she's staying over to be with me tonight."

He kissed her thin dry lips, and left them together.

♂

His mother had kept his room the way he'd left it, hardly changed since he was a boy. His faded posters of the planets still hung on the wall. The bookcase still held his old astronomy books and a few worn and tattered volumes of science fiction. His model spacecraft still hung from the ceiling in the corners. The bed seemed smaller now, too narrow for him. Restless in it, remembering too much, he lay awake till the grandfather clock in the hall struck two.

"Hew?"

LeeAnn's soft whisper woke him. In the faint glow from the window, he found her standing nude by the bed. He lay silent, too startled to speak. He had known her too long and too well, admired her too much, to want any casual affair. Closer than brother and sister, they had examined each other's bodies before they were five. A few years later, they had attempted their first experiments at sex. They had danced together, and kissed in her car. He had wanted her hungrily—and willed the desire out of his mind when he fixed his life on Mars.

"Hew?" He saw her bending closer. "If you must go, I came to say good-bye."

"The verdict isn't final," he whispered. "But you know what I hope—"

He felt her searching hands.

"LeeAnn?" Her body was live and exciting against him, her breath warm on his face. He felt her eager lips. "Have you thought—" He tried to hold her away. "Don't you know I may never come back?"

"That's why I came. I want this moment to remember."

"If you do—" His breathless whisper caught. "If you really do—"

Trembling, he sat up. Her nimble fingers helped strip off his pajamas. She was with him in the bed, upon him, quick hands exploring him, her hot mouth on his. His hesitation and fear of hurt for her drained away. He entered her, and she seemed as wonderful as Mars.

"You've learned." She chuckled softly when they lay resting. "Since that time we tried."

"So have you."

When the old clock struck four, she whispered that she had to go, yet she let him keep her. Dawn was gray beyond the windows before he fell asleep with her in his arms. He woke alone and yearning for her, and went down late.

♂

His father had eaten and gone. He found his mother sitting alone in the kitchen, staring at a newspaper his father had left on the table. He leaned over her to read the bold red headline:

'PROTOLIFE' OF MARS
MAY KILL EXPLORERS!

She shivered when he put his arm around her.

"More likely," he told her, "our Earth bugs can kill the protolife."

She shook her head, saying nothing.

"Mom, I wish—"

"I know what you wish!" Her voice was suddenly sharp. "We've talked too much about it."

"Please, Mom! I have to leave in an hour."

"Forever," she whispered hoarsely. "It will be forever."

"Or I may be back next week. If I don't make the crew."

She gathered herself to give him a pale smile and sip her tea when he poured hot water for her. Without much appetite, he got coffee for himself and they tried to talk. She'd had a rough night in spite of the tranquilizer. She still felt queasy, but she would try to eat something when LeeAnn came down.

Still she didn't want to hear anything more about the Moon or Mars, but LeeAnn had made an appointment for her to get her hair done in the afternoon and promised to go shopping with her, to look for a new carpet and curtains for the guest room. LeeAnn, she said, was like a daughter to her.

Suddenly she wanted to talk about Marty. He was too ambitious, too eager to crowd better men out of the company. Austin had always trusted him and Lucina too far. Houston saw that she was begging him to stay to shield his father from them. Her wan face quivered when he said he must go up for his bag, but she rose to give him a quick little peck on the cheek.

She was still sitting there alone when he came back. Staring at him blankly across the cluttered newspapers, she didn't speak or move until he waved and grinned and borrowed words of his father to say, *"Adios, madre mia."*

Roused by that, she nodded at a foil-wrapped package on the sideboard.

"A gift," she whispered. "To help you remember."

A hard constriction closed his throat.

"One of my Alamo roses," she said. "Red and very lovely. LeeAnn helped me write directions for it and we had Roberto wrap it. Plant it on Mars."

He kissed her silently and picked up the package. Walking out of the kitchen under her stricken eyes, he had a hollow feeling that the visit home had been to his own funeral.

Roberto drove him to the airport.

8

The Crew

No two alike, the eight-person crew of the *Ares* had been selected and trained to become the nucleus of a new human society, able to survive and grow in a little-known and difficult environment, even trained to think and speak with their own telegraphic economy of meaning. The sardonic critic who called them a society of polymaths and egomaniacs had never really known them.

In flight back to White Sands, Houston felt a mix of relief and guilt. During his childhood, while they still lived west of Fort Worth on the old Bascomb ranch, he had been happy because he thought his parents were. His mother was still beautiful, at least to his eyes. His father seemed dependably jolly and kind and strong, with time for cookouts and ball games and weekend hikes or hunts.

He blamed Lucina for the change, blamed the company and his father, but also himself. His mother had loved the ranch, which had been in the Bascomb family for a hundred years. When she let his father sell it because the company was in trouble, it was a tragic blunder, he thought, because she had never seemed happy in the huge old Kelligan mansion. After his father admitted the affair with Lucina, he'd asked her if she wanted a divorce. She burst into tears and told him sharply not to speak of it again.

Perhaps he should have been a better son, but his efforts to make peace between them had always failed. His mother had retreated into bitter silences and his father was often bleakly stern. He had planned since his teens to get away. Mars could be the ultimate escape, yet he felt unexpectedly saddened to be leaving them now, probably forever.

A glow of pleasure came when he relived the night with LeeAnn, and then an ache of guilt. He tried to shrug it off. He had made no promises. Surely, she would get over him.

His spirits lifted when he began to glimpse the brown-and-green checkerboard plains of West Texas giving way to the naked gray New Mexico mountains and the promise of space.

All that's past and gone, he urged himself. *Think Mars!*

♂

Reporting at headquarters, he gave Colonel Orbeliani the required salute.

"Well, Kelligan?" The colonel returned it stiffly, scowling across his desk. "You're aware of the unfortunate publicity on the Martian protolife?"

"Yes, sir. But—"

"White has relapsed." The colonel didn't pause. "Hospitalized again, under experimental treatment. Prognosis not yet certain."

"Not certain?" He peered into Orbeliani's hard brown face. "White's my friend."

"His relapse creates a question. Let's get to it." The colonel's voice sharpened. "Knowing the danger, are you resigning?"

"Of course not."

"In that case, congratulations!" Smiling bleakly, the colonel rose and came around the desk to grip his hand. "I've just reviewed your final profile. You qualified for Mars."

"Thank you, sir!" He wanted to sit, but the colonel offered no chair. "A great relief."

"The other American is Ryan. You two will report to Commander Lavrin for duty on the *Ares.*"

"For Mars?" His head felt light. "With Jayne?"

"With Ryan." Amusement flashed on the colonel's face, instantly gone. "I wish you luck."

To Mars with Jayne!

He stood there blankly until the colonel frowned and he realized that he had been dismissed. Walking out of the building, her image in his mind, he was blind to everything around him until they met on the walk outside.

"Lieutenant Kelligan?" She stopped to survey him, her green-gray eyes appraising him as keenly as if he had been an unexpected stranger. "You've heard?"

"That we're the two Americans?"

"A surprise." Her tone reflected nothing of his elation. "I think we should talk. Let's get a drink."

They found a table in a quiet corner of the Starways Lounge. He ordered bourbon and water.

"A farewell to my father," he told her. "His favorite drink."

"Dad liked Scotch." Her voice slowed for a moment, before she shrugged as if to shake off the recollection.

"Drank anything he could afford. Generally cheap gin or vodka, and too much of that."

She ordered white soda, glanced back at him, and turned to the window as if hesitant to come to her point. He sat admiring her, straight and clean and hard in the neat blue uniform, bright Corps ribbons on the curve of her breast, hair cut short. *Earth's selected best.* An image, he thought, perfect for the slogan.

"My favorite view." The drinks came, and she raised her glass toward the endless strip of gray concrete that cut as far as they could see across drought-browned desert toward the blue-hazed hills and the high space beyond. "Our road to Mars."

"To Mars!" He held his glass toward hers. "And us!"

She smiled for just an instant, and let the glasses touch. In his mind, the moment was almost a marriage. She looked lovely. He loved her—in spite of himself, and even if she despised him. He needed her near him, no matter how, and now she was going to be a close companion, perhaps for the rest of their lives.

She sipped her drink and pushed the glass aside.

"I had my own day at home before the Moon race." A grimace wrinkled her nose. "Long enough. I found Dad married again, to a woman I don't care for. Both brothers are doing well enough in business, bitching about the tax dollars they say the Authority has thrown away."

"And no regrets?"

"Nothing to regret." Her voice had a sudden edge. "No fortune left behind."

"My people do have money." Hurt by her tone, he tried to defend himself. "I know how you feel about rich Texans, but that's all past."

"Your name is still Kelligan." He flinched, and she smiled in brief apology. "I'm sorry. That jab wasn't called for, but it's time for plain talk. If we're going out together, we must understand each other."

"I'm trying."

She ignored his hopeful grin.

"You know you aren't my preferred companion." Her voice was bluntly impersonal. "I'll be honest. I want to be fair. Frankly, I never expected you to qualify. When the colonel gave me your name, I asked to see your records. They do seem to show that your promotions and awards were honestly earned. He assures me nobody tried to pull wires for you. In the end, I had to accept you as one of us."

"Thanks!" He muttered the word, with too much emphasis. "Thanks."

"I don't intend to quarrel." Her cool voice reproved his flash of irony, and she paused, a frown creasing her fine forehead. "I didn't report your offer to help on the Moon. Perhaps you expect gratitude, but that was a breach of discipline. Our survival on Mars will require strict discipline."

"I understand," he said. "But I have feelings."

"Which you must learn to restrain." The frown cut deeper. "We've been lucky, but any disagreement now could disqualify us both. Your profile does prove your competence. I see no reason for any trouble later, so long as you remember one thing." She leaned across the table, eyes level. "I'm ranked above you."

"Okay." He shrugged. "No problem."

"I'm glad we've cleared the air." She seemed relieved, as if this had been a dreaded ordeal. "Mars will be problem enough." She rose abruptly. "You'll excuse me now. The colonel is staging a media event before we take off, damage control for the protolife story. I'm to help with the planning."

"I hope—" He stood up beside her, full of too much emotion. Unthinking, he offered his hand. "I hope we can be friends."

"We know our duty." Hesitant for an instant, she took

his hand. Her grasp was quick and firm. "Keep duty first, and we'll get along."

He ordered another bourbon when she was gone, and sat trying to make some kind of peace with his own emotions. She stirred him too deeply; he couldn't help that. She was still no friend, but they had reached a truce. Time might soften her mistrust or dull her allure for him. Or time might not.

Cool it, he told himself. *Think Mars.*

♂

"Sorry, sir." The nurse at the hospital blocked his way. "Lieutenant White is strictly isolated. Corps orders. No visitors allowed."

"Hew!" White had heard his voice through the door. "Come on in."

Houston found him sitting up inside an oxygen tent, his naked body sprayed grotesquely with thick yellow foam that left only hands and face exposed.

"Don't run away!" He beckoned Houston closer. "I'm not as dangerous as I probably look."

"You do look shocking."

"Scared a reporter this morning." He grinned through the foam. "Little guy named Nick Blink. Claimed to be a friend of yours."

"A devious rat," he muttered. "No friend of mine. Or the Authority either."

"I soon saw that. He wanted me to say we ought to abandon the expedition because of the scarlet plague—that's what he's calling it. I told him to go to hell. Told him to get out or he could catch the crud himself. He turned pale and scrammed."

"You said it isn't contagious."

"But I gave him the fright of his life." He chuckled with satisfaction. "What's with the expedition?"

"We meet the media tomorrow. Takeoff next day."

"You're still going?" White pushed foam away from his eyes, squinting at him. "In spite of the crud?"

"We expected risks when we signed on."

"Wish I were with you." A bitter grin. "Still the guinea pig. They need my blood. And the medics are experimenting. Testing this foam now. It does ease the itch."

The nurse was frowning from the door.

"So long, Hew." He reached out of the odorous tent for a farewell handshake. "Don't forget me."

♂

Newspapers next morning carried gruesome color photos of White grinning out of his yellow-sprayed cocoon and a huge headline over Blink's story:

MARS PLAGUE
HITS EARTH!

Reporters and cameramen came swarming in to pack Armstrong Hall in the headquarters tower. At ten o'-clock, Houston found himself seated with the seven other expedition members on one side of the podium. Corps officers and the four Authority directors sat opposite. Colonel Orbeliani stalked to the lectern and stood warily facing the mob, banging a gavel for attention.

"I have an official statement." Poised on the balls of his feet, he scowled into the glaring lights. A Circassian warrior, Houston thought, lean and dark, facing overwhelming foes. "Copies will be available."

Noises subsided. Hard-voiced, with an air of wary defiance, he read from a yellow sheet.

"The Mars Corps deplores and denies the false reports of a dangerous microbe brought back from Mars by the robot explorers. It is true that a sample of Martian dust did contain chemical molecules unknown on Earth. The samples are still kept in quarantine on the Moon for study in a sealed laboratory. Unfortunately, one researcher has become ill after an accidental exposure. He displays symptoms believed to be allergic.

"His infection has afforded us an unexpected opportunity to test the effects of the molecule on a human subject. Though the symptoms are uncomfortable and persistent, they are not believed lethal, nor is the illness communicable. To repeat in simpler terms: careful tests reveal no danger that it might spread to the public at large.

"Corps researchers are now testing treatments and attempting to develop a vaccine. Critics have suggested that the flight of the *Ares* should be delayed, to allow time for the completion of this medical research and the construction of the planned sister ship. Our present launch window, however, has almost closed. Any delay would cost two years of time and funds not now available.

"In these hard circumstances, the Corps has no choice. The *Ares* is fueled for flight. Crew members have accepted whatever risk may exist. Our control and contact links are intact and ready. Departure will take place as planned."

He banged the gavel again to silence a sudden chorus of questions.

"We'll take questions later." He banged again, and turned to the row of officials. "Authority President Hiro Naguchi will address you now."

Naguchi waited for applause that never came and spoke in brief phrases, pausing for translation by a petite young Eurasian woman. He spoke of how, pooling their resources and their best genius for this great common effort, the member powers of the Authority were at last inaugurating a magnificent new epoch in the historic evolution of humanity. The peoples of Earth were about to become the first citizens of interplanetary space.

The four directors followed with comments intended to disarm their critics at home. Politicians well aware of crisis, they spoke glowingly of the ultimate rewards in new science and human pride that might come from the heroic efforts the expedition had required and paused to praise all the millions who had suffered hunger and privation to pay the way for these eight bold pioneers who now went out to seek a more splendid future for all mankind.

With rhetoric of his own, Orbeliani introduced the astronauts and cosmonauts. They, he said, had been selected as the finest of humankind and trained for the greatest adventure the race had ever attempted. Very different from each other, they were humanity at the peak of evolution, daring to venture away from the tiny island Earth into the vast and half-known cosmic ocean.

One by one he had them stand.

"Cosmonaut Arkady Lavrin will command the expedition. He is qualified as space engineer, astronomer, and physician and surgeon."

"I waste no words." Lavrin rose to grin amiably into the lights. "Wait for what we do."

He bowed modestly to a patter of applause and quickly sat again.

"Astronaut Jayne Ryan is second in command. She is qualified as space pilot, biologist, and nuclear engineer."

She stood to nod and wave toward the cameras, and sat again, silently.

"Dr. Ram Chandra ranked first on the East Asian team. He is a qualified physicist, space engineer, and lander pilot."

"We go to open a new world." A tall dark man, very straight, Chandra bowed deliberately into the lights. "A

better world, we hope, able to survive all the ills that
challenge our old one."

"Dr. Irina Barova ranked second on the Russian team.
She is the official historian and communications tech-
nologist for the expedition. Also a qualified biologist."

Made up for her role, Barova wore a sleek blue skinsuit that clung to every line of her magnificent figure. Her
blonde hair shone; her face was a perfect oval. She glided
to her feet, smiling for the cameras and speaking into the
microphones, her voice almost a song.

"We go for knowledge of the universe and the coming
greatness of humankind."

"Dr. Larissa Kolvos."

Lisa, they called her. She sat next to him, a small quiet
woman, dark and slender and intense, looking too young
for all the ribbons on her breast.

"Dr. Kolvos is qualified as architect, biochemist, medical technician, and nuclear engineer."

She stood very briefly, with a small grave bow for
Orbeliani and another for the cameras.

"Dr. Otto Hellman, ranking first from United Europe,
is qualified as lander pilot and astrophysicist. He is already a renowned authority on his specialty, the geology
of Mars."

A dark, heavy man, Hellman stood blinking for a
moment as if the glare had blinded and confused him.
"We go out—" He gulped and began again. "On Mars
we expect to read the geologic history of our own Earth.
Time has erased most of its record here, but we shall find
it written in rocks as old as the planets themselves."

"Dr. Kim Lo is from East Asia. She is a space engineer, a biochemist, and a qualified medical technician."

Tiny beside Chandra, neat and quick as a bird, she
rose to bow shyly to the cameras, and sat back without
a word.

"Dr. Sam Houston Kelligan is the second-ranking

American. He is qualified as lander pilot, geologist, and space engineer."

Houston stood, reaching for the few words he had rehearsed, but Nicholas Blink was suddenly standing, shouting at Orbeliani:

"Question time! Question time!"

Houston shrugged and sat.

"Question!" Blink kept bawling at the colonel. "Forgive me, sir, but I want proof of your statement that this Martian plague is not contagious."

"I repeat what I said." Orbeliani flushed with anger, scowling. "The disorder is carried by Martian dust, not by its victims. There is no danger to Earth—"

"But, sir—"

"Listen, Mr. Blink!" Orbeliani shouted. "I resent the reckless falsehood in your newspaper story, which can cause undue alarm. Lieutenant White's reaction to the Martian agent is not yet entirely understood, but the safety of the public is a fact proven in the laboratory. Healthy rats stayed healthy when caged with infected rats."

"I question that." Blink raised his defiant voice for the hall to hear. "When I visited White in his hospital room, he ordered me out with the warning that I could contract this insidious alien pathogen."

Orbeliani stood silent, glaring, till Houston spoke.

"Sir, may I explain?" When Orbeliani nodded, he rose to go on. "I've talked to Lieutenant White, who is under treatment here for the infection. Mr. Blink had broken security to badger him for an interview. He made the threat in anger, to get rid of Blink."

"And he did look ghastly!" Unabashed, Blink gestured to his cameraman and shouted again at Orbeliani. "Sir, most of the world is sunk into bitter poverty, with millions sick and starving. Our robot explorers have found nothing but dust and death on Mars. Why, then, must we squander billions of dollars to send these brave men and women out to die there, with nothing at all to gain?"

Orbeliani swung his gavel again, against a rising clamor.

"The billions are spent. The *Ares* is ready. Our explorers are eager to go." He paused a moment and looked away from Blink. "We stand at a moment of choice. We can stay shut up on Earth, subject to all its hazards. Or we can make this first long leap toward the stars, perhaps to let our race survive forever. We may not have another chance."

He waved an imperative hand at Blink. "Now sit down."

"Fine rhetoric, sir," Blink sniffed. "But I have one question for Mr. Kelligan." He swung to Houston. "You, sir? Is that your choice? To throw away your inherited empire for that crazy dream? Or why have you volunteered for Mars?"

Houston stood silent a moment, facing the rows of critical faces and staring lenses.

"If you have to ask," he said, "you'll never know."

9

The *Ares*

The *Ares* was spidery but huge, a thick-rimmed wheel on a long axle, spun slowly to simulate gravity. The rim held living quarters, greenhouses, and animal cages, inside the magnetic torus designed to shield them. The axle, which did not rotate, carried the control dome on its forward end, the fusion-electric rocket engine on its longer tail.

When the media event was over late that afternoon, Houston called Fort Worth for LeeAnn and got her mother, who told him curtly that LeeAnn was out. Roberto answered at the Kelligan mansion and put his father on the line.

"Father? How's my mother?"

"Do you care?" Kelligan was harshly hostile. "We watched you on TV this morning. Upset her awfully. Crying in her room when I went back to the office."

"I left them hurt," he said. "Her and LeeAnn. I hate hurting them."

"If you do, why don't you show it?" The sharp concern surprised him. "Lucky she has LeeAnn. A daughter to her now. Roberto says LeeAnn came after I left and took her out in that red car. Never said where."

"Dad—" The word was hard to say. "Be good to her."

A moment of silence.

"I try," his father said. "I always tried."

Silence again, till he was about to hang up.

"Sam—" His father's voice came back, suddenly warmer, unsteady as his own. "Remember? I once tried to explain about Lucina. You didn't understand."

"I never did. Not even now."

"I wish—wish you did. I want you to know I did love your mother. Perhaps I still do, though she makes it difficult. She expected me to play the saint. I never was a saint. Or tried to be." A half-defiant tone. "Can't say I'm sorry for what I've done. It was what I had to do, because I'm what I am.

"Won't you—won't you try to understand?"

"I'll try," he whispered. "If it matters."

"It does. Because you used to be—" His father caught a raspy breath. "Used to be my son. Before I lost you, Sam. Now I hope—hope you won't go thinking too hard of me."

"Thank you, Dad." He had to gulp for his own voice. "I guess—I guess I've begun to understand."

"God bless you, son!"

Hanging up the phone, he had to wipe his eyes.

♂

Next day he packed his five kilograms of allowed personal possessions and got on the spaceplane with his seven companions and a handful of Corps technicians for the flight out to the *Ares*.

In the next seat again, Lisa Kolvos had a quiet smile for him.

"Glad to have you—"

The jets drowned her voice and the plane rammed forward, roaring down that long runway, climbing at full thrust. Watching the dry mountains rush at them and peel away, watching the flattened Earth grow round and shrink, he shivered.

Good-bye! Elation wrenched him, mixed with pain. *Good-bye, Earth, home, all I ever loved. Forever!*

The pilot cut the thrust as they escaped Earth's gravity well. The sound subsided. He relaxed in the seat and looked around the cabin. A grin for Lisa; though they were never close, he had always liked her. A nod for Hellman and Barova, across the aisle. A wave to Lavrin and Jayne, two rows ahead.

"An odd feeling." Lisa's words, a soft-voiced echo of his own emotion. "A lonely feeling, when you think of the odds we'll ever be back."

"Don't think back. Think Mars."

"I do," She nodded. "But still—"

She sat moodily silent till he spoke.

"Aristo Kolvos." He knew her father's name. "I've read his research on magnetic plasma compression, the key to helium fusion. He should have had the last Nobel."

"Always unlucky." A wry little shrug. "Even with women."

The cabin was windowless, though the pilot used the cabin screen to show them eastern America and then the whole round Earth already dwindling in dark space behind, telescopic glimpses of Goddard Station and the still-small Moon and finally the toylike wheel of the *Ares*. They watched the screen, and she spoke again of her father.

"I loved him." Her voice had become oddly impersonal, almost as the world behind had become a work of fiction. "I was an only child, totally happy with him—at least when he was between women. He spoiled me, and the women must have been jealous. They hated me. I left home whenever I could, spent one summer with my mother, who never really liked me. Boarding schools. Finally, of course, the Corps."

♂

At low-energy thrust, they were ten hours out to the *Ares*. Out of the seat restraints, they wandered around the half-empty cabin and the lounge, renewing old friendships and reviewing plans for Mars.

"Harmless fun," Chandra murmured. "If we knew what to expect, we wouldn't need to go."

Otto Hellman darkened the cabin to run a computer simulation of the origins and history of Mars. A supernova exploded. Its shock wave struck a dark molecular cloud. Compressed, the cloud shrank till gravity lit nuclear fire. Its hot heart became the Sun. The spinning fringes condensed into planetesimals that collided and grew into planets. Scars from those old impacts still marked the planet's south hemisphere.

"The computer story," Hellman finished his lecture. "We'll be reading the reality."

The robobar in the lounge dispensed no vodka, but Houston bought a beer for Lavrin and suffered another quick defeat at chess. Barova curled her lip at beer but drank enough to entertain them with dramatic passages from Pushkin's *Yevgeny Onegin* declaimed in Russian he hardly understood.

He joined a little group talking of their duty stints, building the *Ares.* Lavrin had headed the crew that installed the computer systems. Houston had helped assemble and seal the interlocking plates of lunar aluminum that walled the control dome. Jayne had programmed the computer pilot.

"Can we trust it?"

He asked her that not from any real concern about the computer, but out of the urge to know her better, to penetrate her cool remoteness.

"We'll watch it," she said. "I trust nothing."

And nobody, he thought. *At least not me.*

♂

A guest in the copilot's seat, he had his first glimpse of the completed *Ares.* A bright metal top spinning very slowly against black space, it looked at first too small and fragile for any use, but grew so huge as the shuttle nosed in to dock against the axial core that he felt a thrill for his own small share in her building.

In duty stints, he had operated a dragline gathering moondust for its helium-3, and worked six months on its bright aluminum hull. Yet he felt a shock of the alien as they came through the lock into the axle's hollow core and he swam again in free fall to reach the doorway into the turning wheel.

This was his world now: the *Ares,* space, far-off Mars. Earth was past, lost, memory. His mother's passive desolation, his father's affair with Lucina, Marty's ambitious schemes, LeeAnn and all he had ever felt for her—all erased.

Perhaps.

He shrugged, caught his breath and climbed down to search for his cabin in the great wheel's rim, where the centrifugal pull matched the gravity of Mars. Austere and cold, the small room held all he needed. Berth and computer station, lavatory, even a tiny shower with monitor valves to limit overuse of precious recycled water.

Still in orbit, Lavrin gathered them into the wardroom.

"Long flight ahead." Under stress, his Texas English reverted toward his native Ukrainian. "Commander not from choice. Understand?" A Slavic shrug. "More pleasure in math and astrophysics. Mars Command put me in charge. Okay?"

He grinned as if relieved by their nods of agreement.

"Hard test, the flight. Maybe more severe than Mars. Here aboard, we face each other. Confinement. Monotony. Danger from ourselves. Get it?"

He paused to scan them, blue eyes grave.

"I know you all. Strong enough. Bright enough. Chosen for individual competence. Trained for free decision. Okay? But now we become single unit. Must accept discipline, follow rules, obey order. Under hard penalty. Understood?"

They nodded again.

"Rules not mine." He shook his head and frowned. "Rules of the ship. Rules of space. Rules of Mars. Rules we all must learn, beginning now." His red eyebrows lifted. "Question, Hellman?"

Hellman had no question.

"Five months to Mars." His brittle tone made that a challenge. "Time to lose our edge. Or time to hone it. Must improve special skills. Learn to work together. Or else—you know what else."

He formed them into three watches of two persons

each to serve four hours on duty, eight hours off. Houston found himself paired with Lisa Kolvos, she assigned to run the nuclear engine, he to con the ship. On another trial orbit around the Moon, all went well.

They lifted out for Mars.

♂

Stretched thin, the ties to Earth were painful to break. Every twenty-four hours, a radio link was open through Farside Station, with priority for one crew member to place a three-minute private call. When his first turn came, Houston called his mother and waited through the endless seconds for his voice to reach her and hers to return. All he heard was her breathless gasp and then the clatter when her telephone fell.

On his next turn, he tried his father. Farther out, he had to wait longer.

"I'm okay, son." His father's voice came back at last, strange and faint. "Your mother is not. Heart condition worse. Hospitalized after you spoke to her. Better not call her again."

Collecting himself, he asked how his father was, asked for news of LeeAnn, but the operators cut them off before he heard any response.

When another turn came, he decided not to call LeeAnn.

Sometimes the flight seemed forever. Quietly efficient, Lisa kept the fusion-electric engine running. The thrust of the plasma jet was small but steady; it would continue throughout the voyage.

On duty in the control dome, he had nothing much to control. The pilot computer used inputs from guide telescopes fixed on Sirius, Vega, and Capella to make needed course corrections. Off duty, he worked out in the high-gee gym. He stood his duty shifts in the galley and the greenhouse and the animal tanks. He sat through planning sessions and training lectures and gave lectures of his own.

Nothing unexpected ever happened, yet he was never bored. He watched the rust-red fleck of Mars swell day by day in the telescope. Its hazed and tiny face sharpened into details that whetted his imagination. Lecturing on its geology, he and Hellman debated where to land.

"Not that anybody knows enough," he finished one talk. "All we have is the data collected by the explorer craft in orbit and those few robot landers. At the best, our first landing will be a gamble."

"Lieutenant Kelligan?" All the others were using his first name by then, but Jayne still kept a carefully formal distance. "Commander Lavrin is asking for advice. Otto argues for one of several sites he likes in the north hemisphere. Have you a landing spot to recommend?"

"Not yet." He shook his head, surprised that she might want his advice. "You can call the hemisphere north and south, though they're skewed across the equator. Certainly they're very different. Summing them up, the south is mostly highlands. Ancient crust, still scarred from the hail of impacts that made the planet. Not much changed in the last three or four billion years."

He hesitated, pleased in spite of himself by her interest, yet puzzled. These were facts she must already know, yet she sat watching him intently, waiting for more. He shrugged uncomfortably and went on.

"The north is younger, smoother, more varied. I suppose it's more scenic. Olympus Mons is the biggest mountain in the solar system, twenty kilometers tall."

He paused again, till she nodded impatiently. Her level stare seemed critical, weighing him, perhaps, rather than anything he said.

"Most of the north is lava plains, relatively recent, only lightly cratered. Floors of vanished lakes or seas—

there are gorges cut by floods when Mars was wetter. Valles Marineris slices five thousand kilometers around the planet. Even the polar caps are not much alike, the north cap probably water ice, the south cap largely frozen carbon dioxide."

"So?" A crisp question. "Have you a site to recommend?"

"I know too little to make a choice, but I'd like us to look at the southern hemisphere. The old *Vikings* and most of our robot probes put down in the north, out of caution. Much of the south may be too rough for safe landings, but there are promising sites. And we haven't found much we need in the north."

"Water? Otto says we've sure of water in the north cap."

"True. But we'll do better to get it out of permafrost. The robot probes found evidence of that."

"So what else are you looking for?"

"An open surface where we can land, dig radiation shelters, set up a radio beacon and solar power units; ores we can work—if we're lucky enough, though the probes didn't find them. Clays for ceramics and buiding brick. Sand for glass."

"You think we'll find such a site in the highlands?"

"I've located possible spots."

"Let's take a look."

She followed him back to the control dome. Dressed now for the ship's controlled climate and low gravity, she wore very brief white shorts and a blue blouse so sheer he saw her nipples. Her nearness tantalized him.

Did she know how deeply she disturbed him? Beside him as be brought his maps and data charts up on the monitor, she leaned so close her breast brushed his arm and he caught the scent of her hair. He moved a little away.

"Sorry," she murmured. He thought he heard amuse-

ment in her voice, but her manner stayed briskly impersonal. What, he wondered, did she feel for him? Still that
scorn for the rich playboy? Some spilled-over share of
her contempt for Marty Gorley? A lingering doubt that
he had really earned his berth on the expedition?

He was never sure. She always kept the same emotion-
less remoteness.

♂

To fill empty moments, he began a journal.

"In spite of Lavrin's plea for a team, we are still human
individuals." So he wrote, three months out from Earth.
"Hellman and Barova had been together on duty and off,
but now some sort of tiff has broken the union. Otto
began haunting Jayne, briefing her on his chosen landing
sites. Irina was often with Lavrin in the dome, trying to
learn astrophysics.

"Interesting attempts, but Lisa says they've failed.
She says Jayne and Lavrin are still sleeping together.
Otto and Irina are trying now to break up Ram
Chandra and Kim Lo. Up till now they'd been insepa-
rable, but today I found all four in the wardroom, Ram
and Irina rehearsing a *pas de deux* that would be impossible in the gravity of Earth, Kim and Otto for audience."

On duty with him, Lisa ran the engine by remote control, her monitors and console just across the dome from
his pilot station. At first he found her hard to know. Deft
and sure with everything she did, she observed everybody
with alert intelligence in her mild brown eyes and seldom
said a needless word.

As time went on, she became his best friend on the
ship. She told him more about her father.

"A genius—I believe he really was—but never happy

with himself. He did his great work in high moments that never lasted long. In between he was low. I used to cry for him when he couldn't work and got so terribly unhappy. He needed love, or at least the pretense of it, and got it from too many women. He drank too much and always quarreled with them. He was never faithful long—but always good to me.

"I suppose I was the only person he ever really trusted. He loved me. I never knew how much, or even knew he'd lost his appointment at CERN till after he was dead. We'd been out of touch for months when his body was found in a cheap hotel in Panama, drowned in his own blood with a stab wound to the lung, empty pockets pulled inside out, and empty bottles under the bed. His last woman had left him there a couple of days before."

A sad little shrug.

"I was twelve that year, in a private school in Switzerland. He'd paid for it and had a lawyer I'd never known about who took me to Panama for the funeral and told me about the trust fund he'd left for me; money from his fusion patents. Women had got most of it, but there was enough to pay for the education that finally got me into the Corps."

When Houston told her about his own life, she didn't care what he had been in Texas. She understood his father's long affair with Lucina and wanted to know about the women he had known. With nothing he wanted to say about Jayne Ryan, he showed her the billfold picture of LeeAnn he had carried for years.

"Beautiful! Is she waiting?"

"I hope not," he said. "I told her I'd probably never get back."

"She'll be hoping you do."

♂

Watch by watch, Lisa crept into his imagination. She was never flirtatious. Entertained by the shifting relationships around them, she was never involved with anybody else. He never courted her, but he found her often in his thoughts, sometimes in his dreams. With LeeAnn left behind forever and Jayne only a carefully distant enigma, there was nobody else.

Her soft voice spoke in a dream, calling his name.

"Hew?"

He sat abruptly up, lifting off his berth in the ship's light gravity. He found her standing in the open doorway. At first, still lost in the dream, he thought he was back on Earth, back with LeeAnn. He blinked and recognized her in the dim corridor light. Here with him on the ship, looking almost nude in the blue skinsuit she wore for a sleeping garment.

"Lisa?"

"I've been wondering." She stood beside him, whispering. "With all the others pairing off, we're left the odd numbers. I was wondering if you need me."

10

The Company

Growing from a Texas cattle spread and the oil found under it, Kelligan Resources became an international empire with interests in energy, metals, finance, Latin American trade, and aerospace manufacturing. The company was a power in Texas, at least until the Mars Bubble burst.

All three ranches belonged to the corporation now, manned by *vaqueros* from Chihuahua, but they had still been separate when LeeAnn was a child. The Halloran Lazy H, the Bascomb BB, and the Kelligan K Bar K. A happy time as she recalled it, with the pony she loved and the wide range to ride and Houston her best friend.

She had always been a little afraid of Houston's father, but fond of him too. Gruffly abrupt with most people and too severe with Houston, he had always babied her, calling her his little lady and surprising her with gifts. The best was the calico pony the year she was five and dying for a calico pony.

Not long after, things went bad. Her father had to sell the Lazy H. They moved to Fort Worth. His law practice there never prospered, and only her mother's small income kept then afloat.

Kelligan had done far better. His deep wildcat struck oil. His wife inherited the Bascomb ranch. He set up the new corporation and moved into the big town house his grandparents had built. He was suddenly a state senator and a Texas tycoon, but no longer very happy.

Vacation visits to his ranch were still good times. She rode with the *vaqueros* and learned how to rope and brand a calf. He and LeeAnn's father still took them on hunting and fishing trips, at least until Houston refused to kill anything again. Later, he had loaned her father the funds to send her through law school. Finally, she suspected, even money to buy her the red convertible.

But Fort Worth had never been a happy place. She and Houston had gone to different schools, and all he wanted to think about was space and Mars. His mother seemed miserable in the huge old Kelligan mansion. That puzzled her, till she learned about Kelligan and Lucina.

The convertible had been her father's gift when she passed the bar, a sort of bribe to get her to take over his law office. Even that was a pretty dismal place. The building was as old and shabby as most of his clients, and the income barely paid the bills. With Houston gone, she saw no future there or anywhere.

Not till Kelligan called.

♂

"Lady Lee?" His voice had the warm affection she remembered. "Can you come up to the office?"

Wondering what he could want, she drove uptown and parked the red car under the new Kelligan Tower. Staying busy to keep her sanity in the months since Houston left, she had visited his wife half a dozen times, but Edna seemed to want no comfort and she hadn't seen Kelligan himself. Smiling now, he rose from his desk to greet her with a hug. She caught the scent of the fine cigars he used to give her father.

The fragrance brought a flood of memories: the times he used to jog her on his knee; the day he let her drive his new Cadillac, when she was still far too young to drive; the gentle way he picked her up when the calico bucked her off. She felt a surge of warm emotion.

"Mr. Kelligan—"

She had always called him Austin, but here in his office she felt awed. It was a huge corner room on the top floor, great windows looking down across lesser towers to green suburbs and the silver glints of the lakes beyond.

"Well, Lady?" He had dropped the "little" when she said she'd grown too big for it. "Want a job with me?"

She hesitated, stepping back to study him. A big man, still powerful, handsome with his Roman nose and flowing silver hair. A shrewd man, used to getting what he wanted, but almost deferential now, as if her answer really mattered.

"We aren't doing much at the office," she said. "My mother has a little money of her own, and she wants Father to retire. I've been thinking I should find something better, but—"

"But what?" He had seen her frown.

"If you want the truth—" She waited for his nod. "I wouldn't want to work with Lucina."

"I suppose you resent her." He shrugged. "I'm sorry."

"I'm sorry for Edna. She's so bitter. I've thought I ought to hate you."

"I hope you don't." His sober smile almost disarmed her. "I'm no angel. Or Satan, either. Let's talk." He caught her arm and propelled her toward the great windows. "Look out at Fort Worth. Dallas may be bigger, but this town's mine. I've fought hard for it. I want to keep it."

Arrogance, but she knew him and wanted to forgive him.

"Sit down." He waved at a chair, his voice grown softer. "I know you miss Sam. Edna does."

"Too much." An unexpected tightness caught her throat. "Not that I can help her."

"Nor I." He flinched as if with actual pain and waited for her to sit before he settled back behind his desk. "About Lucina, I hope you'll hear my own story before you decide anything."

"I'll listen."

She waited, her feelings mixed. Kelligans and Hallorans has been friends before Texas became a state. If this offer came out of sympathy, she would have to refuse. She watched him fingering an odd paperweight, an old gold coin in a lucite block cast in the shape of the Aztec calendar stone. His deep-set eyes were fixed on her.

"I want a lawyer." Nodding at last, he spoke abruptly. "One I can trust."

"Don't you have lawyers?"

"Lots of lawyers. But let me explain."

♂

He rose but stood a moment frowning at her across the big desk. She waited, still wondering. He had always been hard to know. So kind to her, so severe with Houston. Her father's close companion, though her mother hated him. The laughing, loving hero of her first recollections, happy on the ranch with Edna and their son. Not this impatient, grim-faced autocrat.

"Mr. Kelligan—" She spoke uncertainly. "If this is charity—"

"No charity." He moved abruptly. "Call me Austin. And come along. Something to show you."

He opened the unmarked door behind his desk and beckoned her to follow. She stopped behind him, staring into shadows. The long room beyond was windowless and gloomy, but she caught a faint odor of old leather and a stronger scent of his cigars.

"My secret retreat." His pleasure seemed boyish. "Not many have seen it."

He touched a light switch and she drew back, startled. A huge mural covered the high wall before her, painted in vivid Mexican colors. Two enormous squat pyramids loomed against a vivid turquoise sky. Worshipers in endless rows knelt around a great red-drenched altar. A naked victim lay sprawled there beneath a savage-featured priest slashing down with a red flint blade.

"Aztec." He gestured. "Done by Lucina's brother. A painter till he drank himself to death."

He turned silently to show her the rest of the room, the massive oak conference table in front of the wide fieldstone fireplace that broke the opposite wall, six tall leather chairs around it, the sofa and easy chair in front of a wall screen at one end of the room, the kitchen alcove and wet bar at the other.

"My father's." He waited while she read the name still lettered in peeling gilt on the chipped black paint of a massive steel safe in the corner. *Kelligan Oil, Inc.* "A sentimental relic." He turned to nod at the mantel and the walls. "Lucina's touch."

She followed him around the room to see the polished Taxco silver on the mantel, the bright-striped *zarapes* hung on the walls, and a huge and ornately framed painting of the sun rising over a castle on a hill, with two snow-capped cones in the background.

"Chapultepec." He nodded at the painting. "As Lucina's grandfather imagined its young heroes holding out against the Americans in 1847. The volcanos are Popocateptl and Iztacihuatl, the way they must have looked before the smog."

"Austin?" She turned to frown at him. "Has Edna been here?"

"She wouldn't want to come."

"I don't like it."

"I can't expect you to, but I thought this might help you understand." He smiled persuasively, nodding again at the *zarapes* and the silver and the paintings. "Lucina—" His voice grew softer as he murmured the name. "I met her in Mexico City a couple of years after I married Edna. I'd gone down with Jay Gorley, one of our field men, to look over a new branch office. Lucina was assistant manager."

Kelligan paused, keen gray eyes fixed on her, until she nodded uncomfortably.

"Daughter of a very able Pemex geologist, Adolpho Conejos. A proud old family, down on their luck. Her mother died when she was born. She'd worked and traveled with her father. Learned the oil business from him. Ambitious as I am. She wanted a better job. Soon wanted me. I brought her back to Texas."

"Your mistress?"

"Shocked?"

"Not really. Edna told me what she knew, long ago."

"A hard thing for her." His voice fell deeper, and his

regret seemed real. "Our marriage was never much good, because sex was just a dirty word to her, yet she wouldn't let me go. I think she conceived Sam in hope a baby might win me back."

His big hands spread, a helpless gesture.

"She wouldn't even talk about divorce. Saw it, I guess, as public scandal and surrender to Lucina. She's never been happy, not since she knew, but we try to get along." His big shoulders stiffened. "That's how things are." He frowned into her eyes. "Now you've heard, do you want to work for me?"

"Or you and Marty?" She shook her head. "Not for him."

"He's the problem." Lips compressed, he turned to lead her out of the room. "Always has been, since Lucina knew she was pregnant. She always claimed he's mine. I thought he could be, till I got his blood tested. He isn't."

"Gorley's?"

"I imagine." He shut the door behind them and beckoned her back toward his desk. "He met her before I did. I made them marry and shipped him off to Arabia. Just to give the kid a name."

"Where do I come in?" She searched his cragged face. "You expect legal trouble?"

"Quién sabe?" He shrugged. "Lucina can be a bitch. Still fond of me, but fonder of her son. And a very shrewd businesswoman. More executive assistant than mistress these last few years. She has her own office and her own secretary. I owe her for all she's done to help me build the company—and for all she used to be. But now, with Sam gone perhaps forever, she's making demands."

"Which is why you called me?"

"You're a lawyer. Sharp enough, your father says." He paused to search her face. "So? Do you want the job?"

"Let me talk to Edna." She stood up. "I'll let you know tomorrow."

♂

She talked to Edna, and Kelligan let her move her father's law library into an office across the corridor from his. On her second day at work, she heard a knock on her door and saw Marty Gorley already striding into the room. A thickset, restless man, with a glassy stare and a sullen mouth. A bully when he used to play with Houston, he had learned to be ingratiating.

"Good morning, Miss Halloran." He and Lucina had always spoken Spanish together, and he had a slight accent. His words now sounded as if he had rehearsed them. "Welcome to the company family. Speaking for my mother too, we're happy to have you aboard."

"Thank you, Marty." Reluctantly, because she thought the occasion required it, she rose to take his offered hand. It felt limp and cold and damp with sweat. "I'm glad to be here."

"I know how close you were to Mr. Houston." His voice seemed innocent, but she saw his shrewd eyes dart at her belly. "We were contractors on the landing craft, and of course we're all concerned for the expedition. I'm arranging for the company to pick up some of the *Ares* transmissions for commercial broadcast."

"I'll be watching." She nodded stiffly, ready for him to leave. "Kind of you to come in."

"Something else, Miss Halloran." Not going, he stepped closer. "I don't know how much the old man has said about our setup here, but you'd better understand that I head our legal staff. My mother is our chief financial officer. We'll certainly call on you if we need your advice, but I really don't expect to need you."

"I see."

"Glad you do." His eyes narrowed slightly. "It was good of the old guy to lend you a hand when you need it." His voice took on a hard undertone. "I just dropped by to warn you that he doesn't really need another lawyer."

11

Reaction Mass

A rocket motor expels a small mass of hot gas at high velocity to propel a larger mass at lower velocity. The reaction mass of the *Ares* was common water, turned to superheated plasma by the energy of helium fusion.

Sitting up on the side of the berth, Houston caught Lisa's hand and drew her down beside him. She moved closer, warm and firm against, him, her expectant face turned to his. Waiting, she smiled in the dimness.

"Lisa," he whispered, "do you need me?"

"To be my friend." Leaning to hear her gentle murmur, he caught odors that stirred him, the sweetness of her breath, the clean natural scent of her hair. "I ask because I believe a man's need is more urgent than a woman's—"

"Lisa, Lisa!" Deeply touched, he drew her closer. "I'm a man. I do need you, but not this way. When the moment comes, we won't need to ask."

He heard her muted laugh, felt her snuggle closer. They sat there silent for a time, listening to the faint sounds of the ship: a far electronic chime, a muffled clang from the galley, the tiny hum of the gears that kept the dome in place while the ship spun beneath it.

"I've been in love." She spoke at last, very softly. "Or

thought I was. Once with a mathematician at CERN. He was my tutor while I was back there for a crash course in quantum engineering. We skied together in the Alps. He wanted me to marry him. Insisted I had a good head for physics. Used to call the Authority an international boondoggle. Told me he'd computed zero probability that I'd ever get back if I took off on the *Ares.*"

"But here you are."

"No regrets," she whispered. "Even if I don't get back."

"That's the way I feel." Relaxed with her, he told her about LeeAnn. "She's beautiful, with enough brains. A truly good person. We might have been happy together, if—" He shook his head. "She never understood what I wanted on Mars."

"Nobody does."

She kissed him at last, lightly and quickly, and slipped away.

♂

Sharing the same watch in the dome, sitting only meters apart, they seldom felt together. The ship claimed them both. Though computer systems ran it, he had to keep on guard against the unexpected. Another set of systems ran the helium engine that kept them all alive, but minding that was just as demanding.

Off watch, they drew shifts in the galley and in the greenhouse, washing pots, recycling waste, nursing mutant seedlings. They fed the pigs and goats and chickens and rabbits, and cleaned their cages. They worked out in the gym and vacuumed the decks, ate their meals and caught what sleep they could and went back to duty in the dome.

To Houston the flight sometimes seemed endless. The same bland foods, frozen and dehydrated and synthetic, eaten from the same self-warming ration packs. The same companions, until their quirks and cranks became obnoxious. Hellman's body odor and his egotistical anecdotes. Barova's syrupy sweetness when she wanted to be sweet, and her powerful perfume. The strange-toned wail of Kim Lo's Oriental music. Lavrin's unbeat-able chess, Ram's sardonic humor, even Jayne's untouchable allure.

At the telescope, he shrank sometimes from the dread-ful splendor of the cosmos, the killing cold outside the ship's fragile skin, the withering vacuum, the lethal radia-tions. The universe became a terrible engine, running forever without control or goal or engineer, creating suns and consuming galaxies, unaware of anything alive.

"Brighten up!" Lisa urged him once when she saw him depressed. "We're alive and bound for Mars! What more do you want? Icing on the cake?"

"Thanks."

He grinned and fought the mood. He was alive, after all, and happy for it. Aware or not, the cosmos had given birth to humankind. Their flight was a second birth, from the womb of Earth into a new human sphere. Mars did hang ahead.

They passed turnaround. Flipped over, rocket engine forward, the ship began the long braking glide toward parking orbit. Lisa took turns with him at the telescope, watching the planet swell, a red dot, a bubble of drying blood, a ball of battered, red-rusted steel.

Could it ever really become a second human home?

♂

Still a month out, Barova asked for a meeting of the crew. Lavrin called them together in the dome. She had prepared herself, long blonde hair brushed into lustrous waves and lips bright red, tight blue skinsuit molded to her perfect figure. Positioned by the main computer, she gathered Hellman, Chandra, and Kim Lo like defenders around her.

"Commander, we have a crisis to face."

Her voice was practiced music, but he heard a hard ring in it. She flashed her bright-toothed smile at Lavrin and turned to her companions. Hellman nodded, grinning warmly. Chandra shrugged. Kim Lo's girlish face looked innocent of anything except affection for him.

"A critical decision." She turned back to challenge Jayne and Lisa and Houston, standing with Lavrin beside the pilot console. "We are proposing a radical revision of our flight plan."

"So?" Lavrin waited gravely.

"We want to cut the flight." Emotion flushed her fluid oval face, and her smooth voice lifted. "We ought to abandon any attempt at a permanent surface station. Instead, we want to survey the planet, gather data that might help some future expedition, and head for home."

"Why?" Lavrin recoiled, astonished. "What's wrong?"

"We want to get back alive."

A moment of silence. Her eyes swept them, alertly bright, narrowed a little and already hostile.

"We're on schedule." Lavrin kept his voice level. "No major malfunction reported to me. What's your problem?"

"Yours, too." Her trim body stiffened and her pale tongue brushed her lips. "Otto says we had to leave a lot of cargo in the rush to get off ahead of the panic."

"A few tons of spares and extras," Lavrin shrugged, "Nothing essential."

"Don't forget poor Luther White." She gestured at the red disk glowing in the telescope monitor. "Sick and maybe dying of that poison dust. Otto says two years on Mars means sure death for us."

"Don't you forget reaction mass." Lavrin scowled at her. "The water we need to load on Mars. We can't get back without it."

"We can manage." She smiled at Hellman, waiting for his nod. "Otto says we have reserves enough to get us back to rendezvous with the *Nergal* when it's finished, wherever it can meet us." Hellman frowned and she added quickly, "That is if we don't spend too mass on needless exploration."

Lavrin shook his head and swung to look at those around him.

"Commander?" Houston waited for his nod and turned back to face Barova's cold stare. "For myself, Irina, I knew the risks before I joined the Corps. We all did.

"We've trained to meet them. It's true we could die. So what? So long as we lead the way, others will follow."

"I admire your spirit." She spread her sleek blue-clad arms as if to embrace his spirit. "But such rash courage will never conquer Mars."

"Irina—" Lavrin paused as if to temper his reproof. "You disappoint me. I was not prepared for this."

"We're not prepared for Mars." She glanced around her for support. "Otto agrees that we can't establish any surface outpost where we can survive a Martian year. Let's admit it." She spread her fine white hands. "Do what we can. Get home safe. Report our data. Which will be a monumental achievement."

Hellman moved closer to her, lover as well as ally. Jayne whispered into Lavrin's ear. He frowned and shook his head. Chandra and Kim Lo stood a little aside, observers still neutral. Lisa shrugged at Houston, as if to deplore Barova's proposal. There was silence in the dome, till Lavrin spoke again.

"I came to stay."

"So did we all." Barova nodded, smiling too brightly.

"Back when we expected to have the *Nergal* with us or ready to follow, with more supplies and more people. In the confusion of the takeoff, we had no time to estimate the risks." She appealed again to Hellman and paused for his mutter of assent. "Now we see the situation as it is. Suicide!"

"Our survival was never insured." Jayne touched Lavrin's arm and raised her own voice. "We accepted uncertainty and agreed to make the best of whatever we might discover."

"A noble goal," Barova purred. "No longer possible. I don't need to review the media panic over White's illness, or list the equipment that nobody likes to talk about because it never got aboard. The balloon-wheeled transporter. The induction furnace. The big radio dish. The spare fusion engine left at the factory because it wasn't paid for."

"Things I wish we had." Lavrin shrugged. "We can do without."

"Think so?" Hellman muttered. "I don't."

Barova caught his arm to restrain him.

"Please, Commander." She produced a luminous smile. "Please consider our proposal. Dr. Chandra agrees that we can remain in Mars orbit as long as four to six weeks. Long enough to gather data. Right, Ram?"

"If that's what we want." Chandra nodded, dark features gravely impassive. "We can take time enough for a rather extensive survey, but we'll have to watch that closing window. Or wait for the next."

"Wait to die!" She paused to soften her voice. "Forgive me, Commander, but we've so much at stake! Science worth more than our lives, if we can get it home. Six weeks should give us time to send landers to both satellites and make at least two actual surface landings, one near the equator and the other on a polar cap. Time enough for an adequate survey, before we have to go."

"You're serious?" Lavrin frowned. "Really serious?"

"Deadly serious, Commander. Our lives depend on it."

"If that's how you feel—" He looked at the three around him. "How do you stand?"

"I came for keeps." Houston turned back to Hellman and Barova. "And I have a question. The *Ares* can't make that return flight without reaction mass. How do we refill the water tanks in just a few weeks?"

"Otto?" Barova nodded for Hellman to answer for her.

"We have a reserve," he said. "Surplus water we loaded instead of all the weight we had to leave. Enough to get us back."

Houston stared at him.

"With severe economy," he added hastily. "If we attempt no more than two surface landings. If we leave with enough margin of time and make the return flight at minimum thrust." He glanced at Chandra. "Ram has checked my computations."

"It's possible—barely." Chandra nodded doubtfully. "I can't promise we'd all survive." He frowned at Lavrin. "Commander, please understand that Kim and I are not committed either way. If the first landers come back with promising reports, we're willing to take our chances with you. If not, the more prudent course is to get back home while we can."

"We really think we can?" Lavrin asked him. "With the water aboard?"

"With luck." He paused to frown at Hellman. "We computed a series of return orbits. Stretching the return window, we can wait six weeks at most. Helium power may let us bend the rules, but still it isn't magic. Stretching the reserves, we'll have to follow a parsimonious orbit, minimizing fuel drawdown. That means at least a year before the rendezvous, on half rations. We'd have to eat the livestock and the feed we brought for them."

"That's what you want?" Houston scowled at Barova. "A year on famine rations to let us tell the world how we lost our nerve?"

"It's the better choice." Her smile was coldly defiant. "Better than death on Mars."

"I'll take my chance at life on Mars. It's better than slow death in space."

Inquiringly, Lavrin looked back at Chandra.

"A painful decision, Commander." He shrugged uneasily. "I'm glad it's not mine to make. Perhaps we could survive on Mars till the next window opens, if we could all agree on the effort. We know there's water. Certainly in the polar caps—"

"Don't forget the protolife virus," Barova cut in. "As for Martian water, it's a gamble for our lives. All we find will be ice or permafrost. Can we thaw it? Purify it? Get it aboard the ship? All of us sick with the virus?"

"Who knows?" Chandra shook his head at Lavrin. "I don't."

"We'll know more," Lisa said, "when we've landed."

"Maybe." Hellman shook his bullet head. "But even two touchdowns will deplete reserves to the danger point."

Jayne and Lavrin turned away, murmuring together. Barova smiled at Hellman, still brightly defiant. Kim Lo stood with her eyes fixed blankly on the monitor image of Mars till Chandra caught her hand. She clung to his. Lisa winked at Houston, seeming somehow amused.

"A painful situation." Lavrin shook his head somberly at Hellman and Barova. "I can't agree to give up all we came for, but we're in trouble unless we can all work together."

"In more trouble," Barova said, "if we miss that window."

"Irina, please!" Chandra caught her arm, with an apologetic nod at Lavrin. "Let's hold everything. Decisions can come later, when we know what's waiting on the planet."

♂

Lavrin let them scatter out of the dome, and the big ship swam on. Watch by watch, Houston and Lisa turned when they could to look again at Mars, ever larger in the monitor, polar caps glaring white, the southern highlands a maze of ancient craters, the north a riddle of lava fields and dead volcanoes, of dunes and pits and deep-slashed canyons.

Spring had come to the south hemisphere, the south snowcap shrinking fast. They watched Martian weather changing. On the floor of the vast Hellas basin, a storm front lifted a plume of yellow dust. High winds swept it around the planet. Thick yellow haze spread north, filling the Valles Marineris rift and dimming everything until only the great cones of Olympus Mons and the Tharsis ridge rose above it.

"Dust storms happen." Lisa tried to be philosophic. "Back in 1971, Mariner 9 found the whole planet hidden. Photography was delayed for months."

"If we're delayed—" He scowled again at the vast red-brown blur that filled the monitor. "Barova's six weeks will soon be gone. What then? Do we just grab a few rocks off the satellites and scuttle for home?"

12

The Cost

Though fusion rockets promised new worlds in space, they cost more dollars and rubles and euros and dolphins than the old world cared to pay. The four powers were slicing funds even before the *Ares* took off. Receiving no good news from the expedition, they voted to dismantle the Authority.

In a ritual established before her son was born, Lucina waited for Kelligan in that back room precisely at eight every business morning to serve her hot *café con leche* and review their plans for the day. As her own story went, Marty had been conceived on the big conference table.

"Señor?" Unhappy now with LeeAnn on the payroll and established here in an office just across the hall, she wore an ironic air of respectful martyrdom. "May we speak of the expedition?"

Kelligan sat bleakly silent, staring across the table at the huge mural of Aztec sacrifice, while she poured the coffee and hot milk from polished silver urns. Whatever she wanted to say, it could hardly be anything he wanted to hear.

"Martin has something for you, *Señor.*" Even after twenty-odd years in Texas, her accent was not entirely gone. "A matter of urgency."

"Okay," he muttered. "Call him in."

Marty came in through the hall door, armed with a heavy leather briefcase and a long yellow legal pad.

"Thank you, Senator." His mother had taught him to please Kelligan with the title. "News for you, sir."

"So?" He scowled at the bright violet necktie that matched the violet stripe in his wide-shouldered velour jacket. She had failed to restrain his taste for color. "What?"

Maddeningly, Marty took time to arrange the pad and briefcase like fortifications to defend his place at the table, and waited for his mother to fill his cup.

"I speak to people, sir." He paused again to sugar and stir. "I cultivate insiders. I stroke them right and they talk because they know who I am."

"So? What do they say?"

"Nothing good." Too solemnly, he shook his nearly hairless head. "Sorry, sir."

"Let's hear it."

"A delegation from White Sands, sir. Acquaintances I made when we were fabricating skin sections for the landers. I saw them with our bankers yesterday. They were all down at the mouth. They'd been to London and Moscow and Asia Island, begging for funds to save the Authority. Turned down cold.

"Not that they wanted to say so. They were trying to hush up the problem, still hoping for a break. I took them to the Astro Club for lunch and margaritas. The English and Japanese guys had a plane to catch, but I kept the Russian long enough. The Club Paree for dinner, with their Texas beauties."

Marty winked, happy with his recollections.

"So what's the point?"

"Mars Authority's up the creek. Sad thing for Mr. Houston."

"How?"

"Bankrupt, sir. Running on loans and promises since

the *Ares* took off. Their funds are dried up now, since news leaked out above this bug in the Mars dust. The powers and the bankers are shutting them down. My Russian wanted me to endorse his Authority check. Swore it was good, but said it might be his last.

"He's a cosmonaut, just back from Farside and bragging about his luck. Could have been stranded on the Moon when the station shut down, with no way home."

"What does this matter to Sam?"

"Hard to say, sir." Marty shrugged and made a long face. "I guess you know the Authority was funding Farside. With the money gone, they're calling their people home. Cutting our link to the *Ares.*"

"So that's your point?" Kelligan stiffened. "They could lose contact with the expedition?"

"They've lost it, sir."

"Bad news for Edna." Kelligan stared blankly at the naked victim sprawled beneath the sacrificial flint. "She's been living with the TV, praying for Sam." He scowled at Marty. "When can they get contact back?"

"Maybe never." Marty fiddled with the yellow folder and looked hopefully up at his mother. "Unless—"

"Unless what?"

"Unless they get a break. They were asking for at least funds enough to keep the station going, but Polokof said all they got was *nyet.*" Gloomily, he shook his sweat-filmed head. *"Nyet* and *nyet* again."

Lucina was ready with the urns, but Kelligan waved her away.

"They're trying to sit on the bad news, but Polokof wasn't used to margaritas. Finally told me the expedition is running into a big dust storm. It hides all the planet, a haze so thick they can't land unless it clears."

His thick shoulders lurched into a shrug.

"Poison dust, if they ever breathe it."

Kelligan wanted a cigar, but Lucina had suddenly

found herself allergic to tobacco. Edna and her doctor had tried to forbid them years ago. Now he tried to limit himself to one a day, after lunch and alone in his office.

"Don't tell Edna," he said. "She's already sick from brooding."

"Trust me, sir." Marty nodded piously. "But such news gets around."

He was about to rise, ready for Marty to go.

"Something else, *Señor.*" Lucina bustled again with the silver urns. "Martin has urgent business."

"Reason I wanted to see you, sir." Marty found a handkerchief and mopped his sweaty crown. "The delegation offered me a deal, right after lunch. They're desperate just to save their jobs. The thing can be a gold mine for us."

"So?"

"They've got to have a loan, just to meet next month's payroll and get Farside back on line. Hoping for a break, Polokof said. Anything that might revive the promise of Mars. I told him, sir—" Marty seemed to shrink behind his fortress. "I told him, sir, that we might guarantee a loan."

"To them?" He let his voice lift. "If they're bankrupt—"

"Not legally. Not yet. Polokof gave me a stack of data on their remaining assets. Their rights to the White Sands facilities. Patent rights on the helium fusion process. Their lunar mines. Their spaceplanes. Their installations at Farside. I think they're desperate enough to offer us options as security."

"What would we do with helium on the Moon?"

"He says a time will come when it will be what he calls gaseous gold here on Earth. Replacing oil and coal. Someday. So he claims."

"Someday? Hah!"

"He's a fusion engineer. He admits the costs are still

out of sight except for spacecraft, but he believes the process can be improved. Could be he's right." Marty caught his breath and mopped his wet face. "A chance for future billions, sir, One we can pick up for peanuts."

"Sell it to somebody else."

"Senator—" Marty gulped and sat scowling at the jungle pyramids while Lucina filled their cups. "Think about your wife. Think about Mr. Houston."

♂

The TV that night reported the *Ares* lost in space, all contact interrupted by a solar flare. When the reporter had no more to add, Edna rose silently and went up to her room. Awake in his own bed, long after midnight, Kelligan saw the slit of light beneath her door and tried the knob. The door was locked, but he heard her moaning Houston's name.

Next day he talked to LeeAnn and his bankers and a company engineer who had been a student under Aristo Kolvos at CERN. The engineer promised that the Kolvos patents might someday be priceless. He had no idea when that day might come, but Kelligan let Marty call White Sands. Polokof returned with Authority officials from London and Asia Island. A hundred million, they agreed, would meet the payroll for a few more months and let them send a skeleton staff back to Farside.

A hundred million was more than peanuts, but Edna wanted word from Sam. LeeAnn urged him to sign and went to White Sands with Lucina and Marty to finalize the terms. Rights were researched, contracts drawn up, checks written, directives executed. Spaceplane crews, staff astronomers and Farside technicians were recalled to duty, tested for indications of paralife infection, and dispatched to the Moon.

And the solar storm subsided.

"At last, sir." Marty called from White Sands. "A report from Farside that contact has been restored. They have relayed a report from the *Ares,* to be aired in half an hour."

Trying to reach Edna, Kelligan got Roberto instead and asked him to alert her. Lucina were already pouring *café con leche* for Marty when he and LeeAnn joined them before the wide screen in the private room.

"Our first signal from the planet Mars!" the announcer burbled. "Or at least from Martian orbit. Most of the first transmissions were astronomic observations and technical details about the flight characteristics of the ship, but we can now air a brief public message from Dr. Irina Barova, official historian of the expedition."

Barova's radiant image came on the screen, sleek in the bright blue skinsuit and poised as if she were a galactic goddess standing in starry space on the huge red-glowing image of Mars.

"Hello, Earth!" She waved a compelling arm. "Captain Arkady Lavrin sends his hearty greetings from the first expedition to reach the Red Planet. For long weeks past we seemed in danger of failure because of a huge dust storm that veiled the whole planet. Landings looked impossible."

She turned like a dancer to look up at Phobos gliding just above her, a huge dark crater-scarred potato shape. In a moment it was gone, and her smile flashed again into the lens.

"I'm happy to say the dust has cleared," her lilting voice went on. "All Mars is now revealed, awesome with its geologic records of cataclysms past, terrible with all its alien unknowns. With Deimos, the tiny outer satellite now behind us, we have now dropped into the orbit of Phobos, only six thousand kilometers out.

"A triumph for mankind! We have already written a bold new chapter in human history. Even our safe arrival in Mars orbit is a monumental scientific event. Recording our observations and our data, we are taking long strides toward claiming the planet for a second human home. We do, however, have one concern."

Very briefly, her smile dimmed.

"Two volunteers, Jayne Ryan and Sam Houston Kelligan, left the *Ares* sixty hours ago on the landing craft *Magellan* to attempt our first landing. The aerobraking maneuver took longer than expected. Their craft disappeared behind the planet. Radio contact was broken. Unfortunately, nothing further has been received. Surely, however, they were able to get down safely while they were out of visual range. Captain Lavrin is confident that contact will soon be restored."

13

Mars

A world of threats and riddles, Mars is small and cold and dead. The fourth planet out from the sun, it has about half Earth's diameter, a tenth the mass, and two fifths of the surface gravity.

The image of Mars expanded on the telescope monitor until Houston thought he could have seen human footprints, if human boots had ever been there. Searching for a landing site, he scanned boulder fields, lava fields, crater fields, glaring ice and ink-black shadow. Different everywhere, everywhere alike.

Dead.

Swinging down toward their planned parking orbit, the *Ares* came close to Deimos, the outer satellite. The name means "Fury." Swift imagined it, in *Gulliver.*

Aseph Hall first saw it, in 1977. Ram Chandra wanted to explore it now.

"Just a dead comet," Hellman objected. "Black rock buried in black dust. Not much chance of anything we need."

"Water? Comets are mostly such volatiles as water."

"Too heavy for water." Hellman wore his habit of professorial authority like a coat of mail. "The high density says it's mostly rock. Volatiles cooked out long ago, except maybe buried deep in the core and out of our reach."

"We don't know," Chandra insisted. "And a look will cost us very little fuel."

"I want it on video," Barova told them. "Landing should make a good action sequence. Something to help us win the PR wars again, when we get contact back."

Hellman yielded to her, meekly, and Lavrin let Chandra and Kim Lo take the *Colon* to Deimos. They came back to confirm that all they found was powdery black chondritic dust fallen to blanket a cratered black chondritic mass. No available water anywhere.

"We did find oxygen in mineral oxides and hydrogen in heavy hydrocarbons," Chandra added. "But we brought no equipment to get them out and turn them into water."

♂

They slanted down into the orbit of Phobos, so low that the polar caps were out of view, hidden below the planet's curve. Chasing that moonlet around it every seven hours, they searched the unending brick-red panorama rolling close below, desolate and changeless, vividly revealed but yet infinitely mysterious.

Gathered in the dome, they debated where to land. Houston spoke again for a site in the southern highlands.

The probes had found little they needed in the flatter northern lowlands, and the south was still almost unknown.

Barova wanted action, drama, something spectacular. A touchdown on a polar cap, one of the great volcanos, or preferably deep inside the Marineris rift. "Something to wake the world," she said. "Something to make us look heroic and put our achievements in the history books."

Lavrin listened and finally settled on Felis Dorsa, south of Coprates Chasma. Not too far from Marineris, it looked level enough for safety, and Hellman supported Barova with his opinion that the geology favored available permafrost.

"The honor of the first footstep goes to Jayne, as second in command," Lavrin said. "She'll go down in the *Magellan,* with one companion."

Houston raised his hand when she asked for volunteers. She looked inquiring at Lavrin instead.

"I'm out," he told her. "The captain stays aboard."

She turned to Chandra.

"We've had our turn." He nodded at Kim Lo. "The Deimos touchdown."

"Not me." Hellman said glanced fondly at Barova. "Not without Irina."

"Okay, Kelligan." Jayne shrugged at him, with a cool wry smile. "We're the first Martians."

Barova wanted them to get everything on video disks.

"Everything?" Houston protested. "We'll have more urgent things to do than pretending we had cameras already there to catch our lander coming down."

"Nothing's more urgent." She smiled past him, as if for the millions back on Earth. "We're living an epic. The greatest story in human history, but only if we get it told. When we get Farside back, I want disks that will excite the world."

"Building the permanent habitat would make a better story."

"Not if we die there before we get it sent."

"We'll take the cameras," Jayne agreed. "If you really think your broadcasts can help save the Authority."

♂

When at last they were ready to board the *Magellan,* Barova posed them clinging to the holdfasts beside the air lock.

"Smile! Show us the spirit of the *Ares.*" The media expert, she was calling orders even to Lavrin. "Wish them Godspeed, Commander."

Reluctantly, Lavrin made a little speech for the camera. This first touchdown on Mars might indeed later come to be recalled as an epic turning point in human history. Planting an outpost here, the race was a long step closer to its magnificent destiny.

She thanked him, no hint of irony in her trilling voice, and disked him shaking hands with Houston, kissing Jayne, gliding aside in free fall as she turned her lens to Jayne.

"How does it feel?" she asked. "To be chosen to make those historic first footprints?"

Jayne shrugged. "We aren't there yet."

She put the same question to Houston.

"Quite an honor, if it happens to us." He grinned at Jayne. "To one of us."

♂

The heavy valve thunked shut behind them, and Barova panned her camera across the control board to Lavrin. "Regrets, Commander? Don't you wish you were aboard?"

"Let history happen." Lavrin laughed. "My duty's here."

"You and I might have made a better cast."

She cocked her head, surveying him with open admiration. His boyhood had been spent in a military school; he knew the art of command. On the long flight out, he had grown a lush red beard. Muscular and tall, with vivid blue eyes, he looked like an heir to the Vikings. Perhaps, she thought, he really was; the genes for the eyes and the beard must have come down from the Norse trader-warriors who founded those first Rus states on the Volga and the Don.

Was she another modern Viking? The notion pleased her. Her eyes were blue like his, her fine skin white enough, her well-kept hair the color of honey. No matter now. The lander was gone. She shrugged, conscious of her own grace even when she played only to herself. No matter who stepped down first into that deadly dust, the whole world would see her videos. Back on Earth, they would surely earn the fame her mother used to promise her.

It was a reward she intended to enjoy. Let Houston dream his impossible dream of a permanent colony, one she had never shared. Her own mission was simply to record the saga and carry it back. Even if dead Mars was destined to remain forever dead, her disks and data could make her fortune now and her name forever.

"I suppose Ryan and Kelligan are good enough technicians." She dropped her voice for Lavrin. "But I don't think they're . . . well, really right for the drama they're about to play. Kelligan looks too young, not tough enough for all the hardships they have ahead. As for Ryan, she's too careless with her hair. She wouldn't even make up for the camera."

She let her gaze linger on him. She wished them nothing bad, but Kelligan had never warmed to her and Ryan had slept with Lavrin half the way out. If they didn't get back, he might want another mate. He certainly smelled better than Otto.

"You and I are surely superior actors." She gave him her most seductive smile. "With greater roles to play."

"If you think so." He shrugged, with only the faintest reflection of her smile. "Our role right now is to support the landing party."

When he was gone, she carried the camera back to the dome for a panning shot of Lisa Kolvos, buckled into her seat at the console. No rival for stardom, Kolvos was still attractive enough and certainly good at her job. Athletic and slim, with straight dark hair, she looked up with a friendly nod at the lens and turned quickly back to the monitor where she was following the *Magellan* down toward Mars.

♂

Eyes on the lander, a small fleck of brightness already shrinking fast, Lisa felt a stab of envy for Jayne and a glow of hope for Houston. The first on Mars! She admired Houston for his total dedication to Mars, liked him more for something boyish and quizzical in his smile.

Was it love? She had always shrugged off that question. The mission had demanded too much to let her think of it. Yet she felt a nagging wish that she could have been with him on the lander, and a fleeting regret that he had never asked her into to his berth.

Jayne? That one was certainly no rival; her dislike for Houston seemed almost irrational. She was a fine human specimen, however; her devotion to the mission was as keen as Houston's. Perhaps she had earned her place on the *Magellan*. She had been hard for Lisa to know, but nobody was more competent.

♂

Lavrin came with Barova back to the dome.

"Forgive the intrusion." His pleasant tone had a ring of command. "If you don't mind, this is an occasion we must record."

With enough to do tracking the lander down to Mars, she did mind. She was the lifeline if something went wrong with the lander. Yet, with the camera on her again, she managed a smile.

"Lisa Kolvos, navigation officer." Barova's trained radio voice had a rhythm and precision she envied. "Officer Kolvos, will you explain the landing procedure for our audience on Earth?"

"Okay." She turned to gesture at the monitor displays. "In the *Ares* we're following the orbit of Phobos, the inner moon. Which means we're six thousand kilometers out, moving two kilometers a second and circling the planet in less than eight hours.

"To get down safe, the landing craft has to kill that velocity. It will use the helium-fusion rocket engine to steer it into the atmosphere, which is thinner than Earth's but still dense enough for aerobraking. The pilot can deploy a parachute to slow it more, and finally land on rocket thrust."

"Can you show us the landing point?"

She shifted the telescope away from the lander to bring a wide slice of Mars into the monitor.

"The target site." She pointed with a pencil to the flat floor of a vast brown bowl. "Of course getting there isn't altogether certain. Not on this first descent."

"They'll make a vertical landing?"

"Right. They must set down tail first, in position to take off again. That may seem awkward, but the craft has only one main rocket engine, located in the tail. There are

thrusters, of course, smaller rockets for steering and maneuver. Those alone are not strong enough for lift-off."

Barova wanted shots of the lander in flight.

"Not just the monitor images. I want the actual
lander."

"It's already too far away for that." She adjusted shut-
ters and filters to open a window for the camera. "All you
can see is the jet. That bright little arrow. Condensing
steam, really."

Mars still filled the monitor, immense and mysterious,
flattened by distance into a red-shadowed map.

"A new world!" Barova chanted into her microphone,
speaking to the faraway millions. "All unknown! Can
you imagine the awe our intrepid pioneers will surely
feel? The wonders they will discover? Can you imagine
building cities here?"

Houston could, Lisa thought. A pang of dread held
her silent for a moment, until she had to respond to the
camera returning to her face.

"Officer Kolvos, what are your own emotions?"

"Confused." She shrugged. "I'm anxious for the *Magellan.*"

For Houston, though she didn't say his name, and the
whole expedition. Glad when Barova was gone, she
searched the endless rust-patched reach of Mars and
found the bright arrowhead of the jet again, even tinier
now as it crept ahead of the ship on its shortening path
around the planet. She magnified the dimming image
again and again, until finally it was gone.

♂

There was still Houston's terse radio voice, reporting
orbital velocity and indicated altitude. She wanted more,
wanted to share his own emotions, but he had time for

nothing unnecessary. The signals grew fainter, the static louder, until his words were hard to hear.

In their Phobos orbit, days were seven hours. The small sun dropped fast behind her toward the planet's enormous mottled swell of bright and darker rust-red. Its harsh light changed as they moved. Flat brick-hued landscapes sprang into sharp relief. Craters became rings of shadow.

Eastward, night was falling over the Marineris rift, a river of blackness flowing down it. Orange dusk squeezed the sunlit west into a narrow crescent, a dim crimson streak, a rosy glow. When that was gone, the two dark and tiny moons shed too little light to matter. Mars had become a black enormous pit beneath her, domed with splendid stars.

Houston had fallen silent, and she called him again.

"All okay." His voice seemed hurried and faint. "Descending as planned from approach orbit. Indicated altitude now 2900 kilometers. Position somewhere over Tithonius Lacus. Volcanic cones on Tharsis Ridge in view ahead. Expect to deploy parachute on the next low pass."

She felt drained by tension and emotion, glad when Barova came to relieve her. In the galley, she heated a ration packet but suddenly didn't want it. Too keyed up for rest or sleep, she returned to the dome. Barova sat at the controls, calling the *Magellan,* waiting and calling again. All they heard was static.

"Relax." Barova shrugged at her anxiety. "No hint of any problem. Contact was lost, of course, when they went beyond the planet. They'll come back."

They didn't come back.

Hours dragged, till Lavrin came to take the con.

"There's nothing you can do," he told her. "Except take a break."

She went down to work out in the gym tank and crawl

into her berth. Sleeping restlessly, she dreamed she was on the lander with Houston, sitting at the controls. At his command, she deployed the parachute. It opened too hard, split, and whipped in tatters behind them. They fell into the night side of Mars.

Waiting to die when they struck, she turned to look back at Houston. His eyes on her, he shrugged and shook his head. His eyes looked sad. Feeling sad for him, she wanted to call out to him, to tell him she loved him, but she had no voice. She couldn't move. Frozen, waiting for the crash, she couldn't even breathe.

But they never crashed.

They simply fell forever into a black and bottomless pit. The stars behind them crept together, into a shrinking circle, a single point that dimmed and disappeared. They fell on and on through the featureless dark, and still she couldn't move.

She woke chilled with sweat, showered in the thin spray of recycled water, and went back to the dome. Ram Chandra had the con. Hoarsely calling the lander, he got only a rattle of static.

"What do you think?" She was afraid to hear the answer.

"Dunno." Like Lavrin, he had learned American English and Corps "tech talk" in Texas. "They should be back in the line of sight, but I dunno."

"Could they be down somewhere out of radio range?"

"Depends on the parachute." He shook his head. "It's never been tested in this atmosphere. Could have dragged them down nearly anywhere—or ripped off and left them up in orbit." He jerked his shoulders at the planet's vast blind face and murmured again, "Dunno."

Another endless watch, and still she heard no signal. With the monitors at full amplification, she searched clay-red ring mountains and ember-red deserts, red-brown canyons and red-gray boulder slopes, until the darker splotches came to look like drying blood. She saw no gleam of metal, no glow of signal smoke, no flash of a solar mirror. Again she tried to sleep, and dreamed that the dead volcanos were erupting blood.

Kim Lo was at the controls when she came back.

"I'm afraid." A bitter whisper. "Afraid they're dead."

"We can't give up." She shook her head and tried to smile. "Because they never will. They're good. They're trained. We have to hope."

Alone on the dome, she met the face of Mars again. It glared back at her, every pock and wrinkle sharply etched. There was no sign of the lander anywhere. Searching, she remembered Houston's useless battle to choose a landing site in the southern highlands, far from Marineris.

The contrast between the hemispheres was vivid now, the north mostly darker, smoother, younger, much of it leveled by lava flows. Flooded by vanished seas perhaps, back before the lavas erupted. The south was brighter, higher, pitted like the moon's far side from the hail of early impacts.

Could they have turned to touch down on the highlands, closer to the south polar cap and out of view beyond the sharp horizon line between the planet's dust-red glare and dead black space? Were they hurt, perhaps, the lander disabled, unable to call? All she could do was keep on searching.

Mars rolled below her, a globe of old iron splotched with the bright hue of new rust and the dark of old rust, scarred everywhere by the wounds of unthinkable time. Yet the telescope and the shifting light uncovered contrast everywhere, deserts of wind-rippled dunes vaster than the Sahara. The great Hellas basin, formed perhaps by a protoplanet's fall, rimmed with the channels and deltas formed when it held a sea. The huge volcanic bulge of Tharsis, Olympus Mons climbing from its flank. The endless canyon maze of Marineris, where slow tectonic cataclysm had split the planet's crust.

It was all sullen enigma, and terror of it swept her. Mars had been her life, the goal of hopes and dreams that kept her life alive. But now, creeping back beneath her, it looked too vast and strange for any human use or even human understanding. Too alien to harbor Houston's city—

She shivered and called the *Magellan,* called again and yet again as the planet turned, hearing only the dead rustle in the speaker.

♂

"Can't somebody go down to search?" she asked Lavrin when he came to relieve her. She saw his frown, and added hastily, "I'll volunteer. I'm sure Ram will join me."

"He has asked." Jaw set hard, he shook his head. "It's no use, because we don't know where to look. We can't cover a million miles of Mars."

"I thought we'd planned one more landing."

"We have." His voice was brittle and abrupt. "On the south polar cap. Barova wants it for the record."

"So we just abandon Jayne and Houston?"

"If I saw any possible chance—" She saw the pain in his haggard eyes. "I don't."

"Surely—" Her voice caught. "We do know where they were to land."

"Near the Marineris rim, which is five thousand kilometers long." Hopelessly, he spread his arms. "South of Coprates Chasma. The possible target area is half the size of France. They may be there—or anywhere."

"Can't we look?"

"And kill the expedition?"

"How could that happen?"

"Talk to Barova." He scowled at Mars, lips set hard behind the fiery beard. "This disaster seems to prove her point. Unless the *Colon* can bring more fuel mass back from the polar ice—" He shrugged. "Its touchdown will be the last."

She stared at him accusingly.

"Listen, Lisa." His voice fell. "With no information from the *Magellan,* we've no assurance that the *Colon* will fare any better. I won't throw it away."

She could only shake her head.

"We must accept a hard situation," his voice had a bitter edge, "and salvage what we can. The *Colon* can carry laser spectrometers and penetrator probes to make a new survey from circumpolar orbit. We've touched Deimos. We've fuel to reach Phobos. Hellman and Barova are collecting good data. If we get back with that, it's enough to justify the expedition."

"So we just forget Jayne and Houston?"

Face bleak, he made no answer.

14

Magellan

Magellan and *Colon,* the two landing craft, were all carbon and titanium, streamlined for atmospheric operation, powered with helium fusion, designed for vertical takeoff against the gravity of the Moon or Mars.

Nudged away by the catapult, the lander drifted slowly out of the ship's sun dazzle, into black space. Houston sat at the controls, Jayne behind him at the cockpit computer. Frowning down at the back of his sandy head, she wondered why he had to be here.

She had to admit he was able enough. His records showed glowing evaluations and high scores on every test. He had trained faithfully, even ranking first in lander training off the Moon. Yet he was still a Kelligan.

Was he fit for the hard push to Mars?

Or had he come to bring his cruel world with him, the world she had grown up hating. The hard world where mighty corporations owned everything and got their dividends from strikes and lockouts, from smog and rats and filth, with never a thought for the poverty and pain they gave little people?

Was he another Marty Gorley, bent on making Mars one more Shangri-La, one more family island of arrogance and greed and lust? Not that he looked in any way sinister. The actual money men seldom did; the ugly ones were mostly the servants and the yes-men and lawyers who jumped to do what they were told.

He was handsome enough, too, with his lean athletic frame and open smile. It made him harder than Gorley to hate. He was spoiled, though, by gifts he had never earned, by inherited brains, inherited body, inherited money. Nothing, apparently, had ever been hard for him, nothing seemed to ruffle him. She heard him whistling softly now, a tune she didn't recognize. Maybe musical, it still annoyed her.

If he expected something easy here . . .

She shrugged and looked past him, into the blackness beyond the thick quartz heat shield. The *Ares* shrank and drifted away beyond it, lost in infinite night. She felt an odd fondness for it, and a sudden unexpected pang of loneliness. Her home for nearly half a year, filled with friends she had learned to love, it was suddenly dearer than the shabby streets of Lakefield.

Mars hung ahead, a vast brick-brown ball already so near she couldn't see the polar ice, so bright she had to squint. They had come so many months, so many million miles, to stake their lives against its stark unknowns. Were they ready? She felt sure of herself, of most of the crew.

Kelligan, however . . .

She spoke his last name. Discipline in the Corps and on the *Ares* had always been informal. To everybody else, he had become merely "Hew," but she had to keep her distance.

"Yeah?" His own quick grin seemed too warm. "You okay?"

"No difficulty yet." She firmed her tone to remind him who was in command. "We're now clear enough. Position the lander for computer-controlled insertion into Mars braking orbit."

"Okay."

The computer she could trust. Kelligan, however, would have to make the actual touchdown. There were no sensors fine enough to search the actual site for the unexpected rock or slope or dune or pit that might be fatal. Perhaps he had proved his skills on ski slopes and hang glider flights and parachute jumps, but landing the *Magellan* would be something graver than any useless game.

Behind them, the *Ares* had crept back into the center of the narrow shield. The alert gong chimed and the rocket fired. A huge white vapor cloud exploded to hide the ship. The lander shivered and surged against her. Heavy with its thrust, she sank back into her seat until the steam jet vanished and again she was weightless.

"Hello Barsoom!" He turned to grin at her. "Here we come!"

♂

Elation had turned him almost tipsy. At last, after all his boyhood dreams, all the years of training, all the months in flight, they were going down to Mars! It spread vast beneath them, a world of enigmatic promise: water—if they were lucky—to keep the ship alive, the means to keep them all alive when the habitat was ready; space and building stuff and promised wealth for the shining cities of his boyhood visions.

"At last!" He laughed aloud. "We're the lucky ones!"

He and Jayne!

In the little mirror above the control board she looked lovely in the snug blue skinsuit. Her red-gold hair was as short as his, and her gray-green eyes shone with joy. He longed for her to like him, to love him if she would, but he was a realist. She owed him nothing.

In time, however, she might. The chance of that looked brighter since they were companions now, alone together, flying down to Mars! The risks ahead were beyond prediction, perhaps enormous, but they would share them. Her life might depend on him, his on her. For the moment, that was enough.

On impulse, he tossed her the Corps salute. Her own hand lifted as if she shared his mood. But then her gaze grew sharper. He saw no smile.

"Lucky?" Her grave tone sobered him. "Our luck will be what we make it."

♂

They were to orbit five times around the planet. That first burn had sent them into a long ellipse that would take them down to graze the atmosphere and then far out again. Each pass would carry them lower. On the fifth, perhaps the sixth, they could attempt the touchdown.

Their first circuit took five hours, but each was shorter than the last. Between passes, he called his brief reports back to the *Ares*. They relaxed in their seats or climbed in turn to the tiny toilet and pantry alcoves off the nearly empty cargo space behind them. He passed a water bottle. She opened ration packs, and they shared a lunch.

"Sleep," she told him once. "If you can."

"Can't." He gestured at Mars. "Not now."

"Better try. You'll need to be your best."

♂

Trying, he found only a broken doze. Mars was passing too close. He had begun to feel the electric tension that always caught him at the moment of a parachute drop or a hang glider landing. Rounding the planet faster than it turned, they would come down from the west to meet the rising sun.

Mars swelled as they neared it. Searching its enormous dome on the first daylight pass, he found the endless gorge of Marineris sliding out of orange-red sunlight into the dark. High as they were, he picked out Olympus Mons and the three great cones along the Tharsis ridge, yet everything was flattened by their great altitude, hard to recognize.

Lower on each pass, he picked out more detail. A wisp of fire floating out of the dark became a feather of sunlight cloud above Olympus. The endless gorge of Marineris was a dark snake coiled far around the planet. He found Coprates Chasma, and their target site.

"Another time around," he called to Jayne. "And touchdown!"

♂

They plunged again into the dark, and the computer initiated the final approach while they were still behind the planet. Weight came back as it reversed the craft to fire another braking burst and tipped it up to maximize atmospheric drag.

When sunlight met them, he turned in his seat to look back at her. She gave him a fleeting smile, as if she shared his own elation, but he caught a stark tension that surprised him. Risk had always exhilarated him, yet he saw reason enough for her evident unease. This was the first actual field test of everything: the tiny *Magellan* itself, airfoils and helium rocket and parachute; the computer program written to fly it down; the altimeter and gyrocompass; even the landing struts and his own untried skill against the different air and gravity of Mars.

He grinned and waved to show a confidence he didn't fully feel.

"Stick to business, Kelligan." Her tone was abrupt and hard, edged he felt with veiled distrust. "Deploy the parachute."

Too soon, he thought. He tried to quench a flash of anger. This was not the moment for a quarrel, and he could understand her mistrust. He had grown up rich. His name was Kelligan. He couldn't expect her to forget Marty Gorley at Shangri-La.

Yet here they were together, about to land on Mars!

What else could matter? His heart beat faster. When the moment came, the final touchdown would be his to make. Till then, of course, she was in command. He tightened his seat belt and peered into the rearview monitor to see ahead.

Felis Dorsa was crawling into view, a shadow-mottled brick-red waste that spread forever toward the red-hazed horizon, the selected target point still far ahead. He glanced at the instrument readouts. Altitude 120,800 meters. The air here probably still too thin, he though, to catch the pilot chute.

"Kelligan!" Her voice was sharp. "I told you—"

He deployed it, braced himself, and felt no drag.

"Can't you obey?"

"Look!" he called. "In the monitor."

The pilot chute was there, a twisted huddle of fabric and cords, drifting uselessly behind. They were still too high, the air too rare. He overrode the computer to angle their flight down more sharply and watched the tangled chute. At last it whipped open. The main chute billowed after it.

"Now!" he yelled at Jayne. "Hang on!"

He heard no answer. The filling chute spread across the monitor and its drag jerked the seat against him. He watched the air speed plunge, the altimeter spin. 110,000 meters. 90,000. Yellow-red desert lifted in the rearview monitor, sliding faster, always faster, as they neared it. 60,000 meters. 50,000.

The target was still too far ahead. He hit the red lever to detach the parachute, saw it dwindle to a vanishing atom in the black space behind. Jayne's face looked white and strained when he glanced at her, teeth sunk into her lip. He felt a stab of regret that she seemed not to share his elation.

AUTO OFF, the pilot was flashing. CONTROLS ON MANUAL.

He whooped with sheer delight. Here at last was Mars! Dead wasteland, foreign, frowning, all unknown, yet the goal of his oldest dream. It was perhaps a deadly challenge, yet he felt ready. Here at last was the chance to justify the years of training, the rich repayment for all he had left behind. He laughed aloud.

"Kelligan!" He heard Jayne's startled gasp. "Are you crazy?"

Tipping the rocket nozzle forward again, he set them on a long glide and watched the fretted rims of Marineris crawling under them, seven kilometer deep, five thousand long, still only a scratch across the planet. Red sunlight burned along its ragged cliffs.

He heard her tight voice again, and still ignored her. Here, coming down through air too thin for the wings, toward the first human landing on a surface still unknown, the task demanded everything he had.

Ten thousand meters. Five. Four. Mars swelled beneath, the basin floor nearly free of impact pits but rippled with long yellow dunes that swept like ocean waves beneath them, faster, always faster. Hazards, perhaps, but they could be avoided. The landing point came into view, a wide level dark-red stretch among the dunes, a line of darker bluffs and crater rims lifting beyond it.

Now!

This first attempt had to be the last. Any overload, Lavrin thought, would add unacceptable risk. They had loaded no reserve mass to let them lift and try again.

This had to be it!

He lifted the rocket nearly level, ready to drop them when the moment came, and watched the monitor. Indicated air speed still almost a thousand knots. Altimeter three thousand meters. Two thousand. They were skimming the wind-drifted dunes, already too low, dropping too fast.

He angled the rocket down, fired a short burst. They lifted. Enough? For a moment he was back in training, bringing the old *Da Gama* down to the Moon. Yet, here in this deeper gravity well, nothing would be quite the same. His pulse thudded. The target spot looked clear, an open island in the sea of dunes. It might have been leveled to receive them. Time for the braking burst, before they passed it?

Not quite yet; they must not drop short.

He waited, one tense finger on the key.

"Kelligan!" Her tight voice seemed desperate. "Fire! Now!"

A few more seconds. He had no time or breath to say so, but the long yellow dunes could be a deadly trap. Wind had whipped them into graceful curves, but their loose sand or dust might let the lander tumble.

His breath slowed, his whole body tense. The critical instant was only seconds away. Waiting, loving the test, the proof of nerve and skill, he watched the dunes rising like a yellow flood to meet them.

"Wake up!"

"Not quite yet." He whispered it silently and held his finger still until the target island lay just ahead, the crater ridge grown tall in the monitor, hardly a dozen kilometers beyond.

"Now!

Breathing again, he hit the key.

Nothing happened.

He heard no jet, felt no thrust. Still too high, they plunged ahead like a falling missile. The target slid away. The bluffs rushed at them, jagged black lava masses like broken teeth. A warning chime. In the monitor, the projected instrument readouts flickered and changed.

MANUAL ABORTED, green letters blazed. COMPUTER IN CONTROL.

He jabbed the key instinctively, jabbed again. All he heard was the muted rush of wind, and then a faint sigh from the microthrusters repositioning the craft. That took too long. The computer program had no sense of urgency, no sensors for all the hazards below them. He cursed it, eyes on the monitor.

The boulder slope thrust at them, dark jagged masses blown from some old volcano. A shadow-pooled crater swelled ahead, opening to swallow them. Falling fast again, faster, they drifted toward it. Too late, the jet ignited. White jet steam billowed under him, hiding everything.

Full power, stunning thunder. It drove the seat against him, yet they still fell too fast. The jet lifted dust, and the steam turned red. Blinded, he still could sense that crater wall stretching cragged arms to catch them. The computer throttled down the thrust, and he could see. Not breathing, he watched the shallow bowl beyond the crater wall.

Level enough, perhaps, if they somehow reached it.

Just maybe . . .

They crashed. The lander shuddered. The jet coughed and died. Twisting metal screamed. The craft tipped, rocked, stopped. He heard silence like a second crash, and then a thin shriek of leaking air. The lights were out, the instruments dark, the monitor dead. Beyond the heat shields, all he could see was a narrow strip of yellow-pink sky.

"Kelligan!" She rasped his name like a curse. "Kelligan!"

"We were okay." He laughed, a mirthless explosion. "Till you cut me off!"

"Laugh if you like!" her hot voice flared. "You've killed us! Probably killed the expedition."

"I did?" Silent for a moment in the tilted seat, he tried to swallow his own anger. "I know it's no joke." He turned to look into her furious face. "But we aren't dead. With any sort of luck, we'll get up again. If we can't they can send the *Colon* to pick us up."

"The games you play!" Her scorn was still savage. "Can't you realize—"

"Listen, Ryan!" His voice lifted. "Call it a game if you want, but the bad move was yours. I was setting us down. Right on the designated target. You cut me off. Let the computer crash us."

"Setting us down?" She mocked him. "You'd frozen at the controls."

"You think so?" Wrath made her beautiful, he thought, nostrils white, green eyes savage. He wanted to seize her, shake her. "I never froze, landing the old *Da Gama* a dozen times on the Moon. I was only waiting, to keep us out of the dunes—"

"Too long!"

He drew a long, uneven breath.

"Commander Ryan, we had altitude left. All we needed, or else we'd be dead." He couldn't help his sardonic tone. "Your computer took too long to fire—or not long enough. Too long for the target. Too short for the crater floor."

"Think so?"

"Think what you like." He shrugged and grinned at her, painfully. "Here we are, Commander. Down on Mars. I'll even take the blame, if you think that will get us back to the *Ares.*"

"Okay, Kelligan." She nodded stiffly, eyes still cold. "We're down on Mars."

♂

The lights were out, but a thin rose-tinted beam struck through the heat shield to fill the cabin with sickly shadows. Through the tilted shield, she saw a red-hazed horizon and a thin scrap of Mars. Jagged points of dark volcanic rock jutted like decayed teeth though banks of saffron dust.

Dismal, dead.

She shivered to a fleeting vision of the *Magellan* as it might be forever, half buried under new drifts of dust, Kelligan's bones and her own lying exposed, dyed rust-red. She shook the image off and sat staring down at him. He had bent to fiddle with the dead controls, trying to bring them to life. As if he knew how.

Down on Mars.

The words echoed in her brain like a sentence of death. Down with Sam Houston Kelligan. The billionaire playboy, forever in search of one more reckless thrill. Always a Kelligan, never jobless or hungry or desperate, forever free to seek some fresh way to risk his idiotic neck. Ski jumps, hang gliders, high mountains. Fast cars and fast boats. Probably fast women too, not that she cared.

She bit her lip, wishing for somebody else.

Though not Otto Hellman. He was too loud, too arrogant with anybody who ventured to question his dogmas, his odor too strong and even worse with the cologne he wore to cover it. Always too close to Barova. How did she endure him?

Ram Chandra? She admired him for many things. His rugged optimism, his sardonic insights, his dark good looks, his total competence. Landing the *Magellan,* he could have been trusted to the final second. But he and Kim Lo had been devoted companions since they joined the Corps.

Arkady Lavrin? Her first choice, if he had let her choose him. He could match Ram at nearly anything, and she liked him even more. Never quite in love—the philosophy he called biotopic rationalism had little room for love—but they'd had fine times in bed. If that stoic philosophy hadn't kept him on the ship, he might have been here with her, celebrating a triumphant touchdown.

When she looked back at Kelligan, he was leaving his seat. A little awkward on the slanted deck, he stopped with one hand cupped to his ear, listening for that thin whistle of escaping air. With a wry expression, he shook his head at her.

"Commander?" She heard ironic challenge in his tone. "What now?"

She took a long breath and tried to quench her flash of anger. With everything at risk, they could not afford to fight. She pushed out of her own seat, frowning at him.

"Kelligan—" The words were hard to say. "Perhaps—perhaps I was too hasty. Maybe I misjudged you. If you think the crash was my own fault, I hope—I hope you'll let me apologize."

"Forget it, Commander." He shrugged. "Let's get on with the job."

"Thanks." She tried to smile, though this was only an uneasy truce. "The job is survival. To repair the damage if we can. To keep alive and hope for rescue, if we can't."

"So where do we start?"

"We find and fix the air leak." She groped for more authority than she felt. "We restore the power and radio contact. Call the *Ares* and report our situation. Prepare for takeoff, if that's possible. And proceed with our mission—to prospect for mineable permafrost and disk the canyon rim."

"A big enough order." His grin seemed oddly innocent. "Let's get at it."

He found a switch, and the battery lights came on below them. He scrambled past her, down the narrow metal stair. She followed him through the cargo space and past the water tanks. The hiss of air grew stronger. She saw the doors of the locker that had burst open and found him gathering a clutter of tools and helium cylinders off the deck beneath it.

"Hull dented in." He nodded at the locker. "There's the leak."

The locker was built against the hull, which was crushed in behind it. She saw twisted metal shelves, pushed out by a bulge two meters long.

"Double hull," he said. "Honeycomb and sealer foam between. It has nearly closed the rupture. I'll get spray sealant on it."

"Do that."

She turned to the rocket engine, which jutted up through the center of the deck. It looked intact: pipes and valves, helium pumps and water pumps, computer controls, the magnetohydrodynamic generators. Nothing wrong that she could see.

But they were dead.

"Problem one," she told him. "Power."

"Thumbs up!" He made the gesture. "I'll get at the leak."

♂

She heard him whistling softly as he climbed the stair to look for sealant. She bent over the engine. Even with the rocket throttled off, the unit should have been running at low output to power lights, computers, radio, and the whole operation of the lander. With battery power, she tried to start it. The dead control panel glowed. The fan whirred. The helium pump whined. And amber letters burned across the monitor.

IGNITION FAILURE.

She tried again, and the letters flashed again.

"We came down pretty hard." Houston stood behind her, holding a sealant capsule. "Rocket nozzle probably fouled. Maybe crushed."

"Spray the leak," she told him. "And we'll take a look."

She felt a flash of admiration for his calm, yet it vexed her. He seemed to take disaster all too casually, as if escape from Mars was only one more game. He was too reckless, she thought, too confident, simply not responsible. She watched him pull a crumpled shelf from the locker, spray a vapor cloud across the dented hull to see where it was sucked away, and finally cover the leak with thick gray foam.

"Okay, Commander?" He listened and grinned at her. The hissing had ceased. "Moon suits? Or are they Mars suits now?"

"Hew, you know my name." On impulse, she put out her hand. "No more Commander."

He stood a moment staring at her before he gripped her hand.

"Jayne it is."

She caught emotion in his voice, but this was no play-time. They were down on Mars, and his name was still Kelligan.

"Let's go." Too abruptly, she pulled her hand away. "Mars suits they are."

They climbed to the air lock on the cargo deck. Before they got into the pressure suits, he fished in the pocket of his skinsuit and found a worn silver coin.

"Antique Mexican peso," he told her. "Dad gave it to me the day I was five. Said it was lucky. *Con suerte.* Maybe it is." He nodded at the air lock. "First one through will be first on Mars. Toss you for the honor."

Only one more game, even if it killed him. A game they would win or lose together. His coin spun a long time before the lesser gravity pulled it to the back of his left hand. He clapped his right over it and waited for her call.

"Heads," she called.

"Luck's all yours." He grinned. "Heads it is."

15

Quarters

Creating the Authority, the Treaty of Mars divided the entire planet like a quartered orange among the four founding powers. Treaty rights were subsequently transferred to Mars Con-Quest, Inc., which claimed sole ownership.

Spanish had always been their special language, spoken in that room of their own when they met for her *café con leche* and a moment of love. It was more melodious than English, and something *la mujer* Edna didn't know. He had always been *Austino* or *El Señor,* and she his *Chiquita Bonita.*

No longer.

The fault was not her own. Perhaps she had gained a few kilos, but she had kept her figure, dieting when she had to and working out in the company gym. Her skin was still white and fine, and her black hair shone. Even now, he had need of her business sense, even if his passion was dead.

Perdido. Lost in the surgery. *Que lastima!*

In the beginning he had been a wild bull, *un toro salvaje,* taking her every day on the sofa or the big table or sometimes on the floor. Now he could do nothing, except to fail and curse himself. *El Viejo.* The old man. So she called him, speaking to Martin. What could he hope to do with this gringo *puta* Mr. Houston had used and abandoned?

She pitied him. Sometimes she hated him.

Stubborn old bull, he had always refused to accept Martin. Instead, cunning as a coyote, he had bribed that gringo goat to claim the child and marry her and run away to Asia. Even when he used to say he loved her, he hated to hurt *la mujer,* the sickly wife who had nearly killed herself to give him a gringo son.

Mr. Houston. She had always made Martin call him that, because she didn't want the boys to fight. Too often, *El Señor* wanted to side with the gringo son. She had been pleased to have him gone to Mars and out of Martin's way until she saw *la bimba* pregnant.

Mr. Houston was certainly the father. Would *El Señor* choose the child to be another heir if he did not return? Was that the reason he had brought *la bimba* into the company? She could never ask him, but the worry was a festering thorn. He laughed at prayer, but she kept begging the Holy Mother to humble Martin's hateful rivals.

♂

LeeAnn enjoyed her job, most of the time. She'd loved Kelligan all her life, and he was always generous. When Marty and Lucina gave her nothing else to do, she spent the days with her father's law books. Perhaps she really had a good legal mind. The cases at least helped keep Houston out of her mind. Happy with the child, she had told Kelligan as soon as the doctor was sure.

He had her tell Edna. That was a painful mistake, because Edna burst into tears and spent two days in bed, grieving that Houston might never come back to give her grandchild a name and a home. She went to bed again when Barova's bulletin made wide headlines:

MARS EXPLORERS
REPORTED LOST!

Trying to cheer her, LeeAnn found no cheering news. She stopped Marty one morning in the hall to ask if he heard anything from his White Sands friends.

"Sorry, Miss Halloran." She felt herself flush from his sharp glance at her belly. "Nothing new, even from the mother ship. At last report it was still in orbit, still waiting for the lost landing party. But that was days ago. It's out of reach half the time, around beyond the planet, and they still have problems getting Farside back on line."

One morning Kelligan called her.

"Meeting with Marty and Lucina. *Una cosa importante,* she says. Better come along."

"Okay." She hesitated. Marty always eyed her too shrewdly, and Lucina had been calling her *una belleza,* praising her too effusively for the beauty of her skin and the color of her hair and the grace of her motion. "If you really want me."

"Come along." An abrupt command.

She followed him into the inside room and stopped a moment to stare at the Aztec sacrifice. Its stark brutality always appalled her. Lucina was bustling about the kitchen alcove. Sweating as always, Marty was shucking off a yellow-checked sports jacket. He sprawled into his favorite chair behind the long conference table where his mother swore he had been conceived. He was reaching for his stuffed manila folder before he saw her and stood up to greet her, thrusting out his black-haired hand. It felt lax and damp and cool. She was glad to let it go.

"Is there something new?" she asked. "From the expedition?"

"Nothing good." He shook his head with an air of funereal sympathy and sat back at the table. "No more news of the lander."

"Café, Señor?" Lucina came out of the alcove, fine teeth gleaming through her smile. *"Mi señorita querida!"*

She waved them into the great leather chairs across from Marty, set cups for them, and poured the fragrant coffee and hot milk. LeeAnn pushed hers aside, looking anxiously at Marty.

"Patience, Miss Halloran." Marty's eye teeth were gold, and she thought they had a wolfish gleam. "They're safe enough, for all we know. Just out of contact."

"When will we get contact?"

"Hard to say."

"Well, Marty?" Kelligan frowned expectantly. "Something for us?"

Marty stared back for a moment and looked down to arrange the stacked computer printouts like defensive bulwarks before he stared back across the table. Like a spoiled child, LeeAnn thought, afraid but yet defiant, anxious for advantage and gloating when he found it.

"News for you, sir." He nodded smugly, happy with himself. "Actually, the Authority has regular contact with the Mars ship now. Bad news for Mr. Houston." He darted a keen glance at her. "Bad for the Authority, but a billion-dollar gold mine if we play it smart."

"Bad for Sam?" Kelligan shoved his cup aside. "How do you mean?"

"Farside now has steady contact with Mars." Marty nodded his slick wet head to emphasize the revelation. "People at White Sands have been delaying news of trouble, hoping to save their hides. But the expedition's about to fold. They're planning to spend just a few more weeks taking a quick look at the planet before they head for home."

"Will they—" LeeAnn couldn't help the catch in her voice. "Can they search?"

"Lavrin says no." Marty stared blankly at her. "Not if they want to get home. The flight back will take all the fuel they have, except what they'll need for one more landing. They'll make that at the south pole, to complete the survey—their orbit's too low to let them see the poles."

"You called us here to tell us that?"

"More, sir." Marty's eyes fell before Kelligan's glare. "A chance to save the expedition. Here's the situation. The old Mars Authority's dead, though they hate to say so. Out of money again. Credit dried up. Which opens up our chance."

"What chance?"

Marty sat with eyes fixed on Kelligan. Black, blank, warily expressionless. The eyes of a poker player, LeeAnn thought, hiding what he had and trying to read his opponent.

"I know Barova, sir." His stubby forefinger tapped a sheaf of printouts. "Dr. Irina Barova. Met her on our media junket to Shangri-La. She always said the Authority was bungling the whole expedition. Working with her and my own White Sands contacts, I've laid out a new campaign."

Nervously, he licked his thick lips and looked down at the printouts as if for inspiration.

"Here's the deal, sir." He glanced at his mother and caught a long breath. "The Authority's kaput. We're going to replace it with a new corporation. No international boondoggle, but a sound commercial enterprise."

"So what?" Kelligan grunted. "If the Authority failed—"

"A new deal, sir. New management and a new approach. Barova says the Authority failed because it never sold itself. She knows PR. She'll be a director."

"When she gets back?"

"We need her where she is, sir. Reporting facts to publicize Mars ConQuest—that's our new corporation. We've got a great staff here on Earth. People out of the old Authority, with the know-how to make it fly."

"What does that do for Sam?"

"Gives him a chance, sir." He shot another glance at LeeAnn. "At least a chance. We're going to finish the *Nergal.* My White Sands engineers they can have it ready for takeoff with a rescue expedition when the next window opens. With help on the way, Lavrin shouldn't have to run for home. He can send searchers down. Build a habitat. Explore the planet."

"So?" Squinting at Marty, Kelligan nodded at LeeAnn. "What do you want?"

"We'll need funds, sir, to exercise the options. They're drawn up to cover all the assets." He ticked items off on thick damp fingers. "The White Sands installations. The spaceplane leases and terminal rights. The Farside facilities and the helium mines on the Moon. The fusion engine patents. The treaty rights on Mars. Investments carried on their books at upwards of forty billion dollars."

"Which nobody wants."

"So we get 'em cheap."

Kelligan sat for half a minute frowning at the writhing victim on the altar stone. His gray eyes returned to LeeAnn and Lucina and finally to Marty.

"How cheap?"

"Depends on other bidders, sir." LeeAnn thought she caught a glint of glee in his eyes. "Our best guess is something under a billion."

Kelligan's face tightened grimly.

"Not all at once, sir. We're authorizing ten million shares at a hundred American dollars a share. Enough, we hope, to pick up the options and complete the *Nergal.*" He reached for his folder. "We're asking Kelligan Resources to buy five million shares and renew the loan guarantees for half a billion dollars."

"That's all?" A sardonic scowl. "For so much pie in the sky?"

"Little enough, sir. When you think of Mr. Houston."

Looking at LeeAnn's tight face, he nodded slowly.

"Show us the details," he said at last. "I'll consider it."

♂

Lucina offered more *café con leche.* They spent an hour over Marty's documents. When LeeAnn and Kelligan were gone, Lucina gathered up the empty cups.

"El Cabron." She nodded happily at Marty. "And *El Cabrito.*"

"El pobre cabrito!" He grinned his gold-toothed grin. "Always saying how much he wanted Mars. Never dreaming the actual final owner would be me."

16

Planum Australe

The polar caps of Mars form in the long winter seasons from freezing water vapor and carbon dioxide. Much of the carbon dioxide returns to the atmosphere in the spring, but residues of water ice remain.

Before Barova and her crew took off in the *Colon,* Lisa went to Lavrin with one last plea for Houston and Jayne.

"We know the planned target area for the *Magellan.* If we have mass for another flight, can't we make at least a few low-orbit flights across it?"

"Talk to Barova." His red-shagged head shook impatiently. "She's convinced that her polar landing is their best chance."

"I don't see how."

"*Magellan* failed." She saw the new lines cut behind his fiery beard, heard his brittle temper. "We can't gamble more lives, asking why. Barova will land on the south polar cap and try for water there. If she finds it, that can save us."

"To search for the *Magellan?*" She felt relief. "To land the colony and build the habitat?"

"The best chance left." Very deliberately, he nodded. "If she does discover available water."

"If she doesn't?" She searched his face. "We head for home?"

"No other choice."

"No choice!" Her voice lifted bitterly. "A year in flight, Ram says. On half rations. Maybe less. I'd rather go down to look for the *Magellan,* no matter the risk."

"So would I." He scowled through the beard. "But I've other lives to think of."

Unable to move him, she begged for a place on the *Colon.*

"Sorry." She thought he really was. "But it's Barova's flight. She wants disks of the polar cap for her documentary. Her companions will be Hellman and Chandra. Hellman's taking equipment to get geologic data. Chandra's our best lander jockey, at least since we lost Kelligan. He'll get them back alive."

Admiring Ram Chandra, she thought he should have been the star of Barova's disks. Handsome enough, dark and tall, he had wavy black hair and a cynical sense of humor. Sharp as anybody, yet he was no show-off. She knew total dedication.

"You'll really try?" she begged him. "For water mass?"

"Of course." His sober smile encouraged her. "Barova wants to create an epic of exploration. Hellman's first interest, I think, is gathering data for his monograph on Mars. But what I want is the planet itself."

♂

Chandra paused, reflecting, dark eyes on her face.

She looked more a college student, he thought, than a Martian explorer. Petite, dark-haired, quietly efficient at everything she did. He liked her, and he felt a sudden impulse to share himself.

"I wish you'd known my father," he told her. "An engineer who spent his life on little bureaucratic jobs that let him hatch grand schemes for the future of India. He was always planning enormous dams to stop the monsoon floods and store the water for crops and power. Most of the dams never got built, but he used to take me with him to let me see why he wanted them. Misery in the streets of Calcutta, riots in the Punjab, starvation in Bangladesh. He taught me most of what I know, and I guess Mars is my own Himalaya."

"My own Mount Olympus," she told him.

♂

The *Ares* had almost overtaken Phobos. Barova and Hellman wanted to touch down on that little moon before they dropped out of orbit to attempt the Martian landing.

"We're after water," Chandra objected. "It won't be on Phobos. It's a sister to Deimos, carbonaceous rubble and dust. Any water will be chemically bound or deep in the core, out of our reach."

"Land us," Barova commanded him. "I want Phobos on disk. We'll do voiceovers to dramatize its mysteries, its origin. Its orbit. The old notion that made it a huge spacecraft, somehow wrecked or abandoned in orbit."

"Okay," he muttered. "Okay."

"Otto will get off with me to lay out his instruments and man a camera. The tiny gravity should give us great shots. I'll do high jumps off the surface with the lander in the background. And you—you can prospect for water with the laser spectrometer and the penetrator probes."

"We've only ten probes," he said. "I'd planned to save them for Mars."

"We'll fire three or four here." She looked past him, her voice grown professional. "I want space adventure! The drama of us exploring a desert moon. Searching for the precious water that might keep the ship and our bodies alive."

"Even if you already know we'll never find it there?"

"Has anybody looked?" Her voice sharpened. "We'll circle the satellite, a couple of kilometers out, and see what we find. I want shots of you firing the probes."

She was in command. A few kilometers out, he used the thrusters to bring them into orbit around it. A great black potato shape, twenty kilometers thick, it was pocked with impact craters and streaked with fracture grooves. She brought a camera to the cockpit to catch it on the monitor and record his words when she questioned him for her future audience on Earth.

"That big crater?"

"Stickney." He spoke into her microphone. "Eight kilometers across. The impact object was nearly too big for Phobos. Almost shattered it. You can see the cracks."

He fired three penetrators. They were slender arrows, rocket-driven, with ground-piercing points. Trailing antenna wires relayed their sensor readings to recorders on the lander. Barova disked him at the launcher and asked for the readouts.

"No happy surprises," he told the microphone. "Phobos is in fact a dead black rock. Darker than coal. The penetrators went through a dozen meters of impact dust and debris. No sign of available water."

"We're landing, anyhow." She gave him the camera and smiled into the lens. "Space pioneers! Dr. Hellman and I will be stepping down on this tiny world where humankind has never been! An exciting moment for us both, because it will be one more historic first."

They landed on the lip of Stickney. Barova disked him at the controls, easing the lander down. She had him record her and Hellman getting into their pressure suits and entering the air lock. Left alone aboard, he shot their monitor images, floating down to the loose black rubble and dust.

Landing in slow motion, she kicked off again, leaping

and soaring and leaping until she vanished beyond the near black horizon. Otto stayed to lay out his array of magnetometers and gravitometers, seismometers and particle detectors and radiation detectors, and the transmitter that would relay their readouts to the lander.

In two hours, they were back aboard.

"Wet your feet?" he asked Barova.

"Sensational shots!" She ignored his sardonic inquiry. "The *Colon* in silhouette against the red face of Mars. Otto tossing a ten-ton boulder. And both of us jumping off the satellite into black space."

"An interesting object," Hellman added. "In a very remarkable orbit that dooms it to fall on Mars in thirty million years."

"Imagine!" Barova whispered. "What a shot, if we could get it!"

"Let's not wait."

♂

The lander lifted out of billowing dust. Phobos shrank and vanished. Dropping out of its orbit, they veered into a path that crossed the poles of Mars. The north cap was still lost in the long winter night, but blazing sun had come to the south.

They stayed a day in circumpolar orbit, filming the planet as it rolled beneath them. Now, early in the southern spring, the south polar cap was dazzling and enormous. They were still too high for the laser spectrometer, but Chandra fired the remaining radio probes.

"One malfunction," he reported the readouts to Barova. "Perhaps it smashed into a boulder before it could transmit. Two struck surface dust, with permafrost beneath. All the others on the cap indicate water ice."

He projected a map to show her the sites.

"Layered terrain." He pointed to a zebra pattern on

the image. "Strange country, with ice in the white stripes."

"Otto?" She frowned at Hellman. "You're the geologist."

"A layer cake," he told them. "Strata of ice and insulating dust, laid down thousands or millions of years ago. Carved since by wind. The layers are terraces sometimes thirty meters high. Winter has hidden the whole polar region with carbon dioxide snow, but that's sublimating fast."

"The ice you want?" She smiled inquiringly at Chandra. "If we land there?"

"Not the best site." He shook his head. "The dark streaks are permafrost: frozen mud, full of water we can't extract. I'd suggest we land here on Planum Australe." He indicated the test point. "The permanent cap, which never thaws. The ice there could be kilometers deep."

"It looks too flat." She frowned at the chart. "I want something scenic for the record."

"This third site?" He tried to please her. "Still on the Planum, with a fair chance for available ice."

"How about this canyon?" She leaned to read the map. "Chasma Australe. Those cliffs should give us a spectacular panorama."

"But no water we can reach." He shook his head. "There must be water ice, but down below the bluffs where the sun has hardly struck. Still covered with meters of carbon dioxide snow. Getting at it could be a problem."

"You're good at problems." Her voice caressed him. "I trust you, Ram."

"I'd very much prefer—"

"I'm with Irina." Hellman leaned to peer at the readout. "Here close to the pole, those layers of ice and dust have recorded many million years of climate change. I want to drill for specimen cores."

"Otto, please!" He saw Hellman recoil, and tried to soften his tone. "We're looking for fuel mass, if you remember. Which means our chance to search for the *Colon,* explore the planet, build the habitat—"

"Priorities, priorities!" Barova spread her tapered hands to waft his words away. "I think the Chasma site is our best compromise. The ice cliffs along the canyon wall should offer exotic backgrounds." She gave him a bright-lipped smile. "I'm sure you'll find water ice as you cut the geologic cores."

"Not very available," he objected. "Whatever we find will be buried too deep. We don't have equipment to secure and melt and refine it."

"Your own priority." She shrugged and leaned to touch his arm. "You're a gifted engineer. If there's water, I'm sure you'll find a way to recover it."

"A risk we shouldn't take."

"Oh?" Suddenly she was frosty. "My responsibility."

"Sorry if I was out of line."

"No grudges." Her voice had softened, and she leaned to plant cherry lips on his cheek. "We're all dear friends on the *Ares,* and we can't afford to quarrel."

He muttered a thank you.

"Set us down on the next pass." Her voice was again crisply commanding. "As near as you can to the Chasma site."

"As you say, Commander."

He deployed the parachute in the dark above the moonless north cap. Correcting for the planet's rotation, he steered toward the line of probes as they came back into daylight over the vast boulder-littered desert of Utopia. Tilting the craft into braking mode, he brought it low across the darker dunes and craters of Syrtis Major, lower still over the endless ocher floor of the Hellas basin, finally skimming the winding ridges of ice and dust of the layered terrain.

The sunlit snow beyond was glaring blankness. Eyes narrowed against it, he detached the parachute, tipped the craft into landing mode, fired more braking bursts. The blank white dazzle raced fast beneath them, faster, faster. Landmarks were hard to see, but at last he found the canyon, a faint shadow streak on the blinding horizon.

The probe itself was nothing he could see. Squinting at the pilot monitor, he steered for its charted position. The Chasma was suddenly close below, a wide canyon whose snow-drifted walls climbed like the steps of a gigantic stair. Older layered terrain, he thought, buried under deeper snow.

"Yonder!" Barova pointed past him. "Above that steepest cliff. The vantage point I want."

He fired another burst. White steam billowed under them. Flying blind, he brought the craft vertical. When he could see again, the snow seemed close below. Too close? He couldn't tell, because the world was a featureless cushion of soft pink-lit cotton, all features buried.

He let them settle toward it, thrust throttled down. Steam against the frigid snow, the rocket jet condensed into an exploding cloud that covered everything beneath. He blinked against its glare and squinted to read the altimeter.

50 METERS . . . 30 . . . 10 . . . 5 . . .

He cut the rocket. In a burst of silence, the lander swayed from a soft impact, righted itself, swayed again. Metal creaked and groaned, until finally they were still. He sank back in the seat, breathing again, rubbing his eyes.

"Magnificent!" Barova had a camera on him. "Congratulations, Dr. Chandra. You've set us down safe on Mars!"

♂

"First thing," she announced, "we get into pressure gear. I want us emerging from the lander for our first glimpse of Mars. Wave to the camera. Register elation. We'll inspect the craft and scout the terrain around us. Otto, you and Ram will set up the drill as soon as you can, to cut the cores. I hope to get away within twenty-four hours."

"Huh?" Chandra blinked. "That soon?"

"Unless the drill strikes available water ice," her creamy voice continued. "Don't fret about it. If we do find water, you'll have your chance. But get into your gear."

She sent Hellman off first, carrying a camera to get her emerging from the lock and climbing down the ladder. He followed her, heart thumping with a very real elation. Here at last, after all the hope and effort, all the tests and waiting—here was Mars!

Out of the lock, standing on the narrow metal grid above the ladder, he stopped to look. His breath caught. The lander stood in a deep bowl, formed as the rocket jet swept the fluffy snow from beneath them. Beyond the rim, the red sun was a smoldering coal, small and pale and heatless, lying low in a dense haze that glowed sullenly crimson near it, fading into magenta dusk on the farther horizon.

Overhead, the sky dimmed to gloomy purple, almost black. The snow in every direction lay featureless and flat, eerily dyed in the light of that uncanny sky. Even in the insulated suit, he felt a chill of alien strangeness. The cycles of time were frozen here, with no room for change or life or mind. He felt that ominous sky sinking down upon him, the haze closing him, overwhelming.

"Ram!" Barova's radio voice broke the spell, cooing in his helmet. He saw her camera on him. "Give us a wave."

He broke the trance, waved obediently, and climbed down to the snow. It had a brittle crust that crunched beneath his boots. New ice, he thought, where jet steam had frozen on the surface. Ahead of him, the others were already climbing a long slope where the jet had compacted the snow. He followed. The crust grew thinner as they climbed, until Hellman broke through and sank to his waist. Barova stopped to record his floundering struggle back to firmer crust and turned to pan from the dull sun to the lander in its pit.

"Mars, Ram!" For a moment she was mocking. "Want to put your habitat here?"

"It might be possible," he told here soberly. "If we do find water."

"Unload the drill," she told him. "Otto will help when he gets his sensors out. I'll shoot everything. Nothing very scenic here, but I got a magnificent shot of the Chasma as we came over." Her voice rang louder when she thought of her far-off audience. "A river of scarlet fire flowing down the canyon. Fog, of course, formed by cold air flowing off the ice and lit by that blood-colored sun."

The core drill was stored in a bay outside the pressure hull. It was heavy and clumsy to manage, even in this lesser gravity, but Barova laid her camera aside to help them set it up. Powered from the ship's helium reactor, it cut fast through the snow, slowed when it struck something harder. Remote sensors logged the hole.

"Water ice!" Watching the readouts, Chandra grinned through his faceplate. "Enough for a city!"

Barova switched off the microphone.

"No good for us," she murmured. "Not unless you can get it in the tank."

She tramped around, recording everything. He kept the drill going, stacking the frozen cores. Hellman sealed them into insulated tubes and stored them in the unheated cargo bay. Saving weight, they had brought only forty meters of drill tube. He reached that limit and showed Barova the readout.

"Four meters of snow," he told her. "Ten centimeters of dust, and then—see it!—meters of pure water ice."

"But buried under all that snow." Her cool voice fell. Somehow graceful, even in the pressure armor, she leaned to stroke his shoulder. "Sorry, Ram, but you know we left all the power tools on the *Ares*. We've no way to get at it. Pure ice or not, it might as well be ten kilometers down."

"Irina, please! If the snow's a problem, we can solve it."

"With no tools?"

"We do have hand tools in the emergency locker. And the jet has already cleared a lot of snow around us. It can burn off the rest."

"Are you crazy?" Her voice went sharp. "You want to squander our last fuel mass melting snow? And strand us in this frozen hell?"

"Who's crazy?" He caught himself and tried to see their faces in the helmets. "Let's stop to think. We landed for water. Here it is, only four meters down. Water enough to refuel the lander and then the *Ares*. Just give me a chance to refill the tanks."

"With what?" Hellman scoffed. "Bare hands?"

"I've checked the emergency bay," he told them. "We have picks and shovels. Heater coils that can melt the ice. Pumps and hose. It will take some hard work—a week or so, I'd imagine. But we can save the expedition." He dropped his voice, appealing to Barova. "Our last chance, Irina—"

"Listen, Ram!" Her words came cold as that frigid haze. "Maybe your instruments are accurate. With superhuman effort we might just possibly thaw enough geologic ice to get us back to the *Ares*.

"But I won't bet our lives on it."

"You—you never wanted Mars!" Hands clenched in the stiff pressure gloves, he swung toward Hellman. "Neither one of you! All you ever came for was one quick look. Enough to let you run back home with the data disks that you think will make you famous."

Hellman grasped a heavy drill chain and lumbered toward him.

"Cool it!" Barova swayed between them and shook her head reprovingly at him. "Ram, let's really stop to think. Look around us!" Her yellow-clad arm swept across the thick-hazed desolation toward the cold red sun. "We're six survivors now—if we do get back aboard alive. Do you really think we've got a chance to plant human life in this ghastly wilderness? As for me, I didn't come to leave my bones on Mars."

"Irina—"

"Enough back talk. Get aboard!" She swung to Hellman. "Both of you. Otto, we'll abandon the drill. Dead weight we'll never need again. We're taking off at once."

Helpless, he dropped his empty hands.

17

Coprates

Coprates Chasma is a central section of the Valles Marineris rift. Formed like the ocean floors of Earth by the slow separation of two great tectonic plates, it consists of deep parallel troughs with a ridge between them.

They climbed down to the air lock.

"Make history, Commander." In spite of him, Houston's voice had a faint sardonic edge. "Your footprints, the first on Mars."

"History?" she whispered bitterly. "We're fighting for our lives."

The lock was a little coffin-shaped box that rotated to open inside or outside. The power off, they had to work it with a clumsy wheel. In the stiff yellow pressure gear, Jayne went through first, and paused on the narrow step outside to look at Mars.

The sun was red and small, still low in the dust-dimmed sky, the crater floor still dark with shadow. They had come down in a tangle of boulders on the crater lip. The lander leaned against a high black cliff of uplifted volcanic rock that had kept it from tipping over. She couldn't see beyond, but cold terror touched her.

In her imagination, this first touchdown had been a simple, well-planned procedure. They would set down on some likely spot, disk whatever they saw, lay out the instrument array, collect rock and soil samples, drill for permafrost, and get their data back to the *Ares.* That easy dream was dead now, mocked by this alien stone, this eerie sky, this land where life had never been.

Whose fault?

That no longer mattered. She shrugged against the unyielding fabric and climbed down to a slope of loose brown dust. Houston had cycled out behind her. Glancing back, she saw him leaning with a camera to disk her sharp-printed tracks in the dust. With a laugh that was half a sob, she beckoned him down to join her.

Plodding a little away, they turned to look back at the crippled *Magellan.* The cliff had saved it from a longer fall, but the struts and the rocket muzzle had been driven deep into the slope in the lee of the cliff. Houston shook his head ruefully and lifted the camera to disk the damage.

"Well, Commander?" His nonchalant tone woke the anger she had tried to stifle. "What next?"

"Get serious!" Her tone came too sharp, and she paused to smooth it. "However it happened, Kelligan, you've got to realize the danger we're in."

"Never doubt it, Commander." His face in the helmet was hard to see, but his voice seemed oddly cheerful. "Let's get out."

"If we can." Dismayed by her own uncertainties, she groped to recover her role as leader. "First thing, let's see where we are."

The crater opened below them, a vast bowl still filled with saffron shadow. She was climbing toward the rim, a wall of fractured stone uplifted by the impact. He scrambled after her and they stopped to see what lay beyond. Ejecta littered the westward slope, jagged masses of dark volcanic rock banked with wind-blown dust. Farther, the land lay almost flat, mottled with rust-reddened yellows and browns, reaching out to the dust-hazed horizon and a bright lemon sky. A better pilot would have set them down somewhere there, but she held herself from saying so.

"Ideas?" she asked him.

"Only the obvious." He shrugged again, still far too casual. "Fix the lander. Call the *Ares* when we recover power. Look for water. Lay out Hellman's sensors. Disk the landscape for Barova. Take off when we can."

"Good enough." She had to agree. "I want you to clear the rocket nozzle."

"Will do." He turned to peer down at it. "I'd guess the obstruction stopped the fusion engine."

"I'll check."

He waved a careless half-salute and plodded back down toward the crippled lander. She stayed on the crest a little longer, trying to pick out the nearest spot where a rescue craft might land, if rescue ever came. It would be a few kilometers west, down below the boulder slopes.

He had opened the tool bay before she followed him. With the power tools useless, he was turning to the buried nozzle with pick and shovel. Even in the clumsy suit, he moved with the dexterity and grace of a natural athlete. He had too many gifts, she reflected ruefully, and too much money.

Or had her own spirit been stunted, because she had too little? Troubled by that sudden doubt, she wanted to call out some word of encouragement, but he ignored her.

♂

He dug into the slope under the lander. The surface dust was loose and fine, easy to lift against the lesser gravity, but it seemed to dissolve when he tossed it into the stagnant air. Dust hung around him in a yellow cloud, so dense he could hardly see the lander.

Half a meter down, the shovel grated on a thick dark crust that he had to break up with the pick. He was soon sweating in the heavy suit, blinded by dust on his faceplate, dismayed when he saw the damage to the rocket. Loose dust poured like a yellow liquid back into his pit, and the sun had reached the ocher zenith before he had the struts and rocket nozzle cleared.

He climbed at last back to the air lock, slapping to knock clinging dust off his suit. Some of it came with him when he cycled through. Unsealing the helmet inside, he caught an acrid whiff of it. Sharp and bitter, it doubled him over with a coughing fit and left an odd metallic taste on his lips.

Under the pressure gear, his skinsuit was dripping. He peeled it off, coughing again and suddenly shivering as if the cruel cold of Mars had followed him aboard. He longed for a hot shower, but the lander had no such luxury. He toweled his body and tried to wash the strange hot taste of the dust out of his mouth. In a dry skinsuit, he looked for Jayne and found her huddled over the computer in the pilot bay. She turned to him with a distracted stare.

"The nozzle's cleared," he told her. "Bottom sections badly damaged."

"Beyond repair?"

"I don't know." He shrugged. "I can trim them, but not accurately. There may be too much lateral thrust. I want to test the rocket when we have power—"

"We won't have power." Dismally, she shook her head. "You were right, Mr. Kelligan. The obstructed jet seems to have knocked out everything."

"We can fix things."

"Not these things." Wide eyes fixed on him, she wiped a wisp of pale wet hair off her forehead. She looked like a hurt child, and he felt sorry for her. "The blockage evidently sent a voltage spike through the system. It burned out the helium injector and knocked out the main computer. That I can't fix."

"So we're stuck?"

"Stuck." She nodded bleakly. "No power. No computer. No radio. No way to get off the ground. Nor any likelihood of help, so far as I can see.

"Unless—" She paused, frowning soberly at nothing. "We do have the navigation strobe."

"You think it can reach them, out in orbit?"

"Not likely, I guess." She pushed again at that stray wisp of hair. "But it does work on battery power. It's one thing we can try; the only thing, I'm afraid."

"If they're looking—" He tried to sound more optimistic. "They do know our target site."

"Accurate to maybe a few hundred kilometers." But then she sat abruptly straighter. "We can try, Mr. Kelligan. We can hope, but we'd better face reality."

"Admit that we're the first Martians?" He managed a stiff little grin. "Probably here to stay."

"If we are—" Her saw her teeth sink into her lip. "Kelligan, I'm sorry," she whispered. "Sorry if you blame me."

"Forget it." He shrugged. "About reality?"

"Thank you, Mr. Kelligan." She nodded soberly. "First of all, reality means food and oxygen to keep us alive. I've been taking stock. On half rations, we can eat for maybe a month. The charge left in the battery system would soon be gone, but we have the solar panels we brought for Hellman's data array. Hooked up to the ion-exchanger, they should keep us breathing. As long as we can, we'll carry on."

Tears stung his eyes as he looked at her, lovely as ever in the snug blue skinsuit, even with a smudge of something dark across her cheek and foreboding in her eyes. He stood a moment thinking of all their times together. His first tantalizing glimpse of her, dancing with Arkady

Lavrin at the Authority ball. Their encounter on the spaceplane. Her scorn for Texas tycoons. Their race on the Moon. His envy of Arkady Lavrin, always with her on the long flight out.

He wanted to take her in his arms and tell her what he felt, but of course that wouldn't do. To her, he was still the playboy fellow of Marty Gorley, who had tried to rape her at Shangri-La. She was still the Lakefield rebel and his superior in the Corps, certainly in no mood for love. Even here alone with her, the rules of the game had to be observed.

"Okay, Commander," he told her. "We'll carry on."

Silent for a moment, she blinked as if her own eyes were blurred.

"Okay." He saw her gulp, but then she rose, her voice suddenly firmer. "Please get the solar cells hooked up at once. I'll bring a camera out to disk you for Barova."

"We can't forget Barova." He grinned, and spoke more gravely. "Commander, we've got to pretend we're going to get out alive, whether we believe it or not. Otherwise—"

"No otherwise." He saw her lip quiver. "We'll carry on."

"I want to take the rover out," he told her. "With no power, we can't run the core drill, but there is a soil probe I can use to test for permafrost. I'll look for minerals that might be useful and a likely site for the habitat."

"Do that, Mr. Kelligan." And she repeated, "Carry on."

♂

They came together off the lander and picked a site for the solar array on a rocky knob the sun would reach. She brought her camera to disk him mounting the panels and laying a cable back to the craft. The door of the rover bay hinged down to make a ramp, and she shot him again pulling the spidery little vehicle down to the ground and testing its tiny helium engine.

It came to life. He loaded tools and drove west, toward the open plain where they should have landed. Looking back, he saw her standing on a point of rock, still following him with the camera. In silhouette against the orange horizon, she looked small and proud and vulnerable. He had to gulp at a lump in his throat.

She was gone when he turned again. Even the lander was out of view, down behind the cliff. He felt suddenly lost in that wilderness of drifted dust and broken rock, overwhelmed by its eerie desolation, so terribly helpless and alone that he shuddered and stopped the rover. They would die here, their fate never known.

Why go on?

Because this was Mars?

Because it was here?

He laughed at the thought, the sound a strangled snort in the helmet. Yet it was true. Here he was on the rover, driving out into this unearthly landscape where no life had ever been, the magic place he had longed for since he was a child. No matter what the aftermath, this was Mars. He laughed again, not at fate but at himself, and drove on down the slope and out of the ejecta field.

This wide basin must have been a lake, perhaps a billion years ago. It spread to the strange horizon, nearly flat, scattered with low yellow dunes, but most of it rust-red clay, scoured bare by ages of wind. He kept off the dunes. The clay should make good bricks for the habitat, he thought, perhaps even fertile soil for the greenhouse.

If this had really been a lake, could its water still lie here, frozen under the dust of a million storms? Or had all the ancient seas of Mars been lost to space, leaking atom by atom out of its feeble gravity well? That riddle had been debated for years. Now at last he could look for the answer.

Without the core drill, however, all he had was the probe. He stopped on a likely bit of bare clay to try it. A slender, sharp-tipped rod, mounted in a flimsy plastic guide, driven by a power hammer. Sensors along it relayed their readings to a tiny monitor.

On his first test, it struck a hidden boulder only half a meter down. On the second try, however, the hammer drove it farther, through nearly a meter of clay, two of dry gravel, then another layer of impermeable clay, so hard the point almost stopped. He kept the hammer pounding. It went abruptly deeper, and he leaned to read the monitor.

$$H_2O \ldots 49\%$$

Water ice!

The lost seas located! He scanned the full printout. The ice was far from pure, laced with heavy concentrations of a dozen salts, but it could be refined. If water was so near the surface here, within twenty degrees of the equator, it must be abundant all around the planet.

Water for Mars!

Drunk with the thought, he stopped the hammer and danced around the rover. A clumsy dance in the stiff yellow suit, but he wanted to yell with triumph. What news for Jayne, for *Ares,* for the Earth! Water for the habitat! Water for a colony, even for the city of his childhood dream!

If— He stopped and shook his head. If they lived to tell about it.

He stood a moment by the lander, staring back the way he had come. The wheel tracks in the hard red clay wound through the yellow dunes toward the far crater slope and the rocks along its lip. Great black rocks that bit like snaggle teeth into the pastel sky. The lander and Jayne were still swallowed in the crater beyond them. He felt lost and alone in this alien land where life had never been.

Yet he was here. He pulled his body upright in the suit and filled his lungs. The air in the helmet had a thin sharp plastic stink, but it would do. He and Jayne had to live and keep the news alive. The permafrost justified his life and the Authority, all the billions spent, all the risk and effort of the expedition. It could bring another ship, whole fleets of spacecraft, to remake Mars into some kind of paradise.

They would not, could not die.

He dismounted the probe and drove farther into the basin, stopping again and again to run another test, elated again and again by the readouts, until the lowering sun warned him to retrace his way. It had almost touched the lurid horizon before he came back across the crater rim. He found Jayne outside, resetting the solar panels to catch the morning sun. She came down to meet him as he parked the rover, and stopped when she heard his news.

"Magnificent!"

She whispered that single word. In the fast-thickening dark, they cycled aboard. She scanned the printouts he had brought from the probe. Raising cups of precious water brought all the way from Earth, they drank toasts to Mars reborn, and made a banquet on their single ration pack.

In the pilot bay that night, they took turns watching the sky and trying to sleep. They saw no flash of any signal, got no sleep at all. Instead, they spoke more freely than they ever had, about themselves and the lives they had led, about the wonders of Mars and their hopes for what it might become. Carefully, they said nothing of their fears.

"Kelligan, I never understood you." The lights were out to save vital power, and he heard her low voice near him in the dark. "I'm here for a reason. I've told you about me and Lakefield. I joined the Corps to get away."

"Glad you did?"

"Glad enough." She kept probing. "But you had more than enough. A Texas tycoon, if you'd wanted to be. Power if you wanted it, women to love, millions to squander. And now you're here." Her voice held ironic challenge. "Fair trade, Kelligan?"

"The one I made."

He lay listening to her breathing, feeling grateful for this close moment, whatever it had cost. Afraid he might spoil it, he said no more till she asked, "Why?"

"I never really wanted all the millions, except maybe to get into space." She said nothing, and at last he went on, "There was a girl. I'd loved her since we were kids. She wanted to marry me."

"Yet you left her?"

"She's always known what Mars meant to me. And never understood."

"They never understand."

He heard her moving to the telescope to sweep the orbit where they had left the *Ares.*

"Only the stars." But her voice quickened. "But what stars! So steady and so bright, all colored with the dust. A sight you never see from Lakefield."

Next day she took the rover out, trending south across the basin to make another line of tests, while he stayed to keep the solar panels facing the sun. Back in the later afternoon, she came through the lock in a cloud of bitter dust off her pressure suit. It set them both to coughing.

"I tried—" she gasped. "Tried to brush it off, but it gets everywhere."

"Nasty stuff!" he muttered. "Because it's so very fine. Ground to powder by all the ages it's been drifting in the wind."

"But it should—" Her voice was gone again. She made a face and wiped her streaming eyes, and he thought she tried to smile. "Should make rich soil," she whispered when she could speak. "When we have water—and we will. I found water ice everywhere under the clay, as far down as the probe could reach and as far south as I had time to go."

♂

Next morning he went north.

"I'll disk Coprates for Barova," he told her. "If I get that far."

"Pretty far." She shook her head. "You know she already has good pictures taken from space."

"But you know Barova." He grinned at her wry expression. "She'd want the view from the cliffs. Anyhow I want to see it for myself. It ought to make the Grand Canyon look like an irrigation ditch."

"Careful!" she told him. "You'll be running into rough country close to the rim. Kelligan—" Something caught her voice, and she went on more softly, "I think you're too much in love with risks."

Or too much in love with her? Aching with his dread that nobody on the *Ares* would ever see their feeble beacon, he wanted to take her in his arms, to cheer her if he could. But that was out. She had never forgotten who he was. What they had was a way of coping, a truce, he must not spoil. With luck enough, even now, it might help them stay alive.

And if they stayed alive—

"Okay, Mother." He grinned and tried to tease her. "I'll be careful."

"Do it, Hew." She hadn't called him Kelligan. "Please!"

♂

The canyon rim on their charts was two hundred kilometers north. He drove west first, curving north as he left the rugged country that had edged the lake. He pushed the rover hard, but the old lake floor was no highway. With the water gone, the winds had carved jutting bluffs and unexpected pits between the dunes. At midmorning, when he found the land sloping abruptly up, he was only a hundred kilometers out.

The north shore, he thought. The country grew rougher beyond a narrow ridge, sloping down. Stopping again and again to test for permafrost, he had to probe farther to reach it until there was none at all. The surface here had been warmer in some earlier age, he thought, heated perhaps by vulcanism. Nearer the rift, the permafrost must have thawed and drained away.

No water here, nor hope of it, yet imagination carried him on. There was ice enough under the basin, enough to let Mars live again. Lost in his visions of that, he was startled to see the sun at the zenith. So soon? He drove up the rim of an isolated crater to look ahead. Still he saw nothing of Coprates, but he couldn't turn back. Not when it should be so near. Pushing on, he came too fast into a wind-cut fissure.

He reversed the wheels, but the rover skidded down a slope too steep for it, struck a rock, and tossed him off. He fell on a bank of wind-drifted debris and lay there a long time, dazed and breathless, bitterly recalling Jayne's injunction to be careful.

Taking stock when he could move, he heard no hissing air, found no harm to the suit. The rover lay on its side, the locker knocked open, gear scattered in the dust. He gathered up the disks and the camera, the repair kit, the shelter balloon and spares for the air unit. Climbing out of the hollow, he heard Jayne's urgent voice in his mind.

"Turn back, Kelligan. You love risk far too much."

It was time to turn back, certainly, if he hoped to reach the lander by sunset, yet—

Could he risk the Martian night?

It would be colder than Earth had ever been, but the thin air should not steal his body heat so fast as the heavy air at home. The shelter balloon was insulated. The power cell and filter would keep him breathing through another day. The pouches in his suit held water enough, and energy wafers. Regardless of Barova, he wanted to see the great rift for himself.

He drove on.

The going got worse. The slope was steeper, the fissures deeper. Cracks, he thought, where tectonic forces had stretched the crust. They jolted the rover. Twice it stalled in dust too loose for the wheels, and he had to push it on to firmer ground.

Finally a wider crevasse stopped him, a secondary gorge, impossible to cross. He drove west along it for many kilometers. The crimsoned sun was low before he found a way around the end. In the sudden dusk, with no warning, he found himself on a sharper brink.

A few meters farther—

He braked the rover and sat there trembling, until awe overcame his shock.

♂

Coprates Chasma!

Black shadow had already filled it. Beyond the jagged rim, all he could see was darkness and the strange tinted stars. When at last his breath and pulse had slowed, he backed the rover to a patch of smoother ground a little farther from the rim.

Waiting there for daylight, he inflated the mirror tent around him and took the helmet off. He felt cramped in the suit and his whole body ached from the fall and the long trek on the jolting rover, but he left it on for warmth.

Trying to sleep, he woke once from a dream that he was a child again, drowning in a frozen pond. The ice had crumbled under him, and he was too numb and stiff to swim. His mother was running on the shore, calling in Jayne's voice that he had always loved risks too much, but she was too far off to help him.

The cold got to him. Clammy and shivering, he hammered his gloves against his thighs to warm himself and lay wondering about the odds for rescue. The strobe was never meant for signals into space. Would anybody at the telescope on the *Ares* ever happen to be sweeping the right point on the night side of Mars at just the right moment?

Not very likely.

♂

Grateful for the sun when it rose, he stirred stiffly to replace his helmet and deflate the tent. Outside, he caught the seat of the rover to pull himself erect. His breath stopped. He stood beside the machine on the tip of a narrow tongue of rock. The planet's crust was sliced away on both sides of him, dropping into an abyss so vast and deep that he stumbled instinctively back.

East and west, it fell forever. Abrupt cliffs of iron-red stone towered over yellow shelves above bottomless gorges of old black basalt. A flood of red fire poured down it out of the west, a fog-laden hurricane flowing around buttes and towers of wind-carved rock on its rush to meet the rising sun. Far mountains loomed out of gold-red haze beyond it. The central ridge, he thought. The rift's farther wall was too far to see.

Stiff-fingered, still numb and swaying, he found the camera and caught those giddy walls, that flood of red-lit fog, the iron-red range beyond. He waited for the sun to find the canyon floor and clear the clouds, so that he could get the faults and craters and landslides that would reveal its tectonic history.

Scenes to delight Barova. Data to make Hellman happy. Splendor worth all his risks. Perhaps he stayed too long, watching the changing glow of sunlight on the cliffs, exploring the canyon floor as the fog revealed it, trying to capture every change. The morning was half gone before he started back, and the long slope away from the rim seemed harder to climb than it had been to descend. Taking what he hoped would be a shortcut to avoid that secondary gorge, he lost himself in a maze of crevasses.

Midafternoon had passed before he found his wheel ruts again, on that long ridge between the old lake bed and the slope toward the rift. A race with the reddening sun. It had sunk low, and he was still twenty kilometers from the lander, when the faint whine of the helmet fan became a fainter drone and a red warning burned across his faceplate.

REPLACE POWER CELL!

He stopped to open the locker and find the spare cell. The fan died when he pulled the life-pack release lever. The air seemed instantly bad, his fingers instantly numb and clumsy. Awkwardly fumbling, he changed the cells and secured the life-pack. A new warning flashed.

WARNING!
POWER CELL DEAD!
REPLACE AT ONCE!

Damaged, he thought, when it spilled out of the locker. At least a little life was left in the old one. Gasping at the stale air in the helmet, he scrabbled again for the release lever. It evaded him at first, and the dead cell slid out of his gloves, but at last the fan droned.

Breathing again, he drove on faster till the rover bucked him off, the way LeeAnn's calico pony had bucked him off the day his father gave it to her, back when they were small. Luckily it stopped to wait for him, as the calico had, but a fit of coughing staggered him before he could climb back on.

Dust in his helmet?

That couldn't be, but the coughing left him breathless and bewildered, uncertain of direction until he found the setting sun. It was lower and dimmer in the red-glowing west, but he had the ruts to follow, and he wouldn't have to think. Just keep his seat on the jolting rover, keep his eyes on the wheel tracks, keep his mind on getting back to Jayne.

He had to cough again, and sob again for breath. Nausea filled his belly. He set his jaws and gulped against it. Don't upchuck. Not in the helmet. Just go on. Follow the ruts in the clay—though they were growing hard to see. The blood-colored sun was dull in the thick copper haze, eaten to only half a disk, suddenly gone.

The sky turned purple-black, closing down to smother him. Gasping, coughing again, he lost the ruts and couldn't see to find them. But there was the crater rim, a ragged gap bitten out of the stars. The lander was just beyond it. Swaying in the seat, he shifted gears to climb.

And the engine stopped.

The helium engine? It shouldn't stop, but perhaps it

wasn't right for Mars. He tried all the levers and switches he could reach. Still it didn't start. He had to leave the rover. The dusk had turned to midnight, but the pink-tinged stars could light his way. Coughing and wheezing and gasping again, he stumbled up the slope.

He thought he remembered the rocks along the crest, stacked like black dominoes against the tinted stars, but then he wasn't sure. He tripped on something he couldn't see, tripped and fell again. Lying with his faceplace against the dust, he thought Jayne would be sitting in the pilot bay, watching the sky for an answer to the strobe.

Or perhaps the *Ares* had already answered. Had Arkady already sent Ram and Lisa down to rescue them? To drill for permafrost? To begin the habitat? Would he live to see great crystal city domes shining in the dark across the basin, and Mars grown magnificent?

"We'll respect—" The words were hard to think. "Respect it, more than we ever did the Earth."

18

Periapsis

The point on an elliptical orbit closest to the primary body. More specific terms are perigee when the body is Earth, perihelion for the sun, periastron for a star. Moving beyond periapsis, the object in orbit recedes toward its farthermost point, apoapsis.

When they were back aboard the *Colon,* stowing their gear for takeoff from the polar snow, Barova told Chandra to lift them back into circumpolar orbit.

"To look again for Jayne and Hew?"

"If we're ever near their target point." He had to admire the fluid flow of her shrug, but her limpid voice reflected no concern. "But you know we have higher priorities. Otto wants low passes back over the ice."

"To access my sensor array," Hellman explained. "I can do it from fifty kilometers."

"From that altitude we might be able to see—"

"I want an ellipse," Barova broke in. "Eight hundred kilometers above the north cap."

"That's too high—"

"Not for a photo survey," Hellman said. "We want to cover all the planet. Dropping back to fifty kilometers over the south, I can try the laser spectrometer for more geologic data there."

"Geologic data?" He stared at Hellman, unwashed since the Deimos landing, unshaven and odorous. "Does that matter more than Hew and Jayne?"

"In fact," Barova said, "it does."

Frowning into the smooth oval of her face, camera-perfect even here and now, he set his jaws to hold back another angry outburst.

"We came for science." Her voice turned crisp. "At least I did. So did Otto. To study Mars and get our data back. If colonists come later, our surveys may bring them—or warn them away."

Her sleek blue shoulders tossed again.

"I see." Chandra bit his lip. "At least we'll be passing over Coprates?"

"Briefly. Once."

♂

The orbit carried them north around the planet's night side, through sunless winter above the north polar cap, south again down the day side. Sitting at the controls in the nose, Chandra felt motionless while Mars seemed to roll beneath, a rust-red wilderness as vast as all the continents of Earth.

Houston and Jayne stayed alive in his mind, the quiet American who had surrendered an empire to come here and the green-eyed girl who seemed to scorn him. He imagined them lost somewhere on below, hurt and desperate, scanning the empty sky for any hint of help.

Close to hating Hellman and Barova, he was at the telescope on every daylight pass above the latitude of Marineris. Never feeling any actual hope. They were far too high, moving too fast. When he magnified the image enough to find any sign of them, motion blurred everything.

Anyhow, what was there to look for? A new crater in the dust? Fragments of burnt and twisted metal scattered here and there across a thousand kilometers of desert? If they were down somewhere safe, why hadn't they signaled?

Every orbit took them lower across the south cap, still a blinding dazzle. While Hellman queried the radio array, Barova had him try the laser spectrometer. Even at fifty kilometers, however, they were too high for it. So he told her when she wanted his report.

"Nothing worth reporting." He displayed instruments and readouts to her camera. "Most of the laser bursts returned no reading at all. A few from the polar cap do show the same mix of carbon dioxide and water ice we found there. A couple off the cap hit the same lithospheric rock the probes brought back. One show of nickel-iron, which may have been a meteorite. The others are wild. Spectra of sulphur, tin, hydrogen cyanide. One rich in iridium, if you want to believe it."

"Do we?" She looked at Hellman, fine eyebrows arched inquiringly. "It could get media attention."

"Ignore it," Hellman told her. "Scientists would laugh, because we see very little evidence of the geologic processes that concentrated ores on Earth. Our whole study might come into question."

"Forget it," she said. "I expect us to go down in scientific history as the first here and the last. Our survey will stand forever."

♂

On the flights back north behind the planet, they floated between the pink-tinged stars and a sea of total darkness. With nothing for the cameras, Hellman and Barova napped and rested, but Chandra was always awake and watching when they came back across the latitude of the selected target point. The darkness promised nothing. He expected nothing, yet he kept on watching the dark telescope monitor—until he finally saw a pulse of light.

A signal of distress?

Almost too faint to see, it slid fast across the screen. He blinked and looked again. It was really there, flashing twice a second. He shouted to rouse Hellman and Barova, but it was gone before they came to look. Still groggy with sleep, they refused to believe him.

"A signal?" Hellman snorted. "If they had survived to make any signal, they'd use the radio."

"I know what I saw. Their navigation strobe, flashing twice a second. Which means they're down alive."

"Get some sleep," Barova advised him. "You're tired. You fret too much. I think you dreamed."

"It was the strobe! You will see it when we pass the spot again."

"Dear Ram!" She shook her head, patiently reproving. "The planet turns. We don't pass that point again."

"We can, if I shift the course for our next night flight."

"You will not." Her patience was gone. "We've no time or fuel to waste. You will hold us on our present course."

"Irina!" He was appalled. "For God's sake! They're

our friends, begging for rescue. Do you want to abandon them to die?"

"Not I, Ram. Our enemy is Mars." Again she was sweetly reasonable. "Remember Martin Luther White?"

"I remember. When I think of Houston and Jayne, down in the dust—"

"Are you that stupid?" Hellman interrupted him, harsher than Barova. "You know the fuel mass left on the ship will barely get us home. We've none to throw away. And I remember White. Speaking for myself, I don't want to die."

"Neither do I. But we left White alive. We've found water. Surely—" He caught his breath and touched Barova's sleek blue arm. "Surely, we can somehow recover water enough—"

"Surely?" Hellman mocked him. "All the water we've found is near the pole, not where you think you saw that light. We must get back to the ship. While we can."

"Irina, please—"

She waved a slim white hand to stop him.

"Listen, darling. I know how much you care for Jayne and Hew, but caring can't help them. You've simply had too little sleep and too much stress. What you saw—or think you saw—is certainly illusion. Give Otto the controls and try to relax."

"Relax? While they're dying?"

"Cool it, dear. Truly, there's nothing you or we can do."

Herself calm enough, she went to the galley and returned to offer them ration wafers and squeeze bulbs of hot coffee. He had to accept his in silence. Too angry to sleep, he kept his seat at the controls. She and Hellman were soon snoring again, the north cap soon sliding beneath, a ghostly blur under the stars.

Fatigue crept over him. He stretched and rubbed his eyes and blinked to see the instruments. Could that winking light have really been illusion? Hellman and Barova were, after all, able scientists. In the end, their data and their disks might matter more than a few human lives.

Yet doubt still tormented him. What illusion could flash twice a second, like the *Magellan's* navigation strobe?

♂

Half a day later, when the planet had turned Coprates Chasma back toward the sun, he begged Barova to let him shift their course to let him search the target spot by daylight. Silkily, she refused.

"Ram darling, you know I'd love to."

They were still in the winter night above the north cap. With nothing to disk and too high for the spectrometer, they were all afloat in the cargo space behind the cockpit, brewing black tea and warming ration packs.

"Would you?" He tried not to sound sardonic. "Really?"

"If we could." She glided to slide a slim blue arm around him. Even here, after all their days in space, he caught her perfume—the name he had seen on a discarded vial was *Attar of Paradise.* "If we had time and fuel to spare."

"I've plotted the point where I saw the strobe," he told her. "On a cratered ridge a couple of hundred kilometers south of Coprates, just out of the saucer-shaped depression where they meant to land. Why can't we—"

"Because time's running out." Her limpid voice cut him off. "Our survey must be completed before the return window closes."

"Just a few hours," he begged her. "There's fuel mass enough, if we're careful. That ridge is pretty rough for a landing, but we could get down safe a few kilometers west. Long enough to pick them up."

"If they're packed and ready, waiting for a ticket home." Hellman's laugh was harshly scornful. "Standing on a hill and waving white rags, like you saw them in your dream."

Trembling, he made a fist.

"Ram dear, please!" Barova reproved him. "You really must relax. I'll let Otto take the controls for a couple of orbits."

♂

Hellman took the controls. Exhausted, he fastened himself in the low-gee hammock and slept a few hours. A little refreshed, he washed his sticky eyes and drank a bulb of bitter tea. Back at the controls again while Barova napped and Hellman was accessing the radio relay, he veered their orbit without permission to pass again above that crater ridge. Again he saw a faintly flashing point that crept across the monitor.

"The strobe!" Breathless, he called to wake Barova. "See it?"

"You've changed our course?" She rubbed her eyes and snapped at him angrily. "Against my explicit orders?"

"If Jayne and Hew are still alive—"

"A tragic thing, if they are." Peering at that feeble flicker in the monitor, she shook his golden head. "I pity them."

"Pity?" he muttered. "When they're back in daylight, I want to land—"

"Impossible, Ram." She watched that fading flash till it was gone. "Out of the question."

"You saw the strobe."

"Hard to say what I saw." She shrugged at the dark monitor. "Could have been lightning. Hot lava. Anything."

"Flashing twice a second?"

"Emotions deceive us." Hellman had followed, intoning the words with an unctuous certainty. "We see what we desire."

"Ram, dear, please remember why we're here. In pursuit of knowledge. We have made great discoveries. Our top priority now is the safe return of our disks and data to Earth."

"No priority of mine," he told her. "I—and most of us—came to colonize the planet."

"A fool's errand!" Hellman snorted. "Only eight, against a hostile world! A thousand people with ten thousand tons of gear could still fail."

"Ram darling." Barova shook her head. "Just look at the odds. Do you want to maroon us to die here? Or do you want to stay alive?"

"Are you afraid—"

"Idiot!" Hellman shouted at him, and turned abruptly to her. His voice fell. "Irina, we must swear ourselves to forget this signal—if it is a signal."

"What?" Chandra was incredulous. "Why?"

"You know the media. How sensation outruns truth. Any report of companions abandoned on Mars—"

He spread his grimy hands.

"We can't forget—"

"Don't you see?" Her voice turned icy. "Our disks and records can make us all heroes, unless we let some baseless rumor spoil everything."

"Rumor?" he whispered. "I know what we saw."

"Better forget it." Hellman gripped his arm, and he caught the rank body scent. "We have too much to lose."

19

Paralife

Also called pseudolife or protolife, paralife is a virus-like self-replicating molecule still surviving in Martian dust, its evolution halted by the severe environment. Infecting human tissue, it became a grave hazard to the exploration and colonization of Mars.

Sick and shivering, Houston had fallen off the rim of Coprates Chasma into the freezing river that ran down the bottom. He was drowning in it, fighting to breathe, till Jayne caught his grasping hand. She pulled him out of the cold and the sickness and the darkness, somehow back into his seat in the lander's pilot bay.

He could breathe again.

"Hew?" her anxious voice was calling. "Can you hear me?"

He tried to nod.

"Thank God! I was afraid—afraid you were dying."

His throat hurt when he tried to speak, but he managed a feeble croak. She brought him water he couldn't swallow and a wet cloth to wipe his mouth when he coughed. He lay there a long time, watching her face when he could see her in the dimness, feeling happy to be with her. All he wanted was the pain in his throat to stop and her to stay with him.

The pain had begun to ease when he woke again. The leaning lander was brighter, lit by a shaft of yellow sun.

Feeling stronger, he raised his head to look for her. She was nowhere on the slanted deck. He rasped her name and heard no answer.

Panic seized him. Without her, he was all alone on Mars. He tried to climb out of the seat to search for her, but even the small gravity was too much for him. He fell back. Cold sweat burst over him. He lay there helpless, breathing hard, afraid for her, till he heard the air lock cycling.

"Jayne!" He sobbed her name. "Jayne."

Her face was over him then, stained with red dust yet always beautiful.

"Sorry," she told him. "I was resetting the solar panels."

"The strobe?" He could whisper now. "Did they answer?"

She shook her head.

"But you're alive." She looked worn and pale, but she could smile. "You're getting well."

She brought a cup of cold water and wanted to open a ration pack for him. He gulped the water with little pain now, and shook his head at the pack. Next day he felt able to share it and ask how she had found him.

"Waiting was hard." The words hurt because he had to blame himself, but her voice was music. "I watched with binoculars on the second day. Finally saw you crossing a ridge, far off in the north. When you never came I set out walking, following your wheel tracks."

"In the dark?"

"It did get dark, but the stars are so bright here. My eyes adjusted."

"You carried me back?"

"The light gravity helped. I thought you were dying."

"I was." Painfully, he nodded. "Near enough."

"From the dust, I think. Like Luth White."

"Still alive, at least when we left." He lay quiet for a

moment, looking for comfort in that and even his memory of the rift. "Coprates!" he whispered. "A splendid thing to see, but I stayed too long. If you can forgive me—"

"Forgiven." She caught his reaching hand, and he saw her tears. "It's I who should be asking. I listened while you were out of your head. Sometimes you thought I was a girl named Lee. Sometimes you knew me."

He waited, loving the warm pressure of her hand and the shape of her face.

"You kept saying—" She paused as if abashed. "Saying—well, that you loved me. Begging me to understand that you never wanted to be born a Texas tycoon."

"You do? Understand?"

"Does it matter?" She shrugged, but her face looked impish. "We've come a long way from Texas."

"It does—does to me."

He lay a long time clinging to her hand, until she had to leave him to turn the solar panels. Next day he got out of the chair to climb across the deck, and that night he watched the sky while she slept. The tawny stars were splendid, but he saw no signal answering the strobe.

♂

Sometimes they talked. At first he was afraid to say much about his family and his life in Texas and the expensive sports and hobbies he had enjoyed, but she urged him to go on.

"You're they first tycoon I ever really knew." She grinned wryly through the red stains on her face. "Still that poor kid back in Lakefield, I used to envy the rich. Tell me everything."

He told her more about his parents, about Lucina and Marty and his mother's long unhappiness.

"My father's a hard man when you cross him. We always fought, but I guess I really love him."

"Lee? Did you love her?"

"At least since her sixth birthday, when we undressed to inspect each other." He paused to savor the recollection. "If you can call it love. She's bright and beautiful and kind. We were always friends. Never—well, passionate. I could tell her anything. She always understood. Except Mars. She wouldn't believe I'd ever get here. She planned for us to marry."

"Were you tempted?"

"Sometimes." He watched her face, still amazed that she could smile. "Before I saw you."

"Now? Regrets?"

"I left her unhappy. I'm sorry for that."

He asked about her family.

"Simon Ryan came through Ellis Island sometime in the last century to shovel coal for Lakefield Forges. A black Irishman from Cork, my grandmother said. His son was my grandfather, a union man who won a strike against the company—it was Lakefield Steel by then.

"My own father helped organize a less successful strike. It crippled the union and broke the company, back before I was born. Unemployed, he got religion; became a preacher and a secret alcoholic. He killed my mother in a traffic accident. He was a good man, sober, but a mean streak showed when he was drunk. He never physically abused me, but I grew up in terror of him. My grandmothers kept me till I was grown."

"Boyfriends?"

"Not really." She shrugged. "Unless you count Arkady."

"He's okay."

"A friend." She nodded, a hint of warm amusement in her eyes. "Now so are you."

Happy with her, he sat silently content till she spoke again.

"I've had a few bad episodes, like that one with Gorley." She made a face. "But not many chances at men. My grandmothers watched me like a pair of hawks, and a preacher's daughter gets a bad name unless she's pretty prim. Early on, anyhow, I fell in love with science and the stars. Beginning, I guess, once when my father took me to the planetarium, trying to make up for another spree." A small sad smile. "Later, when I heard about the Authority, Mars was all I wanted."

"Are you in love with Arkady?"

"In love?" She teased him with a little grin, and went on more gravely. "I like him. The same way, I guess, that you say you like LeeAnn. He's good for me. I admire him. We've enjoyed each other. But what always mattered most to both of us was Mars."

"We all wanted Mars." His laugh was half ironic. "Now we have it."

"Don't laugh." Gently, she reproved him. "I'll never be sorry we're here."

♂

He was soon able to get into his pressure gear and take his own turns dusting and adjusting the solar panels. Appetite returning, he relished the synthetic and dehydrated stuff in the ration packs and stubbornly refused more than his fair share. He watched the sky through half the nights and clung to his last vanishing hope of rescue.

The bleak injustice of their fate, and even Jayne's stubborn cheer, brought him sometimes to despair. The bungled landing had killed them both. It had crippled and probably defeated the whole expedition. In the wake of its failure, no other attempt was likely to come. The first human beings here, they might be the last.

In dark moments, he imagined the wrecked *Magellan* as their tomb, a monument that might endure to hold their bones intact even after the last traces of humanity had vanished from the changing Earth.

More often, however, he felt a strange contentment. The planet lay all around him, splendid even in its ageless desolation. He had seen Coprates. He could watch the flow of light and color everywhere, always enchanting, as the different sun crossed a different sky. Here with Jayne, he had reached his goal. These few weeks were their own, and nothing was forever.

"Enjoy!" The word became a joke they shared. "Enjoy!"

Together when he felt strong enough, they went down the ejecta slope and out into the basin, following the wheel tracks where he had driven north. They found the abandoned rover a few kilometers out, among his wandering footprints in the dust. And her own, when she had come to carry him in.

The helium engine started when he turned the key. Ruefully, he laughed at himself, and they rode the rover back over the crater rim. The camera was safe. They viewed the disks and found Coprates Chasma still magnificent.

Now that he getting better, they could talk of paralife.

"There's a small secret I can tell you now," she said. "About Luther White's accident. It wasn't quite an accident."

They were in the pilot bay, sipping the hot black tea that seemed to dull their hunger pangs. He frowned at her, waiting till she went on.

"I was on the research team with White at the Farside labs when the last probe brought back the samples of dust. We isolated those odd molecules. They were puzzle because they could replicate themselves much as DNA does, in spite of such a different structure.

"In warm water, with nutrients dissolved out of the dust, they multiplied like live organisms. When we tried to culture them in any other medium, they seemed inert. Chemically stable, hard to kill. I guess they had to be, to survive here.

"When the Authority asked if they could be a threat, we ran tissue tests and animal tests. The results were not conclusive. Some rats died, some came through okay. We talked about human tests, of course just among ourselves. Publicity then could have been deadlier than the dust. We agreed, though, that a test had to be run.

"Luther White wrote a random number program to let the computer pick the lucky volunteer. When his own name came out, I wondered if he hadn't rigged it to shield the rest of us. He never said so, but he has a sentimental side. Anyhow, he injected himself and told the story about the lab accident.

"You saw him after."

"You—" He shook his head at her. "It could have been you—"

"The same chance we're all taking now." She shrugged and somehow smiled. "Remember, we did leave Luth able to give blood for the experimental vaccine."

"Nice," he said. "At least for the next expedition."

"You're getting well." She reached to feel his forehead for fever. "And some of the rats did seem immune."

Later, when she had come back from turning the solar panels, he heard her coughing.

20

Biosphere

A human biosphere must provide breathable air at tolerable temperatures, pressures, and humidities. It must offer shelter from harmful radiations and maintain the whole system of biochemical and zoological balances required for a benign ecological environment.

It was their love nest no longer, that windowless room with its bright-striped *zarapes* and gleaming Taxco silver and the twin volcanoes behind the fortress of Chapultapec and twin pyramids above the ceremonial sacrifice. Now itself a field of war, it saw new battles joined nearly every business morning. Lucina and sometimes her son came with thick folders of legal and financial armament. Kelligan brought LeeAnn with him to face them.

"It's hard on Lucina," he muttered to her one morning before they went in. "My loyal right hand all these years. Used to getting her way. But now, when she makes the choice, it has to be her precious Marty."

On the surface, not much had changed. He sat as always at the head of the big table beneath that huge mural, a dead cigar clenched in his black-stubbled jaw, LeeAnn often at his elbow. Lucina still bustled to pour her *café con leche*. When Marty was there, he squinted shrewdly at LeeAnn's pregnant figure and asked how she felt.

More often now he was away with his new associates

at White Sands or visiting cities around the world, scrambling to claim the assets of the dying Mars Authority. In the Fort Worth meetings, he kept pressing Kelligan for further funding.

"Not yet." Kelligan always put him off. "My bankers tell me we're already in too deep."

"They haven't read our prospectus. Senator, have you really studied it yourself?"

Kelligan grunted.

"Talk to our organizers, sir. They can show you it's the best investment off the Earth—that's our new PR slogan."

"Hah! The Authority was a cosmic rathole. How can you do better?"

"Because we know how to sell the planet, sir. In ways the old Authority never did. We'll own it all, by treaty right. Our shares of stock will be deeds to Martian lands. Ownership of all the wealth that may be discovered there."

"Wealth?" Kelligan grunted again. "Lavrin has found nothing but trouble."

"Sir, you don't know Dr. Barova." Marty smiled and licked his lips, glancing briefly up at the blood-splashed priest. "A remarkable woman, with a gift for PR. As I told you, she's with us now. Doing commercials for Mars ConQuest right on the spot."

"What has she to sell?"

"Senator, you're a businessman." Marty grinned, squinting at him. "You built one great corporation. Did it by taking risk. Selling risk to others."

"Limited risk," Kelligan said.

"You're shrewd, sir. You understand why people gamble."

"Stupidity, commonly."

"Partly." Marty shrugged. "But Barova says it's instinct. The primitive chances of the jungle and the hunt."

The thick-lipped grin grew wider. "We have a team of master marketeers, merchandising that instinct. The chance of winning big, because Mars is big. If they face a chance of loss—" He shrugged. "Barova says people need the pain of loss."

He shuffled his folders. "If you'll just look at our new prospectus—"

Kelligan shook his head at it.

"You're asking for more than we can prudently risk. A whole lot more."

"Escuche, Señor!" Lucina came around the table with her silver urns. "Martin's no fool. I've been working with his new associates. They are competent, *Señor.* There will be no actual risk. Not for you."

"Don't crowd me. I want more time to check—"

"It's now or never, sir." Marty was mopping his sweaty head. "Because the Authority's already falling apart. Engineers coming home from Farside and the lunar mines because they don't get paid. Our options are about to expire. We've got to act now, sir, or we'll be sorry."

"Señor!" Lucina urged him, "think of Mr. Houston."

"I think enough of Sam." He glanced at LeeAnn's tight face. "I think of Edna, too." He scowled at the red altar stone and then again at Marty. "Before we get any further, let me talk to the ship."

"That takes time, sir," Marty grumbled. "Everything has to go through White Sands and Farside. There's a long delay to Mars. And the ship's out of reach half the time, around behind it." He caught a hard look from his mother. "No problem, sir," he went on abruptly. "I'll round up a camera crew."

♂

The camera came. Sitting at his desk, LeeAnn beside him, Kelligan reviewed what he knew of Marty's scheme. "Now, Commander Lavrin," he finished, "I have urgent questions. First, I want your best opinion, sir. Is there any actual possibility that my son and Miss Ryan are still alive? Down somewhere on Mars, waiting for rescue?

"Regardless of that, what are your own plans for the expedition? I understand from Martin that some of your people want to cut it short and return through what they call the current window? Or will you try to establish a habitat and wait two years for another window?

"What is your own best estimate of any actual gain, either scientific or commercial, from the heavy investment that would be required to complete the *Nergal,* mount a relief expedition, and try to establish a permanent outpost on Mars?

"Or do you agree with the critics here who say you ought to cut your losses and get back while you can? Because you've done the science? Because you found nothing worth hauling back to Earth? Because you see no actual reason to stay?

"I'm counting on an honest report. You'll understand why. Now here's Miss Halloran."

The camera swung to her.

"Just a word—" The lens was a cold, unfeeling eye, and she had to gulp before she could go on. "A word to Houston Kelligan, if he—if he is there." She leaned a little forward, hopefully smiling. "Hew? We miss you. You mother prays for you. And I—I won't forget."

The desk hid her body, and she said nothing of his son.

♂

When the reply came back next day, she and Kelligan saw it on the TV in the private room. It began with a telescopic montage of the great, red-mottled globe of

Mars, swept and swept again by the shifting sun as it spun beneath the racing *Ares.*

Lavrin came on, standing by the control console in the control dome.

"Greetings, Mr. Kelligan." Fiery hair and beard untrimmed, he looked a little wild, but he began with a gravely courteous bow. "You ask for a status report. *Ares* remains in Phobos orbit. I'm now aboard with only two companions, Lisa Kolvos and Kim Lo.

"We have still heard nothing from your son and Jayne Ryan since they were about to land the *Magellan.* I'm sorry to say, sir, that I can't offer you any real hope that they survive. That's still possible, of course, but their failure to communicate is most alarming. They were supplied and equipped for only a brief exploratory touchdown.

"There's better news from the *Colon.* Dr. Barova has reported a successful landing with her two companions on the south polar cap. They confirm the existence of abundant water in the cap and in permafrost around it. They are now back in low circumpolar orbit, completing a detailed survey of the entire planet. Since they are overlapping the images for stereo, with supplemental laser spectroscopy and radar altimetry, the survey will require several more days.

"Right now our future plans remain uncertain. We came planning to build a habitat and stay two years. I myself am still convinced that we could and should do this. Our duty, in fact, to the ideals of the Authority and the old human dream of space. Kolvos and Lo agree. Your son and Ryan surely would, if we could reach them.

"But they are lost. Searching the area where they were to land, we find no sign of them. Lisa wants to land a search party, but we can't be certain where else to look. Hellman and Barova suspect that they have been disabled by the protolife virus. They're afraid any other landing party will go the same way.

"In fact, as Gorley may have told you, they are pressing to start home immediately, before the current window closes. They feel that, with the polar landing and their orbital survey, they have carried out our scientific mission.

"They have a very sharp concern that the water mass left aboard is barely enough to take us home on the best transfer orbit we can follow now. Reloading the lander for a third touchdown would force us to stay until Martian water can be extracted and purified to refuel the ship. Another two years, a prospect that daunts us all.

"Amid all these uncertainties, Mr. Kelligan, clear answers to your questions are not yet possible. Our future depends on whether we do or don't make that third landing. That critical decision must be made immediately after the *Colon* gets back, because our return flight window is closing fast.

"Barova and Hellman are bent on an immediate return. I myself am prepared to remain. We have barely touched the surface of Mars. At this point, I can't even guess at the science a full exploration may reveal, or the natural wealth it might discover. Speaking for myself, I'm convinced that a permanent Martian station will be worth whatever it may cost, just as a symbol of human greatness.

"If we do remain, we'll certainly need the *Nergal*. If we are forced to abandon the expedition, however, I would advise you to cut your losses as soon as you can."

♂

With a farewell gesture and a slight apologetic smile, Lavrin was gone. The mottled globe of Mars returned, spinning from day to night and back again. Kelligan turned to LeeAnn and saw her still watching the screen.

"An unexpected postscript, Mr. Kelligan." Lavrin's image had returned, his voice more urgent. "News you will welcome. I'll let Lisa Kolvos report it."

Lisa came on the screen, sitting at the console. A small neat woman, her lean figure molded to the blue skinsuit, intense black eyes smiling into the lens.

"I'm excited, Mr. Kelligan." Her voice was quick and eager. "The Commander warns us not to get our hopes too high, but I believe Hew and Jayne may be alive. I'll try to sum up what we know—which I guess isn't really much.

"The Commander's message was recorded while we were on the dark side of Mars. I stayed in the control dome afterward, waiting to transmit it when we got back in line of sight. We happened to be passing over the target area—the spot where the *Magellan* was to land. With nothing else to do, I took one more look.

"Without much hope. I'd been searching the site as often as I could, but generally only by daylight. Not really expecting to see anything by night, I swept the area again. Still nothing, not till the sweep carried me out of the saucer where they meant to land, to a cragged ridge east of it.

"I saw a flashing light.

"Very faint, even in the telescope, but it winked twice a second like the lander's navigation strobe. At first I wasn't sure, but it kept on flashing. I called the commander and woke Kim Lo. It was nearly out of range by then, but they did confirm it.

"We called the *Colon* when it got back in contact. Ram Chandra answered. He said he'd seen it himself. Or at least he'd thought he had—though Hellman and Barova couldn't see it and tried to convince him it was only his imagination.

"We're excited, of course. It seems to mean they did

get down alive. The lander must have been disabled so badly they couldn't take off or even reach us by radio. We've no idea what went wrong, but I hope we can land now and find out.

"Here's the commander."

Lavrin was back on the screen, blue eyes lit.

"We are elated! Yet, Mr. Kelligan—" More soberly, he shook his head. "I must repeat Lisa's warning. This sighting does not yet mean that your son and Ryan are still alive, or that they can be rescued. However, it does let me give better answers to some of your questions.

"I have spoken to Chandra. He agrees with us that we must make a rescue attempt, though he expects opposition from Hellman and Barova. As I told you, this third landing will draw down our reserve so far that the return flight to Earth must wait for another window.

"So we now intend to remain on Mars. Whether or not the rescue is successful, we will use the results of Barova's survey to select a site for permanent occupation. We'll build the habitat, survey the surface as far as we can, and begin work to refuel the *Ares* with Martian water. In time, with luck, our outpost can become the initial human biosphere on Mars.

"With that bright future in view, we urge you to complete the *Nergal.* I hope it can be ready to come out when the next window opens, with supplies and another group of volunteers. We'll try to be ready for them, hoping that our first small biosphere can grow to make the whole planet a second human world."

The screen went dark.

"Well?" LeeAnn looked at Kelligan. "What do you think?"

"I was thinking of Edna." Gloomily, his heavy shoulders sagged. "She takes this hard. I try to make her accept that Sam is gone forever, but she can't give him up. I'm afraid this new uncertainty could put her back to bed."

"About Marty's deal?"

"Oh!" He blinked at her. "If they're all still so eager to gamble their lives on Mars, Sam and the rest of the crew, I guess—" His cragged features softened. "I guess I can take another risk."

21

Mars Time

Orbiting farther out than Earth, Mars takes 687 Earth days to complete its year, its track around the sun. Its day, however, the sol, is only 37 minutes longer than Earth's.

Jayne got sicker as Houston recovered. Her croaking cough persisted, her fever climbed, she couldn't eat. Chills shook her. Shivering in the reclined pilot seat, since the lander had no other berth, she sipped the water he gave her and let him sponge her fevered face.

"A hell of a way to die!" she muttered in one low moment. "After all we came for."

"We aren't dead yet." He grinned into her red-splotched face. "I got well. Nearly well, anyhow. And we've got the blinker going."

"Keep it going." Her hot hand fumbled for his, and she whispered, "I need you, Hew. I really do."

"It took you long enough." Her cracked and blistered lips tried to smile. "They'll see the strobe," he promised her. "They'll come. They surely will."

"But if they don't—" Her fingers tightened. "We must leave records somebody can use. Everything we've disked. And all we can learn about this damned illness."

She made him strip her bare and let him disk the red and swollen blotches that now covered most of her body. Some of the blisters had turned brown and grown crusty at the edge. They itched, she said, but denied that they hurt too much.

"Poe should be here." Staring at her discolored arm, she shuddered with a fever chill. "Remember *The Red Death?*"

"We won't—won't die!" His voice cracked, but he tried again. "We can't. We've worked too hard and come too far."

"Brave words, Hew!" Through tears welled out of her red-rimmed eyes, she managed a hoarse little laugh. "I didn't mean to sound so dismal. Even if we die, we've led the way. Others will be coming. They'll want to know what became of us."

She turned her body for his camera and spoke into the microphone.

"The third red fever case." Her raw throat hurt, and she coughed again when she tried to smooth her raspy voice. "Our second here. The first was Martin Luther White's, contracted on the Moon. Caused, we believe, by a virus in the Martian dust. We found it impossible to culture in the laboratory, unless Mars dust was mixed in the medium. I suspect that we're getting it from some unidentified factor the dust carries into our lungs.

"Which will make infection hard to avoid."

She was beautiful, he thought. Even mottled with those scarlet blotches and drawn thin with hunger, even with her hair matted to her scalp and her face pinched with pain, she was beautiful. He wanted to tell her so, but a painful ache had closed his throat.

♂

A sonic boom?

He was outside, resetting the solar panels, when that sharp concussion echoed against the rocks around the lander. Not breathing, he stopped to listen. All he heard, faint in the helmet, was the thin and bitter wind that blew out of the west every morning after sunrise. He climbed a rock to search the sky. Nothing broke its dusty glow.

Perhaps the lander's impact had disturbed some balanced stone to let it fall. Change was glacial here, but the wind-carved dunes and broken boulders were proof enough that it could happen. He listened and scanned the sky again and finally went back to care for Jayne, saying nothing about it.

When he heated water next morning to mix with the dry soup mix in a ration pack, she was able to swallow a little. Himself invigorated, he turned the panels to face the rising sun and climbed past them to look beyond the crater rim. Black rock. Gray rock. Iron-dyed rock. Rust-colored dust. The pink-hazed horizon. Nothing looked different—until he saw a tiny yellow flame far out across the basin.

What could burn, here in no oxygen? Here where no plant grew?

Perhaps—

Perhaps a plume of sunlit dust? Stirred by something moving? Afraid to believe, he watched until it changed and lifted in the shifting wind, still creeping slowly toward him. A small bright insect crawled into view beneath it. A rover!

And the lander!

He found it at last, kilometers beyond them. A glint of light in the sun. An unbelievable silver exclamation mark standing on the dust-dazed horizon. He shaded his faceplate and stared again until tears dimmed his eyes. Breathless and trembling, he ran back aboard to snatch off his helmet and shout the news to Jayne.

"They've come! We don't have to die!"

She wouldn't believe, not till he shucked off his suit to persuade her that the fever hadn't taken him out of his head. They sat together on the side of her chair, sobbing with relief, until she told him he must go out to welcome their rescuers.

♂

Outside again, he stood waiting on the crater lip to watch the rover following his own wheel ruts out of the basin. He waved when they reached the boulder slope and he could recognize the driver.

"Arkady! And Lisa!"

"Hew?" He heard their radio voices and saw them smiling in the helmets. "Thank God!"

They got off the rover to meet him. Lavrin gripped his glove. Lisa threw her arms around him and he felt her body quiver, even through the heavy fabric. Her helmet, against his, carried her breathless whisper.

"We were afraid—afraid we'd never see you again."

"So were we!" He squeezed her against him and turned to ask Lavrin, "How did you find us?"

"Lisa saw your blinker."

He hugged her again.

"Permafrost?" Anxiously, Lavrin was asking. "We saw where you drilled. "What did you find?"

"Water ice," he told them. "It seems fairly abundant all across the basin."

"We're betting on it." He heard the commander's relief. "Can't take off without a refill."

"You took that chance?" His voice quivered. "To save our lives?"

"To save the expedition."

"I've worse news." They stood silent while he told them about Jayne's illness and his own. "The paralife virus," he finished. "Made us both pretty sick, though I'm almost recovered. Jayne seems better today."

As if already stricken, they stared at each other and then back at him.

"Sorry about it." He caught Lisa's stiff-clad arm. "With no contact, we couldn't warn you. You may be already infected."

"Already?" Doubtful, Lavrin shook his head. "Nobody caught it in the lab on the Moon till White injected himself."

"It's in the dust," he said. "That gets everywhere."

"I've asked about White," Lavrin said. "His infection was recurrent. He seemed to recover, but got sick again. He was back on the Moon the last I heard, under treatment with the experimental vaccine. Results not yet evident."

Lisa turned to stare back across the desolate yellow dunes and naked red clay of the basin, and Houston saw her shudder.

"Ugly stuff!" he muttered. "Everywhere!"

"We talked to White before we left." She turned back to brush dust from his sleeve with her dusty glove. "We knew the odds. I don't regret the risks."

$$\male$$

They came aboard the *Magellan.* Jayne had washed her red-scarred face and put on the blue skinsuit. Waiting at the lock, she received them with a one-sided smile. Lavrin produced a stethoscope from his suit pack and made her lie down again while he examined her.

"No damage to the heart," he announced. "Pulse slow, however. Rales in the lungs. Without the vaccine—" He shook his head, frowning at Houston and then at her, "We can't do much but observe you."

"I'm already better." She sat up again, trying to stifle

another cough. Still weak, Houston saw, even against the gravity of Mars. "I'll be okay."

Lavrin wanted their story.

Houston began, "I botched the landing—"

"I botched it," Jayne's rusty voice broke in. "Before I learned to trust him."

"We managed it together." He grinned at her. "We're lucky, I guess, to be alive. The rocket nozzle is damaged, but not beyond repair—I hope. With a few spare parts, I think we can take off again."

He told about their explorations.

"I scouted the basin and struck north to Coprates Chasma. It's awesome!" He smiled at the recollection. "Deeper than you can imagine. Sheer cliffs dropping down forever to narrow shelves and steeper cliffs below, all layered red and gold and black, blazing when the sun hit them. A river of fog down on the floor, cold air flowing to meet the sun.

"I stayed almost too long, shooting it for Barova. Night caught me on the way back. Air unit failed. I passed out down on the desert. Jayne brought me in, and nursed me through my own bout of this fever."

He stopped to grin at her again, and swung back to Lavrin.

"What now, Commander?"

♂

Lavrin and Lisa told their own story of the agonizing wait for the *Magellan* to signal or return, of the brief touchdown on Phobos, of the polar landing.

"Hellman and Barova report finding thick strata of water ice," Lavrin said. "But out of reach under carbon dioxide snow. They didn't recover liquid water."

"In fact, they didn't even try." Lisa's voice had a bitter

edge. "All they want is to get home safe with the disks and data they think will make them famous."

"Lisa, please." Mildly, Lavrin reproved her. "You know how bleak the odds were, with no actual proof we'd ever find available water. Now we're committed, they'll be loyal enough."

"We'll see." Uneasily she stared at Jayne's scarlet-blotched face. "We'll see."

♂

Crowded together in the slanted pilot bay, they made a banquet of four full ration packs and a bottle of brandy Houston had found in the aid locker.

"To Mars!" He raised his plastic cup. "And all us Martians!"

"To mark the occasion," Lavrin said, "let's change to Mars time."

They pressed buttons on the timepieces the Authority had issued them. Green numerals flickered and shone red with the different hours and minutes and seconds of Sol 19, Mars month Sputnik, Mars year One.

Afterward, Lisa stayed aboard with Jayne to inspect the damage from the crash and Houston went with Lavrin down the crater slope and out across the basin to the *Colon*. They set up the core drill and sank a test hole.

"Two meters of this red clay." He summed up the readouts. "One of dry sand and gravel. Another meter of hardened clay, almost shale. Then the permafrost. Sand and gravel saturated with frozen water, as far down as we can drill. Water enough!"

"A billion years old?"

"Or likely older. The basin must have been a lake, frozen as the climate changed. Dust drifted over it. Enough to insulate it and seal it against sublimation."

"Can we recover useful water?"

"Can do." Houston nodded. "I've thought about it, and looked at the gear you brought. We'll run everything with power from the lander. Drill and boiler and osmotic separator. Steam to thaw the frozen mud. Steam pressure to drive the water out."

The water came out heavy with minerals, unfit for the engine. Osmotic refining was a slow process. They were five days getting the lander loaded and trimmed and ready for takeoff.

Back aboard the *Magellan,* they found Jayne insisting that she was well as ever, though the red eruptions on her face had not entirely healed.

"Commander," Lisa said, "I think you should send her back to recuperate on the mother ship."

"We'll do that." Lavrin swung to Houston. "Hew, you and Jayne will take the *Colon* back and remain on the *Ares.* Leave your surplus water in her tanks—I want her fueled and ready for home." He grinned through the unkempt beard. "Our security blanket."

"Barova's, anyhow." Chandra was sardonic.

"Send her back on the lander," Lavrin told him. "Along with Hellman and Lo. Have them bring repair parts for the *Magellan* and what supplies and equipment they can carry."

Lisa had listed the repair parts she wanted. The computer was beyond fixing, she said, but there was a spare. Lavrin worked with Houston to list what they needed to begin construction of the habitat. Next morning they all rode the rovers back to the *Colon.*

The habitat, they agreed, would be here where they had drilled for water.

"Other spots may be more scenic," Lavrin said, "or offer more resources. We can search for them later. Here we have water, and clay that ought to make brick. Sand from the dunes might make glass. Later we can look for more."

They paced off the selected site, on a little rise where the drill had found only dry clay, no permafrost. He let Jayne try to drive the first metal stake to mark it, though her strength gave out and Houston had to take the hammer.

♂

When the *Ares* came back in radio range, Lavrin called Barova with his orders for her and Hellman and Kim Lo to return with the *Colon*. Houston helped Jayne up the folding ladder. Inside the lock and out of the cumbersome suits, they climbed again to the pilot bubble. Half a kilometer away, Lavrin and Lisa stopped the rovers to watch them off.

Houston opened the injection jets. The helium motor roared. The rocket blast raised a hurricane of rust-colored dust that rolled out to hide the rovers. The lander quivered and lurched and lifted, slowly at first but accelerating fast. The dune-streaked basin shrank. He caught a glint from the leaning *Magellan* on the crater lip. Faster, faster, the mottled globe of Mars shrank and rolled away below.

Jayne slept through most of the flight. Kim Lo answered his hail, and her signal gave him a radio fix. The *Ares* came into view, a faint star that brightened as they climbed, became a sun-glinting toy and at last the great ship itself. Kim opened the lander bay to let him dock.

"Already?" Jayne was flushed and feverish when he woke her. "I was dreaming." A wistful smile crossed her fever-marked face. "Dreaming that the habitat was finished and the *Nergal* already here."

Hellman and Barova recoiled when they saw her.

"Arkady told us—" Barova paled beneath her makeup. "But I didn't imagine."

They kept away, uneasy, while Houston took her

down to her cabin. It was spinning at nearly twice Mars gravity, and he had to help her into her berth. Back with them in the control room, he gave Barova the list of items Lavrin wanted.

"This paralife fever?" Barova studied his face. "Arkady said you'd had it?"

"It nearly killed me." A rueful shrug. "Caught me away from the lander. Jayne carried me in and nursed me through it."

"How'd you get it?"

"Breathing, I guess."

"You breathed the dust?" Her voice was sharp with shock. "When you knew what happened to White?"

"No choice."

"How? When you were sealed in the lander and the pressure suit?"

"Tricky stuff," he told her. "It sticks to everything and comes with you through the lock."

"So it can hit us all?"

"A chance you take." He tried not to grin at her alarm. "The game we came to play."

"Not me!" She shrank from him. "If Arkady expects us to go down there—"

22

Habitat

A Martian habitat should be easily built of local materials with the simplest possible equipment. It must be sheltered against hard radiation and designed to hold air pressure. It requires dependable sources of power and water, greenhouses for food production, and facilities for air regeneration.

Barova's filmic face was cold as her theatric voice.

"I didn't come to leave my bones on Mars."

"Orders from Arkady," Houston reminded her. "You are to take the lander down, with Otto and Kim and a full cargo. I brought a list of what he needs."

"Kim can speak for herself, but Otto has already collected his data and his surface specimens. I've completed my orbital survey. My own work here is done."

"Done?" Incredulous, he blinked into her bright ambiguous smile. "Do you think you know Mars? Have you climbed Olympus Mons? Crossed Coprates Chasma? Seen the north cap? Irina, you can't even guess what you haven't seen."

"Others may come." Her blue shoulders lifted. "We can't do it all."

"But we didn't come to touch and run." Her cool smile bewildered him. "We're here to plant a colony. To establish humankind on a second planet. Something—well, historic."

"A noble dream." Her voice had an ironic undertone.

"I shared it once, but I've been down to the planet. So have you. We've seen at least enough to know it's too small and dry and cold for human life." She turned persuasive. "Face the truth, Hew. There's nothing there for us."

"Science, at least," he argued. "A world of unknowns."

"We've done the science. Drilled the south ice cap. Otto set his sensors out. We've resurveyed the middle latitudes. You disked Coprates. We've scanned the whole planet from low-level orbit. We've got it all. All except this fever—" She shuddered. "I've had enough."

"Lavrin sent orders—"

"I'm here aboard." She shrugged. "He's down on Mars."

"You took an oath—"

"To serve the old Authority." Her cool smile mocked him. "Now dead as the planet."

"I see." He found his fists clenched and squelched the impulse to drive them into her face. "Are you willing to kill the expedition?"

"Mars will do that." Suddenly sober, she reached to grasp his arm. "Imagine it, Hew. Nothing rots down there. Nothing oxidizes. A million years from now the frozen mummies will lie there among their broken tools and scraps of empty plastic in drifts of the dust that killed them."

A grimace of terror had fixed her fluid face.

"Not for me."

He recoiled from her clutching hand.

"Don't you see?" she begged him. "So few of us, against all the odds. Now this fever. The only sane thing is to cut our losses. Get back home with our records—data worth more than all our lives."

"Do you mean it?" He shook his head, wondering.

"Irina, do you plan to spent the next two years shut up in the ship?"

"If I must." She caught her breath and her voice fell confidentially. "I wasn't to say—not till it's public—but you may as well know I have a new position with the successor corporation. Mars ConQuest, which is taking over from the Authority. I have work to do here aboard. Work that matters more than anything happening down on Mars."

Her smile turned triumphant.

"Your friend Marty Gorley is the man in charge. I'm to produce commercials and publicity disks. If we get Mars ConQuest off the ground, he's promising to finish the *Nergal* and have a relief expedition ready to come out when the next window opens.

"That ought to convince the commander."

♂

She spoke to Lavrin when the ship came back into radio range. Houston didn't hear it all, but Lavrin agreed to let Barova remain aboard with Jayne. When Hellman grumbled that he had come as a scientist, not a space jockey, Houston volunteered to pilot the lander down again. Beside repairs for the *Magellan,* he loaded a small fusion generator, machine tools, and all the supplies the *Colon* could safely carry.

Ready for takeoff, he went down to Jayne's cabin. She woke when he bent over her and sat up to catch him in her arms.

"I'm better." She had to muffle a cough. "Much better."

He saw tears in her eyes when he told her he was already going back, but she brought a stiff little smile to her splotched and swollen face and whispered that she'd be fine with Irina.

On the flight back down to Mars, Hellman slept in the cargo space and Kim Lo sat with Houston in the pilot bay. He had never known her well. A slim, attractive woman who did her job and said very little, she had been Chandra's companion and always on another watch. He enjoyed her now. Watching the planet roll and grow beneath them, she seemed as eager as a child waiting for Christmas.

"I've lived for this." She leaned to touch his arm. "A dream since I used to try to see the stars through the glare over Asia Island. Coming true!"

She wanted to know all about his first flight down, the landing, his trip to Coprates. Gravely, she asked how sick the paralife virus had made him.

"Sick enough, but I've made a good recovery." And he asked, "Afraid of it?"

"Of course." She nodded. "I'd be a fool if I wasn't. But I never expected things to go entirely right." Troubled, she frowned. "Barova's a sad surprise, because she has so many gifts. I hate to call her a coward, but she's terrified of the virus. Desperate now." She sighed. "I thought we'd all agreed to take our chances."

"Barova did. I guess she changed her mind."

On their passes around the night side of the planet, with nothing to see except the stars, they talked about their own lives. Her birthplace was Shanghai, but her home had been Asia Island, which he had never seen.

"A city in the sea!" Pride and affection for it echoed in her voice. "Anchored to a seamount. Built so well no typhoon has hurt it. The new capital of the East Asian Union. Two million people now. My father was one of the designing engineers. I grew up there."

Her voice had slowed as she spoke, and she sat silent for a moment, staring out through the heat shield, perhaps at her own fond recollections.

"I loved to watch the construction crews," she went on

more softly. "And we used to dive in the central lagoon before the docks were finished and ships came in. Illegal, of course, but when my father caught us there he only told us how to avoid sharks and police.

"I was an only child. I came there with him when I was six, when my mother wouldn't leave the mainland—she'd been a marine biologist, and she never liked the island because she said civilization was killing everything in the sea. She was in a back-to-nature cult by then, and she stayed ashore. When he had to tell her good-bye, it was a very sad time for me because I really loved her. I couldn't understand how she could give us up, any more than I understand Irina."

Her lips set tight for a moment, but then her shoulders tossed Barova's mutiny away.

"We never heard from my mother again. Her cult was the sort that tried to cut all its ties with a world gone bad. Yet my childhood on the island was happy enough. My father put me through school, and I worked in his office till I won the Authority fellowship. I went home to see him before we took off. Another bad time."

Her face tight, she was silent for a moment, staring out into the splendid dome of stars.

"He's old now." Her low voice grew wistful. "Retired. He lives alone. He cried when I left him, because he was sure I would never get back. Yet he never wanted me to stay. He'd trained me for the expedition, he said, since I was a child. Building our city on the sea had been my school, he said, had taught me how to build on Mars."

Houston told her about his own childhood dreams of city domes on Mars.

"Though not right now." He laughed. "The habitat first."

"Even that can't be easy." Her voice grew sober. "Our cities on Earth grew out of ten thousand years of progress on the world where we evolved. Everything there was right for us. Wood growing in the trees and stone underfoot. On Mars, nearly everything will be wrong. Air we can't breathe. Materials we don't know how to use. Dangers like the paralife that we never even imagined.

"But here we are!" She caught his arm again. "We're engineers, trained to meet the challenge." She laughed. "I'm babbling like a salesperson for business rights on the Island, but it's true.

"We're making history."

♂

He timed their descent for an early morning landing. Bursting out of the dark on their last pass, they flew to meet the rising sun. The high crowns of Olympus Mons and the great cones on Tharsis Ridge rose out of the dawn like islands of fire and soon Marineris was flowing below them, a wide river of black shadow through orange-yellow desert.

He pointed out Coprates Chasma and the crater ridge where the *Magellan* had crashed. Lavrin had set up lengths of drill stem to support a radio beacon. They followed it down into the basin, but the landing site was hard for her to see.

"The white cross," he told her. "There on the desert, west of the crater ridge."

He pointed, and at last she found the tiny X in a rust-brown hollow lost among the yellow dunes. Riding down on a roaring cushion of white steam, she made out the core drill, the tiny boiler, the osmotic separator, and a few crates of supplies wrapped in mirror plastic. Beside them, two wide strips of white plastic film were pegged out for a landing target.

"That's all?" Her voice was hushed, nearly drowned in the thunder. "It looks pitiful. Could Barova be right?"

He caught her dread. The scattered bits of equipment

looked useless as toys some child might have abandoned on a lonely beach. The dunes were waves of an eerie ocean, rising to overwhelm it. He felt a moment of baffled foreboding, and a savage bitterness against Barova.

"Sorry, Hew." She raised her voice to make him hear. "But it seems so—so little."

A shock for her, perhaps, but he had no time for dismay. A great pancake of yellow dust was already spreading under them. Squinting through it, he brought them down on the plastic cross. This time very gently, though he felt a painful jolt when he thought of Jayne and the landing they had botched. He killed the rocket thrust and waited in the sudden silence for the dust to clear.

"A small start." He grinned at her. "But we've begun."

The site did look hopelessly forlorn, but the sunlit dust was bright above it. He showed her the wheel tracks that twisted away through the dunes. Soon they found two tiny clouds, turned to golden flame beneath the rising sun, creeping down the slope below the crater rim.

"And this is really Mars!" Caught up in a sudden elation, she threw her arms around him and kissed his cheek. "After so long!"

Hellman was awake. They got into their suits and went out through the lock to meet the two rovers, Lavrin on one and Lisa on the other. Chandra had stayed with the *Magellan,* they said, welding cracks in the rocket nozzle.

Houston took the commander aside to speak of Barova.

"She panicked," he said. "Afraid of the virus. Refuses to leave the ship."

"She called me," Lavrin said. "Told me about Gorley's project to carry on for the Authority and finish the *Nergal* to follow us. She says she's hired to do commercials for him."

"Which may be true. Or perhaps it's her excuse to stay aboard."

♂

They walked over the clay hill where the habitat would be.

"Kids could build it," Hellman muttered. "Back on Earth."

Here it would be harder. Here, without free oxygen or fossil fuel, every engineering process had new dimensions. Ores of iron might be abundant, since the whole planet had its color, but blast furnaces required coke or charcoal as well as oxygen, all products of life on Earth.

Most of the habitat would have to be underground for shelter against hard radiations. It would have to contain manufactured air under many times the tiny outside pressure. It would need water and power and waste disposal.

"Common brick?" Hellman hadn't come to be a builder. "How can you make it with no fuel to fire the kiln?"

"We'll find ways." Lisa seemed undaunted. "The kiln will be electric, fusion powered. There's clay we can use in a bank out there." She gestured toward the pink-hazed horizon. "I've ground a sample of it, mixed with brine from the water plant and baked under a solar reflector."

She showed him a small hard red cube.

"It will do."

She took a rover to her pit for the first load of clay. Lavrin and Kim Lo drove the other back up the ridge with the spare parts for the *Magellan*. Hellman grumbled that he hadn't come to be a robot, but he helped unload the rest of the cargo and pitch a mirror-plastic tent to give it a little shelter from dust and temperature extremes.

The first item off the lander was the helium reactor. An able engineer when he wanted to be, Hellman got it going. Houston ran a cable from it to power the water plant and refuel the lander. He helped Hellman assemble the power shovel to begin the excavation. A buried rock broke the blade. Repairing it took the rest of the day. They stayed aboard that night.

Lavrin came back alone next morning.

"Ram's got the bug," he reported. "He'd worked late, welding a patch on the rocket nozzle. Kim found him passed out under it, vomiting into his helmet. He coughed all night. Covered with red spots now. Kim stayed to look after him."

Chandra was worse next day. Kim Lo cared for him, distressed because they knew no treatment. Lavrin took the power shovel to dig clay. Lisa set up her little mill to grind it, the power press to shape the brick. Grumbling about a blister where the suit rubbed his knee, Hellman took them off the conveyor and laid them out to dry in the sun.

♂

Loading the *Colon* took three days. Houston slept aboard and spent his days with the boiler and the separator and the pumps. He had to stop at dusk, draining pipes against the bitter cold and using heater coils to thaw everything again before he could start next morning.

When the tanks were full, he took the lander up alone. Barova was waiting when he came out of the lock, long-limbed in her blue skinsuit, oval face and fair hair done for him. She caught him in her arms to kiss him on the mouth, her hot body melting against him.

"Hew, Hew!" Her perfume wrapped him, stronger even than his own stale sweat. "We've been so worried. Afraid you'd never come."

"How is Jayne?"

She clung for a moment when he moved to disengage himself, and abruptly stiffened. He heard the sharp catch of her breath and saw her crimson lips twist into a snarl. Her eyes startled him. They were the eyes of a trapped coyote he had seen long ago on a hunting trip with his father. Fixed on him, wary, terrified, desperate, they almost frightened him.

After one stark moment, that look was gone. He felt an instant of pity for her before her smile came slowly back, like a mask she had to reach for.

"Jayne?" A hollow echo. "She's better. Much better." Laughing at nothing, she drew away from him. "An impatient patient. Anxious for you."

He found her with a pocket computer in one of the cargo holds, taking an inventory of the supplies left aboard. She cried out when she saw him.

"Hew?" She stared at him anxiously. "Are you sick?"

"Okay." He stood searching her for the spots and blisters of the fever. "You?"

"Fine." Most of the marks had faded. Smiling, she was beautiful. "But you surprised me. Irina didn't tell me you were coming."

He took her in his arms and they said no more about Barova till she came into the hold to ask him to help her unload the lander. They hooked up the pumps and hoses, and he left her to transfer his surplus water to the big tanks of the *Ares*. Looking again for Jayne, he found her in the galley, making coffee for him from the precious stock aboard. They drank it, and shared a ration pack.

"I'm well again," she insisted. "I'm going back with you."

He had to shake his head.

"Not till next time. Lavrin's orders. Life on Mars is going to be hard, at least until we get a habitat we can move into. The fever can be recurrent. We want you to come back really well."

"Next trip," she agreed at last. "Right now, you stink." Her nose wrinkled. "And you're bristly as a bear. You need to shower and shave."

He shaved and showered and found her waiting for him in her cabin.

"If you aren't afraid of me . . ." She hesitated, eyes on his face.

"Afraid of you?" The fever-splotches had almost vanished, and she looked lovelier than he recalled. "When I had it, you didn't seem afraid."

"I remember." She laughed. "I even remember the Texas tycoon."

"So long ago."

She shed the robe and helped him peel off his skinsuit. He was tenderly tentative in the beginning, not sure she was really well recovered, but her ravenous eagerness convinced him. They forgot the fever and all the hazards of Mars until they heard Barova calling on the interphone to say that she had the lander ready to return.

"Won't you take me?" she begged again. "Don't you think I'm able?"

"Very able!" He laughed. "But Commander Lavrin doesn't need another act of mutiny."

She pulled him down again to her fever-scented sheets, and then he had to go. She got into her skinsuit and came with him to the dock. They found Barova waiting there.

"Kelligan, you're clear to go." Again he caught a fleeting glint of something feral in her smile. "Before you take off, I have news for you to take Commander Lavrin. Something that should interest you."

She paused as if to tantalize him.

"Your father has agreed to finance Marty Gorley's Mars ConQuest. And Marty says the *Nergal* will be coming out with supplies and more volunteers, two years from now."

The two stood together when he left them. Jayne's lips

moved in a silent farewell. He saw tears in her eyes. Barova waved, smiling as if for a camera till the closing air lock shut them off.

♂

On the long flight down, he relived all he knew of Jayne. The first exciting glimpse of her dancing with Lavrin at the graduation ball. The race on the Moon, when she beat him in. The pain of that bungled landing. Their days alone afterward, when she carried him out of the desert and nursed him through the fever.

Napping when he could, he had a dream of her and Barova. An actual wolf in the dream, green-eyed and gaunt, Barova was hungry because the food supplies were gone, and hunting her through the empty ship. He woke cold and trembling, half angry with himself for his hatred of Barova.

After all, she must feel desperate. Afraid of the fever, trapped aboard the ship, two years and more away from the acclaim she thought her science would earn. If she expected any great rewards from Marty for whatever help she gave him—she didn't know Marty. He could almost pity her.

Perhaps Jayne could bring some reason to her.

Mars spun under him, nightside and dayside. Coming out of the dark on his last circuit of the planet, he picked up the beep of the radio beacon and found the first sunlight on the tall volcanic cones. They slid behind. The endless black-shadowed slash of Marineris swam into view. Searching for the crater ridge where the *Magellan* had fallen, he met a frowning wall instead.

Dust.

A boiling dun-colored barrier, it blotted out the coral-hazed horizon and towered to the top of the atmosphere.

It turned the morning sun a baleful red and hid the ridge and the basin floor where he had to land.

"Colon to Magellan." He tried the radio. "Landmarks all obscured. I need a homing beacon."

All he heard was a storm of static.

"Colon to Magellan." He tried again. "On landing leg. Tanks near empty. Coming in."

23

Gardens

"Gardens in the Sky," title of promotional brochure from Mars ConQuest, Inc. It pictures a lush garden city under a crystal dome standing on a red-cragged hill. The text invites readers to "take stock in paradise!" The par value of preferred shares is high, ten thousand American dollars, but each certificate is also a passport identifying the registered owner as a citizen of Mars.

Edna slept poorly now. She was already half awake that morning when Maria tiptoed in to whisper the news. It brought her trembling downstairs in a pink silk robe to see the morning paper. Silently, Kelligan showed her the bold headline.

MARSMAN FOUND!

"Dear Hew!" The paper quivered in her blue-veined hand. "I've prayed so to keep him safe!"

"Safe?" he muttered. "You know he'll never be safe."

"It says he's alive. He's seen Mars now. He'll come back home."

"You're crazy, Edie, if you think he ever will." The paper slid out of her fingers, and he leaned to pick it up. "You've let his harebrained stunts keep you sick too long. Mars is where he wants to be, even if he dies there."

"I pray the Lord to bring him home."

She had come down without her glasses, and she begged to know what the paper said. He grunted and read the story. Radio bulletins received from Mars reported that the venturesome astronaut son of Fort Worth industrialist Austin Kelligan, thought to have been lost in the first attempted landing on Mars, had been discovered safe with his crewmate in the wreck of his lander.

"Alive today." Kelligan shrugged and gestured for Roberto to pour hot water for her tea. "Likely not tomorrow. Better quit your fretting, Edie. He's gone for good."

"Don't—" She stared at him, pale eyes pleading. "Don't say that."

He grunted and let Roberto refill his coffee cup. A sad time for her. She had already abandoned her garden and quit her bridge group. She kept Houston's old room like a shrine to some saint, with his Aggie pennant still on the wall. He sometimes found her on her knees beside the empty bed, whispering prayers.

"Austin." She raised her voice, and a glint shone in her watery eyes. "If you're giving Hew up for dead, why are you putting all that money into Marty's scheme to send the rescue ship?"

"Huh?" The ghost of a smile appeared and vanished. "The funds aren't committed yet. If I do commit, it will be because I expect to get every penny back." He frowned. "Really, Edie, it's no use fretting. Even if the *Nergal* does get to Mars, it will never bring him home."

♂

LeeAnn had her own part-time secretary now, Anora Karp, the same hearty little woman who had managed her father's office before he retired. Anora asked her about the baby when she came in that morning and told her that Mr. Kelligan wanted her with him for a meeting with the Gorleys.

They found Lucina already rattling pots and cups in the kitchen alcove. Sitting at the big table beneath the red-splashed priest, Marty sported a maroon velour jacket and a huge diamond blazing on his wide floral tie. He darted a glance at LeeAnn's body and turned affably to Kelligan.

"Morning, Senator. Thanks for coming in."

"Got a problem?"

"With your bankers, sir." He looked at his mother, waiting for her approving smile. "They're dragging their feet on the investments you agreed to. Demanding facts that are none of their business and guarantees we can't give. They want their own directors on the board."

"So?" Kelligan shrugged. "Common sense."

"They're killing us, sir. Asking awkward questions. Up in arms now over that our little scam about the lost lander—"

"Scam?"

"Our tragic tale about the *Magellan,* sir." Marty grinned. "The report our PR people put out that it was missing with Mr. Houston and that girl aboard."

"All that—a damned lie?"

"Business, sir. Very good business."

"You let me believe—" Red in the face, Kelligan glowered. "You let Edna believe her son was down on Mars? Probably dead?"

"Sorry, sir, but we had to let the media believe." Marty nodded smugly. "They did. After that disaster report, we were able to pick up the last holdout options for next to nothing.

"But the rescue can ruin us now." His shiny head shook with seeming regret. "It's got sellers unhappy and rival bidders screaming. Which means we've got to close a lot of deals while we can. That's why I'm here, sir. Trusting you to talk some sense into your bankers before they murder us."

♂

Lucina had stood listening. They both looked up at her as she came around the table now, pouring coffee and hot milk, Marty with a question on his sweat-bright face. He murmured something to her that Kelligan didn't catch.

"Hijo mio!" Nodding fondly, she filled his cup and came around to Kelligan. Though she fought to keep her figure that of the dark enchantress he had found in Mexico, her smile was no longer so entrancing as he recalled it. Her vivid lips were often pouted now, the lines around her eyes drawn harder.

"Seguro que sí, Señor." Even her voice was sharper now, often impatiently strident, yet in spite of everything he sometimes itched for the woman she had been. "I have examined the documents and spoken to the bankers. I mix margaritas for Martin's new associates when they are here in the city. Perhaps they know little of Mars, but they are men of knowledge and shrewdness."

"Maybe too much shrewdness." Kelligan swung abruptly back to Marty. "Listen, kid, let's get this straight."

Marty flushed at the word. "Sir?"

"You've got your signals mixed. You've been saying the expedition really was in trouble. When I heard from Commander Lavrin and Miss Kolvos, they'd been terribly discouraged—"

"Sure they had. Nobody promised Mars would be a pushover. Mr. Houston and the girl were really out of touch, but things were never so black as we let the media believe."

"You lied about them? Why?"

"A hard word, sir." Marty shook his head. "Barova calls it media management. We report what we need to put the spin we need on world opinion."

"If Sam and Miss Ryan never were in trouble, I say you lied."

"Call it what you please." Marty shrugged. "We never knew of any actual trouble, but our contacts through Farside were broken. And of course Mr. Houston and the girl had more to do than hang on a radiophone. At least you should be grateful now to know they're safe."

"Can you really call it safe?"

"They say they're all okay. Commander Lavrin assures us that the whole expedition can now land as planned."

He paused to sip his coffee, muddy eyes squinting at LeeAnn and again at Kelligan.

"That's if we get the funding, sir. If we get Mars Con-Quest afloat. If we're able to complete the *Nergal* and get the relief expedition off the ground. It all depends on you. What about it, sir?"

"I must see my bankers."

"Marty—" LeeAnn pushed her coffee aside. "I've a question."

"Fire away, Miss Halloran." He gave her an ingratiating grin. "Anything you want."

"That virus in the Mars dust? Houston told me what it did to poor Mr. White. I've been afraid—"

"No wonder, Miss Halloran!" He laughed at her dread. "An ugly accident, but all for the best."

"For the best?" She searched his sweat-bright face. "Hew wouldn't talk about it, but I know he was uneasy—"

"Of course he was. But did he tell you White was giving blood to make a vaccine? The whole crew had their shots before the takeoff. The good news that is the vaccine works. Mr. Houston and the girl report they never felt better. Not even a cold in the crew, Lavrin says, since they left the Earth."

His mother had settled in the chair beside him, and he glanced at her as if for inspiration.

"No question, Senator." He wiped a handkerchief across his wet face and swung back to Kelligan. "Mars is ours, if we want it. A penny on the dollar! Your penny can buy Farside to keep us in contact with Mars. Complete the *Nergal* and send out the relief expedition. Buy the planet for us and pay you billions back."

He shrugged, murky eyes shifting to LeeAnn and back again to Kelligan.

"Do we get the penny, sir?"

24

Alien Air

Mars once had a far thicker atmosphere, now largely lost to space. What remains is nearly all unbreathable carbon dioxide, its pressure too low for unprotected life or even liquid water to exist. Yet the winds are sometimes violent, and savage dust storms sweep the planet.

He came down blind.

The great volcanic peaks had dissolved in the dust, gone with the endless ragged slash of Marineris and the cratered ridge where the *Magellan* had crashed. Roiling yellow-brown clouds had blotted out the basin floor.

"In a way," he muttered to himself, "you can't blame Barova."

All he had was the beacon's feeble beep. He followed that down through battering winds that ripped away the rocket plume. 400 meters, the altimeter read. 200. 100.

His breath stopped, but at last the white target cross broke into view. A final burst hid it again. A jolt. A creak of the struts.

And he was safely down.

The rocket silent, the wind's shriek came faintly through the hull. Peering through the heat shield, he looked for the mirror film they had stretched to shelter the supplies. It was gone, but shadows loomed through the dust. The little stack of crates and cartons, the drill and the boiler, the small red mound that marked the excavation for the habitat. All abandoned to the storm.

He tried the radio again, calling the *Magellan,* and again he heard no response. Wondering, he could only stay aboard. He had no rover, and the ridge was a dozen kilometers way, too far to walk in pressure gear.

The dust, anyhow, was cruel to pressure suits, as it was to everything mechanical. It clung to surfaces, covering faceplates and windows. It got into joints and bearings to lock or grind them out. It invaded the suits, carrying the paralife virus into human lungs.

This should have been early morning, the small red sun rising through red-gold haze, but no real day had dawned. The sky was a murky brown. Watching a corner of the white plastic marker flapping in the wind, he wondered if it would go, and wondered what harm the storm had done. He thought of Jayne, happy she was still safe on the ship, even with Barova. He ate a ration pack and updated the lander's log and tried the dead radio and napped in his seat and watched the wind again.

When the brown dusk thickened to drown the shadow shapes around him, he knew night had fallen. The wind still shrieked outside the hull, and still he got only a rattle of static when he tried the radio. He found a narrow space in the cargo hold where he could do sit-ups and push-ups, ate another ration pack, and slept in his seat.

♂

By morning, the weather front was gone. The wind's howl had died and the plastic marker had stopped flapping. The sky was still a sullen dun, stabbed with dim red disk of the sun. The crater ridge was only a dim brown outline against darker brown, but at last he found a faint gray fleck creeping below it, Ram and Lavrin on a rover, when he could make them out. He got into his pressure gear and went out to hail them.

"Houston?" Lavrin answered with a tight-voiced question. "Have you seen Kim Lo?"

She was missing.

"The storm caught her." Ram's voice was sick with foreboding. "She'd gone out early that morning to open a new clay pit for Lisa. Arkady and I came down later with the rock drill—there's a boulder we'll have to blast out of the excavation. Halfway here, we met the storm front rolling out of the west."

"I saw it from space," Houston said. "Never imagined anything so rough."

"We had to turn back," Lavrin went on. "Called Kim from the lander. She's been down in her clay pit. Hadn't seen the storm. I told her to come in. She answered that she was on her way—and the radio died."

"It was on sun power." Ram was still hoarse from the fever. "We'd borrowed the batteries for the beacon. Wind blew the solar panels away."

"Kim never got back?"

"Never." Lavrin's body seemed to sag, even in the stiff and bulky suit. "Ram and I searched yesterday, or tried to. Blind in the dust, but we got as far as the clay pit. She wasn't there. No trail we could follow. Not a trace when we circled the pit. Finally had to come back, just to save ourselves."

"She'd been losing sleep, looking after me." Ram's rusty voice. "And of course she'd breathed the dust. She had a coughing spell that morning before she got into her gear. I'm afraid—" Emotion caught his voice. "Afraid for her now."

"Two days." He heard the dread in Lavrin's voice. "And she had no spare power cell or filter for her air unit. They're awkward to carry, and she said she'd never need them. We're all afraid."

"Ram?" he called. "Won't you let me go in your place?"

"I'm well enough." A raspy croak. "Good of you, Hew, but we're on our way."

They drove north along the wheel tracks toward the new pit. He watched until they vanished in the murk. Feeling a cold unease, he remembered the brief life story Kim Lo had told him on the flight down, and her own bright vision of a new Asia Island afloat on this sea of yellow dunes.

Perhaps, just perhaps, she was still alive.

Afraid to hope, he had to remind himself that she had been a volunteer. Mars would never be easy, and the job must go on. Stirring at last to inspect the site, he found no major damage. Savage as the storm had been, the Martian winds had less force than those of Earth.

Whatever the cost, the job must go on. He moved the drill to sink another hole into the permafrost, heated the boiler, and started another trickle of water through the separator and the hoses into the lander's tanks.

He felt a throb of hope when he saw two rovers creeping back out of the dust, but it died when he couldn't see Kim. Ram drove on past him, with only a stiff Corps salute. Lavrin stopped, sweat-streaked face pale in his helmet.

"No Kim." His voice was tired and flat. "Only her rover, where she's left it stuck in the lee of a dune a few kilometers beyond the pit. She must have walked away, already sick, Ram thinks. Maybe out of her head. Wind erased her tracks."

"No chance?"

"None." He heard Lavrin's heavy sigh. "She couldn't have lasted through yesterday. Ram finally agreed we had to give up. Himself—" Lavrin's voice fell. "So sick he had to quit."

Lavrin drove on, and he stood staring past the little rover into the dust-brown sky, remembering Kim on the flight down to Mars, so young and strong and bright, so eager for the future. He ached for her aged father, waiting back on Asia Island for news that would never come.

Was Mars too tough?

He caught his breath and set his jaw. She hadn't come to quit. Nobody had—except perhaps Hellman and Barova. With a shrug against that bitter mood, he plodded back to the pump and the separator and kept them going till cold and darkness stopped him. He ate a ration pack and updated the electronic log. Trying to sleep in the pilot seat, he dreamed Kim was still alive, lost and wandering through the savage night. Somehow in the dream she changed to Jayne. Afraid for her, he didn't sleep again.

Next morning the four came back on the rovers, Lavrin and Hellman, Ram and Lisa. The replacement computer had been installed, Lavrin said. He and Hellman had winched the *Magellan* off the cliff, to stand upright for takeoff. The fusion engine was running again, powering everything.

"Except the lander engine." He turned to frown through the haze toward the crater ridge. "We've welded the damaged nozzle. There's no way to test it except to try a takeoff. That won't be till we refill the tanks."

Lisa drove her rover back to the new pit for another load of clay. Hellman ran the mill and press, molding

brick. Lavrin blasted the stubborn boulder into fragments he could move with the power shovel. Ram
worked an hour, stacking sun-dried brick to build the
electric kiln till a spell of coughing stopped him. Houston
wanted to bring him aboard the *Colon,* but he refused.

"I'll be okay," he kept insisting. "When I can breathe
again."

He lay beside his stack of brick, gasping for breath, till
Lisa came back with her load of clay. Lavrin sent her to
carry him back to the *Magellan* on her rover. She returned looking troubled.

"Fever again," she said. "And he'd vomited. I got him
out of the suit and cleaned him up. He still says he'll be
okay. I hope so." Tension slowed her voice. "I wish we
knew more. All we've got is hope."

Next day, and the next, they kept him aboard.

"He misses Kim," Lisa said. "They'd been together
since they qualified for the Corps. I'm afraid his spirit
died with her."

When the tanks were full again, Houston lifted the
Colon out of the thinning dust toward the mother ship.

♂

Watching the storm from the *Ares,* Jayne and Barova
were dismayed when the radio died. Jayne kept her consternation silent.

"No great surprise." Barova talked, her evident concern mixed with something almost self-complacent. "But
I won't say I told you so."

Jayne listened without comment; she didn't want to
fight.

"It does go to show," Barova added. "Mars is too
much for us. If we can just get back with our disks and
records, that's the best I hope for."

After days of waiting, the radio came alive with Houston's call from the climbing *Colon.* Jayne tried to hug him in his suit when he came through the lock, but he waved her back.

"This damned dust!" he warned her. "Sticks to everything."

Out of the suit, showered and shaved again, he opened his arms for her.

"I'm good as new!" she said. "I've called the commander, and I'm going back with you."

With him in her cabin, she stripped bare to show him that the fever spots were gone. For a few precious hours, they forgot—or tried to forget—the virus and the dust and all the hazards of Mars. He had to stifle a curse when he heard Barova on the intercom, calling to say the water load was all transferred.

Jayne came aboard with him, and the hours of the flight down to Mars were a honeymoon in space. She was lovely. She loved him. They were going to be together on the world they'd longed for. If uncertainties waited ahead, life was never certain anywhere. Swinging around the planet, through racing days and nights, they talked of their families and shared their lives.

"An only child, I grew up lonely," she told him. "At Weigel High, back in Lakefield, I was a female nerd." She grinned at herself. "Proud to be at the top of the class, but I cried when nobody asked me to the senior prom."

"I was the rich kid." He chuckled with her. "Nobody knew I had to mow the lawn to earn three dollars a week to spend as I pleased. I used to skip lunch to save for a book or a movie or some gadget I wanted. My nickname got to be Tightwad."

"I never imagined." She shook her head and reached to touch his shoulder. "I had four dollars a week—at least when my father paid it."

They talked of instructors they had loved or hated in

the Corps, of friends washed out of school, of hard tests and long field trips, of training on the Moon and the final race to Farside. Wistful recollections, till the flight out of the dark on the landing leg jolted them back into hard reality.

Into the dust.

On their first descent, Mars had been an enchanting wonderland, its never-trodden crater fields and lava plains a flow of color and shadow as the sunlight shifted, but now a yellow-brown blanket covered it all, with only the great volcanos visible. Diving, they followed the beacon, seeing only golden haze above and white steam below till the white plastic cross loomed dimly through it, nearly too near.

Lavrin met them when they came off the lander.

"Welcome home," he called. "All okay."

♂

Not quite okay. Lisa had stayed on the *Magellan,* wheezing and aching from her own bout of fever. Ram was finishing the kiln to fire the first batch of brick. He said he was well again, but Houston heard him coughing. Still untouched by the virus, Hellman had been running the drill and boiler and osmotic separator.

"Water mass for the *Ares,*" Lavrin said. "Which creates another problem. We'll have to haul it up there on a rover. That means we'll have to build a road."

Eager to work, Jayne went with Ram to dig another load of clay and learned to run the mill and press. The dust slowly cleared, until at last the zenith turned purple again.

The *Colon* loaded again, Houston flew it back to the mother craft. Barova met him at the lock in an aura of charm and perfume. Jittery, she urged him toward the galley.

"Coffee, dear? It's ready for you. I'm dying for news. Nothing more from Earth, I don't know why. I've spoken with Otto since the radio is fixed, but he's never very social. Arkady's huffy. Won't call back."

"We've work to do," he said. "Not much time for talk."

"I know. I really do. And Hew—" He heard an anxious quaver in her voice. "I hope you understand my own priorities."

"I'm afraid I do."

Her fair skin flushed, but she held her smile while her long eyes measured him. He thought she was about to ask him into her berth. To help her make up her mind, he refused a second cup of coffee and offered to help transfer his cargo.

"I'll do it." She stiffened. "Get your shower."

He got his shower and took the lander back down to Mars.

♂

Ram was still recovering when he landed, but Lisa was very ill. Lavrin had finished cutting the new road up the ridge. Hellman had begun refueling the *Magellan.* Jayne was happily making brick, happier to come aboard the *Colon* to share ration packs and spend the nights with him.

"News from Earth!" was Barova's greeting when he got back to the *Ares* with another load of water. "You can tell Arkady I haven't let the expedition down. Marty Gorley's a great friend of mine since I met him at Shangri-La. I've been transmitting reports to him when I could get through Farside, and he's giving me an executive position with Mars ConQuest."

She saw his puzzlement.

"I mean now." She had a air of triumph. "We're

mounting a really slick professional promotion, with Mars citizenship as a bonus for every investor. I'm using our files to produce commercial spots and disks right here on the ship. Your own disks of Coprates made one of the best.

"Arkady calls me insubordinate." She made a quick grimace. "Just because I won't leave the ship. I don't intend to. I want you to urge him to join us. If Marty's Mars ConQuest gets off the ground, he can finish the *Nergal* and mount a relief expedition. If not—"

Her fine shoulders lifted.

"Tough talk."

"Tough times," she said. "But I want to get home alive."

♂

On Mars again, he delivered her message.

"So?" Lavrin shrugged, his blue eyes bleak. "I expected better of her. I'm not sure just what she wants, but we're too few to fight. For now at least we need her where she is, to keep the ship alive and in contact with Earth."

Hellman had the *Magellan* refueled by then, though only lightly loaded. He lifted it safely off the crater lip and took it up to the mother ship. Barova, Houston thought, would be well pleased to see him.

With the power shovel, Ram and Lavrin had dug a pit for the habitat. They were laying brick now to wall the first small cell, which would be the entry lock.

"Testing everything," Lavrin said. "The brick. The mix of dust and separator brine we're using for mortar. The plastic liner film and wire reinforcement to hold air pressure."

Houston had the *Colon* loaded again by the time Hellman brought back the *Magellan*. They took turns in flight, the water processor running steadily. Ram was insisting by then that he was fit as ever, and Lisa was recovering, already well enough to run the power shovel, digging clay.

That first cell completed and sealed, they tested it with fifteen pounds of the native atmosphere. When it held, they set up the catalytic regenerators to fill it again with a mix of oxygen from carbon dioxide and argon and nitrogen from the Martian air. Ram and Lavrin moved in and began laying brick for a larger cell, to be the first greenhouse.

They had found no sand to make transparent glass, and it would be lit with fusion-powered lamps. Leaving its air rich with the carbon dioxide the plants would need, they sterilized Martian dust for soil, seeded it with benign bacteria and brought purified water from the separator. When it was ready, they hopefully planted tomatoes, potatoes, and test samples of the hybrid fruits and grains and vegetables the Authority experts had bred for Mars.

Back from one more flight, he saw the billowing steam cloud of Hellman's takeoff a few minutes before he landed. Jayne met him when he came off the lander, looking well and happy when he could see her face.

"Hew! I'm so glad to see you home!" Her voice was bright and her face looked well and happy when he could see it through the faceplate. "You know," she added, "Mars is really beginning to feel like home."

Seed had sprouted in the greenhouse, she told him, and young plants were thriving. Ram and Lavrin had sealed and tested another habitat cell, with a third for the livestock already begun. Lisa had gone on a rover to search the buried shore of the ancient sea for sand that might make transparent glass.

She returned late that afternoon, with no sand in the little cart the rover pulled. Instead, she had Kim Lo's body, frozen hard in her pressure suit. She parked near his lander, her voice a hollow murmur in his helmet.

"Found her half-buried by the storm. Must have wandered most of the night to get where she was, blind in the dust and already sick with the fever."

They dug a grave in dry clay and gathered around her body, still in the suit and lying on the cart. Lavrin read a short formal service, and they all spoke briefly of what she had been to them. Lisa knew her father's address on Asia Island, and Lavrin called Barova with a message for him. Ram set up a short length of drill stem for a marker, with a welded crossbar that bore her name and the date and a single word, "Pioneer."

Houston spent the next three days filling his lander's tanks, but he never took off. He was waiting for Hellman, and Hellman never returned.

25

Motion

Isaac Newton's laws of motion govern everything from falling pins to rockets in flight and planets in orbit. First law: motion in a straight line continues until changed by an acting force. Second law: the change is proportional to the force and the time it acts. Third law: every action has an equal and opposite reaction.

Barova was hungry for Hellman when he arrived with his last load of water mass. She had first met him when she came to stay with an aunt in Berlin during a troubled time in Russia, and they had been occasional lovers in the Corps. A social misfit before she taught him to bathe twice a day and keep himself doused with cologne, he had become an apt student in the arts of sex. And she, expert at love but indifferent at math, had found him a useful tutor.

Now, after three vigorous and sweaty hours, she slid out of her berth and evaded his black-haired arms when he reached for her again.

"Gut! Schon gut!" she breathed. "But now our time has come."

"Nein!" They had spoken German in the Bavarian training camp where she first tempted him to break the Corps rules of conduct. "Not yet!" He looked at his watch. "Though they are ready for the first livestock—"

"Let them wait!"

"Liebling, they're all on edge since Lo was lost. If I'm late—"

"Otto, you aren't going back."

He stared at her, his penis sagging.

"We're flying home to Earth."

"In two years, perhaps." He laughed at her. "If the expedition survives. If we can refuel the ship—"

"We're departing at once."

"Are you mad?"

"Going mad, shut up here on board." She shrugged. "Though not quite so insane as the fools below us on the planet."

"You want to abandon the expedition?" He stood over her, a thick-muscled and odorous tower, shaking his head in unbelief. "When we still have so much essential cargo aboard? The commander seems willing to leave you here to care for the ship, but he wants a pig and a coop of chickens now—"

"Unfortunate." She sat up on the edge of the berth, reaching to prod his black-furred stomach with a red-nailed forefinger and smiling when his penis stirred again. "But cannot let you risk another landing. Lavrin might keep you."

"Don't you know?" He stared into her tantalizing smile. "We're already far past opposition. The return window's gone."

"So Lavrin assumes." She shrugged, an enchanting flow of perfect flesh. "We must surprise him."

"Irina, you are sometimes a child and always adorable." He eyed her white body, his tone fondly tolerant. "But we must accept the laws of the universe. Helium propulsion may be a great advance, but it is not miraculous. *Ares* cannot return until our next window—"

"Two more years in this dreadful prison!"

"A kinder life, Irina, than they're enduring down on Mars."

"We're going home." She gestured to sweep aside his consternation. "You're the astronaut. Make an orbit to take us there."

"I can't unmake the laws of motion." His penis hung limp, but his own voice lifted. "The ship has too much mass and too little—"

"I'm not a total *Dummkopf*." She smiled again, too sweetly. "There must be fuel enough, from all the water you and Kelligan have brought. With only the two of us aboard, the mass will be quite small." No longer flirtatious, she reached for a robe. "Secure your lander and write a new pilot program to take us back to low Earth orbit—leaving at once."

"I'll do the math just to please you." Grudgingly, he nodded. "But I know the answer."

♂

She showered and perfumed herself again, and waited for him in her cabin, still in the filmy robe. Science had made Hellman a cautious skeptic, but she knew how to move him.

"You are the *Dummkopf*." He came back to thrust a flimsy yellow printout at her, an undertone of trouble in his fondly teasing voice. "The laws of Newton forbid any return departure now. Under penalty of death."

"So?" She shrugged. "We shall appeal."

"Irina, you never change." He shook his head in mild reproof. "The equations allow no appeal."

"Then our mass must be reduced. The livestock can go. And whatever cargo is still aboard—there's the standby power plant, and all that metallurgical equipment Lavrin said he wasn't ready for."

"Not enough." Hellman shook his head. "I made a trial routine for the empty ship, and still we do not overtake the Earth."

"Then some of the ship must go." Her eyes fixed on him, as if he might be needless mass. "Every gram we can live without."

He shrank from her eyes, slowly nodding.

"If we were really crazy," he muttered reluctantly. "The *Ares* was assembled in orbit from prefabricated modules. Some sections, perhaps, are no longer essential. The cargo bays. Most of the centrifugal modules. Livestock cages, living quarters, common room, the gym. The magnets for the torus. I suppose we could survive here in the dome, though at some risk from radiation—"

"Get back to the computer." She cut him off. "You'll have mass figures for the modules. Make us an orbit for the naked frame. The rocket engine and fuel for it, food and air for us."

"If you're that desperate—"

"*Liebling,* we are desperate together." Her bare arms caught him for a moment. "I know you'll get us home."

"If we live—"

"If we die—" She drew him closer. "We die together."

♂

Hellman was back in an hour, his dark face glum. Her opening arms dropped again when he shook his head.

"The verdict?"

"We do get back." He grinned bleakly. "The only possible transfer orbit will take us within a few hundred thousand kilometers of Earth, but we pass on by at twenty kilometers a second. No mass left to brake that velocity."

"Can't we brake in the atmosphere? As we've been doing here?"

"The *Ares* is not titanium. Air friction would burn it up."

"Let it burn." She shrugged. "We can fly the lander down."

"We'll have no lander. It must be jettisoned, with everything else."

"Then Gorley must send one to meet us and take us off."

"Why so frantic, my dear?" He was scanning her body, and she straightened to lift her perfect breasts. "If you don't want to risk the surface, we might report a problem with the lander and stay here together—"

"For two years?"

"Better, I think, than a dozen months on the bare skeleton of the ship, trying to nurse it home. We can let Kelligan come in the other lander for the livestock and—"

"Kelligan's against us." She stiffened, moving with the insolent grace of a hunting leopard. "An enemy, if he ever suspects. I have seen distrust on his face. I don't want him aboard again."

"Irina, think about it." He sat down beside her. "Suppose we do reach Earth alive? People will know we deserted the expedition. What kind of a future is that?"

"Otto, you fret too much." Her smile seemed serene. "I can work with Gorley. After we depart, those idiots below us will have no contact with anybody. We can report whatever we please."

He sat silent, eyeing her as if she had been a stranger.

"Am I a *Dummkopf?*" She laughed at him. "We can invent any fate we like for Lavrin and his crew."

"Except survival." He nodded, rather grimly. "Left there alone, without the livestock and equipment—"

"I feel for them, but they asked for what they have. If you wish to help them, think what our reports can do. Make them heroes. The martyrs of Mars! Our story can simply be that Lavrin sent us home to for supplies and medications. Sadly, too late."

"Irina—" He paused to eye her again. "I'm glad you are my friend."

"Trust me, Otto." She leaned toward him, smiling tenderly. "If you have doubts, let me tell you more about Marty Gorley and Mars ConQuest."

"But, Irina—"

Her white arms had opened, and she let him pull her back into the soiled and odorous sheets.

♂

She was lovely, eager, skillful. Her perfume enveloped him. Yet, even in her hot embrace, misgivings killed his libido.

"Sorry," he muttered, sprawled on the tangled sheets beside her. "But it's such a dreadful thing. Really, Irina, we can't abandon Lavrin and Lisa and the rest."

"I might worship them, but I know Marty Gorley." She smiled, remembering. "A dear friend, since our first night together at Shangri-La. We can trust him because he must trust us. He hasn't been to Mars."

"Call him. I want his promise to rescue—"

"You want more delay? Till we can reach Farside? Till engineers complete the link? Till he finds time to talk and the engineers get his voice back to us? With Earth farther off every hour?"

"We'll wait as long as it takes, Irina." Sternly, he

scowled at her nude perfection. "Without an understanding with him, I won't let you throw our lives away."

She studied him, with a slow and tantalizing smile.

"Always the cautious scientist. That's why I need you with me, *Liebling.*"

She peeled off the thin red robe and drew him into her berth.

♂

Waiting for Gorley, they heard instead from Lavrin.

"Calling *Ares!* Calling *Magellan!*" His hoarse and anxious voice came from the *Colon,* still sitting on the pad. "Are you in trouble? Please report your situation. With no more delay."

Hellman asked her uneasily, "What can we say?"

"Nothing." Barova shrugged, unconcerned. "They'll guess the truth soon enough."

Lavrin called again, and still again. If they were sick with the virus, if there had been an accident, if perhaps the *Magellan* had failed to reach the dock, the *Colon* would be on the way with help.

"If you plan mutiny," he urged them, "don't do it. Your return window has already closed. You can't get home. Even if you could, you'd arrive in disgrace. The murderers of Mars! Come back to duty, and we can all survive."

"Nothing they can do," Barova said.

When Lavrin begged for the livestock and equipment still aboard, Hellman wavered.

"They are friends!" he muttered. "The best I ever had—"

"Otto, please." She slipped her arms around him. "We're not wicked. Merely intelligent. If we die here, all our precious science is lost. If we get it safely home, it survives forever. Our own names with it!"

She kissed him, and he made no reply.

Cautiously, however, Hellman watched the landing site whenever he could. The *Colon* and the habitat were too far and small for the telescope to see, but before any message had come back from Gorley, he saw a faint white plume that stretched for a few minutes across that scrap of tawny desert out toward the *Ares* before it dissolved in the wind.

"Colon," he warned her. "Coming out after us."

26

Anomaly

Natural laws prevail. The cosmos seems uniform, all perhaps resulting from a single Big Bang. Observing it, science has woven a theory of everything—always under revision when some unpredicted anomaly fails to fit that universal pattern.

The *Ares* was visible at night, a white star racing from west to east against the creeping constellations. Houston and Lavrin sat together till dawn aboard the *Colon,* tracking that star with the radio antenna, calling the ship, calling and calling again.

Receiving no reply.

"Sickness?" Lavrin turned uneasily to him when daylight had erased the star. "From the virus?"

"Mutiny, more likely."

"More likely." Bleakly, Lavrin nodded. "Otto's been Irina's lover—or madly jealous when she had somebody else—ever since they joined the Corps."

"If they hold the ship—"

"Disaster." Behind the flowing beard, Lavrin's jaw set

hard. "We've got to keep it if we can. I'm going out there."

"Do you expect a fight?"

"Perhaps." Tight-lipped, he scowled through the heat shield into the crimson east. "Though we've no weapons and they should have none. Irina's the leader. Headstrong and resourceful. I don't know that to expect."

"I'm your pilot, sir."

They were off in an hour, climbing through the lingering yellow haze. When the stars burst into view above the atmosphere, they found the bright white point of the ship and called again. Again with no response—

Until a sudden sunlit plume exploded behind it.

"Rocket steam!" Houston whispered. "They're climbing out of orbit."

"Leaving us marooned."

"Shall we follow—"

With a grimly silent headshake, Lavrin beckoned him to turn back toward Mars.

♂

At the habitat, he gathered them in the bare, white-walled cell they had readied for the pigs and chickens. The air was icy cold. Fans whirred softly in the air unit above them, but it had not yet cleared the bitter stink of sealant spray. Ram coughed when he breathed it, and Lisa slid her arm protectively around him.

Looking at them, Houston felt a wave of sympathy.

Ram had come from the brickyard, an ocher streak of dust across his jaw. Sweat stained his blue skinsuit and matted his dark hair flat. Ignoring Lisa, he stood hunched against the chill, his body sagging forward as if even the gravity of Mars had become a burden. His hollow eyes were blankly fixed on Lavrin, and Houston saw the Commander's lips pressed white with concern.

Kim Lo's loss had hit him harder than the fever.

"Five of us left." Hardly needing seats here, they stood together on the empty floor. "Now on our own." Turning from Ram to the others, Lavrin somehow managed a stiff little smile. "The original Martians."

"So long as we live," Ram muttered bitterly.

"We may die." Lavrin shrugged and paused to scan their faces, his voice oddly gentle. "We may not. For now at least, we've been abandoned. Our friends have lifted the ship out of parking orbit, but perhaps not far. They'll have to wait a year and more for any possible return window. Time enough to think better of what they've done."

"I know Barova." Ram looked bleaker. "She won't be back."

"Perhaps she won't." Lavrin swung calmly to the others. "We did need her and Hellman. Certainly needed the ship and all that's still aboard. But we came prepared for the unexpected. We'll carry on."

Jayne and Lisa were nodding, with murmurs of assent, but Ram stumbled forward, bleakly scowling.

"How?"

"Really, Ram, we can cope," Lavrin urged him. "Complete the habitat. Learn to stay alive. Explore as far as we can. Keep good records of all we learn for whoever follows."

"Whoever?" Ram was still hoarse from the fever, his voice a sardonic rasp. "We know Barova. She won't be begging for rescue—not for us."

"So?" Patiently, Lavrin nodded. "We spend the rest of our lives here."

"Which won't take long." Ram spread his empty hands, a hopeless gesture. "A few miserable months—"

"Ram, please!" Lisa caught his arm. "We have to hope."

"And work." Lavrin's voice fell soberly. "Work to

finish the habitat. Work to develop more water. To make glass when we find the right sand. To build a larger greenhouse. We can get to know Mars and record what we learn—which is what we came for. And wait for a break—"

"What break?"

"Maybe none." Lavrin dropped his voice. "Face it, Ram. Nobody promised us milk and honey."

"Sorry, Chief." With a painful little grin, Ram put out his hand. "I'll try to face it."

They all joined hands, silent for a moment, and went back to the tasks of staying alive.

♂

Houston drilled deeper wells, finally into gravel strata that held unfrozen water. On the power shovel, Ram dug a long trench for another greenhouse. A dozen kilometers away, in a pit on what had been the shore of that ancient lake, Lisa found silicon sand that she hoped would make useful glass.

Jayne came back to live with Houston on the *Colon*. Watching the sky at night, they sometimes saw Phobos climbing out of the west, but never the *Ares*. Scanning the radio spectrum, they heard no signal.

"Give it up." One Martian midnight, when his muscles were still aching from a long day in the brickyard, Jayne called Houston away from the console. "They aren't coming back."

"I guess you're right." He paused to study her, and slowly smiled. "You don't seem to mind."

"Why fret?" She caught his hand. "We're alive. And here where we always longed to be."

Following her down the narrow steps into the cargo bay, he felt a sudden surprise at his own contentment. Day by day, they had to battle crisis and disaster. The fever was recurrent, one or another always spotted with it, coughing and weakened. Their dwindling supplies strictly rationed now and the greenhouse only beginning to produce, they were always hungry, often groggy from sickness and punishing toil.

Yet somehow he didn't really mind.

"It's true," he whispered to her as they unrolled the bed they shared. "We're alive. We have Mars. We have each other. While we last—"

"Don't say that!" Her kiss stopped his voice.

One of the crates brought down off the ship contained the experimental laser surveyor he had tested in his training flights around the Moon on the old *Da Gama*. When the second greenhouse was finished, Lavrin had them install it on the *Colon*.

"Looking for gold?" Still haggard from the fever and grieving for Kim, Ram was bleakly sardonic. "Where would you spend it?"

He saw Jayne's face, and apologized again.

"Forgive me!" Houston saw his tears before he turned away. "I know what we came for. I try to face the fix we're in. I know Kim was never sorry. It's only—only that I can't—"

A sob cut off his voice.

Jayne and Houston did the survey together. She ran the spectrometer while he flew them on a circumpolar orbit that carried them fast through red-glaring day into star-fogged night and swiftly back again. The useful range of the instrument was only forty kilometers. It was more accurate at twenty, and he kept them low.

For him, it was unforgettable adventure. After all his years of dreams and training for the corps, even after dust and fever and defeat, Mars was still a magic panorama, every cliff and crater still exciting as it unrolled below the racing lander. The northern winter was now far advanced, and a heavy haze had spread off the ice cap and down across the vast dune fields around it, but the summer hemisphere blazed flame red by day and lay open by night to the laser bursts from probe.

Jayne seemed entirely well again, and happy as he was with all they were seeing, though with little time to look. Bent over the spectrometer on the nightside legs, she spent most of the daylight time reviewing and recording her results. Only now and then did she steal a moment to share the windows and the telescope with him.

"Otto and Irina?" Flying south through daylight, they had crossed Syrtis Major and the edge of the great Hellas basin. The retreating fringes of the south polar cap swept into view below, mottled now with dust-stained ice and darker rock where Barova had disked dazzling frost. "Running away from all we came to find. How could they?"

"I guess they never knew what we came for."

Her shoulder brushed him when she leaned to see through the heat shield, and he bent against her body, so vitally alive, so good to feel and smell and love. With only a fleeting smile for him, she looked ahead again, her mind still on Mars.

"Wonderland!" she whispered. "Always different, always new. A picture of the planet's history. It lets me imagine the crust cracking to open the Marineris rift, and Olympus exploding."

"The south." His arm went around her, and she settled back against him. "That's what fascinates me. Olympus is new; it must have been erupting in the last billion years. Even the old sea floors are young beside these craters under us. Four billion years since the last of the falling protoplanets made them.

"I get gooseflesh—"

She shivered against his shoulder. Perhaps only to tease him, but she was warmth and life and youth, suddenly more wonderful than planetary science. He took

her in his arms, and for a moment they forgot spectroscopic analysis and all the hazards ahead.

♂

They were three days in orbit, climbing for a few hours
to a safer altitude when they had to sleep. Flying south
over Elysium on the third day, he found her frowning at
her readout monitor.

"Something wrong?"

"Something very odd." Brushing red-gold hair off her
furrowed forehead, she looked up at him. "Maybe a
glitch in the software, though it checks okay. If not—"

She shook her head.

"What's so odd?"

"Readings I can't believe. Readouts from the floor of
one old crater in the oldest of the highlands."

He waited while she bent to squint at the monitor
again.

"Free metals!" Baffled, she shook her head. "Metals
that shouldn't be here, not in the abundance I'm reading.
How they could have gotten here, I can't imagine."

He waited for her to look up.

"Spectra of precious metals." She spoke slowly, half to
herself. "Osmium, iridium, platinum, palladium, gold.
Alloyed with one another, sometimes with a little silver
and copper." She caught her breath. "If you believe the
readout."

"Why not?" He shrugged, frowning at the monitor.
"We don't know what's impossible. Many meteorites do
contain microscopic inclusions of platinum and other
refractory metals."

"And the asteroid that killed the dinosaurs!" Her eyes
widened. "It left a layer of iridium-rich fallout all around
the Earth."

"Didn't Ram report a similar readout? From almost the same spot?"

"Yet it's hard to see how—" She took a long breath, staring at him. "I want you to change our course, to let me run another test."

♂

He took them down to fifteen kilometers on the next nightside leg, and she spent a long time over her readings when they were back in sunlight.

"Hew, it looks—looks real!" She looked up from the monitor with awe in her eyes. "No glitch I can find in the software. "But—" She stared back at the instruments, shaking her head. "How could it be?"

"Hellman's the geologist." Houston frowned. "He laughed at Ram's anomaly."

"Let's look again by daylight."

They waited for the turning planet to bring the crater back into sunlight, and he brought them across it again. Hardly ten kilometers below, it slid by too fast. An age-worn crater ring, a glint of frost left in the shadows, something not frost that shone. He swept it with the telescope while she tried to get it on a video disk. Too soon, it was gone.

She looked hard at him, a silent question in her eyes.

"Bright objects scattered all across the crater—" He straightened from the hooded monitor, rubbing his eyes. "As if from a meteor fall."

"Meteorites?" She shook her head, whispering. "Of precious metals?"

"Solid objects." He shook his head. "They cast shadows. "Something fallen since the crater formed, because they're scattered over the rim and the slopes around it. But I can't believe—" He frowned at the empty blur on the monitor now. "I'd like a closer look."

"Can we touch down to get an actual sample?"

"Not among the boulders." He bit his lip. "I didn't see a level spot."

♂

Back from the splendor of space and the wonder of discovery, they landed back at the habitat, back in dust and hardship and hunger. Ram came from the bricklayer to meet them, moving in his clumsy yellow-dusted pressure suit with the slow, rolling lope that Martian gravity enforced.

"Welcome home to paradise!" He was still hoarse from the fever, and harshly ironic. "Did you find the mother lode?"

"Something, anyhow," Jayne told him. "You'll hear about it."

His mood still bitterly bleak, he recited dismal news. Still no signal from the *Ares*. Lisa's silica sand had too much iron for useful glass, and she had found no flux that would melt it in her experimental furnace. Now she was coughing again, though still trying to work. A fungus was wilting the greenhouse beans. The kiln was cold, a heater coil burned out.

In the habitat, Lisa welcomed them with mugs of hot tea brewed from a mutant maté thriving in the greenhouse, and proudly served the first small ripe tomatoes. Lavrin listened silently to Jayne's report, and wanted to see her video of the crater. A dark rim-wall when they viewed it. A flattened central peak. Scattered flecks of something brighter, blurred a little by the lander's motion.

"Near where you got your own anomaly," he told Ram. "When you flew with Barova."

Ram shrugged and Lavrin turned toward him with a noncommittal grunt.

"I had a better view," Houston said, "through the telescope. The objects do look like meteorites, fused enough to round the edges when they fell. Heated I guess from air friction—the atmosphere must have been thicker then. They lie on the surface or are only partly buried. Perhaps there was more ice then, thick enough to cushion the fall. They do look bright, I don't know why."

"The noble metals don't oxidize." Lavrin peered again at the image on the screen. "Pure enough—if that's possible—they might stay bright."

"Is this fairyland?" Ram demanded. "Or how the hell do you think they got here?"

"I'd like to know." Jayne frowned. "All we have is what we've told you."

"You want to know what it is? I'll say a bug in your software."

"Could be." Houston shrugged. "I'd like to know."

"But we can't risk the lander." Lavrin turned from the screen. Lisa had coughed again, and his troubled glance settled on her. "Not since we have just one—"

"Ironic!" Ram's laugh was a hoarse explosion. "If it really is a treasure field. And Otto and Irina ran away before they knew—"

27

Propulsion

Action equals reaction. Energies must balance. $V^2m = V^2m$ when the V's are velocities and the m's are masses. The propellant mass of the *Ares* was water turned by high-velocity plasma by the fusion of deuterium and helium-3.

Hellman balked when Barova told him to start the engine.

"Must we?" They were in the control dome, floating gravity-free. He caught a holdfast and swung to shake his head uneasily at her. "Can't we still compromise and try to save the expedition?"

"If you wish to die."

She hung poised in the air, a radiant shape in the blue skinsuit, laughing at him. A scientist, a man of method and reason, he distrusted all emotion. Yet, ever since that day when she asked him to picnic with her in the Alpine forest, he had been her eager slave, rejoicing when she wanted him, bitterly enduring all the painful times when she chose to find her fun with some other.

"The *Colon* wasn't built for combat," he tried to argue now. "All they can really hope is to get the animals and the other cargo still aboard. Food, equipment, medical supplies they'll die without. Can't we make some kind of truce?"

"With Arkady?" Her face tightened. "I'm through with him."

"If he gives his word, he'll keep it. We can say I had to stay aboard because of trouble with the *Magellan*. When they get here—"

"I told you." She cut him short. "I won't let them on the ship."

"To save their lives—"

"I think of ours." Her voice changed when she saw the stubborn set of his jaw. "No crisis yet. We've time to talk." She was suddenly bewitching. "Let's drink a toast to Arkady."

In the galley, she mixed stiff drinks from powdered orange juice and Russian vodka she had found in Lavrin's locker. After two rounds of that, and very little talk, she let him strip off her skinsuit and carry her down to her berth. A clumsy lover in the beginning, he had learned what she wanted, and the giving was worship for him, a liberation always from his rigid world of science and now from gnawing guilt.

"Time to think of Arkady." In the midst of his passion, she pushed him abruptly away. "Think what he must be planning if he suspects—and start the engine now!"

He stood over her gaping, caught between lust and anger. She sat up on the berth, laughing at him, maliciously preening her naked loveliness.

"Life with me?" she teased him. "Or death on Mars?"

"You know me too well." He was tipsy from the vodka, his words slow and slurred. His anger contained, he shrugged ruefully. "I have no choice."

"I love your organ of choice." Wickedly, she grinned at his lifting penis. "It guides you right."

His arms were opening for her, but she swayed away.

"Later, *Liebling,* later. Now we must think of finding the optimum transfer orbit back to Earth before our unfriendly friends arrive."

The *Colon* was back in the telescope when he searched

again, its rocket exhaust a faint blue star creeping away from the glaring limb of Mars. It grew. Already two hours in flight, the lander was overtaking them.

♂

He started the helium engine, but tried to balk again when she pressed him to put them on an orbit back to Earth.

"Why so frantic, *Kindlein?*" He was still flushed from the vodka, awkward in free fall when he swung to face her. "We're in love. Here aboard, we have everything—"

"Everything?" Her voice had a sudden edge. "In this hateful prison?"

"Our paradise." He lurched to catch at her arm. "Our own small world, with supplies enough and the splendid universe spread out around—"

"*Liebling,* you're drunk." She evaded his clumsy grasp. "Talking nonsense."

"Sanity, my dear." He blinked at her owlishly. "The nonsense is yours. Refusing to wait for a window. Better just to lift the ship out of Arkady's reach and wait in orbit for the next window—"

"Otto, *bitte!*" She cut him off impatiently, and paused to warm her voice. "Perhaps we are in love, but we don't have years to throw away. I told you about my partner in Mars ConQuest."

"Gorley? Don't you trust him?"

"Trust Marty Gorley?" She snorted. "Better than trust, after those three nights in bed with him at Shangri-La, I understand him."

He flinched from her words.

"When you left me to drink alone?" His hairy fists clenched and opened again, helplessly hanging. "And laughed when I lost a month's pay in that crooked casino?"

"Sorry, Otto." Almost laughing again, she reached to stroke his dark-furred chest. "But you know we were there to serve the Authority."

"That's why you were screwing—"

"For Mars." Innocently, she smiled. "Gorley was always a louse. Stupid in bed and apologetic for his money—said he was only a hired hand of Kelligan's. Drank too much and yammered too much about his darling mother. Hinting about some scheme of theirs to take the resort hotel away from old Kelligan. A thief and a fool—though he has a kind of cunning."

"So why your big deal with him?"

"The fact is he and his mother are more than any hired hands. I got him to talk more than he meant to. Tales of graft in the Authority and rumors it was headed for trouble. He was already planning Mars ConQuest, though then it was meant to be only a scam. When my own turn came, I told him how we could take over Mars.

"And we'll own it now."

Squinting at her, Hellman clung to his holdfast and shook his head in befuddled wonderment.

"That's why we must get back to Earth," she told him. "Because I know Gorley. Unless I get there, he'll rob me blind."

"Irina?" A plaintive query. "Have you forgotten me?"

"We share alike." She gestured at the bulge of the tight skinsuit at his crotch. "So long as you share with me." Her voice grew harder. "I am no *Dummkopf,* and no friend of Arkady's. He's already too close behind us. So get that engine going."

Sobered by the sudden iron in her tone, he reminded her again of the laws of motion. Every kilogram of mass increased the odds that they would never reach the Earth. He didn't want to jettison the lander.

"Without it we are helpless," he reminded her. "We can only beg for rescue when we pass the Earth."

"No need to beg," she said. "We'll be the heroes. The sole survivors. With all our data disks, we can even bargain with the rescue craft. So strip the ship!" she commanded him. "Down to propulsion mass and the food we need."

She gloved her fine white hands to help, and they stripped the ship. Squawking chickens and squealing pigs went through the disposal hatch, along with bedding straw and bags of feed. Metallurgical gear went out: furnaces and forges, drills and lathes, all the tools intended for extracting and using whatever metals might be found on Mars. He kept the lander secured until she made him let it go.

"Every kilo," she repeated. "A time may come when only one needless ration pack could kill us."

♂

He watched the moving star behind until it ceased to grow and suddenly went out. The radio thumped and squawked.

"*Colon* to *Magellan* . . . Lavrin calling Hellman . . . Calling Barova . . . We beg for any kind of truce. We intend no violence . . . For the world's sake, and ours, for all we came to Mars for, please reply."

They did not answer.

"Let 'em guess." Barova shrugged, bright teeth flashing. "The facts are sinking in."

The signals dimmed and finally ceased. The star appeared again, fading fast as it crept back toward the vast bright curve of Mars.

"The end of that." With a nod of satisfaction, Barova asked, "How long to Earth?"

"I'll have to recheck velocity and mass reserve," he told her. "And recompute our orbit."

Busy for three hours, observing the apparent positions

of Mars and Phobos and Deimos, and working at the keyboard, he turned to her with a troubled scowl.

"Not quite enough," he muttered. "We still carry too much mass to overtake the Earth."

Gym equipment went through the hatch, books and musical instruments and electronic gear the colonists had left behind, cartons of ration packs she said they could live without, spare pressure suits and air units for them, surplus helium cylinders.

He observed Mars and Phobos and Deimos again, and ran new computations.

"That may do." He nodded, his face still grim. "We're on a minimum energy orbit that will take us down to graze Earth's atmosphere thirteen months from now—"

"Thirteen?" Her voice went sharp. "Too long!"

"Ah Kindlien!" He shook his head at her concern. "It's better than eternity. Thirteen happy months together. Not that I relish the ending." His face grew bleaker. "We'll still be moving nineteen kilometers a second, with only a spoonful of water left in the tanks."

"Can't you—"

"No more." Tension clenched his fists. "We must breathe. We must eat. Energy is conserved. The laws of motion still apply."

♂

Barova got through to Farside and White Sands, calling Mr. Martin Gorley. Responses were faint and long delayed. At first he was not available, but his voice came back at last on a scrambled beam meant to keep their secrets.

"You're smart to pull out," he assured her. "We'll have Farside alerted to search and rescue craft standing by for your signal."

Mars ConQuest was up and running, he said, with

sales offices already open in a dozen countries, most of them with projection rooms where investors could see the expedition landing and the habitats begun.

He wanted more inspirational material for his sales people now.

"We'll get it to you," she promised him. "The greatest story of our age!" She let her voice ring. "The actual conquest of Mars! An epic adventure of high courage and tragic sacrifice and dazzling reward. Commander Lavrin and his crew will go down in history as the heroes of our race."

"Marty Gorley!" Her lips curled when the camera was off. "A human rat! He'd rob his darling mother, but we must help him keep the company booming till we get there."

To keep the company booming, she edited the records of the expedition with a new narrative in her best dramatic voice. The epic of that first descent. The breathless tension of the first touchdown. The triumph of the first human bootprint in the dust. Houston's daring trek across the planet to see the awesome grandeur of Coprates Chasma on fire beneath the rising sun.

She produced new versions of her own landing on the south polar snow and the touchdowns on Phobos and Deimos, new promotional disks to show the brave beginnings of the colony, the rovers jolting out through the long yellow dunes, the first cores of permafrost, the clay pits and rows of drying brick, the excavation for the habitat, a silver-bright lander dropping out of the coral sky to nestle down in its cloud of steam on the cross-marked pad.

Hellman was no actor, but she could make his heavy features impressive on the screen. She wrote scripts for him and coached him on delivery, describing the scenic splendors of the planet, the allure of its trackless vastness, the promise of wonders yet to be discovered. In her own voice, she painted space terminals and city domes, low-gravity spas and secure refuges from the troubled Earth.

She said nothing of dust or red fever or Kim Lo's death.

"The Martian colony is thriving," she reported. "The first habitat is fully functional. The first crops in the greenhouse are already maturing, growth marvelously accelerated by low gravity and the abundant carbon dioxide. The livestock has adapted well; hens are laying and pigs getting fat. We enjoyed a feast before we left the planet, omelets and a young pig roasted, every dish produced on Mars.

"Dr. Hellman and I are coming home on a special mission for Commander Lavrin. We love the planet and we wanted to stay, but he is sending us back to tell the epic story of the expedition and invite all the thousand or millions who will want follow as development proceeds."

That was for the media, brokers, and investors.

"We left them desperate," she told Marty himself. "Their equipment is totally inadequate to meet the merciless conditions of Mars. When their supplies run out— and that will happen soon—they won't survive for many months. It is unlikely that the planet will ever be visited again."

♂

Hellman's pilot program dropped them sunward from Mars.

"A tricky thing," he told Barova. "We must graze Earth's atmosphere, close enough to slow us down and let rescuers reach us, but not so close we burn up or hit the planet. I've saved twenty tons of water mass for correction."

The long rocket burn completed and the engine dead,

they swept on gravity-free. Mars shrank behind them, a diminishing disk, a sun-lit globe, a red-blazing star. Week by week, long month by month, the hot sun swelled. The blue-white point of Earth grew brighter ahead.

Barova finished her commercials and transmitted them to Farside and White Sands. Hellman worked on his monograph, *Areology: The Geology of Mars.* They spoke on the scrambled beam to Marty Gorley, though he seldom answered. They clung to holdfasts and guide lines when they moved, made their meals, slept in restraining nets, experimented with free-fall sex.

"Thirteen months!" she muttered once when they hung together, breathless and sweating, in the odorous air above her berth. "Thirteen eternities!"

"Patience, *Liebling,*" he protested. "Thirteen eternities in paradise, if you could be as happy as I—"

"I think too much." She paused, lips compressed. "I think of Mars, and—" She broke abruptly off. "Get your shower and check the computer."

Her tone was so sharp that he floated there a moment, seeing her so clearly that he felt startled. She was no longer making up her face. Hard lines had begun to show, and they cut deeper now. Sometimes he thought she was getting tired of him.

"Why?" he whispered. "Do you regret—"

"Nein! I do feel for Houston and Ram, even for the women." Her smooth jaw set. "Never for Arkady. He cared too little for me." She laughed. "I remember how he used to remind me we were all volunteers for Mars. I hope he's happy with it!"

♂

Checking the computer, Hellman said he must make an orbital correction. She waited at the controls in the dome while he climbed down into the tail of the ship to start the helium engine. The engine didn't start. He didn't come back. Searching at last, she found him huddled over the engine in a clutter of twisted tubes and blackened valves and a bitter reek of something burned. He started when she spoke and bent again to the machine.

"Something wrong?"

He ignored her.

"Otto? What is it?"

"The engine." He looked up at last, dazedly shaking his head. "I tried to start it. I believe—" His voice died and he caught a long breath. "I believe it is destroyed."

"Fix it!" she rapped. "You've got to fix it."

"I'm doing my damnedest."

She watched him for a time, but he seemed unconscious of her. Grown impatient, she went back to the galley to drain a vodka bottle before she tried to call Marty Gorley. A brief message from White Sands said he was not available. Long hours had passed before Hellman came to find her still waiting at the signal console.

"Is it fixed?"

Miserably, he shook his head.

"Why not?"

"It can't be fixed." He bit his quivering lip, and she saw blood drying on his black-stubbled chin. "It destroyed itself."

"What do you mean?"

"It burned." Drifting off the deck, he clutched a guide line to secure himself. "Much of it fused. Hard to tell what happened, but the fragments show corrosion. I believe the water injection jets had become obstructed, perhaps by permafrost minerals not removed by the separator. The plasma needs water to cool it. When the water failed, it burned out everything."

"Don't we have spare injection jets?"

"None." He shrugged, and she saw that he was about to cry. "None I can find."

"We left Earth with repairs for everything." Her voice sliced at him. "Where are they?"

"I don't know." He wiped at his eyes. "I've looked—"

Helplessly, his hands fell.

"Dummkopf! You threw them out!"

"Liebling, Liebling!" Blinking, he shook his head. "Perhaps we did."

"If that is true—" She stared at him, eyes fixed and wide. The stare, he thought, of a trapped animal. "Are you certain?"

"Certain."

"So?" Her eyes slowly narrowed. "Where does it leave us?"

"In space." He grinned bleakly, rubbing at the blood on his chin. "Without power, we cannot correct our orbit. It is one that will never bring us within ten million kilometers of either Earth or Mars. I believe we are doomed to drift forever in the space between."

She had snarled like an animal, lips curved back over shining teeth, and he trembled back from her.

"If you must blame me—"

"Relax!" She snapped it like an order. "It's Arkady! He brought us here."

"Lavrin? How—"

"Because I loved him." Her face was a bloodless mask. "Because he hated me."

"Liebling!" He blinked in disbelief. "Arkady hates nobody."

"A beautiful man!" She gazed away at nothing. "His blue eyes lit that first day when he swore me into the Corps. He broke regulations to take me out of the dorm that night. I thought we were going to be—"

Her red lips twisted.

"Next day—" Her voice was a whispery hiss. "Next

day he was changed. I wanted him. Crawled to him. And he has always laughed at me. Called me Contessa or Pavlova or Czarina. And always preferred some plain fool like Ryan."

"Don't you—" Hellman peered into her rigid face. "Don't you care for me?"

"You?" She turned to him suddenly, her voice gone harshly shrill. "You clumsy oaf! Cold as a stone. Don't you know they call you the human skunk?"

He wilted away from her.

"Arkady!" She snarled the name. "I did everything. Begged him on the flight from Earth. All I got was his teasing laugh. Even on Mars, when I was calling from orbit. 'Keep the ship, Contessa,' he told me. 'Just let us have the cargo. What we want is Mars.'

"So let him have it!"

Her laugh was an animal cry. In compassion, Hellman reached to grasp her arm. She started from his touch and turned as if astonished to find him still with her.

"Otto! Can't you fly us home?"

"No hope." Dismally, he shrugged. "I see no hope."

"None?" Desperate, she searched his face. "Not even from Gorley?"

"If you can reach him." He spread his hands as if he didn't care. "If you can keep him bewitched. Perhaps he could complete the *Nergal* and send it to meet us in space."

28

Creation

The mother of the sun was a giant gas cloud, the father a supernova whose shock wave struck and squeezed till gravity shrank it. Nuclear fire ignited in its heart and warmed the spinning fringes that gave birth to planets, asteroids, and comets. Finally to such unlikely creations as life, mind, and humankind.

"A fever dream, Ram." Lavrin pushed the sheaf of yellow printout back toward Chandra. "All of us have had 'em."

They sat around a table in the habitat over mugs of Lisa's bitter Martian maté. Dinner had been raw greenhouse carrots and scanty bowls of cabbage soup. The odor of that still lingered.

"But, sir!" Chandra leaned over the table, jabbing his dark finger at a yellow sheet. "Can't you see?"

Houston ached for him. Still weak from his bout with the virus and depressed after Kim Lo's death, he had grown haggard and gaunt. Yet now the spectroscopic printouts had lit a dark fire in his sunken eyes, and restless energies had seized him.

"They're all a little different, but look at this one." He waved a flimsy yellow sheet. "Gold, 29 percent. Platinum, 27 percent. Iridium, 12 percent. All the noble metals. Does the spectrometer have fever dreams?"

Lavrin frowned through the great red beard. "A glitch in the software, more likely."

"What kind of glitch?" Ram was hoarse and wheezy. "A software bug would give us random errors. These aren't random." He shuffled the sheaf of printouts. "Most of them exactly what you'd expect. Oxides of silicon, iron, aluminum, magnesium, calcium, sulphur."

His anxious eyes flashed at Houston.

"These readings all come from that same spot where we got that first anomaly on the flight with Hellman and Barova. Just coincidence?"

"I don't see how." Houston frowned at Lavrin. "Hard to believe, but here on a new planet you should expect surprise."

"I want to see." Chandra rasped. "This is reality. It will explain itself when we get to that crater." He swung to Lavrin. "Sir, we've got to look."

"I wish we could." Jayne shook her fever-scarred head. "We wanted to land there. It just wasn't possible."

"Rough country, Ram," Houston said. "Old terrain, of course. Churned by impacts. Crater on crater. The bright objects themselves are a hazard to landing—even if they're somehow really all the readouts say."

"They are!" Ram appealed to Lisa, who sat beside him. "Can't you believe the spectrometer?"

"I want to." She reached for the sheaf of printouts and turned soberly to Lavrin. "If all those objects are really precious metals, can't they save our lives? Bring rescue here the way Inca gold brought the Spaniards to the old New World?"

"If they are." Lavrin shook his red-shagged head. "Not likely."

"Sir!" Ram pointed a quivering finger at the printouts. "Won't you believe—"

"I believe in nature," Lavrin answered patiently. "In science. In what we know. Mars is a natural world. We've seen enough to understand the processes that made it. They don't allow house-sized nuggets of the noble metals—or, in fact, even much enrichment of any ores here, the way they were enriched on Earth. Really, Ram, there's no appeal from nature—"

"Arkady!" Lisa spoke suddenly. "Perhaps nature did have a process." She flourished the printouts and turned to stare at Houston. "Remember Doc Sakane?"

"The guy from Mauna Kea?" Houston nodded, with a puzzled frown. "At the symposium on planetary origins?"

"The Nobel winner in astrophysics a couple of years ago." Eyes shining now in her fever-lean face, she looked back at Lavrin. "One evening he invited a few of us to his room for hot saki and kept us there half the night talking about exciting ideas he couldn't prove. One was the notion that the cooling solar nebula must have been a kind of distillery. Fractionating different elements out at different levels, at different temperatures and pressures."

"Of course." Lavrin nodded. "The inner planets are heavy stuff. The giants that condensed farther out are mostly hydrogen and helium. But you never find the heavy elements pure."

"That's why Sakane couldn't prove his theory," she said. "The separated elements were all chemically combined and mixed again. If it were possible—" Compassion in her dark-rimmed eyes, she looked back at Chandra. "If some anomaly—some miracle had stopped that mixing."

"That would take a miracle." Lavrin shook his head. "One that never happened."

"The noble metals are miraculous." Ram's creaky voice rose higher. "Because they don't oxidize. Turbulence in the shrinking nebula must have remixed most of whatever separated, but turbulence is chaotic. Couldn't it be—" He looked at Lavrin. "Couldn't it be that some freak of chaos and gravitation tossed masses of the noble metals out of the ecliptic plane before they fell into some growing protoplanet? And finally brought them here?

"Won't you, sir—" He caught a raspy breath and leaned across the table. "Won't you let me take the lander? To see what they are?"

Inquiringly, Lavrin frowned at Houston.

"Too hazardous, I'm afraid." Houston shrugged regretfully at Ram and grinned at Jayne. "We've had one lesson in the dangers of landing on such terrain."

She gave them a small wry smile. "One too many."

"Sorry, Ram." Lavrin shook his head. "A risk we can't take. Not with our only lander."

"No matter, sir." Ram was doggedly persistent. "If I can't have the lander, let me take a rover."

"That far?" Lavrin frowned. "It must be three thousand kilometers."

"I want to try—" The rusty voice faded and he sat a long time silent, fever-yellowed eyes staring blankly past them at the white-tiled wall until at last he whispered, "When I think of Kim, I want to try."

"Later, perhaps." Lavrin shrugged. "If we ever feel secure. But now we've got to put survival first. Whatever they are, those objects can't be fit to eat. Meteorites of common iron would be more useful to us."

"Still—" His dark-stubbled jaw was stubbornly set. "I want to know."

"If we go looking for anything," Lavrin said, "it ought to be iron. Over all the ages, enough must have fallen here. There's no weathering to hide or destroy it. We've no equipment to smelt ores, but we could work iron." He turned to Chandra. "Want to try for iron?"

Sunk back into dejection, he merely shook his head.

♂

Later, when the second greenhouse had been completed and seeded, and bricks for the third were drying in the kiln, Houston asked permission to drive a rover east.

"We've never been beyond the ridge. We might find anything."

"Or nothing." Lavrin was as gaunt as the others, pinched from toil and hunger, his normal cheer worn thin. "But go if you like."

He mounted the laser spectrometer on the rover and drove east beyond the crater ridge to search for iron or sand for glass or anything that might help them stay alive.

His helmet radio had a limited range. He was out of touch for five days, roving across a wide plateau crossed with ranges of yellow dunes and rock-littered flats. Driving by day, he inflated the balloon tent at night for a chance to eat and sleep outside his pressure suit.

The Martian landscapes still enchanted him. Only broken stone and dry red clay and wind-carved sand, they seemed forever strange in the light of a sun that climbed out of luminous dust on a coral horizon to cross the purple zenith and sink to another coral horizon. Vistas no human eye had ever seen drew him always farther with the promise of rich revelation.

Promises forever denied. The sand in the dunes was never fit for glass. His laser bursts against the boulders revealed no meteoric iron. Nor noble metals, either. Each new view began to repeat the last. Turning back at last when food and water ran low, he felt tired to the bone and heavy with foreboding. If this were a game, as Jayne used to say, the winner was going to be Mars.

The red-hazed sun had almost set before he came down the crater ridge on that last day. An icy wind stirred thin wisps of dust, but nothing else was moving. The *Colon* stood like a lonely silver tower beside the low red mounds that covered the habitat. Or a gravestone, he thought, that might still be standing here a million years from now. Or ten million—

He shook off the thought. It came from hunger and fatigue and disappointment. Down beneath the mounds, life and hope would be waiting. Jayne, with her wry stoicism. Ram, still the competent engineer. Lisa's quiet optimism, and the comfort of her hot maté. Arkady's invincible chess. Even something warm to eat.

He drove into the mirror-fabric shelter and found the other rover gone.

At night? Nobody ought to be out. Puzzled and uneasy, he hurried down the steps to the lock, another balloon with a scavenger pump to salvage precious air. He crawled inside, sealed and inflated it, hauled himself through.

Jayne was waiting for him in the entry alcove. Alive and smiling, thinner since they landed yet still lovely in her blue skinsuit. It took him a moment to see the leaf-shaped fever spot that had come back to her chin, but then he froze, staring at it.

"I'm okay." She came to help him out of his pressure gear. "Find anything good?"

Her tone was lightly quizzical, but he heard the tension in it.

"Not till just now." Stripped to his skinsuit, he opened his arms but she stood still, her face pinched and tight. His voice dropped. "I see the other rover's gone. Is anything—anything wrong?"

"Not now—" She paused to stow his helmet on the shelf. "But you were gone so long. Five days! I thought it would be only be two or three. We were all afraid—"

She looked away.

"I kept hoping," he said. "Pushing on for more than I ever found."

She came at last into his arms, but he felt her shiver against him.

"It's hard." Her voice was quiet, without sobs or tears, but he heard her pain. "Back in training, it was easy to be brave. I wanted to get here more than anything. But—" She shrugged against him. "It's hard to hold up."

"The rover?" He drew away to look into her shadowed eyes. "Where is it?"

"Ram." She paused, lips pressed tight. "The morning after you left he was gone. Must have packed his gear on the rover while we were all asleep. Slipped away sometime before we woke."

"Where—"

He already knew, but he waited for her words.

"He left a note to say he was going after a sample of those noble metals. For Kim's sake, he said." She shook her head, a helpless gesture. "He doesn't get over her."

"That crater's too far for the rover." He frowned, thinking of the odds. "I've just spent five days covering maybe eight hundred kilometers over fairly good country. He'll have many times the distance, there and back. Most of it over terrain that looks impossible."

"Arkady told him that," she said. "Calling on that first day, while the radio could still reach him. Begging him to come back. Even promising to carry him in the lander to some closer point. But Ram—"

Dismally, she shrugged.

"You know how he is now. Stubborn as ever and coughing with the fever. I think half out of his mind. Once he seemed to forget the printouts altogether. Said he was looking for Kim. After that first day, we haven't been able to reach him."

"He'll never get back. Not in the shape he's in. We'll have to go after him, if Arkady will let us take the lander."

♂

Lavrin let them go, and gave them a chart where Ram had plotted the route he was begging permission to follow. They had to spend two days repairing worn valves and pumps and replacing osmotic membranes in the separator, and two more refueling the lander. Taking off early one morning, they climbed to a circumpolar orbit that would carry them low over the plotted route.

Even with the telescope, the rover was hard to spot, but Jayne picked it up on their third pass. A faint metal fleck almost lost against the sullen immensity of Mars, it was creeping south and west and south again across the ancient highlands, still eight hundred kilometers short of the meteor fall.

"Moving!" she whispered. "At least he's still alive!"

"Still with too far to go."

"Colon to Ram," she called. "Hello, Ram! Hello!"

All they heard was static.

"Colon calling!" she tried again. "Houston Kelligan and Jayne Ryan calling Ram Chandra. Do you hear? Ram, do you hear?"

Houston turned up the volume. Amplified static hissed and roared, rising and falling like the waves of a cosmic ocean. Nothing else, until the rover was out of reach again beyond the stark horizon where iron-stained crater walls met dead black space. On the next pass she found it again, a few kilometers farther along.

"Jayne to Ram," she called. "Hew to Ram. Answer, please!"

They heard no answer.

"Perhaps his radio is dead." Houston frowned at the chart where his route was plotted. "Let's try to set down somewhere ahead, where he'll have to pass. If we can find a possible spot."

He marked a site that looked level enough, twenty kilometers ahead, and got the lander safely down in a narrow pass between two ejecta-littered crater rims. The rover was not in sight. They waited, watching the gap where it should appear. The small sun sank lower. Rust-red crags lost their color. Shadows clotted into darkness. The salmon-pink horizon turned slowly purple.

"The splendor of Mars!" Jayne's voice was wryly ironic. "The wonder-world we gave our lives for."

"It gives me gooseflesh now." He stared past her into the descending night. "To think these craters haven't changed in maybe four billion years. It's so—"

Dead.

He decided not to say the word, but it came from her.

"Dead!" she whispered. "Can you really imagine people coming to live here? Mars terraformed? Or even the domed cities we used to dream about?"

He didn't have to answer, because he had caught a reflected glint of the fading sunlight. He found the rover in the telescope, a fragile metal spider crawling out of a black-shadowed gorge. It stopped on the rubble slope beneath a cliff, half a dozen kilometers away.

"Ram?" Jayne called again. "Do you hear me?"

Centered in the telescope monitor, Ram's orange-suited figure clambered off the seat. Every motion very deliberate, he stood up to look down the gorge as if just discovering the lander.

"I hear you." A wheezy rasp. "Why are you here?"

"To help you, Ram. To take you home."

"I need no help, because Kim is with me."

"Come back with us, please, before you have trouble—"

"I have no trouble, because Kim is showing me the way."

"Listen, Ram!" she begged him. "We all of us love you. We must stand together. We need you back at the habitat, to help us all stay alive."

"Kim will keep us alive with the metals on that golden mountain."

"But Ram, you can't get there. It's too far. The country's too rough. You know the odds—"

"Damn the odds!" his hoarse croak broke in. "Kim says she'll get me there."

"Have you food enough? Water? Power cells? Carbon filters?"

"All okay. Kim brings me everything."

"Won't you let us pick you up?" Houston asked him. "To take you and the rover somewhere closer?"

"Close enough," he rasped. "The land's smoother than I thought. And Kim is waiting on the mountain."

"Ram, please—"

The speaker clicked and the static rustled again.

"Out of his head." Jayne turned from the monitor, biting her lip. "But what can we do?"

"Not much."

♂

They sat watching the monitor. Moving laboriously, as if even the Martian gravity had become a heavy burden, Chandra unfastened his water tank and supply locker and wrapped them with him inside the shelter. It inflated slowly, a tiny silver cocoon. Black shadow crept up to swallow it.

In the comparative comfort of the lander, they made their slender meal, one shared ration pack and two greenhouse carrots. They watched night descend, and the blaze of pink-tinted stars across those old impact pits in the timeless stone. A long time sleepless, they thought and spoke of Chandra.

"Hard luck." He shook his head. "A grim way to go."

"For all of us, perhaps." She shrugged. "None of us are sorry."

Dawn found a glitter of frost on the old rocks around them, gone in an instant when the hard sun touched it.

They found that bright cocoon again, already collapsing. Chandra crept out of it, slow but methodical in motion. They watched him fold and pack the balloon, load water tank and locker, mount the seat and drive on toward them.

"We can't just let him die." Jayne rose from the monitor. "I want to try again."

She got into her own suit, and they waited. The rover dropped out of sight. Two hours passed before it labored back into view at the summit of the pass. Jayne went out through the lock to stand where it would have to come. Watching from the lander, Houston saw it lurch on by her, not fifty meters away.

Ram turned to give her a stiff Corps salute, but he did not pause.

"Wait, Ram!" she called after him. "Won't you come aboard? Just for a shower, anyhow, and a mug of Lisa's maté?"

He didn't look back.

29

Sammy

Sam Houston Halloran, boy born to LeeAnn Halloran at Kelligan Medical Center, November 29. Eight pounds, three ounces. Maternal grandparents, Judge J. Mark Halloran and Mrs. Martha Halloran.

When LeeAnn's pregnancy became evident, Kelligan asked her bluntly, "Is it Sam's?"

"He," she corrected him. "But he is Hew's."

"I'd hoped so." He glowed with approval. "Glad to

know the young fool did something right before he ran away to Mars."

She kept her downtown apartment after the baby came, though both sets of grandparents wanted her to move in with them. Her maiden aunt, a retired LPN, agreed to babysit, leaving her free to stay on at Kelligan Resources.

Marty Gorley was commuting now between Fort Worth and White Sands. Claiming what was left of the Authority, he ran Mars ConQuest from its old headquarters there, coming home for weekends with his mother. Kelligan and LeeAnn found him sitting one morning with his yellow pad and stacked folders under that Aztec sacrificial mural, waiting for them and his coffee.

"No more maternity gowns?" He peered appraisingly at LeeAnn. "Your figure did wonders for them. But how is little Houston?"

"A happy baby." LeeAnn tried not to flush. "Thank you."

"Que niñito bonito!" Lucina came around the table with her silver urns and stopped to smile at Kelligan. "Have you another photo?"

Kelligan dug pictures out of his jacket pocket.

"Your own eyes, *Señor.*"

"Or Mr. Houston's." Marty grinned and reached for the photos. "He'll be proud when he gets the news."

LeeAnn sat looking past them at the victim bleeding on the altar stone, wishing in spite of herself that Marty and his mother had been next in line. They were suddenly too cordial, smiling too widely, too eager to praise the child, offended too quickly by any imagined hint that they might be jealous of little Sammy.

Lucina gave her a penetrating glance and leaned to pick a fleck of lint off Marty's loud plaid jacket. Settling down beside him, she whispered something that made him nod in quick agreement. Frowning, Kelligan saw her suddenly as a stranger. In her severe business suit and gold-rimmed glasses, her sleek black hair cut mannishly short, she seemed as remote as the priest with the red flint blade.

Once so bright and slender and seductively appealing, she was matronly now, almost stout. It amazed him to recall the days when this room had been a secret shrine, she its passionate goddess.

And Marty—

Froggy. The thought hit him like a club. With the bulging, dull-colored eyes, the tight, thick-lipped mouth, the bald, sallow head always glistening with dampness, he looked like a frog waiting for a fly. And, with the forward thrust of his head and his heavy-shouldered stoop, more than ever like Jay Gorley.

$$\male$$

"Hoy, Señor," Lucina announced, "Marty has a matter of business."

Deliberately, while they waited, he pushed his coffee cup aside and shuffled through his folders to find a small scrap of yellow paper.

"If I may, Senator, a financial emergency." He turned to his mother to wait for her fond smile before he gulped and went on, "I regret to tell you, sir, but ConQuest has a cash flow crisis."

"Again?" Kelligan scowled. "How come? After all I've found for you?"

"Only temporary, sir." His eyes fell for before Kelligan's hard stare. He caught his breath and blinked again. "A matter of only a few weeks, sir. Until our promotional campaign gets under way."

"Times are tough," Kelligan muttered. "For everybody. The end of the Authority hurt markets all around the world. Debts they'd run up are not worth a penny on the dollar today. Contractors and suppliers failing everywhere."

"Which is how—" Marty glanced at his beaming mother and found a stronger voice. "How Mars Con-Quest was born. Paying that penny for option on all the worth of Mars. Look, Senator! Look at where we stand: finally organized, setting up agencies all around the world, launching great promotions. But now, sir—" He faltered for a moment. "Now, sir, we've run short of working capital. Just a few million more—"

"You had a billion. Where did it go?"

"Most of it, sir, went to picking up our options. Fantastic bargains, really." He squinted at his slip of yellow paper. "You know what we got. White Sands. Treaty concessions on the Moon as well as Mars. The helium mines. The fabrication yards and the *Nergal.* Even most of the Farside facilities."

"Junk!" Kelligan grunted. "Which nobody wanted."

"Worthless, sir, till we picked it up." Marty inflated himself, hitting his stride. "Because the old Authority was such a dinosaur. A dinosaur trying to fly! The four Treaty Powers always pulled four ways. For dollars or rubles or dolphins or euros, but never together.

"We're playing for dollars now, and all set to win. We've got Farside back on line, to let the settlers talk. They tell us plenty! They're down safe and well in the first habitat. We've got Dr. Barova disking documentaries of everything they do."

"Houston?" LeeAnn whispered. "Is he on the disks?"

"From Day One!" Marty grinned at her. "You know he and this Ryan girl were the first people down. We've got his shots of the crater where they landed and his heroic trek across the desert to this spectacular canyon— five kilometers deep and so wide you can't see across it."

He turned back to Kelligan, voice booming louder.

"Great stuff, Senator! We've got them drilling for

water, making brick, digging pits for the habitat, planting the new greenhouse. They're pioneering a new planet, sir. Think about it. Mr. Houston: the Columbus of Mars!

"Here's our latest sales brochure."

He flipped a slip of holo-printed plastic across the table. The front face carried the planet in stereo, a rust-mottled ball suspended against velvet-black space. LeeAnn turned it over. The stereo on the back face showed a tiny vehicle standing on a red stone point at the brink of Marineris. Sheer cliffs fell beyond it, layered red and black, falling forever into a chasm of golden haze. Sunlit fog poured like a river of flame through mountain passes at the bottom.

"Mr. Houston's rover," he said. "He took the picture."

"What about them now?" LeeAnn searching his face. "We heard about sickness and terrible problems. You're certain they're okay?"

"Landing made as planned. That's how Lavrin puts it. He's down with the colony. The first habitat modules are complete and in use, and two greenhouses. They've grown their first vegetables. Tomatoes and squash and some sort of bio-engineered peas. The animals are thriving. They're searching now for ores they can mine for metals and sand to make glass. Getting ready to welcome another group of colonists whenever we can send them."

She stared at the brochure, white face set, tears in her eyes. Watching her, Marty grinned at his mother and bent his forefinger for more coffee. Kelligan sat still for half a minute, drumming on the table with his knuckles, and asked abruptly:

"How much money?"

♂

LeeAnn found Kelligan a new secretary, a lively Dallas girl named Samantha Battle. Last year's Miss Texas, she was a delicious long-limbed blonde who could brew excellent espresso on a shiny new machine in the back room, take dictation on a laptop, laugh enchantingly at his jokes, remember everything he told her, and anticipate every wish as if she read his mind.

Lucina hated *las gringitas* and said so. She moved her silver coffee urns to a side table in her own office. Her conferences with Kelligan were shorter, and usually by telephone. When she served *café con leche* now, it was to Marty on those days when he was back in Fort Worth from his White Sands office.

"I spoke last week to our friends in space," he told her one morning. "Irina Barova tells a sad, sad story." His fat lips pursed. "I could cry for her."

"Dígame!"

He nodded for her to fill his coffee mug.

"She says the *Ares* is disabled, drifting in space somewhere between Mars and Earth. She and Hellman are desperate, begging me to complete the *Nergal* and send it out to rescue them. I told her not to wait."

"The TV said you were rushing construction."

"That was announced." He paused to sugar his coffee, and slurped it noisily. "But cash flow difficulties have forced us to postpone any actual start-up."

"Niñito!" She reproved him as if he were still a child. "When *el viejo* gave you the money, you promised to finish construction and send the relief expedition."

"Madre!" He mocked her tone. "Cash flow is always a problem, and I had other uses for the old man's money. In fact, I'll be asking for fifty million more."

"Hijo!" Her face creased beneath the heavy makeup. "You have already demanded too many millions."

"And you have always made him find them."

"Nada más." The frown lines bit deeper. "He has

grown stubborn, with *la puta rubia* scheming for my place. *Una bruja!* He listens when she calls Mars Con-Quest a high-risk investment. There will be no money. Unless—"

Her eyes narrowed thoughtfully.

"Unless we find another way to move him. I have seen the broadcasts of this actress on the ship. Perhaps she can tell a story to persuade him. He likes such women."

"Barova?" His dark face tightened. "Contacts with her have ceased."

"You said you were just speaking to her."

"Listening." He made a comic face. "She lectured me from space, attempting to instruct me in astronomy. A subject I never cared to learn, not even when we were young and Mr. Houston wanted to show me Mars in his new telescope, a small red blur in the lens."

He shrugged impatiently.

"I called him a fool at the time—and what is he now?"

"I hope you aren't another. If you want more of *el viejo*'s millions, you had better make up with Barova."

"Madre!" His tone was patronizing. "You don't know Barova. Her advice was useful once, but no longer. Since they quarreled, Hellman has called me to spill more than she revealed. He says the expedition is ending in disaster. They escaped in the ship, trying to get out with their lives, leaving Houston and the others to die."

"To die?" Her coffee mug clattered on the desk. "Don't tell *el viejo.*"

"Not a word." He shrugged, self-content. "Not at least until we have his money."

"How do you expect to get it, without Barova to persuade him?"

"With your persuasion, *madre querida.*" A frown replaced his coaxing smile. "The truth is, Barova has become an enemy. If she and Hellman did get back alive, they'd seize the media. The new heroes of Mars! They could steal my company. Or destroy it, with what they know about the colony. Yet—"

He tapped his coffee mug.

"I expect no trouble from them."

Ignoring the gesture, she frowned reprovingly through new gold-rimmed bifocals.

"Hijo," she told him, "you should know that *el viejo* has never been entirely a fool. Not even when he loved me. He was persuaded to underwrite that last loan only because of the *Nergal.* Because you assured him it could carry aid and supplies to his son on Mars. He has now begun to wonder. *La puta* is asking for reports of actual progress."

"Get rid of her."

"If we could—" Her crimson lips set hard, but in a moment she shrugged and went on. *"Niñito,* I think you must do two things. Finish the *Nergal.* And persuade Barova to call *el viejo."*

"Persuade?" He grinned. "She was begging me to let her call. She and Hellman are trapped on the disabled ship, praying for their lives."

"Can't they fix it?"

"Impossible, so Hellman tells me. The helium engine is broken. Even if they fixed it, they couldn't save themselves. That was the point of her last lecture."

He crooked a stubby forefinger for more coffee.

"The problem is velocity. She explained that a successful fix might bring them nearer the orbit of Earth, but they would be moving too fast. Attempting any landing, they would be cremated in the atmosphere. That's why she begs for rescue. A sad, sad story."

Watching her pour, he gestured for more hot milk.

"Happier for me," he added. "She and Hellman are where they can do no harm. And Houston—" With a nod of satisfaction, he paused to taste the coffee. "He's safe on Mars."

"Hijo." She set the silver urns back on the side table and came to stand beside his chair, her arm around him. Her voice was suddenly hushed. "There is something I never told you."

"Que?"

"Houston is your brother."

Startled, he twisted to stare at her. *"Que dice?"*

"El viejo is your father—though he tries to deny it."

"My father?" Squinting up at her, he drew a long breath and sat straighter in the chair. "How can he deny it? There are blood tests to prove paternity."

"There was a test." She shrugged. "He had the doctors make it when you were in the hospital after you fell off your trike. He showed me the document. Perhaps it does support his lie. *Pero no le hace.* Half the people on Fort Worth know how long I was his *mujer.* A good attorney can make the old *toro* regret he ever saw me."

"So?" He nodded slowly, looking past her. "You believed I would be the heir?"

"I always hoped you would be. When Houston went to Mars, I felt almost sure. Though now, with *la gringita* and her baby bastard—"

Her lips moved as if to spit.

"Mr. Houston won't be back to claim it." He grinned and pulled her closer. "I promise you that."

30

Winter

With a year twice as long, and its polar axis tilted farther, Mars has seasons longer and more extreme than Earth's. They are somewhat uneven, the southern winters longer than the northern.

Every evening when they returned to the lander after their meager supper in the habitat, Jayne and Houston climbed into the pilot dome to scan the dusty south horizon.

"There's a chance," he kept on saying. "I always thought Ram was the best of us. He never fails at anything."

"Some kind of chance," she agreed. "I try to think there is."

Yet that grew harder and harder to believe. They were now four alone, cut off from home since the *Ares* vanished. The slow seasons were changing, the cold small sun retreating northward.

"Let winter come." He shrugged when she spoke of it. "Here, we'll hardly see the difference."

"Here we won't." But she shivered. "I was thinking of Ram, down so close to the pole. If—"

She didn't go on.

"If he were coming back," Houston said, "he'd be here."

♂

"No time to grieve," Lavrin said when they were all together in the habitat. His angular frame was drawn gaunter now, his face hollowed behind the beard, his mood grown bleak. "Ram was a strong soldier in our fight to survive, but we'll do what we can with what we have."

With luck enough, he said, they might still discover sand fit for greenhouse glass. Perhaps some chance rock that would prove to be meteoric iron. Even with no such luck, there were bricks to be shaped and dried and fired and laid, tiles made for the septic system, a pit dug for a pressure cistern where water would not boil away or freeze.

"We're okay," he said, "as long as the helium engine—"

He bit the sentence off, but they knew the rest. The fusion engine generated the oxygen they breathed, turned permafrost to water, lit and warmed the habitat and greenhouses. And it was overloaded.

"We've got to have transparent glass," he said. "To relieve the engine of the greenhouse load."

He let Lisa drive out again and again to search for sand. What she found was always contaminated with too much iron, but they carried other projects forward. They laid brick to wall the new greenhouse, laid the plastic liner, stretched wire to reinforce it against air pressure, piled clay over it to shut out radiation. They laid power cables, strung lights, prepared soil and seeded it, installed the septic system, dug and bricked and sealed the cistern pit.

One evening after work Jayne stood a long time gazing south across the red-brown flatness of the old lake basin toward the far horizon they had watched so long. The haze above it was amber now. Stronger winds were lifting dust, and she sensed the coming cold.

"Winter." She flinched away from that darkening desolation, turning back to Houston. "So far, we're okay here. What I can't forget is Ram. The snowcap will be covering his mountain. And then the dry ice frost."

She reached to grasp his arm.

"Hew, I want us to take the lander up again to see what happened to him."

"It's a forlorn hope." He shook his head. "When you think of all the kilometers to search and the odds we couldn't land anywhere near, even if we found him." But he saw the determination in her eyes. "I'm ready," he told her, "if Lavrin will let us go."

♂

Lavrin let them go. The lander in low orbit, they followed Chandra's plotted route again, and once more his rover was too small and far to see against the immensity of Mars. Days had shortened toward the pole, and haze had thickened where water vapor and finally carbon dioxide were freezing from the air.

"We have to fly too high and fast." Jayne sat hunched, peering into the telescope monitor. "Things blur. There's never time to look again."

Yet at last she did pick up wheel ruts, two faint parallel lines cut into the flank of a dune. Once they caught the sun on Chandra's crater, the meteorites glinting for fleeting seconds through the haze. On the third day, she thought she saw wheel tracks again.

"There!" She caught his arm and pointed, but whatever she had seen was already gone from the monitor. "Ram was there!"

"Not likely." Houston shook his head. "That spot's a

good hundred kilometers from anywhere on the route he meant to follow."

"I did see wheel ruts," she insisted. "Inside that rim wall, though it looks too steep for his rover. They led toward the shadow under that central peak. Let's come back across on the next orbit. Lower if we can."

"A narrow chance—"

But he brought them overhead again. The shadow had shifted. She found the wheel tracks where it had lain and caught a momentary red sun-glint.

"His rover," she whispered. "A reflection from the mirror foil around the water tank. Gone now, but I think there's a spot near enough where we can land."

He studied his charts. The crater looked newer than most, not all its floor impact-riddled. He made two more passes to study it before the brief daylight was entirely gone. Back above the habitat he called Lavrin to ask leave to land.

"Your own judgment," Lavrin said. "If you don't get back, we'll know why."

♂

At the first light next day he put them safely down on a flat patch of time-crumbled rubble a few kilometers below the peak. Yellow-suited, they got off the lander and stood searching the wide crater bowl for Chandra and his rover.

"Nothing," Houston whispered. "Nothing I can see."

"But he was here."

"Why would he have been here?"

Her answer was a silent shiver.

The ring wall shut them in, dark rock splashed by that ancient impact into crags that time had never smoothed. The north sun crept low above them, small and red and cold. It pale rays were erasing the frost they touched, but crystals still glittered in the shadows.

"Let's move." He stirred abruptly. "The day will be short."

They searched, plodding across the slope over red-brown regolith, dusty rubble that had been crumbled and crumbled again through the ages of microimpacts and cosmic radiation. Two kilometers away, they found the ruts and followed them upslope till Jayne stopped and pointed.

"He stalled the rover here."

Ruts and bootprints showed where Chandra had found a slope too steep for him, reversed the rover, and turned toward another path.

"Not for long," she said. "He went on."

On a still steeper slope another kilometer toward the summit, they found the rover abandoned. Chandra had backed and tried again, backed and tried again and still again, and finally walked away. His bootprints wandered uncertainly, but they always turned back toward the summit.

Climbing on, they found him in the shadow of a jutting bluff, half a kilometer higher. He had fallen, the dustprints showed, and tried to climb again. His suit still white with frost, he lay face down, both hands reaching to clutch a jagged ledge above him.

"Hurt," Houston whispered. "But he kept on climbing." He stood a long time staring, shivering again. "He came a long way to die."

"The way he wanted," Jayne said.

They carried the frozen body back down to the rover. Jayne got on the seat to try the little helium engine, and it ran. Houston found the water tank empty, the food locker empty except for the camera and disks packed in it. The folded shelter balloon seemed oddly bulky. He moved it, and whistled in his helmet.

"Look at this! He made it to the mountain."

Under the folds of mirror fabric they saw three lumps of shapeless metal, almost mirror-bright, rounded where the heat of friction with some vanished atmosphere had fused them. They looked small, but he grunted when he tried to lift the least.

"Heavy!" he whispered. "Nuggets of those noble metals."

♂

Downhill, the rover ran well enough. They loaded it into the cargo bay, along with Chandra's body and the nuggets, and lifted the lander out of the crater. Back at the habitat, they dug a grave beside Kim Lo's. When it was ready, they all stood around the yellow-suited body where it lay on the rover, still frozen hard, arms stretched out and both gloved hands bent to grasp that higher rock.

One by one, they said farewell.

"He was my friend." Lavrin spoke slowly, choosing his words. "I met him in the barracks on my first day in the Corps. He taught me how to make my bed, taught me to beat him at chess, tried to teach me his philosophy. He nearly always led his classes, yet never felt superior. He might have been our commander, but he never liked giving orders."

Wryly, Lavrin shrugged.

"Officers called him difficult. A better word might have been independent. He went his own way, never caring much for regulations. That's what got him to his mountain."

"I loved him," Lisa whispered huskily. "I loved him."

"So—so did we all." Jayne's voice faltered, but then grew crisp, as if she had thought out what to say. "His death is tough for us to take, because he did die so hard.

Thirsty and starving and maybe out of his head, trying to climb—" Her voice caught, but in a moment she raised her head. "Climbing a mountain peak where nothing alive had ever been. I think finding what he had come for."

"I know he did," Houston said. "Because—"

His voice was failing, and no words were enough. He turned to gaze into the empty pit. He had worked and played with Ram Chandra, flown with him in lander training on the Moon, sometimes envied his fine intelligence and resented his unshakable certainties, yet always trusted him, admired him, even loved him.

"We both—" He gulped to recover his voice. "We both were dreamers. He found his dream."

When the pit had been filled, he cut Chandra's name and dates into the stainless steel marker welded to the drill stem stake over Kim Lo's grave, and added one word.

MARTIANS

♂

Afterward in the habitat, they screened his disks of the meteor field. He had kept the camera running as he picked a way up the slopes of an old rim wall. Driving on down across the crater floor toward another central peak, he had wound among gleaming metal masses larger than the rover.

Watching, Lavrin whistled.

"Millions of tons! Nothing like it in the solar system. A fabulous find—if it's actually real."

He asked Jayne to run a laser test on the nuggets they had found with Chandra. She set up the spectrometer on a bench in the workshop amid the clutter of parts from the battered rover, and they gathered behind her to watch. White lightning dazzled them, and sharp explosions crashed.

"Real gold!" She sneezed from the hot-sulphur reek, and peered again at her readout. "If you can believe a mass spectrometer. Real platinum! Iridium, osmium, palladium, all here. Alloys different in each nugget. A little silver, traces of copper. Not much else."

"A treasure planet!" Lavrin coughed and wiped his eyes. "Who would believe it?"

"Nobody," Houston muttered. "Nobody is going to know."

Lavrin raked the fingers of both hands back through long red hair and stood frozen, staring at the nuggets.

"Hew—" He had to cough again. "There has to be a way to get the news to Earth. I wonder—" His blue eyes narrowed. "If we stripped the *Colon* and loaded it to the hilt, could you fly it back to Earth."

"Huh?" Houston drew a long breath. "I never thought of that."

"Think about it. Now."

"I don't think it's possible." He had to shake his head. "Not when you know the range of the lander and the fuel mass it carries."

"Suppose you carried added mass?"

"If we could add enough—" Breathtaken, he looked into Jayne's startled face and back at Lavrin. "Perhaps—perhaps it might be done." He nodded slowly, calculating. "I suppose we could make a number of trips, carrying water mass up to orbit. Stash it there in plastic tanks. Gather them up on the final flight and take them in tow."

"If there's a chance—" Lavrin worn face came suddenly alive. "Think about it."

♂

They discussed the notion in the shop and out at the brickyard and over a slender meal of greenhouse peas and squash. Houston computed loads and orbits. Lisa wondered if Hellman and Barova could get home with the *Ares*.

"They're fools if they try. Fools anyhow!" Lavrin shook his head. "Too little water mass for the flight, even if they wait two years for a window. Even it they did get home, I don't think they'd encourage a relief expedition. I think the *Colon's* our best chance."

"If Hew wants to try."

Houston looked around the table. They were sitting together in the common room, and Lisa had filled their pottery mugs with her bitter maté. Their eyes were fixed on him.

"Let's play it fair." He fumbled in his pocket for the old Mexican coin. "We're all rated pilots. Let's toss for the honor."

"Count me out." Lavrin shook his head. "My duty's here."

"And me," Lisa said. "I came to stay."

"So you're elected." Jayne gave him a quizzical smile. "Lisa and I don't have that much stamina left. And you're a Kelligan. People may want to doubt the story. You're the one they'd believe."

"Must anybody go?" Lisa stared at him, a shadow in her eyes. "Would you have any chance to get there?"

"Hard to say."

He looked back at Jayne. She sat with both thin hands gripping the rough red mug. Her hunger-sunken eyes met his, mutely intent. He saw her lips move as if to speak, then tighten silently.

"Give us a guess," Lisa persisted. "On the odds."

"Quién sabe?, as my father used to say." He shrugged. "The lander wasn't engineered for interplanetary flight. Or powered for it. The water mass in tow will be frozen,

difficult to handle. There are a lot of things that could go wrong—and likely would."

"So the odds are pretty bad?"

He had to nod, wondering why she seemed so intense. Never seeming emotional, she had endured hardship silently, and worked too hard even when she was pocked and weak with the fever. He thought again of her visit to his cabin on the flight out, her quiet offer of herself. Had she loved him, and never really said so?

Or loved Ram, perhaps, when he was totally devoted to Kim Lo? His death had torn her up. Or had she sunk into despair just because she could see no good ahead for anybody? He wished he had somehow known her better.

She still waited, and he tried to answer.

"If you want a guess, I'll say the odds are maybe one in ten."

She seemed to flinch. "Must you go?"

"Why not?" He shrugged. "Whatever the chance, it's better than none."

"If we just sit here—" Lavrin's nod heartened him. "The odds are zero."

"A cruel thing." Her dark head bowed. "For all of us. But I see you have to go."

♂

Computing orbits, Houston chose his launch date.

"New Year's Day," he told them. "On the calendar of Earth."

"A lucky day." Jayne tried to smile through new fever spots. "We hope!"

Waiting, he overhauled the lander's fusion engine and stripped the little craft of every nonessential kilogram. Making flight after flight, he stockpiled water out in orbit, pumped into big plastic bags where it would quickly freeze.

The lander ready, he joined in the battle for survival. Lisa had finally found sand for glass and clay for a fusion-heated crucible that could melt it. Jayne designed forms that let them cast the melt into interlocking blocks. He ran the power shovel to dig a shallow pit for the solar greenhouse and helped lay foundation walls for the glass brick that would make the arched sun-roof.

His launch date came before it was done. On New Year's Eve, they gathered for a farewell feast. Lisa raided the greenhouses for ripe tomatoes and vegetables for a stew. Lavishly, they opened two ration packs. Lavrin brought out his last hoarded brandy bottle, still half full. Resolutely cheery, they scoured their dishes and drained their pottery mugs and talked of happy times in training. Half tipsy, they sang old Corps songs and laughed at attempted jokes and wrote messages for Houston to deliver. At midnight, Jayne led them in "Auld Lang Syne."

After the song, they sat in painful silence. The food was gone, the bottle empty. Houston's thoughts came back to all the tasks and uncertainties ahead: collecting the masses of ice in orbit, securing them in tow, keeping sane and fit enough through too many months in flight.

Jayne's dark-circled eyes were fixed on him, her face grave and strained. What would her future be? She and Lavrin had slept together on the *Ares*. Perhaps they would again—if starvation left them life enough for passion. Life enough for anything. Pain for them drowned his flash of jealousy.

A tiny smile lit her face when she saw his own intentness. Desperately, he yearned to take her with him back to Earth, back to life and hope and humankind, but he had to quell the wish. The lander's life-support system would not keep two alive on a flight of so many months. Perhaps not even one.

He shrugged, with a silent nod.

"Better go aboard." Abruptly, Lavrin broke the quiet. "You'll need some sleep before daylight."

She went with him to the air lock and watched him squirm into the pressure suit. Waiting with the helmet, she leaned to kiss him, her lips cold on his. Feeling the tears on her cheek, he caught her body in the bulky sleeves and held her for a moment against the stiff fabric.

"You'll make it." Her lips crushed his again, before she drew back to look into his eyes. "Hew, will you come back?"

He saw her desolation.

"I will," he promised. "I'll get back."

31

Regression

Term for a global economic slowdown more prolonged and severe than earlier "recessions" and "depressions" and "stag-flations." It killed the Mars Authority and opened the way for such scams as Gorley's Mars ConQuest.

Cynical critics called the Future Crisis Group a "coven of doomsters." Organizers of the annual meeting at the Kelligan Conference Center invited scientists, economists, and officials from half a dozen nations, though problems at home kept most of the officials away. Those who came saw disaster dawning.

The keynote speaker was Dr. Enos Kohlmar, who had made his name with books and lectures on the darkening twilight of mankind. He liked to dwell upon the Four Horsemen riding again: Conquest and Slaughter, Famine and Death. His ominous rhetoric introduced two days of dismal forecasts.

A demographer asked his apprehensive audience, "Can Earth be saved?"

His answer was a very doubtful maybe. World population had passed nine billion, most struggling against starvation. Mines were worked out, the best soils eroded away, the oceans poisoned. Hunger and disease could only increase, conflict and hatred with them.

"Are we worth saving?" a pessimistic ecologist inquired. "Desecrating our planet, have we not condemned ourselves?"

New data showed global warming still increasing. Forests were gone, climates gone crazy, deserts spreading, sea levels rising as polar ice began to thaw. Nature might take centuries to cleanse the greenhouse gases out of the atmosphere and restore the ozone shield; it might take forever.

"I see us as our own executioners," a political scientist announced. "In the scramble for survival, we are setting nation against nation, faith against faith, race against race. Our only public heroes are the fanatic champions of cults and tribes and nations, enemies of all the rest."

Andre Ducrow had been the founding planner of the dead Mars Authority. Disheartened by its failure, he was aging now, as thin as if he had just escaped a famine of his own. "What might have been" was the theme of his wistful lecture, on the second day.

"Mars was the challenge we needed." His hair was a flowing silver mane, and he still spoke with the ringing eloquence that had inspired the Authority. "No easy challenge, but its difficulties might have united the race. We needed union, needed a common goal, needed a total devotion to something greater than ourselves.

"We might have found our future on Mars. A new frontier, demanding new technologies, it could have created the genius to invent them. Demanding greatness, it would have made common men heroic. Demanding sacrifice, it would have revealed the splendor of the human spirit.

"Did it fail?" With a gesture of tired regret, he swept back his shining hair. "Or did we fail it? We let high resolutions falter. We placed our narrow needs and petty fears above the destiny of the race. We sent a few brave men and women out to claim the planet that might have launched our expansion across space, and we abandoned them.

"Fate will not forgive us."

He left the platform in a feeble patter of applause, which subsided into moody silence as the next speaker was announced.

"Mr. Martin Gorley." Introducing him, the chairman seemed apologetic. "Mr. Gorley is the oddball among us, neither an official nor an academic type. He is, however, a prominent Texas industrialist and financier, and head of Mars ConQuest, Inc."

Marty's mother had come with him. She sat very straight in a front-row chair, proudly smiling and and waving encouragement when he rose. He had dressed for the occasion in a high-fashion green-striped suit, his wide yellow necktie secured with a huge diamond stickpin, yet he looked nervous on the podium, as if he felt overwhelmed by all these unfamiliar intellectuals. Sweat gleamed on his brown bald crown. He barked to clear his throat and glanced uneasily back at her.

"We are hearing bleak predictions—" Nervously, he paused to squint at his notes. "Unfortunately, our Earth does seem sick, but I bring you better news from Mars."

Out in the audience, somebody laughed. Marty cringed, and the chairman scowled reprovingly.

"On behalf—" Marty stalled and studied his notes. "On behalf of Mars ConQuest, I thank Dr. Ducrow. Without his vision, there would have been no Authority, no expedition, no Mars ConQuest. True, the Authority went under. Its failure did leave Lavrin's party down on Mars, without contact or support or hope of relief. Until—"

His throat seemed to stick. He fumbled with his notes and peered uneasily back at his mother. She waved and smiled, nodding behind the gold-rimmed glasses. He caught his breath and found a firmer voice.

"Until Mars ConQuest made the rescue. Thanks to our own efforts, Commander Lavrin and his people are safe. We are back in contact through Farside Station. We have resumed construction of the *Nergal*. We are planning a relief expedition, to take off when the next launch window opens."

Pausing to mop at his dark face with a yellow silk handkerchief, he seemed heartened by a ripple of new attention that ran through the audience. He pulled himself straighter and his voice grew deeper.

"The Lavrin party did meet hardships. Their first landing was a crash. The site was unfortunate. A savage dust storm delayed the search for water and the construction of their first habitat. But I am happy to tell you that they have triumphed now over every setback. They've found water and manufactured building materials. The first Mars biosphere is already complete. They are surveying a site for the second. It should be ready to receive the new colonists when the *Nergal* arrives."

He bent his head toward Andre Ducrow.

"I want the world to know the Authority did not fail. Dr. Ducrow's grand design is still very much alive. We are mining helium-3 on the Moon again, to fuel a new fleet of spacecraft and power the future industries of Mars. New settlers will be expanding these first biospheres. New spaceports, new factories, new cities—"

He was beaming now, and the splendid stickpin shone.

"They are only the dawn of our great vision. The Martian environment may be difficult, but new technologies will come to answer its challenges. ConQuest engineers are already developing plans to terraform the planet, bringing air and water from captured comets, or perhaps from ice satellites steered down from Saturn.

"A new and better Earth! That's the shining goal of our ConQuest engineers. A future world protected from all the ills the conference has been reviewing. We intend to limit population growth, to conserve resources, to preserve the environment. Science will thrive there, because survival will require it. In the grandeur of that inspiring environment, the arts will surely flourish. Mars can become the ultimate human paradise. A playground, too, that I hope most of you will sometime wish to visit."

When the chairman asked him to take questions, they came from the back of the hall.

"Nicholas Blink, now with Global Press." A heavy man who now wore a black eyepatch and a ragged gray beard, he stepped into the aisle, his voice a raspy shout. "You tell a rosy story, Mr. Gorley, but it seems incomplete."

"Ask me, sir." Marty bowed and grinned, arms spread wide. "Anything you want to know."

"I've been on the expedition story since the beginning." Blink strode farther down the aisle. "I covered the takeoff. I got live interviews from Lavrin and Barova on the ship. But now there's nothing." He spread his arms. "Since that crash landing, nothing except canned documentaries. If things are going so well, Mr. Gorley, why can't we get something live?"

"A natural question, sir," Marty answered smoothly. "Many have asked. The answer is simply the misfortunes of the Authority. All contact has to go through the Farside relay link. That was broken when depleted funds forced the staff to be recalled. We have only recently been able to restore it."

"News to me." Blink sounded doubtful. "Can we get

through now? To Commander Lavrin? Dr. Barova? Anybody else on the ground?"

"Patience, sir." Marty shrugged. "Lavrin has no long-range transmitter at the habitat. Messages must be relayed through the landers and the *Ares.* Those contacts are still uncertain. And of course the landing party has more to do than talk. It's simply impossible to set up an interview.

"If you'll try to understand—"

"Understood," Blink rapped. "But I still want the word from Lavrin."

"Give us time," Marty urged him. "He has equipment on the *Ares* to build a more powerful transmitter at the biosphere. When that's complete—and it should be soon—he'll be available to the media.

"Satisfied?"

"Thank you, Mr. Gorley." Not visibly satisfied, Blink stayed on his feet. "I have another question. About your new corporation and your plans for the future of Mars."

"Fire away." With a confident grin, Marty glanced at his mother. "I'm proud to talk about Mars ConQuest and the magnificent future we plan for it. As you may know, we've taken over all the assets of the bankrupt Authority. We own Mars."

"Maybe you do." Blink was not impressed. "My question is about the way you're selling it. I understand that security officials in several nations have inquired into your methods of stock promotion."

"No surprise." Marty opened his hands, begging for patience. "Our shares are only now coming on the market. Their true value is not yet well established. Skeptics still regard them as highly speculative, but early investors have already cleared fortunes.

"Think of it, sir! We have a whole world to sell."

"Pie in the sky!"

"Sir, please!" He bristled. "The planet's potential

value is beyond calculation, but we must wait for its development. That will take capital and time. We're selling shares to raise the capital. If you call that unduly aggressive—"

"Security officials have questioned the source of the dividends you have declared. How can you pay dividends, when you are producing nothing on the planet?"

"Ask our investors," Marty advised him. "Every one an owner and a citizen of Mars. Their properties appreciate. Our shares today are worth ten times the issue price. Our first investors are begging to invest again."

"They may be sorry—"

"Excuse me, Mr. Gorley," the chairman broke in. "This is an academic symposium, not a sales conference."

"If you please!" Blink stood fast, glaring at Marty with that single eye. "One more question."

The chairman hesitated, but yielded when someone in the audience called, "Let's hear it."

Marty mopped sweat off his head, glanced uneasily at his mother, and turned back to listen.

"An odd story out of Scotland." Chairs scraped as people turned to listen, and Blink raised his voice. "A radio amateur says he picked up a distress call from the *Ares.* The voice of a woman in trouble—"

"*Que mentira!*" Marty's mother gasped. "Do not listen!"

"—Barova." Blink lifted his voice. "She claimed to be Dr. Irina Barova, historian of the expedition. She seemed desperate. She was calling Farside, Mr. Gorley, trying to get through White Sands to you. Begging for rescue—"

"An ugly lie!" Flushed and furious, Marty turned to the chairman. "Sir, I won't submit to malicious insult." He stabbed a finger at Blink. "This scandalmonger has no right to make such absurd accusations. Throw him out!"

"Not yet!" someone shouted. "Let's hear it all."

"If you like." The chairman shrugged. "But keep it brief."

"Only a fragment," Blink said. "Though the message was repeated, reception was poor. The radio ham missed words, but he swears he got the sense of it. Barova and Dr. Hellman were adrift and helpless in the disabled *Ares.* She said they had left the landing party down on Mars in desperate trouble, most of them dying or dead from hunger and some strange disease—"

Marty shrank toward his mother, who gave him a comforting nod and a tight little smile. Belligerent, he turned back to Blink. "We were already aware of this cynical fraud. We are investigating the perpetrator. Mars ConQuest is taking legal action."

"Perhaps you should." Blink smiled through the untidy beard and swung to face the audience. "A most plausible hoax, if it is a hoax. But the Scot says he knows Barova's voice from broadcasts he had heard. He swears—"

"Impossible!" Marty had grown shrill. "Barova is still aboard the *Ares,* but she reports no trouble anywhere. She's busy, in fact, producing new video disks to help us tell the epic story of those heroic men and women taming the wilderness of Mars—"

"Sorry, Mr. Gorley." Blink marched farther down the aisle. "That Scot contradicts you." Lucina had risen to challenge him, but he ignored her. "He claims Barova and Hellman say they fled on the *Ares,* attempting to escape the tragic fate of the landing party—"

"Que mentiroso!" Defiant, Lucina shook her fist at him and appealed to the audience. "A diabolic liar! Don't believe him!"

Blink waved her back toward her chair.

"Barova says the ship has been disabled." He swung to face the audience. "The rocket engine is dead. She and

Hellman are drifting somewhere between Mars and Earth, unable to reach either planet. They were begging Mr. Gorley to complete the *Nergal* and launch a rescue expedition."

His single eye fixed on Marty.

"Will you do it, Mr. Gorley?"

"Vicious libel!" Marty croaked. "Mars ConQuest will sue—"

"Excuse me, gentlemen." The chairman banged his gavel. "This is an academic symposium, and our program must proceed."

32

Year Two

Setting up a calendar for Mars, Commander Lavrin began the year with the southern winter solstice, when the sun is farthest north. He named the twenty-four months for pioneer space-craft.

Lisa had first met Arkady and Jayne in the Beta test, designed by the Corps to weed out candidates unfit for the first expedition. On their first day in the Corps, still strangers to one another and given no warning what to expect, eight new trainees were ordered one by one into a lightless, soundproofed examination room. Groping and stumbling through total darkness, they found only seven chairs in the room, facing into a small circle and crowded close together. Outside the test room, the examiners shouted questions through a speaker, watched with infrared cameras, and recorded every reaction.

It was an ordeal that went on forever. Though the chairs reclined, the barrage of questions interrupted any effort to sleep. They posed unpredictable riddles, demanded mental skills few possessed, and asked for judgments none felt prepared for.

Lisa was Number Eight, the last to be admitted.

"Larissa Kolvos." Blundering about until she found all the chairs occupied, she stood in the middle of the circle, answering when the voices called Eight. "My friends call me Lisa."

The examiners wanted more.

"My father? He was Aristo Kolvos. A physicist at CERN."

"Your mother?"

"A poet. She signed herself just Zara. They divorced the year I was eight. I stayed with my father till he remarried. Boarding school then. College. A lab job with my father till I got into the Corps."

Why had she volunteered?

"I grew up dreaming of Mars," she told the dark. "My father showed me the planet when we were in the Alps on my sixth birthday. I asked if I could ever go there. He said maybe. I believed him, because I knew he was already working on helium fusion."

The examiners went on to others, but still she stood trapped there, anxious about her score and longing for a drink of water and finally swaying with fatigue. It was Arkady Lavrin who recognized her predicament and stood to give her his chair. She learned to know him by his voice and his touch when he helped her find the chair. His voice was kind like her father's, and his gentle hand eased a little of her stress.

Listening, she learned his name. His father had been a Ukrainian diplomat who met his Swedish mother in Stockholm. He had lived in many countries and gone to military schools and earned degrees in engineering and astronomy at Moscow University.

A girl named Jayne Ryan sat somewhere beyond Arkady. Already interested in each other and murmuring together about Lakefield and the Moon, they seemed more relaxed than she was. Arkady was soon the leader of the group, asking the others to exchange names and shake hands, to take turns standing in the center, to ease their fatigue with a stretching exercise.

Lisa followed him and Jayne around the circle, reaching to touch the others, giving her name and learning voices. He helped her find the door to a toilet that was equally dark. That helped, but there was no food or water, no sleep, no relief from tension.

She grew hoarse with thirst. Her dry mouth had a bitter taste. She felt weak with hunger. Her body ached when she stood and when she sat. She tried to stay awake and answer truthfully, but the test became a kind of nightmare. Again and again, when the shouted "Number Eight" jarred her out of a doze, she had to wonder where she was.

At last it ended. The questions stopped. The examiners turned lights on and told them the date. Only three days had passed. Arkady laughed and asked if they meant three years. The heavy door swung open and she heard voices, a truck on a mountain road, far thunder. The clean tang of pines brought her back into the live world, the Corps research center in the American Rockies. A sense of liberation lifted her out of fatigue and hunger.

Arkady and Jayne, ahead of her, had stopped in the corridor outside. She knew them by their voices, and she was happy to see them in daylight. Arkady was barely twenty then, beardless, his red hair cut short, so handsome that her breath caught. Even after that long ordeal, Jayne looked fit and vividly alive, admiration for Arkady shining in her eyes. She stood holding his arm, nodding eagerly when he spoke of finding something to eat.

They were a beautiful couple, she thought, discovering and delighted with each other. They hardly noticed her.

Flinching from a pang of envy, she walked on by. She had joined the Corps for Mars, not for romance.

Neither the logic of the test nor her final score was ever revealed, but next morning she was called to the commandant's office, along with Jayne and Arkady, to be congratulated on their selection for continued training.

♂

When the solar greenhouse had been finished and sealed and planted, Lisa asked Lavrin if he planned to build another.

"No more." With a painful grimace, he shrugged. "Tools and machines broken or worn out. Steel wire and liner plastic all used up. And ration packs running out. We'll have to limit activities till we can begin eating out of the new greenhouse."

Yet he let her take a rover west across the basin to search for better sand, or clay to make better crucibles, or perhaps the iron Houston had failed to find. On the second day she came upon a dark and deeply pitted boulder that lay alone on a bare clay plain.

A laser shot verified that it was nickel-iron, almost pure. From the marks of heat and impact, she thought it must have come down hard through a thick atmosphere and probably buried itself, though erosion had left it exposed. Nearly three meters long, it was far too massive to be moved. She used the helium-powered electric arc to slice off sections small enough to carry.

"So you did it!" A grin of delight crinkled Arkady's wasted face when he saw the samples, the grin she had loved since the Beta test. "Something more useful than platinum or gold—at least for whoever comes after us."

They forged a few crude tools out of the metal. It was hard to work, however, without the equipment they had lost with the *Ares*. Arkady hammered one little red-hot slab into a new blade for the power shovel. It refused to fit. He tried again and finally tossed it aside.

"No matter," he muttered. "We may never need the shovel again."

He and Jayne had begun setting more lengths of drill stem while she was gone, to carry a new antenna and give the radio beacon a longer range. When it was done, they tried again to call the *Ares,* and even to call Farside. They heard no response.

"We'll keep listening." Lavrin had settled into a bleak, laconic determination. "And keep the beacon going as long as we can power it. If anybody comes, if Hellman and Barova should bring the ship back, we'd better be easy to find."

"Why should they come back?" They were sitting around the table in the common room, where they gathered for what cheer they could get from one another and Lisa's hunger-easing maté. "After what they've done to us?"

"I try to hope."

"If you can hope—" She made a bitter little shrug. "I wish I could."

"Remember Hew." Jayne managed a wistful smile. "He'll be back."

"If he can." Gloomily, Lisa shrugged. "If he gets to Earth alive. If people believe in our meteor mountain. If he can raise the millions or billions to finish the *Nergal.* If he can find a crew for another expedition."

"You can trust him," Jayne said. "He's a Kelligan."

"If he does get back—" Lisa shook her head, with a searching look at Lavrin. "It won't be before the next opposition. We can't hold out so long."

"I think—I'm sure we can." Lavrin's answer was slow and not very sure. "If we ration the staples we have left. If the new greenhouse produces what we hope." Stiffly, he grinned behind the gray-streaked beard. "We won't be fat, but we should be alive."

♂

Jayne inventoried the remaining ration packs.

"Ten full cartons," she reported. "Sixty packs each. Besides the one we opened yesterday."

"One pack a day." Lavrin frowned at his calendar watch. "Split three ways. With what we hope to grow, it should keep us going through Year Two."

"If the new greenhouse produces."

Every morning they divided that single daily pack very carefully and relished every crumb. Nursing the greenhouses, they harvested what they could and limited their lives to make the best of every calorie. Bitter as the nights were, they ventured out to scan the sky, finding only Phobos and tiny Deimos moving among the pink-tinted stars, never the point of light that might be the *Ares* or another rescue ship.

Listening, they heard nothing from anywhere. Earth, Lavrin said, was still too far away on its faster circle around the sun. As the next opposition neared, perhaps they might get a signal through.

"In time for what?" Lisa asked.

"Whatever." He repeated the word, with a resolute grin. "Whatever."

In the month of Viking, a dust storm howled around the habitat and filled the sky with yellow murk that took many days to clear. The month of Explorer passed, and the cold north sun crept farther southward. The Martian winter changed to spring, with still no ship in the sky, no signal from Farside, no hint of hope. The month of Apollo came, and Vostok.

On Vostok 12, the helium engine stopped.

Lights flickered out. The throb and hum of the air

machines fell silent. Lisa shivered, groping through the sudden dark to find a battery light, but Lavrin was whistling a Ukrainian folk tune as he got into his pressure gear to cycle through the lock. He brought one of the rovers to the habitat and ran a cable from it for emergency light and power while he and Jayne tried to repair the big engine.

Lisa watched them at the job, and searched the solar greenhouse for anything they could eat. Lavrin found her there again next day, and showed her what looked like a small brass bolt.

"The problem." His face looked drawn and grim. "The helium injection jet. There is—or should be—a tiny hole in it. The orifice is clogged. Probably from something corrosive in the water."

"Can't you fix it?"

"Not without the emergency repair kit. A thin green plastic case, about so long." He measured with his hands. "Special tools in it, and I hope spare jets. It should have come down with the engine. You haven't seen it?"

Dismayed, she shook her head.

"We've turned the shop upside down." Helplessly, he shrugged. "It isn't there."

"We've got to find it."

"We've looked everywhere, twice. It's not in the shop. Not in the supply room or the kitchen. Or the well house or the pump house. Nor the tool boxes on the rovers or the drill. Not on the ground where we unloaded the lander. Could it be in the garden tool room?"

It was not in the garden tool room.

"I suppose we left it on the *Ares*. Without it—"

Wearily, he let his shoulders sag.

"Power to light the greenhouses?" She peered into his dust-grimed face. "Can we use the rover engines?"

Bleakly, he shook his head.

"They couldn't stand the overload," he said. "Not for

long. We must keep at least one alive to light and warm the habitat. And to keep the beacon on."

"Will we ever need the beacon?"

"*Quién sabe?* as Hew used to say." He grinned at her, wanly. "We'll keep it on."

♂

Next day she and Jayne mulched and seeded a narrow strip down the center of the solar greenhouse, which had been left for a footpath. The task was nearly done when sunset began to redden the glass arch overhead. They stood up to stretch their backs.

"So here we are!" Jayne turned to her with an odd little smile. "Remember how we met, back in the Beta test?"

"I do." She shook her head, staring wistfully away into the crimson dimness. "I walked past the two of you together as we came out. I didn't know you noticed me, but I fell in love with Arkady."

"You did?" Jayne's brow creased. "I never saw you with him."

"He was always with you. At least till you left the *Ares.*"

"Oh!" Jayne laughed. "I suppose I did wonder if I was falling in love, at least until the staff began to preach their little sermons about egotism and alcohol and sex emotion as hazards to the expedition. Arkady and I have always been good friends, but we never called it love. I never was in love, not before I landed here with Hew."

"Arkady?" She whispered the question. "Not with Arkady?"

"Don't you know his first passion?" Jayne laughed again. "Irina Barova!"

"Not Irina!"

"Ironic! They met when he was home in Kiev and she came there on a promotion tour for the Authority. He saw her on TV and went down to her hotel for an interview. She had him in her room overnight and signed him up for the Corps."

"I never imagined—" She shook her head. "I never saw them together."

"That night was the beginning and end of the affair." Jayne made a face. "You know what Irina is. I've always been sorry for Hellman."

Lavrin and Jayne slept late next morning, worn out from work in the greenhouse and trying to economize calories. In the common room, they found Lisa's empty maté mug on the table, and the day's ration pack opened, with only her share gone. Her narrow bedroom was vacant when they looked, her pressure suit missing.

33

Citizen

The Martian passport issued to each shareholder was bound in limp black imitation leather, embossed with a silver spacecraft and a red image of Mars and endorsed for dual citizenship with any nation on Earth.

The room was tiny and dark. It smelled of fish and strong tobacco and the battered bucket he used for a urinal. From the throb of the engine and the rise and fall of the floor, he knew he was afloat on some sea of Earth.

"Com' está, Señor?" The little black-bearded man bent over him again. *"Soy Francisco. Su amigo, Francisco. Quiere agua, señor?"*

He found no voice to say he wanted water, but he gulped thirstily when Francisco put the cup to his cracked lips.

"Quiere caldo?"

He wanted the fragrant broth, and Francisco lifted his head to help him gulp it. Only one small cup, because at first it had made him sick. He slept and woke and Francisco gave him a brimming bowl. Later he got canned milk and hard bread. Sometimes an orange. Finally a whole broiled fish or a slice of ham.

He seldom tried to talk. His great weight crushed him into the narrow berth, and Francisco seemed strangely afraid of him, hesitating in the doorway when he seemed to be asleep and jumpy when he needed to be lifted.

Mars seemed remote as a dream, no longer quite real, yet the recollections were vivid in his mind. The long flight out. The landing with Jayne. Coprates Chasma and the habitat and the orbital surveys. The search for Ram and the great nuggets from the meteor field. Singing "Auld Lang Syne" and Jayne's farewell kiss.

For a long time he didn't know or care how he had got back to Earth. The lander flight returned in broken fragments, painful to recall. The cruel battles with the ice when he had to kill the engine and seal himself in the awkward suit to chop lumps of it out of the masses in tow and drag them aboard and thaw them in clumsy plastic bags so that he could finally drain them into the tanks and start the engine again.

The endless fasts, when too many ration packs were gone and he had no strength for anything except to sleep. The anxieties, when he ate enough to clear his head so that he could make observations and correct the pilot computer. The suffocating heat from the first braking pass through Earth's atmosphere. The slingshot flight back around the Moon, which seemed so brief because he had been unconscious. The hard fight to stay aware and in control on the last long final glide down across the Pacific. The bad moments when he knew he would never reach land, when the engine failed, when he was falling.

Able at last to sit up, he asked Francisco for his clothing.

"*No hay, Señor,*" Francisco said. "*No hay ropa.*"

He had come from the sea *desnudo.* Naked as a new baby. Francisco brought him a threadbare terry bathrobe, not entirely clean. A gift, he said, from *El Capitán.* The captain himself came in, a nervous little man with a neat white beard and shrewd, close-set eyes.

"Captain Pedro Murchison." He set a half bottle of Scotch and two coffee mugs on the tiny table. "If you feel able, *Señor,* I have questions."

"So have I," Houston said. "I'd like to know where we are."

On the great Pacific, Murchison said. Off San Ambrosio Island. His ship was *El Tiburón,* out of Valparaiso. The catch had been disappointing, but he still hoped for better luck.

"May I ask, *Señor?*" He sloshed generous shots into the coffee mugs and handed one to Houston. "Why do you return?"

"Return?" Houston sipped the hot liquor cautiously, wondering what to say. He knew too little. If he had come naked from the sea without Chandra's precious nuggets, he had no proof of anything. "I don't remember."

"Francisco says you spoke of Mars." Murchison watched his face. "At times when you were very sick. Tell me, *Señor,* have you in fact returned from Mars?"

"Perhaps," he said. "I don't remember."

"I think you came from Mars." Murchison sat on a stool to face him. "We watched you descend. Your machine had no wings. We first saw it when the jet roared beneath it. The jet died. It fell and floated. The engineer went to it in a boat. He opened a hatch and climbed inside to bring you out before it sank."

"Did he find anything—anything else?"

"No golden nuggets, *Señor.*" Murchison squinted at him. "Though Francisco says you spoke of golden treasure while you were sick. If you wonder, the engineer had no time to search your rocket. It was damaged. Sinking fast. Your are fortunate that he got you out. Even naked and half drowned. Nothing else."

"Please thank the engineer." He shivered from a burning gulp of scotch and decided that Murchison must be trusted. "It's true that I was on Mars. If I told you we did find gold and other precious metals, would you believe?"

Murchison shrugged. "You told Francisco your name was Kelligan. Of the Kelligan company."

"I am Sam Houston Kelligan." He spread his empty hands. "With no passport. No money. Nothing."

"Perhaps you have a friend." The shrewd eyes narrowed. "Because I am a citizen of Mars. My passport."

While Houston stared, he pulled the thin black booklet out of his shirt pocket to show the silver craft and the red globe of Mars.

"I received it with my investment in the Mars corporation," he said. "It carries rights of entry and departure if I should wish to go there when the cities are built. My wife has no desire for that, but the shares pay dividends. She likes the dividends."

Marty Gorley. Silently, he nodded. Marty was evidently very busy selling shares in a future Mars that might never exist—not that Marty cared.

"The dividends, *Señor?*" Murchison was asking. "Will the golden mountain you spoke of guarantee such dividends?"

"Not yet." Houston handed the passport back. "I brought nuggets on the lander, hoping they could save my companions and perhaps bring more ships and people. If they were lost—"

Unhappily, he shrugged.

"The engineer brought nothing off." Murchison set his

empty coffee mug beside the bottle and bent intently toward him. *"Señor,* your story troubles me. Because it is not what the broker told me."

"You trouble me," Houston said. "With your passport and your shares in Mars ConQuest. Why did you buy them?"

"For my wife. And the great dividends." Wryly, Murchison pursed his lips. "Because of the bright brochures that show the mountains and canyons and ice caps of Mars. Because the broker has the videos of Dr. Hellman and Dr. Barova, which tell of sweet water and good soil and many useful minerals on the planet. Is that not persuasive?"

"Apparently."

"Now you promise gold." The small eyes narrowed. "Though there was nothing of actual gold in the brochures. Only the promise of future certainties of great wealth for all investors. The new spaceport will be ready when the next spacecraft arrives. New habitats will be waiting for new settlers. New helium ships will cross in five days, instead of many months. True, *señor?"*

"Not if you wait for Marty Gorley."

"El Presidente Gorley? The president of Mars?"

Houston laughed.

"The brochure contains his promises." Still very sober, Murchison frowned. "Mars is to be a veritable paradise, without pollution or poverty, disease or warfare. City domes will be built, with factories in tunnels and caverns beneath them. Highways will cover the planet. Tourist hotels will stand on the canyon rims and the summits of the great volcanos. Great medical centers will save the lives of those grown too old or feeble to endure the gravity of Earth. A new and better world, so he says.

"You laugh at him, *Señor?"*

"I hope for Mars," Houston said. "But not because of Gorley."

"My wife and I own a thousand hectares," the captain said. "In the great Hellas Basin. Even if we never see them—and she has no desire to—I had hoped that our son might build a great *hacienda* there.

"But now—" Dismayed, he shrugged and spread his hands. "If what you say is true—"

"It's true," Houston told him. "Gorley seems to be conning everybody. My friends on Mars are sick and starving. Hellman and Barova stole the *Ares* and left us to die. I flew the lander back, hoping the news of the gold and other noble metals we discovered would let me bring help.

"If you believe me—"

"I do not wish to believe." The captain sagged back against the steel bulkhead, dismally shaking his head. "Yet I saw your rocket fall into the sea. I saw you come aboard more skeleton than man."

He poured more Scotch into their mugs and sat squinting sharply Houston for a long half minute.

"Perhaps I am an idiot," he said at last. "My wife may throw me out, because our shares have been more profitable than fishing. When I left port they were worth eighty thousand new *escudos*. But I must believe you. Believe enough to call my broker."

He clinked his mug against Houston's and gulped the Scotch.

"But I think, *Señor,* that you will find trouble ashore."

♂

Francisco found clothing for him somewhere, a faded shirt and denim pants and a worn brown jacket. No shoes, but a pair of slippers and a shapeless knit cap. So clad, Houston was able to walk the deck as he gained strength and watch the men hauling in their nets, which were never full.

A police launch came out to meet them before they docked in Valparaiso harbor. Captain Murchison pointed him out to the officers who came aboard and looked away while they handcuffed him and took him off the ship.

So this is Earth? He stared out of the police car at the squat, gray-walled concrete fortress where they parked it. *This is home?*

Inside, standing before a fat little sergeant sweating behind a desk in a grimy, poster-cluttered office, he grinned in bitter amusement.

"Your passport, *Señor?* Your name?"

The sergeant sneered at his name.

"Sam Houston Kelligan? Where is your visa? Where are your millions?"

"My father in Texas will send money, sir, if you will let me call."

"Unfortunately, *Señor* we have no budget for international calls."

"May I call the American ambassador?"

Doubtfully, the sergeant shrugged. "If he will accept such a call."

They let him call the American embassy in Santiago. One official voice after another asked him to hold for endless recorded commercials and finally passed him to another official voice. At last he was told that a consular officer would contact him when arrangements could be made.

Lying awake that night on the hard steel shelf in the cell, he tried to see a bright side. Really, except for the roaches, the cell was no worse than his room in the Martian habitat. Jayne and Lisa and Lavrin might have rejoiced at the greasy stew they fed him. The live human voices and traffic noises beyond the bars were better, perhaps, than the dead stillness of space. Tomorrow would surely be kinder.

Tomorrow came. Hard bread and bitter coffee and endless waiting before the fat sergeant came with a jailer to escort him to a larger, cleaner room, where he found Malcolm Baxter impatiently standing. Baxter was a narrow-faced, sharp-nosed man in gray, who clearly had no time to waste on him.

"You want us to call Mr. Austin Kelligan?" Baxter raised a shrill, accusing voice. "We have already called his Fort Worth office. He was not available. We were referred to the information center at Mars ConQuest. They informed us that Mr. Sam Houston Kelligan is still on Mars."

"Sir—" He had taken cold, and he had to clear his throat. "Believe me, sir! I am Sam Kelligan. I can prove it. Just give me a chance to explain how I got back from Mars. If you'll call Captain Murchison, on the fishing boat that brought me in—"

"Excuse me, mister." Baxter moved toward the door. "Frankly, your story seems absurd. I see no reason to believe you, and no basis for intervention. Frankly, I have better things to do."

"I'm an American citizen."

"I see no evidence of that. I understand that you have attempted to enter Chile in violation of immigration law. If that's true, it appears to be a matter for the local authorities."

"Can you find me a lawyer?"

"Not likely."

"Anybody—"

"Good day, mister."

Baxter turned away. The sergeant saw him through the door and waddled back.

"Attorneys expect money, *Señor*. There is, however, a television reporter who wants to speak to you."

"Please! Anybody at all."

♂

The reporter was a loud-voiced, black-eyed blonde who stood conferring with the sergeant in the hall outside while her crew were setting up their equipment and posing him under glaring lights.

"Ramona Castellana of Andes Video," she introduced herself to the camera. "Six weeks ago we exposed a fantastic hoax. Port authorities here at Valparaiso had received a sensational radio report that purported to come from a fishing boat far off the Chilean coast. A man who said he was captain of the boat claimed that he had seen a strange spacecraft fall into the Pacific. He said he had taken aboard a remarkable survivor.

"A man who claimed to be from Mars!"

She gestured at Houston, and a red light burned above the camera lens. He brushed at his shaggy hair and wet his lips and tried to smile. She was speaking Spanish. Her audience was probably only local, but perhaps somebody who had known him would recognize his face.

"This individual has now arrived in Valparaiso. We are interviewing him at the headquarters of the port authorities, who are holding him on open charges." Her voice turned sardonic. "He says he is Sam Houston Kelligan, a son of the American financier and industrialist Austin Kelligan."

The fat sergeant stood watching through the open doorway, an amused smirk on his face.

"Does anyone know him?" she asked the camera. "He has no passport, no documents, no proof of anything. The actual Kelligan was one of the pioneers who set out for Mars two years ago on the *Ares*. According to the Mars information office at White Sands, he is still there."

"They're lying—"

The red light went off.

"Do you wish to tell us who you are, *Señor?*" Her voice dripped contempt. "Or what have you to hide?"

"I am Sam Houston Kelligan. I can prove it, if you will let me call my father in Fort Worth."

"Mr. Austin Kelligan?" She shook her head, with an ironic shrug for the lens. "Unfortunately, *Señor,* he doesn't care to claim you. We have tried several times to reach him since we first heard the story. He is never available. His office always refers us to Mars ConQuest."

"A damned—damned lie!" He gulped to smooth his quivering voice. "I have been on Mars. The colonists there are in desperate trouble. I came back to bring the truth. To beg for help. I brought identification—more than you ask for—but it was lost when my lander went down in the Pacific."

"Most unfortunate!"

"The truth!" He wanted to smash his fist into Ramona Castellana's sarcastic smile. "You can ask Captain Murchison. He saw me come down."

"Perhaps he did." She shrugged again. "We tried this morning to reach him, but again you are unfortunate. Overnight, Captain Murchison sold a large block of Mars shares and disappeared from Valparaiso, leaving his wife with a black eye and his ship abandoned.

"Which leads to another question." Her hard eyes stabbed again at him. "How was Murchison involved in your hoax?"

"There is no hoax." The small red light was on again, and he spoke to it. "But Captain Murchison did save my life. He sent out the boat that rescued me from the sinking lander."

"The captain was very kind," she taunted him. "But it appears that his fishing voyage had been unsuccessful. We are informed of other difficulties. Unpaid creditors were preparing to seize his ship. He left his wife with no money and this damaged eye. Or can you suggest better reasons why he vanished so hastily?"

"Maybe he wanted to avoid your cameras."

She smiled for the lens, fine teeth gleaming, and turned back to ask him, "Did you grow wings to bring you back across space?"

"I came back in a landing craft."

"So he says." She laughed for her audience. "We have consulted space engineers. They assure us that no landing craft could possibly return from Mars to Earth. These small shuttles were designed for flights of only a few thousand kilometers, not for many million."

"The flight was difficult," Houston said. "But here I am."

"With the gold you say you found on Mars?" A mocking sneer. "Or where have you hidden it?"

"We did—" He tried to swallow his anger, to voice some sane appeal. "We did discover a field of meteorites composed of the noble metals. Gold, platinum, and others. I brought a hundred kilos back. I was told they went down with the lander."

"A likely story." She snickered for the lens. "I called Farside Observatory to ask about this tale of golden meteorites. It's absurd, they tell me. I spoke to a man who has collected and analyzed thousands of meteorites on the Moon. He says it's true that some of them—like sea water—do contain trace amounts of gold and other precious metals. Or even tiny diamonds. But only tiny trace amounts."

"There's a theory," he tried to say. "That elements could be fractionated in certain levels of the evolving solar nebula, purified and tossed out—"

She wasn't listening.

"You had the *Ares* there on Mars," she said. "Why didn't you use it?"

"We didn't have—" He caught his breath and tried to

be convincing. "Hellman and Barova had seized the ship and flown it away. I don't know where. They left us marooned, to die there. I came back to beg for help."

Confidentially, she dropped her voice for the camera. "Summing up the story, we have spoken to information officers at White Sands. They assure us that the real Sam Houston Kelligan is still safe and happy on Mars. He laughs at the notion that he might wish to leave.

"The *Ares,* they tell us, still remains in low Mars orbit. All the cargo has been unloaded. The animals are thriving, the frisky goats jumping high in their new low-gravity environment. Dr. Barova is still aboard, taking on fuel mass for a flight back to Earth when the next flight window opens. She will bring Dr. Otto Hellman and their accumulated data on the planet. White Sands is now selecting volunteers for the next expedition."

She looked back at Houston, her face set hard.

"Mister, I don't know your name. I don't know how you got into the middle of the Pacific—unless this Captain Murchison has some share in your fraud. But our staff has spent a good deal of time on this investigation, and we can only conclude that you are very stupid—"

"Very desperate!" He interrupted her. "Because what I say is true—and important to the world. If you would only look for the facts! Captain Murchison may be gone, but men in his crew saw me come down. You can talk to the engineer who pulled me out before the lander sank—"

"We've spoken to the engineer." Triumphant, she raised her voice over his. "We've spoken to the mate who says he gave you his cabin. And the cook, Francisco Torres, who says he fed you and nursed you back to life after they picked you up."

"Surely, that is proof—"

"Proof of all you aren't," she crowed. "They all deny that they saw any spacecraft descending from the sky.

They swear, instead, that they found you drifting in a rubber boat. Do you want to tell us how you really got there?"

"They're lying—"

"Somebody is." Sardonic, she nodded at the camera. "This concludes our interview with Sam Houston Kelligan—for whoever may care to believe him. I am Ramona Castellana, of Andes Video, 'views of today, visions of tomorrow.' "

She signaled her crew to kill the lights.

"*Vengase, Señor.*" The sergeant beckoned from the doorway. "Back to your cell."

34

Olympus

The largest mountain in the solar system, Olympus Mons is three times the height of Everest. The base is 550 kilometers across; the sharp escarpment around it sometimes seven kilometers high; the great caldera at the summit 64 kilometers wide.

Her father had given her a book about the old Greek and Roman myths the year she was five. Her mother said it was too old for her, but he read parts of it to her until she learned to read it for herself. She loved the book because the old Olympians had been so magically powerful but still so oddly like her own parents.

Being Greek, her father wanted to call them by their old Greek names, but the Roman names in the book seemed easier to say. He became Vulcan in her imagination. Not handsome like Apollo, he was a small dark man who wore a beard and limped like Vulcan from a bad ski fall. A craftsman like Vulcan, he could fix broken toys or anything. Vulcan worked in a shop; her father's shop was a lab at CERN, the research center in Geneva.

She sometimes saw a stronger likeness. Vulcan was the god of volcanoes, and her father could erupt when he was angry. That was only at her mother, however, or later at Yvette. Never at her, because he loved her as deeply as she loved him.

Her mother was a little like Athena, beautiful and wise. She had begun as a painter, but nobody bought her paintings. Now she wrote poems and books about art. She was kind and generous enough when she happened to be at home, but that was seldom. She was nearly always away, traveling to read her poems and visit auctions and galleries and lecture about art. She had strange friends and never much time for Lisa.

Nor enough for his father, who never liked her friends. The year she was eight they separated. She stayed with him till he found Yvette. Yvette was like Venus, she came to think, seductive and beautiful and probably unfaithful. He was often angry with her, and he let Lisa go away to boarding school.

She thought of her childhood as she climbed away from the habitat, because everything else hurt too much. She had filled herself with the hunger-dulling mutant maté, but it gave her no strength. Not even enough for the feeble gravity of Mars. She had left the energy wafers out of the helmet dispenser for Arkady and Jayne.

To keep from being found, she left the road before she reached the crater and picked her way higher, always choosing the rougher slope, or the steeper, looking back only when she had to stop to rest. Already far below, the mottled red and browns of the old lake floor spread to far dark hills in the south and the yellow dunes northward and the dust-colored horizon. Empty, dry, dead.

Dead forever?

They had come to bring life, but now that seemed less possible than the family of the gods upon Olympus.

The habitat looked tiny from this height, but still almost at her feet. She found the white cross that marked the landing pad where nothing might ever land again. The sun's pink glint on the glass arch of the new greenhouse. The low red mounds of shielding clay that covered the others. Like graves.

Or actual graves for Arkady and Jayne, unless Otto and Irina decided to bring the *Ares* back, or Houston got to Earth alive and returned with the *Nergal*. Not really likely, but perhaps by walking away she had given them a few more months.

Unless—

She shrugged and turned to scramble on, turning north toward a still higher ridge. So high and steep and far, she thought, that they would have no strength to follow, even if they found her trail.

Perhaps too high and steep for her. She fell and had to lie awhile to rest before she could climb again. Her suit had grown stiffer, heavier, clumsier. Every step became another labor. She had set out at dawn, and the day seemed to last forever. The heatless sun was suddenly high above that northward ridge. It sank westward, reddened in the dust, dropped into the sea of desolate dunes.

In the bitter dusk, she reached an ancient lava flow. From fissures, perhaps, where some old impact had fractured the planet's crust. It had cooled into a maze of hummocks and pits and knife-sharp blades that were hard to see by starlight. When she fell, her body screamed for her to let it lie there.

Why not?

She knew no reason. Her hands were already aching and numb, and her breath had dimmed the edges of the cold faceplate, yet she wasn't ready to quit. Not quite yet.

She caught a jutting rock to drag herself up and stumbled on again until the stars showed her the cliff ahead.

It was a black volcanic wall, impossible to climb. Yet she tried and fell and crawled along its foot until she found the cave. A tube where lava had flowed and then retreated. She crept inside. At last a place to rest, where her body might lie hidden.

Perhaps forever.

Lying in the dark there, shivering with the probing cold, she escaped to better times. She was back in the race on the Moon, triumphantly crossing the finish line at Farside in her own battered rover. She was on the power shovel, excavating for the habitat. She sat again with Houston on the side of his berth on the *Ares,* happy to be with him, happy to discover his understanding friendship, yet feeling a shadow of sadness.

The others had all made couples. Ram and Kim Lo. Arkady and Jayne. Otto and Irina. Why not Houston and her? When they were here alone together, liking and trusting each other, suffering natural needs?

Or had she ever let him know her?

Perhaps she had grown up too close to her father, feeling too keenly the pain his own loves had brought him. Whatever the reason, she had never felt quite free for love. Not even when she spoke to Houston in his cabin.

Of course she had risked experiments, even that strange night with Irina. There had been happier moments, too, the best perhaps that weekend in the Caucasus with Arkady. He had been tender and splendid. It might have gone further, but his orders to the helium facility had come that week, and when they met again he was with Jayne.

And of course they all had sworn to hold their duty to the Corps above everything. A tragic error? Had Mars been really worth all their lives? For Arkady and Jayne perhaps it might be, if help did come while they survived. But for Houston, who would probably die aboard the lander before it ever reached the Earth? For her, if her body lay frozen here through the next million years?

Shivering in the dark, she finally went to sleep.

♂

A sharp ping woke her.

She couldn't breathe. The heavy helmet was suffocating her. Struggling in the dark, she fought to find the safety locks and get it off.

Don't! her training told her. *Without it you will die.*

But she was dying anyhow. The power cell must be spent. Frantic for breath, she ripped the seals open and flung the helmet off into the dark—and somehow gulped a breath of precious air.

Something pinged again.

Water falling! Icy droplets struck her face. Listening in the dark, she heard the ripple of water flowing. Liquid water, here on Mars? She sat up, somehow stronger, not even very hungry. Faint light glowed at the mouth of the lava tube. Unsteady on her feet, she splashed down the shallow stream and waded out into the dawn.

Stars still burned above her, somehow no longer pink. A faint white glow had dimmed them in the east. A soft wind struck her cheek, not so cold as she expected. It blew down the rugged slopes, which fell so steep and so far into the night below that she wondered how she had ever climbed them.

Turning south, she caught her breath.

A blade of light was slicing the sky. She watched it widen, a shining arch that cut across the stars from east to west. She watched it brighten as the rays of the unseen sun revealed it, watched it become a topless wall traced with curving lines. Like—like the rings of Saturn!

Rings around Mars!

Their white radiance caught a narrow scarf of cloud in the blue sky overhead. Blue—because the dust was somehow gone! Breathless, shivering more from awe than the morning's chill, she watched daylight creep down the cragged slopes above her. The size of the mountain amazed her again. The wind-drawn cloud must have blown from a high summit she couldn't see.

Dazed by all she saw, dazed to be alive, she watched the dawn. The sky grew bluer. Night receded from the tortured lava-shapes around and below her. The sun rose at last beyond a remote, sharp horizon. A rim of fire. A burning dome. A hot white disk. It lit the dark lavas, so rugged and steep she wondered where she was.

How, she wondered, had she come so high and far? No summit near the habitat had looked like this. The slope beneath her slanted down for many kilometers to the ragged lips steeper cliffs. Below them, kilometers farther, a gently rolling plain spread away, green when sunlight found it.

Green—on Mars?

Green vegetation, liberating oxygen? Incredible, but this had to be Mars—the gravity still felt the same. The lava tube where she had slept had seemed unchanged, at least until she heard the water flowing. Yet this was no longer the dead world she had known. An impossible time must have somehow passed since she crawled into the cave to die. And somehow she was on this enormous mountain.

Olympus Mons?

The notion staggered her, yet it made a sort of sense. Planetary rings should be in the ecliptic plane, above the equator. The habitat had been south of it; Olympus stood just as far north. The ring plane rose south of her now. The sharp cliffs so far below—could they be the tall escarpment around its base? Staring up again at the ice-white rings, she thought she had begun to understand. Mars had been terraformed!

If the rings were ice, and she thought they looked like ice, they must be fragments of an ice asteroid or perhaps one of the ice moons of Saturn steered into Mars orbit below the Roche limit, low enough to water the planet when gravitational forces shattered it. Searching the far horizon, she found faint blue mirror gleams. Lakes filled again, or seas, poured into basins dry for a billion years!

A brighter glint caught her eye. Metal? Glass? When the full sun caught it, she made out a shining dome on a headland that jutted into the nearest lake. A city dome like those Houston had dreamed about? Built long ago, perhaps before the terraforming was complete, and sealed to contain its own atmosphere?

Trembling to know, to meet the new Martians, she left the helmet in the tube where she had tossed it and started down the mountain, picking a path through black lava ridges, clambering over glassy volcanic blades.

The green plain was farther than it looked. The sun rose higher, hotter than she had known it. This new atmosphere must create a strong greenhouse effect. The rings made a dazzling glare; perhaps their reflected light warmed the planet. Sweating and breathing hard, she felt weak again. Once she fell and slid and bruised her arm.

Wonder spurred her on, yet she stopped again and again to search the world below. A second dome gleamed beyond another lake. She thought she caught the glint of a third on the south horizon. Once she saw sunlight on a vapor trail, almost as high as she was, but angled down toward the nearest dome. It soon was gone, but it had taken her breath again.

Mars was alive!

White cumulus began to form below her, and the sun climbed so high that she knew it must be midsummer here in the north. The puffs of cumulus below spread to make a white-tufted carpet that hid the green landscapes and the distant domes. A taller weather front lay across the north, a darker anvil cloud growing from it. She saw lightning flashing.

A thunderstorm on Mars!

She stopped to get her breath, wondering what could have worked such wonders. Human technology, brought by future colonists? Or total aliens, beings perhaps wiser than men? How much time had gone? Centuries? Millennia? Geologic ages?

And how was she here alive?

Longing for answers, she climbed on down from one slippery knife-edged shelf to another and always another. The sun went down behind the white-scarfed crown of Olympus. Night fell. Shadows crawled out of rifts and canyons to hide the pits and hummocks that tripped her. She fell and stumbled up again and pushed on into the dusk. Far off above the domes she saw a moving light, and then another, flashing steadily blue and crimson, blue and crimson.

Aircraft! If she could make a fire, flash some signal—

A blast of icy wind staggered her again. Lightning lit the lava traps. Near thunder crashed. Stumbling on, searching for any rock or cave that might give shelter, she came at last to the escarpment. An abrupt and jagged brink, falling into boiling cloud. Dazzled with the lightning, she saw no way down.

Wondering, hoping, searching, she crept along the rim till the storm struck. Sudden hail pelted her. A savage wind gust tossed her over an edge she hadn't seen. Clutching at the howling wind, she toppled into fire-riven fog.

35

Bubble

The mad speculation in the shares of Mars ConQuest had historic precedents in the boom and bust of the South Sea Bubble in eighteenth century England, the tulip craze in Holland, and the Florida land boom of the last century. Its scale was simply wider, its outcome stranger.

The fat sergeant's manner had changed when he came next morning with the jailer to unlock the cell.

"Señor." The title was no longer ironic. "You have visitors."

They left him locked alone in the windowless room where Ramona Castellana had grilled him. He waited, wondering, until the lock clicked again and the heavy door creaked open.

"Hew!"

LeeAnn Halloran gasped his name and stopped where she stood. The sergeant beckoned another man to follow her and stood watching from the doorway. She frowned for a moment as if she had never seen him before she caught her breath and ran into his arms.

"I couldn't believe—"

She clung, trembling against him. Her wildharvest scent brought back their last night together, that night in the old Fort Worth mansion when she slipped into his room. Her tears were cold on his cheek, but she was suddenly laughing with relief. Weak-kneed, he staggered to the heavy gravity of Earth and had to catch her arm. "Alex Penning." She pulled away to introduce her companion, a tall, athletic man with neat rimless glasses and a fashionable wave in his flowing golden hair. "Our specialist in international law."

"We weren't certain, Mr. Kelligan." Penning offered a white and well-kept hand. "I'm glad we took the chance."

"I was wondering—" Still unsteady, he looked for somewhere to sit. LeeAnn took his arm to guide him to a decrepit sofa beneath a faded print of Bernardo O'Higgins, and he found breath to go on. "I tried to call my father."

"Don't blame your father. It's Marty Gorley." Her face twisted. "I don't know all he's up to, but he must have heard about your return some time ago. He's ready for you."

He blinked at her, startled.

"Your father was eager to answer when we heard you'd called. Marty scoffed and made us wait to see a videotape, one he said had been secretly shot by security people who'd infiltrated a scheme to break the corporation. It showed men who might have been brokers rehearsing a look-alike for you. Training him to tell your own story about the lander flight and the fishing boat picking you out of the sea."

"I don't see—" He gaped at her. "Why?"

"To discredit you and save Marty's corporation. The plotters intended to sell shares short, and rake in their millions or billions when the world markets broke. So he said."

"Clever enough." Penning nodded. "I myself was almost convinced. And your father, with his deep involvement in ConQuest, saw Kelligan Resources also at stake."

"But I—" LeeAnn's arm was still around him. "I had to see."

"Thanks!" he breathed. "How did you find me?"

"A bit of luck!" She hugged him harder. "Somebody in Santiago recognized you on TV. A man said he'd known you in training. Never gave his name. He called your father's secretary, and she called me—nobody else would believe you'd got home from Mars in just a landing craft."

"Not for sport." Relaxing against her, he saw Penning squinting sharply at him though the rimless lenses. "Can you get me home?"

"Why not?" She looked at Penning. "Alex has it all arranged."

"If Miss Halloran is certain—"

"I'm certain!" She squeezed again. "Can we go?"

"There's paperwork." Penning glanced at the waiting sergeant. "We had another bit of luck, Mr. Kelligan. Your mother had your passport. Thanks to that, I think we'll soon have you on your way." He frowned again, lips pursed judicially. "Though larger problems may come later, if—when we get you back to Texas."

"Larger problems?"

"I do anticipate more difficulties with Gorley." Penning paused to stare at Bernardo O'Higgins as if trying to place him. "I don't know if you've heard of what we call Mars fever?"

"We all had something we called red fever. An infection from the dust."

"Mars fever's something else." Penning's manicured forefinger caressed a slick-shaven chin. "Another shape of human greed. Gorley's spread the contagion with his Mars ConQuest. A multibillion-dollar operation, with investors everywhere going crazy to get aboard while they can."

"That's Marty!" Houston grinned with a rueful admiration. "A con artist since we were kids. Tried once to sell me a map of treasure buried in my own back yard. Slicker now. Even the man who picked me up had bought stock in ConQuest."

"Millions did." Penning nodded gravely at LeeAnn and turned to frown at him. "That's our problem."

"A bigger one for Marty," she added. "If we can prove your story."

"He'll fight. That phony tape was just his first bullet."

"How, Alex?" She stared at him, uneasily. "What else can he do?"

"*Quién sabe?* as Mr. Kelligan says. Gorley has everything at stake, and he's resourceful." He gave Houston an abstracted glance. "You've been at risk, sir. I suppose you still are, but we'll look after you."

"*Señor?*"

The sergeant was beckoning Penning out of the room. Houston watched him go, considering him. Wide at the shoulder and lean at the waist, he had a cleft in his pink chin and an air of conscious charm. An expert, no doubt, with clients and juries. And evidently fond of LeeAnn.

How did she feel?

Left with her on that old sofa, feeling her live warmth beside him, inhaling her remembered scent, he didn't want to search for answers. He simply sat there, glad to be alive and back with friends, not even much troubled about what Marty would do. All he needed was time to recover, to regain strength against the gravity, to relearn the ways of Earth.

"Tell me." She stirred, concern on her face. "If you feel like talking, how bad was it on Mars?"

"It was splendid!" His own words surprised him. Relaxed beside her, he paused for recollection and saw her waiting for him to go on. "Magnificent!" he said. "Exciting to explore, because we were the first. It was all so wonderful, so new, never quite what we'd imagined.

Of course there were bad times. But I don't think any of us ever wished we hadn't come.

"Except, I guess, Hellman and Barova."

She wanted to know about them. He had to tell her how they had mutinied and vanished with the *Ares,* how Kim Lo and Ram had died, how he had left Lavrin and Lisa and Jayne in danger of starvation.

"Dreadful!" She shivered. "But at least you're back." Her arm went back around him. "We'll soon have you home again. Home to stay." She turned to look into his face. "I hope!"

He shrugged. He hadn't come to stay, but he had no will to say so, or even think of any future now. Earth had begun to seem as strange and dangerous as Mars. All he wanted was freedom to rest and time to regain strength and wit to face these new hazards.

He asked, "How are my parents?"

"Your mother missed you." He heard reproof in her tone. "She felt for a long time, I think, that she had nothing left to live for. Your father—" She frowned. "He looks well, but I'm concerned, because he's so reluctant to see Marty for the con man he is. Thanks to Lucina's scheming, I'm afraid he's put too much of his own money into their racket—"

The lock clicked. The sergeant and Penning were returning, the sergeant suddenly another friend.

"*Señor,* I beg you to forgive a most unfortunate misunderstanding. No charges will be placed against you." Heartily, the sergeant pumped his hand. "You are liberated."

He had no energy to ask just how his freedom had been arranged, but the sergeant glowed with satisfaction, shaking all their hands again as he put them into a waiting taxi. It took them first to a clothing shop to replace the rags Francisco and Murchison had found for him, then to a restaurant for breakfast.

He fell moodily silent at the table, amazed at the white cloth and polished silver, wishing Lavrin and Lisa and Jayne were here to share his steak and eggs. LeeAnn tried to cheer him, brightly recalling their childhood times together and suggesting holiday spots where he might like to go while he was recovering.

The taxi took them on to the sleek Kelligan company jet waiting at the airport. By noon, they were ready to take off for Texas. The pilot took his flight plan to the terminal and came stalking angrily back between with two men in military uniform.

"Somebody trying to screw us," he muttered to Penning, and turned to Houston. "Sir, this is Lieutenant Salinas. He wants you back in the terminal. He doesn't say why."

Salinas was a smooth-mannered soft-spoken man who expected to get what he wanted. He smiled very suavely when LeeAnn tried to send Penning with them to the terminal and informed her very firmly that no attorney would be necessary.

A bulky man with a dark Latin face and a heavy black briefcase was waiting to meet them at the building. He gave no name, and Salinas did not introduce him, but Houston saw the red-and-silver glint of a Mars Con-Quest badge on his lapel.

Saying nothing to Houston, he escorted them into a private office and opened the briefcase to set up a compact disk camera aimed at an empty chair. Watching his black-gloved hands, Houston saw the shapes of hard prosthetic fingers under the leather. Ready at last, he clicked a switch to start the camera, sat down with the other officer, and nodded at Salinas.

"Sir, I beg you not to take offense." Smiling blandly, Salinas beckoned him into the empty chair. "We must ask a few questions before you leave Chile."

He sat under the lens.

"Coffee, sir, before we begin?" Quietly courteous, Salinas spoke crisp American English. "Or would you like a beer?"

"All I want is to get back home."

"I understand." Salinas nodded his sympathy and waited for a gesture from the man with plastic hands. "I hope we don't delay you long, but we must ask you to amplify what you seem to have been saying, sir, about the situation of the colony on Mars. And about how you reached Chile."

"I've already explained all that to several people."

"So I know. Unfortunately, sir, circumstances have changed."

"Changed? How?"

With no reply to that, Salinas began a long interrogation. Who had been aboard the *Ares* on the flight to Mars? Who had been the first to land? Where? Would he describe the habitat? What had happened to the *Ares?* Listening poker-faced, with no show of either belief or doubt, he asked for endless detail about the dust sickness, the trips of exploration, the discovery of the meteor field, the spectroscopic evidence of actual noble metals, the deaths of Kim Lo and Ram Chandra, the present plight of the survivors.

"You think I'm lying?" Houston asked when at last he paused.

"I merely ask." Salinas shrugged, with a noncommittal nod at the civilian and his camera. "I make no judgments. But I think you should realize, sir, that you are disputing all the information we have been receiving from Mars ConQuest."

"Apparently."

"Do you understand the consequences?" Salinas glanced at the civilian, who nodded rather grimly. "There are those who doubt. Stockbrokers, for example. Investors with millions in ConQuest shares. Engineers who wonder how you found it possible to fly a landing craft back from Mars."

"I had doubts of my own." He managed a feeble grin. "But here I am."

"How did you happen to come down so near Captain Murchison's fishing boat?"

"Sheer good luck." He shrugged. "I was barely alive. I don't recall even seeing the boat before I woke up aboard."

"Where had you known the captain before you went to Mars?"

"Nowhere."

He heard the civilian's skeptical grunt.

"Why did you persuade him to dispose of his shares in Mars ConQuest?"

"His own idea. A good one, I imagine."

"Did you know he's dead?"

"Dead?" He turned from the lens to stare at Salinas. "I'd never seen him before, but he was decent to me. He saved my life." Salinas stared blankly back until he asked, "What killed him?"

"He was stabbed through the heart last night in a room he had taken under another name in a Santiago hotel."

"You think I killed him?" He turned to laugh at the silent civilian. "When I was safe in jail?"

"Please!" Salinas shrugged. "We merely want to clear up certain—ah, awkward ambiguities about your relationship with Captain Murchison. Selling his Mars shares, he demanded American dollars instead of *escudos*. His wife says that money should have been with him. It is missing." His voice grew softer. "Was some of it for you?"

"It was not." He was on his feet. "If you're accusing me, I have a lawyer—"

"Sir, please!" Salinas smiled disarmingly. "We were

simply verifying the press and police reports of your remarkable story. I thank you for your cooperation." He reached for Houston's hand. "I'm sorry we had to delay you, sir."

The heavy civilian grunted at the other officer and came striding toward them angrily. Salinas raised a hand to stop him.

"You may go," he told Houston. "I find no cause to hold you." He frowned at the muttering civilian. "However, sir, you are likely to face more serious accusations, even in North America, unless you can produce more convincing proof of who you say you are."

♂

At last, late on a warm midsummer afternoon, they were allowed to take off from Valparaiso. The copilot was also the steward. He served drinks and meals and turned seats into berths. With stops at Lima and Panama City, they landed at Fort Worth next morning in the teeth of an unseasonable cold snap. Roberto brought the car through snow on the parking area to take them off the jet.

"Señor?" He gulped and blinked at Houston. *"Señor?"*

"Roberto, *Como 'sta?"*

"Señor Houston!" He grinned with pleased relief. *"Bienvenido!"*

He drove them fast through swirling snow along remembered roads and streets. Drove him home! Sitting with LeeAnn in the back seat, he pointed like an excited child at landmarks he had known.

"Only a couple of years," he murmured once. "It seems a lifetime!"

"Closer to three," she said. "A long time, Hew."

Her grave tone made him look at her. It struck him that time had changed her, firmed her face, given her a habit of authority. No longer the girlish good companion he remembered, she had evidently become a responsible executive in Kelligan Resources. But she was still, he thought, in love with him.

The old mansion looked just the same, far back from the road, snow on the lawn and the gabled roof, winter-bare trees around it. Robert parked in front and unlocked the front door for them. LeeAnn and Penning waited to let him enter first.

In the kitchen, he found his father sitting at the table almost as he had been on that remembered morning when he was leaving for the race on the Moon, the breakfast plate and coffee cup and newspaper clutter spread before him. Yet grown older, thinner, grayer. Deeper lines cut the cragged face, the heavy shoulders bent farther forward. The plate had been pushed away, bacon and eggs and half a biscuit left uneaten.

"Huh?" Looking up, Kelligan gaped and froze. His jaw dropped. Unconscious of the action, he took off the black-framed glasses to polish then on his dark blue necktie. He glared at Houston and stared down at a big red-lettered headline, MAN FROM MARS?

"Sir?" he rasped at last. "Speak!"

"Hello." Houston grinned. "It's really me."

"Sam?" A hoarse challenge. "Prove it."

"Remember—" He searched for a telling recollection. "Remember the last time we went hunting? I shot a rabbit that cried when it was wounded. I threw the gun away. Said I'd never shoot again. I never did. And you were pretty mad."

"My boy—my own boy!" Whispering, his father stood half upright and sat weakly back. "I thought it couldn't be."

He came across the room to grip his father's hand. Mouth trembling, Kelligan nodded at a chair. They sat together, neither speaking. Kelligan polished the glasses again and put them back to study his face, reached almost timidly to touch and grasp his shoulder.

"Your mother—" he whispered, "your mother will be happy."

LeeAnn and Penning had followed him in. She hurried upstairs. Seeming at home in the kitchen, Penning poured coffee and orange juice for them and gestured at the breakfast dishes waiting on the sideboard and the stove. His mouth dry, Houston wanted nothing at first, but Penning's plate of bacon and eggs woke the hunger he had brought back from Mars. He was eating when he saw his mother, thin and frail in the same worn robe he remembered, making her cautious way down the stair.

"Houston?" She swayed and clutched the banister. "Is it really you?"

He ran to take her in his arms. She clung to him, sobbing. With her tremulous voice, her thin-boned feel and her familiar scent, she woke all his childhood. Pity pierced him; she seemed so old and frail, far too old for her years. He had taken her arm to help her to the table when he heard a child's voice above.

LeeAnn had followed, the child in her arms. He waited at the foot of the stairs, breathtaken and staring, till she reached him. Smiling oddly, she shook her head at his bewilderment.

"Hew, meet your son." She held the child out for him to take and spoke gently to it. "Sammy, your dad."

"My son?" He reached uncertainly to touch the child's pale hair, but Sammy recoiled, snuggling back into her arms. He stood blinking at them, dazed. "Why—why didn't you call?"

"I tried when he was born," she said. "Marty said all contact had been cut off."

She set Sammy on the floor and he toddled hastily away to his smiling grandmother.

"Sam Houston Halloran." She looked back at Houston, tears shining in her eyes. "Your mother says he has your mouth."

He looked at the child and back at her, feeling overwhelmed with too much emotion, a mix of awe and pride and tenderness. Again he felt too heavy in the gravity of Earth. He needed to sit.

"I hope you're happy," she was whispering. "This time I hope you'll stay."

♂

They sat a long time in the kitchen. Sammy consented to sit for a time on his knee and went more willingly to stand in Penning's lap and chew on his pen until LeeAnn took him back upstairs for his bath.

"Lee still has her own apartment." His mother smiled fondly, watching them go. "But Maria's fond of little Sammy, and we keep him here while she's at work."

She asked how he had got back from Mars and sobbed again when he tried to tell her. Seeming nervous, his father listened silently, drank more coffee, and finally called the office to say that he would be delayed. Penning finished a second helping of bacon and eggs and said he had better get off to check the market news.

"Things will be happening," he said. "When the truth gets out."

LeeAnn came back downstairs. Sammy was bathed and asleep. She was eating a late breakfast when Samantha Battle called to say the news was getting around. Marty Gorley was about to hold a televised press conference at White Sands. They went into the living room to watch.

♂

The camera panned over the media people packing into Armstrong Hall and swung back to focus on Marty Gorley and his mother, seated on the podium beside a lectern emblazoned with the Mars ConQuest logo, the silver spacecraft diving at the red Mars disk.

A tightly smiling company official stood behind the microphones.

"Most of you know why Mr. Gorley called you here. Rumors!" He snarled the word. "Vicious rumors! The result of a diabolical hoax. A Satanic plot invented to bankrupt a million investors and create a worldwide financial panic. He is eager to counter with the truth." He bowed. "Mr. Martin Gorley, president and CEO of Mars ConQuest."

Marty stood, clutching his yellow legal pad. Paunchier, Houston saw, balder, dark face shining with sweat. His broad-shouldered jacket glinted as if woven from threads of actual gold, and the stickpin on his wide green tie was a huge ruby half-globe, rimmed with diamonds.

"Mars ConQuest—" The two words boomed through the long room, but then he paused to squint at the yellow pad. "We own a planet." He raised his head, confidence restored. "In just the past year, we have become the world's greatest corporation, measured in cash flow. Must we pull back from space to fight an ugly lie?"

Somebody in the audience shouted a question.

"That story from South America?" His face flushing darker, he glanced at his mother, who sat bolt upright, beaming proudly at him through gold-rimmed glasses. "A malicious fabrication! Our colonists report rich prospects for the future of Mars—but no gold nuggets the size of houses!"

He sneered at such absurdities.

"As millions know, we have already found and shared great wealth on Mars. We won't allow this cruel fraud to destroy the corporation or ruin our investors. The *Ares,* our original spacecraft, is now in flight back to Earth. Dr. Hellman and Dr. Barova are bringing their scientific data, their rock and soil samples, their surveys of the planet. Added evidence to expose this malevolent hoax, if anybody wants more evidence.

"We—we are Mars ConQuest." He glanced again at the yellow pad to find the words. "Our colonists are the conquerors. Back in Earth orbit, the *Ares* will soon be ready to load cargo and selected volunteers for her second flight. The *Nergal,* her sister ship, is already near completion. She, too, should be available for launch through the next window."

"Yes, sir?" He paused to listen to questions shouted from the back of the hall. "Please, one at a time."

"One more lie," LeeAnn murmured. "Alex knows an engineer who was working the *Nergal* for the old Authority. He's bitter now because Marty hasn't spent another penny on it. The frame is still in orbit, but he says most of the modules are still only half finished, lying in the yards of the Moon where he had to leave them."

"Sir?" Marty was scowling with annoyance, cupping his hand to hear questions they couldn't make out. His necktie was suddenly askew, his bald head bright with sweat under the television lights. "Sir? Yes, it's true we were out of contact. But only temporarily. The Farside facilities were down for a time after the Authority failed. Problems again when the Sun passed between Mars and Earth."

His mother had gestured, and he paused to straighten the bright green tie.

"But all that—all that is past. We are back in full contact now. Commander Lavrin reports—"

More questions erupted. Houston caught a voice he knew.

"Lavrin's report is in the press kit." Marty mopped his forehead and raised his voice. "You'll see it. He says the habitat is finished. A cozy Martian home, to use his own words. The greenhouses are producing more than they can eat. The livestock is already increasing. Explorations continue. Yet now this—this—"

Anger seemed to choke him, and his mother murmured a word.

"Impostor!" he croaked. "A con man come from nowhere! He asks you to believe he has found a gold field in the sky. To believe he flew here from Mars in a tiny landing craft. To believe the colonists are starving. Finally, to believe the biggest lie of all.

"That he is Sam Houston Kelligan!"

"Con man?" LeeAnn whispered when Marty paused. Sitting on a sofa with Houston, she gripped his hand hard, as if to hold him back from any return to Mars. His father sat rigid, eyes fixed on the screen, hard-bitten face grown grim. "Who's the con man?"

"Sam Houston Kelligan!" Marty was booming the name again. "The son of Mr. Austin Kelligan, one of our most prominent investors. A courageous man, a real hero, Houston Kelligan sacrificed a great fortune here on Earth to go out with the colony. He's still on Mars. If you want proof, we have his own word in recent personal messages to his parents in Fort Worth."

The cameras caught a startled stir in the audience. A gaunt mannish woman with blue-tinted hair was on her feet at the back of the hall.

"Absurd!" Marty shouted. "You've heard the story. You've heard how conveniently the suspect was picked up naked after his lander sank in the Pacific—if there ever was any lander."

The woman pushed down the aisle, yelling hoarsely.

"That's not all." Marty laughed. "The hoax gets uglier. The suspect claims that the colonists are sick and dying from some strange malady. Starving because their greenhouses have failed. He claims he came for help.

"Fantastic nonsense! Yet calculated to damage millions of innocent investors all over the world. Honest people who have put their trust in our grand plan for a magnificent future Mars. Millions have already been rewarded, enjoying our generous dividends and seeing their share appreciate.

"Their trust must be protected—"

The audience was buzzing. He stopped to gesture for silence, and a cameraman caught the woman's arm.

"Investigations of the plot are not yet complete, but we are trying." He squinted again at his yellow pad. "Though Chilean authorities did interrogate the impostor, it seems somebody was bribed to let him go. Certainly he is not acting alone. One accomplice has been identified.

"He was a man named Murchison, said to have brought the suspect to Valparaiso in a fishing boat. Unfortunately, Murchison is dead, cornered in a hotel room in Santiago and killed by Chilean police. Yet the motives behind the plot seem evident enough.

"Greed! Sheer greed! Price manipulation and international blackmail. We are informed that overseas speculators have been selling Mars ConQuest short—selling borrowed shares, that is, expecting to repay the loans with cheaper shares bought on falling markets. Kindling panic now to make those markets fall. They expected the scheme to make them millions. Even billions!

"And ruin Mars Con—"

Rage shook his voice, and his mother raised he hand to calm him.

"We're at war!" Not much calmer, he shook his fist. "To stop this mischief and protect out investors, Mars ConQuest will offer a reward of ten million American dollars each for the apprehension of this criminal and his accomplices, dead or alive. Although their true identities are not yet known, they will be discovered. Police have been warned that they are armed and dangerous.

"A monstrous plot! It must be—will be—crushed!"

With an air of triumph, Marty flourished a fat fist and sat back beside his mother. Beaming with approval, she patted his shoulder. A company man announced that the press kits were available, with photos and descriptions of the suspect. Reporters crowded to the podium. Muttering, the blue-haired woman retreated.

"Hew!" LeeAnn caught Houston's hand. "That looks like—that's you!"

"Couldn't be." Wryly, Houston shrugged. "He says I'm still on Mars."

The conference was over.

"I'm afraid for you," she whispered. "But I must look at Sammy now."

She left him with his father, who sat fixed in the chair, staring at him as if he were still a perplexing stranger.

36

Conjunction

Sometimes the nearest planet, Mars at opposition can come within 56,000,000 kilometers of Earth. At conjunctions, which happen just over two years apart, it has swung around behind the sun, nearly 400,000,000 kilometers away.

"The quiet one." In the habitat, Lavrin searched Lisa's empty room. "Lived inside herself and never let me know her. Now what's she done?"

"Left us." Jayne's voice fell. "I think in one of the rovers. Half the greenhouse lights are out."

"Where would she go?"

They got into pressure gear and cycled out of the habitat. With the main fusion plant disabled, they had been running both of the little rover engines to light the old greenhouses and warm the new one. Now they found both rovers standing in the shelter, the red alarm light on one flickering feebly.

"Dead. Dead from overload." Lavrin gestured at the light and bent to study fresh bootprints in the dust. "She just walked away."

"Because she found the engine down and knew we'd all get hungrier." Jayne bit her lip. "I've just checked the supplies. No rations gone. I think she's trying to die for us."

"Little idiot!" His lips quivered. "Or I should say saint."

"We must overtake her."

"I'll take the working rover." He frowned, his voice sharply anxious. "If you think the plants can live a day in the dark."

"It's a chance we must take." Jayne nodded. "I'll try to fix the other."

♂

Lisa Kolvos.

She came to life in Lavrin's mind as he drove slowly from the habitat, leaning off the rover to follow her bootprints up the rutted road that climbed east, toward the crater ridge. His nagging annoyance vanished as he recalled his first glimpse of her at the Beta test. A slight, shy girl when at last the lights came on, smiling for an instant when her eyes met his. Eyes very blue, though her hair was dark. Something wistful on her pixie face, as if she wanted him to like her.

Already he did, from her voice and her touch in the dark, but she hurried on before he could turn from Jayne to speak. Afterward she had always kept a certain wary distance, friendly yet reserved in a way that puzzled him. He remembered the weekend when they had shared a tent on a mountain training exercise in the Caucasus. With him in his sleeping bag, she had seemed timidly eager at first, but suddenly reluctant or afraid.

Perhaps it was because she had fallen on the afternoon climb, though she said she wasn't hurt. Perhaps because she thought he already belonged to Jayne. Perhaps because of her own ideals. He hadn't asked her why, but he wondered now. She had been a loner in the Corps, never intimate with anybody. Bright enough, and competent at everything, but seeming content within herself, needing no intimate friends.

Or had she needed someone?

Had he failed her? Had loneliness driven her to this? Some private pain he might have helped her heal? If he had tried to reach within her secret shell, to discover what she was and share his own emotions with her—

He shrugged, impatient with himself. Too late for regrets. In the end, unless some miracle took place, what happened here on Mars would never matter to anybody else. He gripped the wheel and urged the jolting rover on.

Halfway up the slope, she had left the road to follow a rocky shelf that held no footprints. He drove on in the same direction till the rover stalled on an ejecta slope too steep for it. He left it and climbed still higher, working back and forth across longer and longer arcs, searching rubble and dust for bootprints or any trace.

He found nothing.

Climbing, he forgot to notice time. The small sun surprised him, already high in the purple north. It astonished him again, low over the northwestern dune fields. The bitter dusk had thickened before he gave up and plodded back to the rover. With only starlight left to guide him down the ridge, he crawled instead into the

balloon tent and shivered through a night of bitter dread.
How long?

Had her air unit been serviced, the power cell fully
charged, the carbon filter cleaned? Haunted, he was back
in his pressure gear at dawn, backing the rover off that
ejecta bank and searching for a better path toward the
crest. In a higher strip of dust, he came upon her footprints. They led him to a bluff she had tried to climb. He
found her where she had fallen, lying still in its frigid
shadow.

Shouting, shaking her, he got no response. Yet her
body had not stiffened. He carried her back to the rover,
inflated the tent around them, unsealed her helmet. Her
skin looked blue, but he felt a faint pulse at her throat.

He kept the engine running to heat the tent, pulled off
her gloves and boots to rub her icy hands and feet. He
heard a sighing breath. Her skin color changed. She
stirred at last, staring up as if he had been an unexpected
stranger.

"Commander?" Whispering, she shook her head. "Is
it—are you really Arkady?"

"Arkady Lavrin." He grinned at her. "An old friend,
if you remember. Since the Beta test."

"I guess—" She shook her head, peering blankly
beyond him at the translucent yellow fabric of the tent.
Another shiver shook her. Smiling uncertainly, she
blinked again at him. "It must have been—must have
been a dream. Quite a remarkable dream!"

She lay flat again, eyes closed, smiling faintly to herself, until at last he asked, "What was it?"

"I'd crawled into a lava tube to sleep." Her words
came slowly, so softly he could hardly hear. "When I
woke there, water was running down it. Without my
helmet, I could breathe. Out of the tube, I found myself
on Olympus Mons. The sky was blue, with shining rings
like Saturn's across it. Mars had been—must have been

terraformed. Green hills and plains below me. Lakes and city domes far away. Aircraft flying. All so very real."

Eyes open again, she shook her head.

"Just a dream, I'm afraid."

"The dream we all live for," he said. "But now we've got to get you back to the habitat."

"No!" She struggled to sit up. "I'm not going back."

"Lisa!" He caught her stiff-clad arm. "Lisa! What do you mean?"

"I wanted—" Her face white with pain. "Wanted to give you and Jayne a better chance."

"You are an idiot!" He felt her trembling and drew her close against him. "If you thought we didn't care."

She closed her eyes, sobbing softly in his arms.

"Remember when we met?" he whispered. "Back at the Beta test. I liked your voice and touch before I ever saw you." He lifted her a little to kiss her cold lips. "Since then I've always cared. Always hoped to know you better since that weekend in the Caucasus, if you remember—"

She flinched as if with actual pain.

"I do remember!" She breathed the words, trembling. "If I had known you really cared—and if the rules of the Corps had left room for private life—"

"We do live for the Corps." Her eyes had opened, blue as ever, and he grinned into them. "But let's not die for it."

The maté in his flask was not entirely icy. She sipped a little of it, asked for more, ate an energy wafer. Strength came back, and her spirits lifted.

"That dream—" She shook her head, staring at the yellow plastic wall. "Crazy! Nothing I believe." She closed her eyes as if trying to recover the dream. "But still—if half of it can ever come true—"

♂

When she said she felt able to hang on to the rover, they sealed their suits and drove down to the habitat. Jayne was standing in the road to meet them. She and Lisa hugged, moving like robots in the stiff yellow gear. She confessed to Lavrin that she had failed to fix the other engine.

"The helium injection jet. Fouled with corrosion, like the one on the main engine. Still no spare." She shrugged in defeat. "Nothing else I know to do."

"Still—" Lavrin was grimly cheerful. "We've still got this one."

He hooked the rover engine back to the greenhouse lights. The plants were wilting from too many hours of darkness, but they revived a little. Jayne found three tomatoes that were almost ripe. Recklessly, they opened three full ration packs to make a small feast in the dim-lit chill of the common room, and Lavrin lifted his mug of bitter black maté to welcome Lisa home.

A savage dust storm in the month of Mariner kept them three days underground. Out again afterward, they found half the white plastic film ripped off the cross that marked the landing pad.

"Better pin it back," Lavrin said, and added wryly, "Not that I expect a lot of traffic coming in."

Leveling the dust to repair the marker, Lisa uncovered a small green plastic box.

"The repair kit!" She held it up for Lavrin to see. "Dropped somehow when we were unloading the landers and hidden since."

Lavrin found spare helium jets inside, along with the delicate tools designed to clean and adjust them. Both the disabled engines were soon running again, lighting greenhouses, powering the radio beacon, rekindling hope.

Another solstice came, beginning Mars Year Three. In spite of everything, they stayed alive. They stretched the vanishing ration packs, nursed the engines, pumped brine and refined water, harvested the greenhouses and seeded them again. Earth hid behind the Sun and crept out again. Searching the dark splendor of the pink-tinged nights for the *Ares* or any ship, they saw Phobos moving, and Deimos, and nothing else.

"If Houston did get through—"
Words they thought but seldom said, because they knew the odds.

♂

In the Fort Worth office, Alex Penning watched Marty Gorley's press conference and spoke to media contacts. Though the telephone at the Kelligan mansion was unlisted, it rang till Roberto left it off the hook. Taxis and TV vans began racing up the drive and parking on the snow-drifted lawn.

Houston's mother wanted to hide him in the attic. His father took him instead into the long room he still called the library, though his gun collection had replaced most of the books. A log of fragrant pine was burning in the fireplace, and he had Roberto bring ice and a bottle of his favorite bourbon.

"Martín!" He mocked Lucina's voice. "A damned liar! Always was a miserable rat. Let's make him squirm!"

He sloshed bourbon over the ice in two glasses and handed one to Houston.

"Stand fast, son," he rasped. "Stand fast!"

They clinked the glasses, and he asked no questions.

Penning returned to stride into the library, flushed and elated.

"Tell 'em, sir," he told Houston. "A showdown now. You or Marty Gorley."

LeeAnn and Penning with him, he went out to face an unbelieving mob. Nicholas Blink strode to stand just behind the arrayed microphones and cameras, shouting the same hostile questions he had answered for Lieutenant Salinas and Ramona Castellana.

"I am Sam Houston Kelligan," he told the lights and the lenses and the bristling microphones. "Ask my father. My mother. Roberto—he's known me since I was two years old."

His father came out briefly to pose with an arm around him, grimly scowling at the cameras. His mother whispered huskily that she knew her own son. Roberto flashed gold teeth into the lights and swore that he was indeed *El Señor* Sam Kelligan.

"Esa es la verdad."

A photographer emerged from the crowd to grip his hand and assure the cameras that he was in fact the same Astronaut Sam Houston Kelligan he had photographed as he boarded the spaceplane on his way out to Mars.

"Okay, Kelligan!" Blink grinned at last and shook his hand. "I'll buy your story—and we'll all watch the fireworks."

"You struck your lick." Penning gave him a nod of judicial approval when they were back in the library, drinking Roberto's scalding coffee laced with bourbon. "Now it's Marty at the bat."

Leaving Edna Kelligan's shrubs and winter-bare flower beds in trampled ruin, reporters rushed away to set off a worldwide financial panic. Stock markets crashed. Brokers were laughing next day at offers to sell Mars ConQuest. Marty and his mother were gone from their White Sands apartment. When police broke into his locked office, they found company records shredded and petty cash missing from the safe.

"So he struck out," as Penning put it. "All his millions and billions gone like smoke, as I get the story. Squandered on sales commissions and new promotion schemes and the dividends he'd paid to bait more suckers into the net."

♂

Kelligan had been hurt.

"But not killed, sir," Penning told him. "Not at all!"

They sat again that evening in the library, a log crackling in the fireplace and the air fragrant with the cigar he lit when his wife was gone up to bed.

"Your loans to Gorley are lost, of course, but LeeAnn had alerted me. We had our brokers selling Mars Con-Quest short while it slid. Recovered the best part of your investment."

"Now what?" Houston eyed him anxiously. "About the *Nergal?* Helium production on the Moon? The treaty rights there and on Mars?"

"They'll be auctioned." Penning sat well away from Kelligan's cigar. "As the bankruptcy proceeds. I can't imagine many eager bidders." He looked the room at Kelligan. "Sir, should we consider trying to pick up the pieces?"

"Give me time." Kelligan scowled at the whisky in his glass. "Wait till we know where we stand."

"That could depend—" Penning had no whisky and no cigar, only a glass of sparkling water. He turned to frown thoughtfully at Houston. "The gold strike you've spoken of could make a difference, sir. If you can establish that your precious meteor field actually exists. Do you know where your lander went down?"

"Eighty-one degrees and twenty-three minutes west," Houston told him. "Twenty-eight degrees and forty-nine minutes south. I asked Murchison when I got well enough to think. He had the figures in his log." He caught his breath to ask, "Can it be recovered?"

"Perhaps." Penning paused to smile at LeeAnn, sitting closer to the fire. "We can charter a salvage sub."

"Hew?" Her own smile gone, LeeAnn stared at Houston, her voice sharp with concern. "You won't think of going back? Not after all you've been through?"

"I left people there," he told her. "People I love, in desperate danger. They need me. I'm going if I can."

♂

In the panic's aftermath, LeeAnn and Penning became attorneys for Mars. They chartered a salvage submarine that brought up the *Colon* with a hundred kilograms of precious metals still aboard.

"Poker chips," Houston said. "Cash 'em in. Get all you can. I want the *Nergal* completed for a new expedition. I want the treaty rights Marty claimed. Revised to guarantee freedom for an independent Mars."

They sat in Kelligan's inner office, Lucina's abandoned Taxco silver still gleaming on the mantel, the bright *zarapes* and the young heroes of Chapultapec still on the wall, the naked victim still sprawled beneath the red flint blade. There was no *café con leche,* but Samantha Battle ran the new coffee machine expertly and smiled as brilliantly as Lucina once had done as she filled their cups.

"Better fold, Sam." Dead cigar clenched in his jaw, Kelligan scowled at the great yellow nugget on the old mahogany table. "It's no royal flush. Not in the middle of this regression. Hard times everywhere."

"Gold's still gold," Houston argued. "Platinum's a catalyst. Palladium a possible key to cheaper fusion. Osmium and iridium—"

"Off on Mars," Kelligan muttered. "Think of shipment costs to Earth."

"Ships will be coming. They'll want return cargo."

"Capital." Penning reached a soft white hand to stroke

the nugget. "If you believe the economists, an influx of new capital might cure the regression." Owlish, he blinked at Kelligan through the rimless glasses. "Hard times, sir, can be good times for negotiation."

"If you believe economists—" Kelligan snorted. "Too many of them believed Marty Gorley."

Yet he negotiated. In the wake of failure, none of the four founding powers of the old Authority wanted rights to anything on the Moon or Mars, or dared to let another power own them. One by one, when the bidding was over, they had ratified a new treaty clause that recognized the independence of the Mars Republic.

♂

Anxious for news of Hellman and Barova, Houston called Farside Observatory. He had to hold for Dr. Sakane, the new director. On the line at last, Sakane was breathless with asthma but eagerly wheezing questions of his own about the noble metal meteorites. Houston told him what he knew and agreed to send him test specimens.

"We'll name a town for you," he promised. "When we get it built. The new mining town at the Chandra crater."

"Thank you, sir." Sakane had to gasp between his phrases. "Thank you very much. I could wish to visit fall area. But old heart and lungs need the low lunar gravity. Can never leave here, not even for Mars."

Houston asked about the *Ares*.

"Signal fragment received. Male voice, in apparent distress, picked up on big dish. Hellman, I presume. Requesting rescue effort. We got radio fix and computed possible orbits. None come in ten million kilometers of Earth."

"Can you tell us where to intercept the ship? If we can complete the *Nergal?*"

"Misfortune," Sakane gasped. "Misfortune for *Ares*.

For Dr. Hellman. Dr. Barova. Single fix insufficient. Received no second signal. No second fix. Regret to say—orbital coordinates incomplete. Actual orbit remains unknown. Inadequate for telescopic search. I think ship forever lost."

♂

A few months later, the *Nergal* in orbit, Houston returned to Fort Worth to make his final farewell. He spent one last night in the room his mother still kept as he remembered it, his old posters of the planets fading on the wall and the time-stained model starcraft still hanging from the ceiling.

LeeAnn and Sammy were staying overnight. Roberto had laid a fire. With Sammy asleep, he sat late with her and the dying embers, talking of Mars and their childhood together and her new career with Kelligan Resources, and finally in silence, thinking more than he could say. Her good-night kiss woke his own emotion, and he lay half the night awake, hoping in spite of himself that she might invade his room again. That didn't happen, but her bright voice woke him early, calling him to say good morning to Sammy's Baldy Bear.

"Hi, Daddy!" Sammy knew and loved him now. Freshly bathed and fragrant in his own neat yellow skinsuit, he raised both arms to be lifted out his crib. "Sleep good?"

Houston lifted him and asked how Baldy Bear had slept and listened to him laugh.

"Can you leave him?" LeeAnn watched with tears in her eyes. "Can you really stand to leave him?"

"If I could stay—" He held Sammy against him, stroking the fine bright hair. "But the *Nergal's* fueled and ready to fly. Sixteen volunteers aboard. One of them

Martin Luther White, with a supply of the new paralife vaccine."

"But—you?" Her low voice caught for an instant. "Can't you send somebody else?"

"It hurts, Lee. It hurts!" He put one arm around her, and Sammy wriggled happily between them. "Because I do love you."

"And always loved Mars more."

"I guess that's so." Sammy was reaching for his chin. "Not—not that I'm sorry." Sammy was staring up at him, blue eyes round and huge. He had to blink back a tear. "Because we did get there."

"Nearly died there!"

"Not quite. I hope—" He had to look away. "Hope those I left will be alive to hear the news."

He felt the warmth of her breath and turned back to smile at Sammy.

"I have to go." His voice quickened. "Thanks in part to Alex. He's has agreed to be our ambassador and business agent here. For Free Mars! We're doing a lot of what Marty promised. The *Thor* is already building. The *Nergal* will be back two years from now with the first cargo of precious metals."

"But not—" Her lips twisted white. "Not with you?" She reached to take Sammy away.

"Not with me." A lump aching in his throat, he held Sammy against his heart. "It isn't easy, Lee. More like—like cutting off an arm. But I do belong there. They'll be expecting me. Jayne and the others. If they're still okay."

"I hope—" She took the child, but then her arm tightened around him. "For your sake, Hew, I hope she is."

"You can be happy." He hugged her and the child. "You do have Alex."

"I have Alex." She drew a little away, nodding soberly. "He loves me and loves Sammy. I can't ask him to wait any longer."

Sammy snuggled against her, wide eyes still scanning him.

"So long, son." He bent to kiss the tender cheek. "I hope to see you someday, with us on Mars."

"See you, Daddy." Sammy grinned. "On Mars."

♂

Dropping into orbit, the *Nergal* found the planet washed in yellow dust, the great volcanoes standing out like scattered islands. The radio beacon was silent. Calling the colony, they heard no answer. Landmarks invisible, landings had to be delayed.

"A sad thing, Hew." Fit again, White clapped his shoulder sympathetically. "Sorry for what I think you'll have to see."

The new colony was to be planted in the great Hellas Planitia basin half around the planet, at a lower altitude and nearer the meteor field. White went down with the first survey party in the *Cortez* when the dust cleared there. Houston had to wait another week before he found that tiny white cross below Coprates Chasma. When at last the dust revealed it, Captain Farah let him take the *Hudson* down alone.

Over two Earth years had passed since he took off on the *Colon,* but the same yellow dunes rippled the barren red-brown flatness of the old lake floor, the same boulder-strewn ridge climbed above the pad toward the crater where he and Jayne had crashed the *Magellan,* the same small brown mounds covered the habitats.

Down safe, he sat a long time on the lander, afraid to climb off. The time was mid-morning, the sun a small gold coin in the rust-yellow sky, but nothing was moving, nothing looked recent. Antenna wires still stretched between the drill stem posts, but no beacon had guided him down and nobody answered when he called from the lander.

Stirring himself at last, he got into pressure gear and cycled out. He found bootprints around the pad and wheel ruts that ran toward the mirror foil stretched over the rovers. A new brine drain pit had been dug near the osmotic separator. All drifted now with yellow dust.

Cold with dread, he tramped past the rovers to the habitats. Dirt mounds like graves—he tried to shrug the notion off, but his new gear seemed stiff and cold, and the south wind's chill fogged his faceplate till he clicked the heater switch. Shivering, he had to stop and nerve himself again to venture down the dusty steps to rap on the utility door.

Nobody came.

He crawled into the air lock and hit the ENTRY button. Dead silence till he shivered again. But then a relay clicked. The light came on. Air hissed. The valve thunked. In the entry hall, he heard the whisper of a fan. Machines at least were alive. Forebodingly, he unsealed his helmet to sniff the air.

It held no taint.

"Hello?" A breathless croak. He tried again, "Hello?"

Only silence.

He skinned off the pressure suit and walked down the dim-lit tunnel to the common room. Lavrin and Lisa sat at a table over small pottery bowls that smelled of boiled beans and cabbage, and steaming pottery mugs of mutant maté. Their backs toward him, they hadn't seen him. He gulped when he saw a single red rose opening in a rough brown pottery vase at the center of the table.

"—your birthday?" Lavrin was asking. "Tomorrow?"

"The eighth of Viking?" Laughing at him, Lisa looked very lean, yet quite alive, even happy. "Will that be September seventh? Dates still confuse—"

She had seen him.

"Hew?" She was on her feet, blinking in startled unbelief. "Houston?"

"Sam Houston Kelligan." He grinned at their bewilderment. "Your beacon's out. No answers when we called. No sign of life I saw. I was afraid—"

"We're okay." Lavrin came striding to kiss him on both cheeks. The same red-bearded giant, gaunt yet vigorous enough, beaming with relief. "We've gone troglodyte, living underground. Killed ourselves too long, listening to nothing on the radio. Shut the beacon down because light for the hybrid soy and wheat needed all our power."

"Jay—" Apprehension caught his throat. "Jayne?"

He saw her then, coming out of the greenhouse tunnel. Thin perhaps, yet lovely still in her faded blue skinsuit and a tattered smock, a handful of carrots in her hand. She cried his name and stood frozen for a moment before she dropped the carrots and ran into his arms.